D0035594

The Carpathian Novels

Anthologies

Specials

Standalones

SAMURAI GAME

CHRISTINE FEEHAN

JOVE
New York

A JOVE BOOK
Published by Berkley
An imprint of Penguin Random House LLC
penguinrandomhouse.com

Copyright © 2012 by Christine Feehan
Excerpt from *Dark Storm* copyright © 2012 by Christine Feehan
Penguin Random House supports copyright. Copyright fuels creativity, encourages
diverse voices, promotes free speech, and creates a vibrant culture. Thank you for buying
an authorized edition of this book and for complying with copyright laws by not
reproducing, scanning, or distributing any part of it in any form without permission.
You are supporting writers and allowing Penguin Random House to continue to
publish books for every reader.

A JOVE BOOK, BERKLEY, and the BERKLEY & B colophon
are registered trademarks of Penguin Random House LLC.

ISBN: 9780515151541

Jove mass-market edition / July 2012

Printed in the United States of America
13   15   17   19   21   20   18   16   14   12

For Kylie and Brandi Magner.

Thank you for coming to FAN;
I miss our wonderful lunches!

For My Readers

Be sure to go to www.christinefeehan.com/members/ to sign up for my PRIVATE book announcement list and download the FREE eBook of *Dark Desserts*, a collection of yummy recipes sent by my readers from all over the world. Join my community and get firsthand news, enter the book discussions, ask your questions, and chat with me. Please feel free to email me at Christine@ christinefeehan.com. I would love to hear from you. Join me for a fun-filled time at my FAN convention. Visit www .fanconvention.net for more information. I hope to see you there!

Acknowledgments

I could never have written this book without the help of several people. Thanks to Brian Feehan for his extremely helpful advice whenever I'm stuck, and of course to Domini Stottsberry, who always works so hard on research and in every other aspect of helping put a book together. Special thanks to Jason Hutton of the 2/75th Rangers for his invaluable work on the military scenes. I have no idea what I would have done without you. Of course, I take full responsibility for all mistakes and greatly appreciate Jason's aid in helping me with terms and planning missions and escapes.

The GhostWalker Symbol Details

SIGNIFIES
shadow

SIGNIFIES
protection against
evil forces

SIGNIFIES
the Greek letter *psi*, which is
used by parapsychology
researchers to signify ESP or
other psychic abilities

SIGNIFIES
qualities of a knight—
loyalty, generosity,
courage, and honor

SIGNIFIES
shadow knights who protect
against evil forces using
psychic powers, courage,
and honor

nox noctis est nostri

The GhostWalker Creed

We are the GhostWalkers, we live in the shadows
The sea, the earth, and the air are our domain
No fallen comrade will be left behind
We are loyalty and honor bound
We are invisible to our enemies
and we destroy them where we find them
We believe in justice and we protect our country
and those unable to protect themselves
What goes unseen, unheard, and unknown
are GhostWalkers
There is honor in the shadows and it is us
We move in complete silence whether
in jungle or desert
We walk among our enemy unseen and unheard
Striking without sound and scatter to the winds
before they have knowledge of our existence
We gather information and wait with endless patience
for that perfect moment to deliver swift justice
We are both merciful and merciless
We are relentless and implacable in our resolve
We are the GhostWalkers and the night is ours

CHAPTER 1

Congressman John Waters stroked his hand up the silken thigh of his companion until he reached the top of her stocking, where his fingers traced bare skin. He leaned toward her and whispered in her ear so he could be heard above the blasting music. "Would you like one more drink before we leave?"

Brenda Bennett sent him a practiced smile and turned her face so she could nip his earlobe with her teeth before whispering back, "Make it a Red Bull and vodka. I want to spend a long time tonight with you. I have so many delicious things I've been thinking of doing with you and I don't want to chance falling asleep." She paused, her breath warm against his ear. "Either one of us." Her tongue teased his earlobe.

"Sounds like a good plan to me," Waters said with what he thought was a sexy leer.

Brenda playfully touched his leg with the stiletto heel of her sexy red open-toe shoes. "I'll visit the ladies' room and make certain I'm looking my best for you."

"You always look your best," the congressman assured

his favorite companion. He patted her thigh and stood up to make his way through the crowd to the bar.

Brenda glanced to her left, her eyes meeting the woman seated at the table adjacent to hers, giving the briefest of nods. Both got up and made their way through the crowd to the bathrooms. The Dungeon was the hottest club in town, where only the elite came together for two purposes—making deals and playing bondage games to get laid. Brenda made very certain her clients went away happy and returned often with very large pocketbooks. She was always especially happy to see the congressman because she was always paid double.

Brenda smiled at the woman who followed her inside, but prudently remained silent while they both checked the stalls to ensure they were alone before they spoke.

"I got your call, Sheila. Getting Waters here tonight wasn't easy on such short notice. He had some big thing going on with his wife. You have to tell Whitney to give me more of a heads-up when something is this important to him."

Sheila shrugged. They both knew it didn't matter in the long run how difficult the task was. Their boss made obedience well worth it. "Whitney wants you to make absolutely certain our good congressman goes through with his vote to approve the research on his new weapon." Sheila Benet handed Brenda the thick envelope, retaining possession when Brenda eagerly closed her fingers around it. "Don't fail, Brenda," she warned. "He doesn't accept failure."

"Have I ever failed him?" Brenda asked, her dark eyes glittering with anger. "I have *never* failed him. You remind him that *every* name he's ever given me, I've found a way to seduce or blackmail them into doing what he wants. I can read weakness, and although he hates working with women because we're so damned inferior, he won't find too many men who can do what I do. You just tell him that, Sheila."

Sheila raised her eyebrow, still retaining possession of the envelope. "Do you really want me to tell him all that?"

Brenda pressed her lips together tightly, but caution

tamped down some of her anger. "I work hard for him. The one time I told him not to press Senator Markus, he insisted, and even then, when I knew what was going to happen, I still found his weakness. Rather than be blackmailed, he killed himself, just like I said he would. Whitney needs to place a little more value on me as a resource, that's all I'm saying."

Sheila gave her a brief, cold smile as she allowed her fingers to slide away from the envelope, leaving it in Brenda's hand. "That's probably the very reason why he padded your pay, Brenda. Perhaps you might consider that he's a brilliant man who rewards those useful to him. He had no choice but to call you when Waters seemed to be wavering on his vote. Make certain the good congressman doesn't even consider letting him down."

Brenda pushed the thick envelope into her purse and gave Sheila a smirk. "No worries. I've recorded every single session with the honorable, upstanding John Waters and I don't think he would ever want the things he's done to come to light—not with his uptight wife and righteous, church-loving family so vocal about all things sinful. He'll do whatever Dr. Whitney needs him to do."

"You have a pretty good thing going here, Brenda," Sheila said. "You get paid by Whitney and by the mark." Her eyes went glacier cold. "Don't blow it." Abruptly she turned and went into the nearest stall, slamming the lock into place to signal she was done. She'd given her warning and if Brenda chose to bitch again—well, that was between her and Whitney. But people who crossed him generally had a way of disappearing fast.

Brenda hummed to herself, a slight smile on her face. She adjusted her silk blouse so that it was just open enough to reveal the enticing rounded curves. The material fell nicely over her nipples, pushed up by the camisole she wore beneath the silk. She glanced down to get her bright red lipstick from her purse. The water in the sink suddenly turned on. Her gaze jumped to the steady stream of water.

She shrugged and looked up, uninterested in why the automatic faucet would have been triggered. In the mirror, just behind her, she was startled to see the face of a woman standing very close to her. There was no sound at all. She had time to register a waterfall of platinum blond hair and Asian features. A hard blow to the back of her skull sent her head forward, slamming her into the edge of the sink. She felt nothing at all as blackness descended.

Brenda's body slipped to the tiled floor from the edge of the basin. With gloved fingers, the woman threw a handful of water onto the floor around Brenda's feet and the soles of her shoes, crouched to snap one stiletto heel, and jerked the envelope from Brenda's purse, all in one smooth, silent move. As she stood, she removed a tiny camera placed just over the mirror and seemed to disappear in the blink of an eye.

"Brenda?" Sheila called out tentatively.

The water continued to run in the sink. Sheila frowned and glanced under the door of the stall. Brenda was lying on the floor. "Brenda?" she said again, her voice cracking. There was no answer, only the sound of the water running.

Sheila continued to stare under the door, frozen in place. She couldn't see any other feet, but Brenda's shoe was off her foot, the heel broken. A thin stream of red ran along the cracks, moving in an ever-widening puddle. She gasped and jumped up. Behind her the toilet automatically flushed and she nearly screamed. Very slowly, with the tips of her fingers, she pushed open the door and peered out. Brenda lay on the floor, the front of her skull smashed from where she had slipped on the water. Her clothes, instead of looking sexy and tempting, revealed her for what she was—a highly paid prostitute, her body obscenely displayed there on the bathroom floor.

Swearing under her breath, Sheila quickly took toilet paper and opened Brenda's purse to retrieve the envelope of cash. It was gone. Her heart jumped. Whitney would never believe her. The money had to be on the body somewhere, and she had to find it or he'd think she stole it. That would be just like him. She crouched down beside Brenda and looked her over. There didn't seem to be a place she could have concealed the envelope.

Voices just outside the door had her jumping up and backing away, back toward the stall door. She let out a scream and stood, covering her mouth, her gaze frantically searching the body as the bathroom door burst open and three women came to an abrupt halt and added their voices to hers. At once chaos erupted.

Harry Barnes, aide to Senator Lupan, scowled as he pushed his BMW to the limit on the curved mountain road. Why in the hell had Sheila Benet picked such a ridiculous place for a meeting? There were plenty of safe places downtown where civilization reigned. He was allergic to grass. To bugs. To stupid cows. He was *finally* about to score with the woman he'd been chasing for three straight months and he wasn't going to blow his chance because Sheila had suddenly gotten paranoid. They could meet under the nose of the senator and the old man wouldn't notice.

He punched a button and music flooded the car. He set his teeth as he glanced at his GPS. Another three miles. Stupid, stupid woman. Maybe he could call and his date would understand he'd be an hour late. Sheila had said not to make any calls, that if someone was on to them, they'd pick up his cell phone call. Damn. He slammed his flat palm against the steering wheel in pure frustration. *No one* was on to them. Why should they be? How could they be? And no one would dare to monitor his cell phone.

"Friggin' Sheila," he snapped and ordered his phone to call the sexy Miss Catherine. She looked very good in her prim little pencil skirts and red silk blouses as she sat behind a desk, her long hair coiled in that uptight little bun. He had images of unwrapping her like a Christmas gift stuck in his head and until he made it happen, he couldn't move on. He talked for the next couple of minutes, persuading her to wait for him, that he'd make it worth her while. He hung up feeling smug, tossing the phone onto the passenger seat. Using the senator as an excuse was genius. What woman wouldn't be impressed that he was so indispensable to a senator that he couldn't get away until the senator was ready to call it quits and go home?

Smirking, he tapped his fingers on the steering wheel, pleased with himself. "That's how it's done," he told himself aloud and grinned at his reflection in the rearview mirror. For a few moments there, he'd forgotten how good he was at playing the game. Now that he knew for certain his evening's fun wasn't lost, his mood swung back to cheerful— after all, Whitney was going to pay him handsomely for keeping the old senator in line. Not hard to do at all these days. It only took a little work on his knees and the man was putty in his hands.

Sheila Benet's car was parked to one side exactly at the mile marker she'd told him, leaving enough room for him to pull over. He slipped out of the car and stretched. It was a beautiful night, the stars overhead and a half-moon shining brightly down on them.

"Hey, Sheila, how's it going?" he greeted as he sauntered over to her car. "Nice night for all this cloak-and-dagger drama."

Sheila stuck her head out the window. Her car was still running. "No one followed you?"

"I don't think there's a cow alive on this road tonight. I haven't seen headlights in the last fifteen minutes." He resisted rolling his eyes as he held out his hand for the fat envelope. "Senator Lupan will do exactly as I ask him. Tell Whitney he has no worries on that score. The old man can barely breathe without his oxygen. I keep him isolated and happy. He has no family; there's only me, and no one realizes just how bad that last stroke really was. He relies very heavily on me now."

"He *can't* step down until this is done, Harry," Sheila reiterated as she placed the envelope in the aide's outstretched palm.

"No worries. He'll hang in there, if for no other reason than for something to do. He's sick, but his mind is active and he needs the interaction and the adulation his position provides. I stroke his ego and a few other things for him and he falls right into line." Harry flashed her his most charming smile. "It's all good, Sheila. He'll vote the way we want him to. I guarantee it."

"Would you bet your life on it?" Sheila asked with a snide curl of her lip.

Harry's smile faded as he turned away from her in disgust. Sheila Benet was a coldhearted bitch. He'd never once failed Dr. Whitney. It didn't matter how distasteful the task was, he got it done. Just because Sheila had the mad doctor's ear didn't make her so damn high and mighty. As many years as he'd been working for Whitney and taking the payoffs from Sheila, one would think she would have tried to be a little friendly.

"Harry." Sheila had followed him to his car. "It doesn't pay in this business to get overconfident. Anyone can be bought. We got to you, didn't we?"

Harry gave her a black scowl and tossed the thick envelope of bills in his glove box in disgust, not bothering to count the money. It was always right. He started his car and then slammed the door closed, flipped Sheila off, and took off fast, leaving her standing there.

"Stupid, uptight woman, probably hasn't gotten laid in ten years," he snapped and glanced in his rearview mirror to see that she'd just gotten into her car.

When he looked toward the road, there was a woman sitting beside him—small, Asian features, hair covered by a tight skullcap. She grabbed the wheel with gloved hands and jerked hard, sending the BMW straight over the cliff, plunging into the deep gorge below. Tree limbs hit the window, smashing the glass, and the car hit another treetop on the way down and began to roll. He shouted, his hoarse voice steadily cursing, although he had no idea what he was saying. When he managed to look again, he was alone in the car—the woman a figment of his imagination.

Sheila saw Harry's car abruptly turn straight for the cliff and drive right off of it as she pulled to the shoulder of the road. She slammed on her brakes, her heart pounding. "Oh, my God. Oh, my God," she chanted.

Her mouth went dry. With shaking hands she drove to the edge of the road where the car had gone over and climbed out. It was a long way down. Whitney hadn't been happy about losing Brenda, a key member of his pipeline to Washington, and he really would be upset if Harry was dead. No one else had ever managed Lupan. The senator believed his aide was the only constant in his life who cared about him. He'd be lost without Harry. She couldn't imagine him doing anything but staying in bed if Harry really died.

She had no choice but to try to make her way down there and see if he was still alive. Cursing both Whitney and Harry under her breath, she changed from heels to her running shoes, put her hazard lights on, and made her way carefully to the edge. The terrain was very steep in some places but with a little work she could make her way down. She slipped several times and cursed the two men over and over when she had to half sit to get over one spot.

Glass was everywhere, scattered around the wreckage of the car. Thankfully she heard moaning. Harry was alive. Breathing a sigh of relief, she clawed her way to the overturned car. Harry hung upside down, blood dripping from his head. His eyelids fluttered and he stared at her with pleading eyes. Without touching him, she considered her next move. Harry was dying. Blood pumped from a gash on his leg and one side of his head appeared to be caved in.

"Sorry, Harry," she said, surprised she actually meant it.

She stumbled her way around the car and, tearing a strip of cloth from her shirt, she pushed what remained of the passenger door open wider so she could lean in without allowing her body to touch anything. It wouldn't be good to be found at another accident scene. Ignoring Harry's moans, she opened the glove compartment. There was no envelope. The money was gone.

Anger surged through her, followed by an adrenaline rush of sheer terror. She *had* to find that money. If she went back to Whitney a second time, reported an accident had killed another in his pipeline to Washington, and that the first installment of the payoff was once again missing, she was dead. He would kill her. She knew him. Whitney didn't allow mistakes.

She swore out loud. "Where is it, Harry? The money. You're bleeding to death. If you want my help, tell me where the money is."

Harry's gaze shifted to the empty glove compartment. He looked shocked. There was no doubt in Sheila's mind he thought it would be there. She shifted out of the car as he gurgled, a little repulsed as blood trickled from his mouth. She didn't like blood. She'd ordered kills many times, on Whitney's behalf, but she didn't actually get her hands dirty. She could hear his breathing, a death rattle now, and bile rose.

The money was gone. Where, she had no idea, but it was gone. She couldn't search that wreckage of a car; like in the bathroom a couple of weeks earlier, the money had disappeared. No officer had reported finding an envelope of money when Brenda's body had been taken to the coroner. She backed away from the crumpled car and the smell of death. All she wanted to do was run, but with her heart pounding so hard, she stood frozen.

Wind rustled leaves in the trees and moved brush so that limbs swayed and creaked. A chill went down her spine. She looked around, suddenly afraid. The night had eyes and she couldn't be seen. She tried to run, a small sob escaping. She slipped and began to claw her way up the steep incline, more afraid than she'd ever been in her life—and for the first time it wasn't Whitney she was afraid of.

Major Art Patterson whistled softly as he ran down the steps of the Pentagon. The sky had turned dove gray, not quite dark yet not light. He loved the time of day when the sun and moon came together. He glanced upward. A few stray clouds drifted lazily by, but were so thin the stars already out had no trouble shining. He grinned up at the moon and stars as he hurried to his car.

Life was good. He enjoyed working for his boss. General Ranier was a four-star general, tough as nails but fair. The program the general was responsible for was one Patterson believed in. The GhostWalkers were men and women trained in every type of warfare possible, in every terrain, in water, in air, in every type of weather. They were the elite of the elite. He thought of them as "his" team. He should have been a GhostWalker. He would have made a great leader, and working for Ranier allowed him to play a very large part. He knew he was a great asset to the GhostWalker program.

He drove a showy little silver Jaguar, racing through the streets toward his meeting with Sheila Benet. She seemed so cool, but she flashed fire when they came together. She liked the uniform and the power he wielded, and he liked melting all that cold ice. He stroked the black leather seats almost lovingly. Yeah, he had the good life. Just because he didn't show psychic ability didn't mean he wasn't a true GhostWalker. Whitney had recognized his abilities and just how useful he was to the program.

Ranier had turned on Whitney, believing he'd gone too far when his experiments on young orphaned girls came to light, but the general hadn't looked with an open mind. Patterson had tried hard to convince him of the truth—those girls were throwaways. No one wanted them in any of the countries where Whitney had found them. Had he not taken them, they would have ended up on the streets as prostitutes. At least they served a greater purpose. Whitney gave the girls clean beds and food. Most were grown now, and Patterson had seen the facilities once where they were housed, and the conditions were very nice.

The women were all educated and spoke multiple languages, had all been trained as soldiers and shaped into useful members of society. The general loved his GhostWalker program and fought for it with every breath in his body, but he blamed Whitney for tainting its reputation. No one wanted the experiments to come to light, but they'd been necessary and Patterson believed in what Whitney was doing, 100 percent.

The major parked in the second-story parking garage at the mall. He rarely went to malls, but Sheila had insisted they be out in the open, in a very public place. She seemed far more nervous than usual, which was unlike her. He whistled as he made his way to the escalator to take it down to the first floor where he was meeting her in the little French coffee shop. At least the coffee was good.

She was already sitting at a small table in a corner, which afforded them a little privacy. She was dressed in her usual style, that pencil-thin skirt that showed off her hips and long legs, so elegant in stockings and high heels. There was nothing cheap about Sheila Benet. She was class all the way. He liked sitting across from her in any public situation. She was a woman who turned heads with her hair in the upswept twist and her prim-and-proper short suit jacket that hugged the full curves of her breasts and small waist. She reminded him of the pinup girls from the forties with her red lipstick and shapely figure.

He bent to brush a kiss along her temple in greeting. He was always careful when he touched her never to take it too far that she could object. He wanted her always wanting that little bit more from him. She was the type of woman who could never fully be in the seat of power or her man would lose her. He wasn't a permanent kind of man, but the affair was fun and ensured his favor with Whitney. He often idly wondered if Whitney slept with her, but she was very close-mouthed on the subject.

"You usually prefer to meet in dark places," he greeted. "What's up, Sheila? You said it was urgent and you wanted to come somewhere very public. Is there some problem?"

"I don't know," she replied in a low voice. Behind her sunglasses her eyes moved restlessly, surveying the crowded shop. "Maybe. There have been unexplained accidents lately, and I don't want to take a chance that you might be one of them."

He had never seen Sheila shaken or he wouldn't have taken the threat seriously. "I can take care of myself, honey, but thanks for the heads-up. I'll be careful."

She looked up as the waitress approached the major. He asked for coffee. Sheila waited until he'd been served before she leaned toward him again. "This is huge, Art, really huge. Orders are going to come down soon to send a team back into the Congo. The president has been asked to help get rid of the rebel problems of the current regime."

Patterson sat up straight, a frown on his face. "How would Whitney know that? *No one* should know about that. Not even him."

"He's got ears everywhere, Art. He's a very trusted man in many circles, and for them, his security clearance is still at the highest level. Until we prove his soldiers are the answer we've all been looking for, there will be skeptics and jealous enemies looking to bring him down. You know that. Look at your boss. He runs a GhostWalker team and yet he despises the man who created them."

Art shrugged, in no way concerned. As long as Rainer didn't approve of Whitney and his ongoing experiments with the women and soldiers, it meant a hefty paycheck for him at the end of the day. The major wanted Whitney beholden to him. Whitney still carried a lot of political clout in some circles and he could help further his career. The women always had been and always would be expendable. They had no families, Whitney made certain of that. As long as they were fed and clothed, who cared? Hell, no one even knew— or cared—that they existed. The sacrifices they made definitely enlightened the scientists, allowing great strides in the medical and military fields. Their lives had purpose, when, if not for Whitney, they would be useless to society, little leeches living off men.

Art took a slow sip of his coffee, savoring the taste, waiting for Sheila to make her bid. It was going to be good, whatever it was, he could tell. She was overly nervous and uncertain of how to present to him what Whitney required of him, which meant much more money than usual. He stayed quiet, allowing her to squirm, drawing out the silence between them.

Sheila cleared her throat. "One mine in the world produces a certain type of diamond and only once in a great while is one found. Whitney needs that diamond for a new weapon he's working on for defending our troops. It's an amazing weapon but not yet finished. Without that diamond, he can't complete the project." She leaned close, her blue eyes steady on his, very earnest. "He tried buying it, offered millions, but Ezekial Ekabela has the diamond. He took over that region of the Congo some time ago after his brother was killed."

Art steepled his fingers and looked at her over them. "His brother was General Eudes Ekabela, the man who had both Jack and Ken Norton tortured. He was killed by a member of the first GhostWalker team. And I believe General Armine took over, not Ezekial."

"That's right," Sheila said, but she squirmed and Patterson knew she was hoping he didn't have that exact information in his head. "General Armine took over the rebel army before Ezekial could get into power, but he has a small group still loyal to him and he still holds that mine. He's trying to cement his position as the leader of the army. Under Armine's leadership, they've been pushed back. Ezekial Ekabela wants his army back and he wants the territory they lost back. He's gotten his hands on a diamond that Dr. Whitney needs."

"I don't understand what you need from me."

"The president of the Congo has asked our president for help." She held up her hand. "*Don't* ask me how I know. The order will be to go in and destroy the munitions and vehicles, and to assassinate both Armine and Ekabela."

Patterson shook his head. He was always astounded by how much information Whitney managed to intercept.

"Whitney has been supplying arms and money to Ekabela, not a lot, but enough to keep him hungry and enable him to defend the mine against both Armine and the president. If the president gets that land back with the mines, we'll never finish this weapon." She leaned toward Patterson. "This one is important, Art. Really important. Ekabela is willing to trade the diamond to be put back in power. Along with that, he wants a GhostWalker. He wants revenge. He preferred one of the Norton brothers from GhostWalker Team Two—mainly, I suspect, because he couldn't identify the one who killed his brother and Jack Norton wreaked havoc on his army, but Dr. Whitney persuaded him that was impossible."

"I don't understand," Patterson said with a small frown. "What difference does it make to Whitney which Ghost-Walker he gives up if he's giving one to Ekabela?"

"The Nortons are no longer expendable, *especially* Jack. He has children—twin boys. His brother is certain to follow his example soon. They need to train their children in survival, and Whitney is absolutely sure that they will. The Nortons are premium, elite soldiers and have proven their worth to the program over and over."

"No doubt," Patterson agreed, trying to look very sincere.

"We need a hero in the program and Dr. Whitney has selected Sam 'Knight' Johnson. It's a terrible sacrifice he doesn't want to make and, of course, it deeply saddens him, but in order to keep the program moving forward, sacrifices do have to be made. Of all the GhostWalkers, Sam is the most expendable. He can't provide us with a child, and the children are more important than the soldiers."

"I still don't understand."

"Johnson is paired with a woman of no use to the program. Unless Whitney can get him back, which is highly improbable, he will not accept another mate, so he'll never produce a much-needed child." She shrugged. "In any case, it was easy to persuade Ekabela that Sam Johnson was the man who killed his brother."

Patterson stretched his legs out and took a casual look

around the coffee shop. As usual, this popular café was packed. His hungry gaze automatically noted the women surrounding him. A harried mother who looked as if she needed a man to make her feel beautiful; a little mouse of an Asian woman who sipped tea and studiously read a book on Zen as she listened to music with an earpiece in her ear and tapped her foot to the beat; two middle-aged animated friends having fun, laughing together . . . so many types. He loved that about women—that there were so many to choose from and right here in this room there was a good cross-section. He turned his head to smile at Sheila. The conversation was going along very nicely.

Did he really care that Sam Johnson was paired with a useless woman? Not really, but what was important, of course, was the fact that the renowned infallible Dr. Whitney had made a mistake or it wouldn't have happened. And *that* was an important nugget of information Sheila had inadvertently given him.

"So you're saying Johnson goes on the mission and doesn't come back. The team takes out the terrorist cell and along the way, Whitney's men are in place to make certain Ekabela gets a GhostWalker to torture endlessly in return for the diamond."

"Not exactly," Sheila hedged. "Ekabela's men will be there to take the GhostWalker, but we'll have a sniper in place to kill Johnson once the diamond is in our hands and the rest of the team is out safely. He won't suffer."

Art was very skilled at portraying emotion he didn't feel. He blew out his breath, shook his head, and took another drink of coffee. "That's bullshit, Sheila, and you know it. That puts the entire team at risk. What's to say Ekabela doesn't go after more than one GhostWalker and keep the diamond anyway?"

"The money, of course. He needs the money for his war chest and he needs an ally like Whitney." She looked around, lowered her voice further, and beckoned him close. "Did you get the intel on the recent jailbreak in Lubumbashi?

Nine hundred and sixty-seven prisoners escaped. It appeared that eight armed men attacked the prison guards, allowing the prisoners to flee, trying to free a militant who had been condemned to death. Unbeknownst to the minister, they had three members of Ekabela's family: another brother, a son, and a nephew. It was only a matter of time before someone gave up their true identities. Whitney arranged to help Ekabela recover them as part of the good faith deal. Ekabela needs Whitney, although his is a lost cause. He'll never find enough followers to keep those mines for long."

"He massacres entire villages and the children, forcing them to join with him or die. This man is no saint. His reputation is terrifying in that region. He's not a man Whitney wants to be in bed with."

"Of course not," Sheila soothed. "Of course Whitney doesn't want to deal with such a man, but he needs that diamond for the defense of our country, and he can't chance that the local military gets enough guts to take back those mineral-rich lands, nor can he take the chance that whoever has the mines next will do business with him. The moment the diamond is in his hands, you know that he'll destroy Ekabela. He'll move heaven and earth to make certain the man dies, and with him, all of his terrible atrocities. The price for this powerful weapon that could end wars, for the defense of everything we hold dear, is one man. *One*, Art. You and I both know it's a small price."

The major frowned and scratched the back of his head. "These soldiers are elite, every one of them. They've trained extensively. Even without their psychic abilities, just the training alone is worth so much to our government. Do you have any idea how many operations these men have run, just this team alone? To give one up to the enemy, that just doesn't sit right."

"Of course no one wants it that way, Art," Sheila said, leaning forward to touch his hand with her fingertips. "Dr. Whitney *agonized* over this decision. The mission *has* to take place. If we don't sacrifice a knight, then many good men will die." She took a small package from her purse and, with one finger, pushed it across the table at him. "Dr. Whitney really needs your help on this. Make certain Johnson is on that team when the orders come through."

The major loved this part. Negotiation—his forte. He frowned. Drew a hand over his face and shook his head. "Ekabela will torture that GhostWalker the way they did Jack and Ken Norton. Ken is covered in scars," Patterson said. "Sam Johnson has served this country time and time again, going above the call of duty."

Sheila withdrew another packet and placed it carefully on top of the other one.

Patterson studied her face. Should he push? Sheila bit her lip when he remained silent. Laughter bubbled up. He had her. He sank back in his chair and shook his head. "Not this time. I've read what Ekabela does to people he doesn't like. If you told him Johnson killed his brother, he'll fuck him up so bad the man will beg for death and I doubt if Ekabela will give it to him—not for a very long time."

She took out a third packet and placed it beside the other two. Her lips compressed tight. Patterson swept up the money. "You'd better have a sniper in place, Sheila," he warned, knowing full well Whitney wouldn't risk blowing the deal by killing Ekabela's prize. "I'll see what I can do, but Whitney blew it when he had me talk to the general. I don't hold a trusted position anymore. He plays his cards close to his chest. He and that aide of his go way back."

"Nevertheless, see to it that the orders change before they get to the general."

Patterson stood up, sliding the packs of money inside his coat in the pocket specially tailored for just such lucrative transactions, satisfaction welling up. He turned from the table to walk out.

Sheila hastily plugged in her earpiece. "He's on the move. Watch him closely. If anything happens to him, we're all in trouble." She had a team in place this time—Whitney's own men, his private army of GhostWalkers on his payroll, men not quite as perfect as the elite soldiers on the teams, but enhanced nonetheless. She'd noticed those men—mercenaries—rarely lasted long. The effects of the enhancements seemed to take a toll on them, making them belligerent and always ready to fight.

Several people in the café had gotten up to pay, cutting across Patterson's path, slowing him down. A tall, slender man in a business suit picked up his briefcase and stood, nearly running into the major. He stepped back with an apology to allow the soldier to continue his line of travel. A small Asian woman turned from the cash register with a small cough, her fist going to her mouth to politely cover the soft sound.

The major glanced back and grinned at Sheila. "See you later." He turned and faltered in his stride, both hands going to his throat. He made a sound, much like a death rattle. He staggered, and took three more steps.

The tall man passed him, heading for the counter, his bill in his hand. Two of Sheila's team paced alongside Patterson but from opposite sides of the room. The major once again turned toward Sheila. She could see his face was nearly purple, his lips blue.

"Move in. Move in," she practically shouted.

Patterson went down on his knees, grabbing at the Asian woman, nearly toppling her as well. She looked frightened and backed away, toward Sheila, bumping her and bouncing off. Sheila tried to get to the major, but several customers blocked her path for a minute, rushing toward the fallen man who appeared to be choking. She was bumped and pushed in the melee, delaying her. Sheila's team reached Patterson first, surrounding him as he fell flat on his face, gasping for breath.

"Call nine-one-one," one of her men ordered her.

They rolled the major over. His eyes were wide-open, sightless, bulging. His mouth was open as well, giving her the impression of a fish gasping its last breath. He was definitely dying if he wasn't already dead. Whitney could not possibly blame her for this. She pushed her way through the small crowd to Patterson's side and knelt over him as her men worked on him. Her fingers found the inside pocket. She nearly screamed aloud. The money was gone. Gone. Right in front of her. In front of the team. It was impossible.

She took a careful look around at the crowd. She'd scoped out this very café numerous times and most of the onlookers were the same people who came in after work for coffee and a chat with coworkers or to relax before they went home. She recognized the little Asian girl who had been reading her book. She and the three Asian men who sat at a table chatting together, along with the tall gentlemen with the briefcase, worked at Samurai Telecommunications across the street. The two women laughing together were secretaries at the law offices of Tweed and Tweed.

She could practically name everyone in the room and where they worked. She'd done backgrounds on everyone including the workers here. What was she going to say to Whitney? Thank God she had been smart enough to place a tracking device in the third packet of money. She knew Patterson, knew his greed. He always managed to sound very concerned for the soldiers, but in the end he'd always been more concerned for his bank account. She read him like a book and she'd known exactly when his breaking point would be.

She looked down at the major. Two of the team members worked on him, trying to bring him back, but he was gone that fast. Disgusted, she stood up and dusted off her hands, walking with great dignity back to her table. The small tracker was there in her purse. She reached inside and turned it on. The green light blinked rapidly, telling her she was very, very close to the source.

Suspicious, she looked around her. Two café employees stood close and one of the two secretaries. An Asian man was on the other side of her. Clearly it could be on any of the four. She moved her hand slightly. The tracker went wild, glowing bright, indicating she was directly over the bug. No one was that *close* to her. Frowning she looked at the floor. Nothing.

Her heart jumped and then began to pound. She put her hand on the pocket of her jacket. The tracker was in her pocket. She sank into a chair, nowhere to go, terrified of what Whitney would do now that she'd failed him again.

CHAPTER 2

At long last the game was on. Azami "Thorn" Yoshiie allowed herself one small smile as she stepped out of the single-engine plane she'd piloted, landing at the tiny airport of Superior. She'd flown over the Lolo National Forest, taking her time, quartering the acreage where she knew the homes of GhostWalker Teams One and Two were located.

Jack and Ken Norton, two members of Team Two, owned twenty-four hundred acres surrounded by national forest and they had leased it to the two GhostWalker teams, forming a nearly impenetrable fortress. From the air, even the houses were nearly impossible to spot. The soldiers had taken great care to incorporate their surroundings, using mountains and trees to hide their existence from the outside world.

Her two most trusted men accompanied her, flanking either side of her, but a foot away, giving all three plenty of room to maneuver should they have need to do so. Daiki and Eiji Yoshiie were both broad-shouldered men, although Daiki stood a head taller than Eiji and a good foot taller than Thorn. Both were impressive warriors, missing little when it came to details. She needed her best for this job, men who were calm, quick-thinking on their feet, and without fear. They were walking into the lion's den and worse—sticking their heads right into its mouth. They were also her adopted brothers, and she trusted them as she did no others.

"Before we go any further," she said softly, "I need to ask one more time if you're both fully committed to this mission. This will be the most dangerous operation we've done to date. Nothing else compares with this. Every man, woman, and child in this compound is enhanced as well as psychic. We don't know what gifts they have and we'll be under constant surveillance as well as intense scrutiny."

Daiki frowned at her. "Why is there doubt in your mind, Azami?"

"You are at the most risk, Daiki, because of the role you must always play. Our company has grown far beyond what we imagined and there is more than enough money for both of you to bow out now, before it's too late. As head of the company, you're a target anyway, but when you walk into the lion's den with me, you and Eiji will have less of a chance against enhanced, experienced soldiers. You've read their files. You know what we face. These men are some of the most dangerous men on the face of the earth today. Even factions of their own government fear them. They will strike against you first, my brother."

"We vowed to help you, Azami," Eiji pointed out.

"And I released you from that vow long ago," she reminded. "I am enhanced, as they are. I have psychic gifts, as they do. This isn't the same as the other jobs we've worked on."

Daiki shrugged. "These people could be innocents and we don't want to make any mistakes. We need to know who our enemies are." He looked his sister in the eye. "We made this vow to our father, not to you. You cannot release us. You never asked this task of us."

"We do not wish to be released, Azami," Eiji added. "It is important that you know that. I am prepared to die. Death means nothing to me. If fate wishes it so, then so be it, but I will work to stop this evil. Like Daiki and our father, I saw what that man did to an innocent child."

"We are sworn to stamp out evil," Daiki continued, "Our father's legacy lives in all of us. He took us in, gave us life when we would have lived as slaves in the sex trade. He gave us his name and his heritage. He taught us the way of the samurai. We have thrived in business following his way. We cannot step off the path when it becomes dangerous. We have prepared for this day."

Thorn took a deep breath, pride for her brothers slipping into her heart. She took another deep breath, drawing in the crisp air coming off the surrounding mountains. She saw the freedom and beauty of nature and always found she felt completely free when she was away from the cities and out in the open. She'd learned calm, to be centered, to know her way and have confidence in herself, but Whitney was a personal demon she'd never been able to fully exorcise in the way that she should. Confronting his evil was necessary, but still, at night—when she was alone—the thought of him, those terrible memories of her years with him, still gave her nightmares.

"Azami?" Daiki inquired softly.

She could hear the genuine concern in his voice, and as always, when one of her brothers showed her unexpected affection, she was touched. She sent him a small, quick smile of reassurance, keeping her features serene. She could tell Eiji and Daiki were both worried about her. They'd been with her since the day they had been with their father and had seen the occupants of a rented car dump her out on the street in one of the worst parts of Kinshicho in eastern Tokyo. Whitney had disposed of her in a place known for pimps, sex trafficking, and pedophiles, just as her brothers' parents had abandoned them. She had been eight years old and her body had been covered in scars already. She'd weighed forty-seven pounds, and the signs of torture, abuse, and multiple operations were significant—signs that she had been systematically experimented on by a madman.

Mamoru Yoshiie had lifted her gently into his arms and looked into her eyes for a long time before he'd nodded, as if seeing something in her that was worth saving. No one had ever made her feel as if she was worth anything until that simple nod. He had taken her home to live with him and his adopted sons. From that day, Yoshiie had raised her as if she were a beloved daughter, not a throwaway found on the dirty streets.

"It's beautiful here. I don't know why I didn't expect that." It was her way of reassuring them, pointing out the beauty of their surroundings as their father had done when her nightmares had awakened the entire household night after night. He would carry her outside where she could breathe, and sit with her, pointing out the distant mountains and the sky overhead. The boys would crowd close, touching her shoulder in that same calm reassurance.

They were walking straight into what might be the heart of an enemy camp. It wouldn't be the first time, and hopefully, it wouldn't be the last. There was little intelligence on the compound, and even sending a satellite to spy over the Lolo National Forest hadn't yielded much in the way of data. She had no idea if this particular group of GhostWalkers worked closely with Whitney or not—but his daughter and grandson were somewhere up in those mountains. Lily Whitney-Miller was married to a GhostWalker. She had worked with her father on some of the experiments. If anyone knew Whitney's location, it would be his daughter.

"These people are professionals with abilities similar to mine," she reiterated quietly. "Do not take chances. If things go bad, don't worry about me, just get out fast."

Daiki frowned at her. "You are repeating yourself, Azami," he reprimanded. "Are you certain you're ready to do this?"

"I've waited all my life for this moment. Whitney is a monster and he has to be stopped," she replied. "It is my destiny to find a way to cut him off from those he manipulates into aiding him, and then I will be able to stop him."

"We've had years to practice our roles," Eiji pointed out. "We've played this out in front of the entire world and we won't make a mistake. Believe in the skills our father taught us, little sister."

Daiki bent close. "We are brilliant businessmen to the world, but our father taught us the way to live, to be, and we are extraordinary warriors. We will not fail you or ourselves."

"Heads up," Eiji warned.

"Mr. Yoshiie?"

Thorn turned slowly, her breath hissing out at her reaction to that low masculine voice. Serenity, she reminded herself as a powerfully built, coffee-skinned man with heavy muscles and an easy, fluid walk approached. His dark eyes were filled with intelligence and his curly black hair invited a woman to run her fingers through it.

Thorn was rarely shaken by anything, especially by the appearance of a man—after all, she'd trained with very fit men for years—but for some reason, this man shook her when no one ever did. He walked with the confidence of a GhostWalker, very skilled, an exceptional warrior who knew his worth. Sam "Knight" Johnson.

She'd studied his file in great detail. He was renowned for his hand-to-hand combat skills and he'd been a member of the team that had gone into the Congo to rescue Ken Norton. There was nothing in his files to indicate what psychic skills he had or what Whitney had done to enhance him, but the way he walked, fluid, his body flowing over the ground, made her think of a great jungle cat. She noticed he made no noise when he walked and when he stopped, he went absolutely still.

Sam Johnson had multiple degrees in molecular biology, biochemistry, and astrophysics as well as nuclear physics. He'd been an orphan, raised in numerous foster homes before General Theodore Ranier and his wife, Delia, had recognized the extraordinary intelligence of the boy who had stolen their car. The general talked the court into allowing him to be responsible for Sam, and then he and his wife had taken the boy in. It was the general who had seen to it that Sam was educated. Only after satisfying General Ranier's demand for a higher education did Sam make the decision to follow in the general's footsteps and join the army.

His career had been—extraordinary. He was highly decorated and had run multiple covert operations successfully, building a reputation in the Rangers before joining the GhostWalker program. There he had received additional specialized training as well as enhancements, once again performing with excellence, honor, and courage. He had run numerous missions in Yemen, searching, finding, and taking out high-profile al-Qaeda targets, again without any recognition or fanfare. He was brilliant, an amazing soldier, and had contributed significantly to his country's safety, and yet this was the man Whitney was so willing to sacrifice.

"Welcome to Superior," Sam said with a slight bow. "Thank you so much for coming."

His bow, though Americanized, was not in the least awkward, she decided. She could see why the GhostWalkers would send him as an emissary. He was almost courtly, his manners impeccable. Intelligence shone in his eyes and, she reminded herself, he was a GhostWalker, capable of things no one would ever believe.

If both Teams One and Two trusted this man to vet visitors, she would have to be very careful. It didn't help that his voice nearly mesmerized her—and maybe that was an enhancement right there. He was the enemy. She had to think of all of them as her enemy. She kept her eyes downcast, presenting one of her best disguises, hiding in plain sight. Few people ever looked past the powerful Daiki Yoshiie, part owner of the largest international telecommunications company in the world. He was a billionaire and a trusted man in the world of business. Like the samurai of old, his word was his bond. Few knew that it was his adopted sister, Azami, who was the brains behind the company and that she developed all the audio communications for the satellites while Eiji developed the lens.

Sam had to force himself not to stare at the woman. She stood between the two men, but slightly behind them, which bothered him on some strange, elemental level he didn't know existed. She was very small, and unlike the traditional businesswomen of Japan who usually wore skirts, she wore the same navy, pin-striped suit as her male counterparts. He'd studied the films on all of them, and she often wore this severe-looking suit, although for him, it made her all the more feminine. Her complexion was smooth, petal soft, her mouth shaped like a little perfect bow. He loved the way she wore her long hair swept up and held by multiple ornate pins, with several long silky strands tumbling to her shoulders and down her back, an invitation for a man to want to take all those pins out just to see that mass of black hair cascade to her waist.

She looked young and innocent and fresh, almost as if she'd been secreted away in a convent her entire childhood and was just coming out into the world for the first time. She appeared quite traditional and far too young for a man as weathered and hardened as he was, with her downcast eyes and long, feathery lashes. His heart slammed hard in his chest and his blood rushed hot through his veins. He kept an expressionless face, grateful for the years of training. He'd never been so aware of anyone in his life.

"I'm Sam Johnson." He didn't offer his hand, but bowed a second time, this time to her—that small woman who packed such a punch he felt her like an electrical current running through his bloodstream.

The taller of the two men stepped forward with a slight bow. "I am Daiki Yoshiie. This is my brother, Eiji, and my sister, Azami Yoshiie."

The woman cast her eyes to the ground, but not before he saw something dark and intelligent swirling there. In one brief glance, she had appeared to take in everything about her surroundings. When she bowed, she looked more a regal princess than the demure woman walking two steps behind the powerful men who ran Samurai Telecommunications.

Sam studied the trio without appearing to do so. He was good at sizing up the enemy, which was exactly why he'd been sent to pick up the three VIPs. Outsiders were rarely allowed inside the compound. The risk of allowing anyone inside where security precautions could be determined was great, but they needed these people and, after all, they were computer nerds—right? His radar had gone off the moment he approached them, and he had no idea why. They looked exactly as they had in every news report and interview they'd done, yet they gave off some strange vibe that set the hair on the back of his neck up just like hackles.

Sam watched the way they moved, that easy flow across the ground. Perfect balance, feet under shoulders, rolling muscles. Even the woman—as small as she was—had that same flow of a fighter. Whoever these people were, they were *not* just computer nerds. They didn't spend days and nights in front of a screen or sitting in a chair. Yet even that could be accounted for. Their father had been a famed swordsman and ran a school training students in martial arts. It would stand to reason that all three would be skilled, but his gut didn't accept the explanation.

Possible Charlie. He raised the alarm reluctantly, sending the alert to his two team members lying up on the rooftops, both armed and very dangerous.

It was the woman whose gaze jumped to his face. She felt that small pulse of energy where neither man had. That meant . . . Sam refused to look away from her. This woman had secrets, and it was up to him to protect the two Ghost-Walker teams and their families relying on his judgment. She aroused his interest; more than that, she intrigued him, but the safety of the compound came first, and she definitely was far more than she appeared with her business suit and her demure expression. A man could get trapped in those dark, liquid eyes, so velvet soft and inviting, filled with intelligence and piercingly bright. Her dark eyes slipped from his gaze and shifted toward the rooftops. Oh, yeah, she was sharp, this one.

What had she missed? Thorn took another slow, careful sweep of the airport and the outlying buildings. Nothing seemed out of place, but Sam was not alone and he'd definitely communicated telepathically with someone else. The spike in the electrical current had been sharp, a certain sign of psychic energy. Although it had been far too long since she'd felt such a surge, there was no way she didn't recognize it. She'd spent a good portion of her childhood feeling that spike when Whitney experimented with the other girls, using her body as his lab rat.

She could almost smell psychic energy. She associated that spike and scent with acute pain. She wanted to press her hand to her stomach to still the sudden churning. She thought she was past all that. All the years her adopted father had put into training her in the way of the samurai. She should feel at peace anywhere she was. She accepted death as part of life. She wasn't afraid of this man or anyone else, but those childhood memories were forever entrenched in her brain.

The lives of both Daiki and Eiji were in her hands. They trusted her—trusted her judgment. Had she started this game before she was ready? It was war, pure and simple. She had declared war on Peter Whitney, and all of them would be at risk until it was finished. He had tortured her, used her for his ghastly experiments, and then disposed of her when he thought her of no more use to him.

Many times her adopted father had pointed out to her the huge mistake Whitney had made. Whitney had seemed omnipotent—godlike—to the orphan girls he controlled in his laboratory, yet had not known the considerable power Thorn wielded. She had been a child but she had managed to keep her psychic gifts secret from him—in effect, she'd defeated him. There was honor in what she'd accomplished, Yoshiie had assured her. She hoped he would think what she was doing now was honorable.

"We so appreciate you making the trip," Sam said, keeping his voice low, showing no emotion, but he watched them closely. Lily had outstanding intelligence on anyone she did business with. She would never have invited these three to the compound if she had any suspicions. "We've arranged for you to stay with us. Do you have your bags?"

He shoved his hand through the thick mass of curls on his head, watch facing out, scanning the faces of each of the three VIPs from Samurai Telecommunications. If these three were imposters, the facial recognition program would catch it immediately. He couldn't explain what made him so uneasy, particularly about the woman. There were no covert looks, nothing to make him worry, yet he couldn't shake the feeling that something was off about them. He was careful, watching them closely, and he couldn't discern a signal between them, but he was certain something unseen by him had passed between them.

"We do not want to impose on your kindness. We will stay in the local hotel," Daiki said with a small smile.

"Unfortunately, our home is miles up the mountain, Mr. Yoshiie," Sam said. "Trying to get you back and forth would eat up most of the work time. It would really be more convenient for you—and for us—if you stayed with us. We have accommodations apart from the main house. You would have plenty of privacy." He wanted them where he could see them at all times, and he wanted Lily to send him the results of the facial scans immediately.

Again, he didn't see them exchange any signal, nor was there a sharp spike in the energy around them as if they were speaking telepathically, but his brain refused to settle. Every nerve ending was on high alert. He watched them all very closely, observing their interaction, and there wasn't a single thing out of place, not one, yet he found himself more certain than ever that something wasn't right.

As strange as it seemed, he was coming to believe that it was the woman, not Daiki, who was in charge. There was absolutely no reason why he would feel that way. The reputation of the Samurai Telecommunications company was spotless, and always, it was Daiki at the helm, Eiji and Azami flanking him, but Sam found he didn't believe it They were almost too smooth.

Of course they would be, he argued silently with himself, they had gone to high-security companies all over the world; yet he found himself certain that the woman was the boss, not the imposing male doing all the talking, which was shocking. Samurai Telecommunications was in the news all the time. It was an international corporation with offices in London, Tokyo, Washington, DC, and San Francisco. They were investing in Africa as well as making headlines by investing in Turkey. Eiji was usually the spokesperson, but Daiki was the undisputed leader and lauded to be the brains. Azami was always with them, but clearly in the background.

Even with Dr. Lily Whitney-Miller, who was an acknowledged genius, Sam was used to being the smartest person in the room, often overlooked because he was a soldier, and people automatically discounted the brains of a soldier. He had the feeling Azami Yoshiie might be the smartest person in the room wherever she was—and those around her overlooked her because she was a woman. She stayed in the background deliberately, just as he often did. He found he could gather more intelligence that way, and he would bet his last dime that she used exactly the same tactic.

He wasn't certain why he was so on edge or felt as if they were in the opening gambit of a lethal chess game, but his alarm system was shrieking at him—loud.

Lily says all three are who they say they are. Nicolas "Nico" Trevane relayed Lily's assurances. He was the undisputed best shot of the team, a sniper renowned for making impossible shots and the man Sam most wanted as a backup at that moment.

It was Sam's call then. Bring them up? Or dump the high-resolution satellite for the time being? Sam let his breath out slowly. There was no doubt the woman felt that small surge when Nico relayed Lily's acknowledgment of the three identities. Her gaze had jumped to his and then once more did a careful survey of the rooftops.

The first and second GhostWalker teams had made their homes in Montana, high in the mountains, their lands bordered by the Lolo National Forest. They were completely self-sufficient and could live for years off the land if they needed to do so. They had an impressive arsenal built up between the two teams as well as vehicles for winter, small planes, and a helicopter. Lily's money had been put to good use. This high-resolution satellite would allow amazing surveillance. They had far too many enemies. They needed a secure way to check every order as well as to communicate with the other two teams making their fortress in San Francisco.

"This way," Sam directed, making up his mind.

Again a flutter of indecision settled in his gut. This had *never* happened before. Sam always recognized an enemy. His eyes were enhanced. He saw tiny details others missed. He was highly skilled in recognizing lies. Their facial expressions remained serene, not giving away anything, yet some tiny flicker of signals his brain caught but he hadn't yet defined told him something was off.

As a rule, he was a gentleman and would offer to carry the woman's bag, but he wanted his hands free. He hoped Nico or Kadan "Bishop" Montague, a powerful anchor and shield, lying up on the rooftops with a sniper rifle, would take note of that precaution. They both knew him, knew the way he worked. Anything out of the ordinary would alert them to possible danger.

Thorn curled her fingers around the handle of her small travel bag. She couldn't spot the shooters, but she knew they were there—she felt them now. The taste of psychic energy was in her mouth, impossible to ignore. Once she entered the SUV that would take them to the very lair of the Ghost-Walkers, she would no longer have a choice, not without killing someone. She would be fully committing her brothers to their course of action. Neither Daiki nor Eiji was enhanced, although they were well versed in the way of the samurai—Mamoru Yoshiie and his school had seen to that. They were extraordinary warriors, and she knew she could count on them. They had worked smoothly together over the last few years, but this would be their most dangerous mission yet. Did she have the right to risk their lives?

"Ma'am?" Sam prompted.

She sent him a small, demure smile, her gaze flicking to his. The moment their eyes met, she felt that hard punch in her stomach. A million butterflies took wing. He definitely had an effect on her. She gripped the handle of her bag and lifted it, indicating she would follow him.

It was now or never. She had already set her plan in motion. She had to know all the players, and this man was a sacrifice, a "knight" in Whitney's game to be given to a ruthless killer to be tortured before he was disposed of. It was possible she could make him an ally. In any case, if she managed to pull this off, she would have eyes and ears in Lily Whitney's camp here in Montana, and the GhostWalker teams would want the satellite software installed in their San Francisco fortress as well. This would be her biggest step in her war against Whitney, and his own daughter could very well be his downfall.

GhostWalkers, as a rule, could detect one another fairly easily, and they always felt psychic energy when it was used. She had learned she was an exception—even Whitney hadn't known she had powerful psychic gifts. So far, that single distinction hadn't let her down, but Sam Johnson might prove to be the one person who was able to "feel" her psychic energy even when she wasn't using it. She knew that was part of the code of identity. They all "felt" that subtle pulse their bodies gave off when they were in close vicinity to one another. She controlled that pulse, just as she could control her heart and lungs.

Sam led the way to the SUV. Had Nico and the Bishop not been watching his back, he would have had a difficult time leading the way across the open parking lot to his vehicle.

The sense of danger grew instead of dissipated. Every step raised the hair on the back of his neck, but he never broke stride or gave away that he was worried. The trio acted the part of businessmen, but somehow they didn't *feel* that way to him. Every sense remained alert, and he actually felt the pulsing of the venom sacs implanted along his wrist from one of Whitney's insane experiments. For his body to react with such intensity, he was certain he wasn't wrong—that something was not right about their three guests.

The facial recognition program would be nearly impossible to beat and certainly would have detected one of them as being imposter, raising the alert immediately, but Lily had confirmed the identities of all three. Clearly, the taller man was really Daiki Yoshiie, founder of Samurai Telecommunications, and the other two were his adopted brother and sister. The company had risen fast, gaining an impeccable reputation internationally. It was said that the company was run by the code of Bushido and that their word was gold.

Sam knew the exact position of all three of the visitors. They had fanned out as they followed, the woman directly behind him. None of them made noise when they walked, not the slap of the soles of their feet, not the soft brush of the material of their clothing. Still, he "saw" them. He had the ability to "feel" and map out anything behind him. He practiced each step in his mind. At the first sign of attack, he would step back and to his left, crowding Eiji, while he disposed of the woman first, believing she was the real threat. He would have to follow through, snapping Eiji's neck and using him as a shield against Daiki's attack. It would have to be one move, not two, killing Azami and then Eiji immediately after.

Nico would definitely take out Daiki. Still, Sam was armed and he added the second move, shooting Daiki the moment he had disposed of Eiji. He practiced over and over in his mind until he knew every move smoothly. All the while he kept his breathing easy and his stride casual. They crossed the parking lot without incident.

Unlocking the SUV, he opened the front passenger door. Daiki slipped inside, much to Sam's consternation. He had expected the woman to take the front seat. She flashed him one look, her expression covered by the sweep of her lashes and went around the vehicle to take the seat behind the driver. A muscle twitched in Sam's jaw. He wanted the woman where he could see her. The two men didn't raise his hackles in the same way she did. The last thing he wanted was for her to be sitting behind him.

Sam took Daiki's bag and stowed it in the back, then gathered Eiji's as well and placed it carefully in the storage space. There were three rows of seats in the SUV, making the luggage space small, but the visitors seemed to be traveling light. Azami had kept her bag very neatly with her. He would have liked to get a feel for the weight of that bag. She was *definitely* the threat his body was reacting to.

He had been fully briefed on them. Little was known of Azami before Mamoru Yoshiie had adopted her. Rumors flew about Yoshiie, yet nothing was concrete. He was reputed to be a direct descendent of a famous samurai and his family had passed down to him all the fighting skills and way of life of the samurai. He was known as a master craftsman of sword making. He seemed a quiet, gentle man who led a family life. He had a good reputation from all who knew him, and yet the rumors persisted until the man was shrouded in myth, becoming a thing of legend.

It was whispered in Japan that Mamoru Yoshiie earned his real living as an assassin. The yakuza were rarely spoken of, especially in polite company, and when it was implied Yoshiie had some association with them, that had been firmly denied by the yakuza itself. They left the man strictly alone and some said it was Yoshiie one went to if they were in trouble with the local crime lord. Sam doubted if any of it was true until he'd met Yoshiie's adopted daughter and his sons. All three moved with the skill of a consummate fighter.

"We were expecting at least two bodyguards to accompany you," Sam directed his statement to Daiki. "We do have accommodations for them as well if you would feel more comfortable."

"Azami and Eiji are my bodyguards when we are installing software for a satellite as important as this one. We know that most companies do not want strangers living and working where sensitive material might be exposed. We endeavor to make our clients as comfortable as possible."

That made sense and it explained the way Azami's eyes had continually swept the small airport and the roofs of the buildings, but it didn't explain the way his body reacted so strongly to her.

"Why are we waiting?" Azami inquired very politely.

Sam couldn't keep his gaze from shifting to the rearview mirror. Azami wasn't looking at him—or Daiki. She peered through the tinted windows, obviously expecting trouble.

"We know a man of Daiki's stature has enemies," Sam said, his tone very matter-of-fact. "We had men in position to cover anyone taking undue notice of your arrival. They'll be here in a moment or two."

He kept his glaze glued to the rearview mirror, observing Azami's reaction to the news. She turned her head slowly and met his eyes in the mirror. He felt the impact all the way to his toes. His blood went hot, rushing through his veins, flooding his groin with need. He kept his expression composed, but only with effort. She was potent, that sweet, demure-looking bodyguard sitting directly behind him. He had no doubt she could take off his head in seconds. So much for the intellectual, computer-nerd types.

She inclined her head, regal princess to the peasant who had just scored. She had known his men were out there all right—she wasn't in the least surprised—but she didn't like them climbing into the SUV and seating themselves directly behind her and Eiji, neatly flanking them, taking away any advantage they may have had.

Nico and Kadan both carried large, solid briefcases, clearly housing their sniper rifles. Neither tried to hide the fact as they slipped inside. Sam kept his eyes locked with Azami's. She didn't even turn her head or flick a glance toward the two men as they entered—and that was more the mark of a professional than anything else could have been. She was too sure of herself. Sam swore to himself. They were in real trouble, but he couldn't figure out how or why.

These were businesspeople. They were known throughout the international community as well as having been vetted by every separate military, CIA, and Homeland Security committee that could possibly investigate them. They were under intense scrutiny, just by the fact that they produced and sold high-resolution satellites. Their software and their satellites were considered the best in the world. How could every agency have made such a mistake?

Sam wanted to doubt himself, he really did. The woman was the first one who had really intrigued him, both mentally and physically. Maybe it was the challenge, but deep down, he knew this woman's destiny was tangled with his. Good or bad, they were somehow intertwined. He'd rather their relationship was positive, but that nagging radar of his wouldn't shut up. Something was very off about all three visitors.

"Kadan Montague and Nicolas Trevane," he offered by way of introduction after he'd identified their guests.

All three gave a slight head bow toward the newcomers. Azami continued to look at Sam through the mirror, her eyes like that of a cat, tilted and wide, fringed with feathery black lashes that swept down demurely when her brother turned his head to look at her. Sam wasn't buying the act. He started the SUV, sending up a silent prayer that Nico and Kadan wouldn't be lulled into a false sense of security by Lily's positive IDs. The back of his neck itched. Azami Yoshiie was more than a damned bodyguard, and it was going to require a fair amount of discipline to keep his mind on his driving.

The mountain road was hazardous, the switchbacks tight and the road narrow once they were away from the small town. Sam set his teeth and drove. He could feel his heart beating in his chest and he did a little slow breathing. It made sense that Daiki Yoshiie would travel with bodyguards who could protect him as well as teach clients the installation and use of the necessary software for their products. Being bodyguards explained the way they all three moved, and if half of the rumors circulating about Mamoru Yoshiie were true, he would have taught his children to defend themselves. So if it all made sense, then why was he so uneasy?

"Would you like music?" he asked Daiki politely. Making casual conversation was usually quite easy for him, but he felt he had the proverbial sword poised at his neck, making it a little more difficult to think up topics of interest.

"It is not necessary," Daiki replied with equal politeness. "I do not require music or conversation to be comfortable. I enjoy the surroundings, and your mountains are quite beautiful."

"And remote," Eiji added. "This road does not appear as if it gets much traffic."

Sam had veered off the main road leading to the Lolo National Forest, to take a private road most of those residing in the complex of homes within the fortress used. The road was a little steeper than the other one, but it cut through the thicker forest, the canopy of trees forming a natural ceiling above them, hiding them from possible eyes in the sky.

"The compound is remote," Sam said. "It affords us privacy. The research is very delicate and security is tight."

"I understand Dr. Miller resides on the premises of her research center," Daiki continued.

Sam sent him a sharp glance and looked in the rearview mirror. Both Kadan and Nico looked as if they were lounging lazily in the far backseats, but he knew their expressions very well. The moment Lily was mentioned in conjunction with her residence, both had gone to full alert. At all costs, Lily's son needed to be protected from any outsiders. He had been born with exceptional qualities, and everyone knew her father, Peter Whitney, would do anything to get his hands on the boy or at least gather evidence that the child was different.

"Have you met Lily?" Sam asked, knowing the answer. He'd been in Pakistan hunting high profile al Qaeda targets when the four GhostWalker teams had made the decision to acquire a high-resolution satellite of their own.

The money in the GhostWalker fund allowed the astonishingly expensive but necessary purchase, but it was the security that concerned all four teams. They had known someone from Samurai Telecommunications would have to spend time at both compounds while they learned to handle the satellite.

"She came in with her husband to our DC office several times," Daiki said. "An extremely brilliant woman."

Why the hell did he feel so damned edgy? That was Lily. Anyone meeting her nearly always used that adjective to describe her, yet Sam's radar wouldn't stop shrieking at him. If anything, it was in full-blown alarm mode. He glanced in the mirror again, then to his right and left. If someone had been behind him, he should have seen dust. Still . . .

"Do you have someone following us?" Sam asked simultaneously with Azami.

His breath caught in his throat as his eyes met hers in the mirror. He saw the same shock and surprise in her eyes that were in his. She felt that same wariness and wrongly had put it down to his crew. If the threat wasn't emanating from her or her men, then where the hell was it coming from?

CHAPTER 3

Sam instantly threw the SUV into four-wheel drive and was off the road, rushing into deeper forest. Nico and Kadan shifted position, weapons fitting into their hands easily.

"The windows are bulletproof," Sam informed the three visitors. "Keep them up. Who knew you were coming here today?"

"I filed a flight plan," Azami answered.

Sam thought it significant that she sounded very calm. He glanced at her in the rearview mirror. Her facial muscles were relaxed. The woman knew there was trouble, but she remained unfazed. Bodyguard, like hell. She was far more than that. She didn't even show tension. He found himself breathing out rather than in. Every time he took in a lungful of air in the close confines of the SUV, he found himself breathing her into his lungs. She seemed to permeate his body, slipping past his guard and lodging herself deep.

"We also leave our itinerary with my secretary in case one of us is needed," Daiki added. "She's been my secretary for many years and would never betray us."

Sam wasn't all too sure about that. As far as he was

concerned, everyone who wasn't part of his team was a potential enemy. It was strange to find himself so divided. He'd always been a decisive person. He had great confidence in his intellect and his physical abilities. He'd trained with nearly every weapon known to man, circled the globe training in every terrain, and he'd been involved in hundreds of missions. He'd never been this damned tense.

The SUV bumped over rotting logs and splashed through rocky creek beds filled with running water. There was the faintest of tracks on the pitted, uneven very narrow trail. Tamarack, fir, western red cedar, and white bark pine trees grew in abundance, a thick, lush forest surrounding them, sentinels providing intertwining canopy to shelter them.

"Bandit, three o'clock," Nico said. "Slow down and let me bail."

"We can't stay inside this vehicle and fight," Azami said. "I want Daiki under cover."

"Hold on, Nico." Sam still wasn't convinced they could trust any of the Yoshiies, but he was tasked with their safety. "I'm getting us there." He zigzagged through the trees, missing wide trunks by inches, knowing the helicopter coming after them would have a much more difficult time in the heavier canopy.

"Incoming," Kadan reported.

Sam jerked the wheel in the only direction he could, scraping the bark from a western red cedar tree and spinning the SUV nearly onto its side. He reversed his direction and took the trail that would bring them closest to the bunkers they'd scattered through the hills. Each bunker was hidden by fallen trees. Brush was encouraged to grow around the entrances so that from air or even on the ground, they were impossible to detect.

The explosion was loud, trees splintering as smoke and debris erupted into the sky and rained down, blanketing the area. Clearly the helicopter was trying to drive them out of cover.

"Bail, now," Sam said. "I'll lead them away."

It was another point in his argument that all three of the visitors were seasoned warriors when neither Daiki nor Eiji hesitated, leaping from the vehicle along with Nico and Kadan. Sam slammed his foot on the gas and spun the SUV, the doors slamming closed. The back refused to latch, swinging open again, but Azami caught the handle and closed it fast before they briefly showed themselves to the helicopter and once again disappeared in a blast of dust and debris under the forest canopy.

"You have to get out," Sam ordered. "Kadan and Nico can protect you three while I draw them away."

Azami climbed into the front seat, dragging her case with her. "Eiji can protect my brother. Don't worry about me."

Confidence permeated her voice. In any case, he didn't have time to argue. Another explosion rocked the ground in front of them and smoke reduced visibility to zero. The helicopter was attempting to herd them, and that meant they had ground forces.

"Get out now," Sam said, as he slammed on the brakes and shut down the vehicle. He was already leaping out, not waiting to look to see if she followed him. She was far too calm and experienced not to realize the vehicle was a liability to them.

He raced through the smoke away from the others, Azami on his heels. As soon as he got to the edge of the swirling smoke, he held up his hand and dropped low into the thick vegetation. Azami dropped with him. The sound of an engine firing up off to their left was loud. A second engine joined the first, from the right. Sam swore aloud.

The trap was a neat little box, and that told Sam this plan had been in the works awhile. Someone had come into the forest and scouted alternate trails the GhostWalkers took and set their ambush. This was no sudden decision hastily put together the moment Azami had filed her flight plan. Well thought out and carefully executed meant experienced warriors. The helicopter and multiple Jeeps manned with soldiers of some sort meant money.

"Get the hell out of here, stay on your belly, and crawl

away from me. Try to make your way back to the others. Identify yourself or Kadan or Nico might shoot you when you come up on them. They've got us boxed in and it's going to get ugly fast."

"I'm familiar with ugly," Azami said. "Lead the way."

Sam turned his head. She had a bow and arrows slung over one shoulder and a very sharp knife hanging from her belt. He caught a glimpse of a gun when she slipped closer to him, using her toes and elbows. Yeah, she was no sweet businesswoman needing protection. He didn't mind being right about her at all. He flashed a quick grin and slithered over the top of the small mound of leaves to slide down the slope into the ravine below.

"Someone knew you were coming," he said as he led the way into an animal maze inside deep brush.

"Or they're after one of you," Azami pointed out. "I don't allow my brother into a situation I haven't checked out thoroughly, and your own government seems to have people who want you all dead."

He didn't turn his head to look at her. What was the use? Her expression gave nothing away. "That's classified and you shouldn't have that information."

"You're not the only people who investigate thoroughly before they walk into the lion's den. I take my brother's protection very seriously."

Sam liked the soft, melodic quality to her voice, and it sucked big-time that he even noticed it, let alone allowed it to affect him when they were surrounded by danger. Maybe that was the problem—wasn't danger supposed to heighten attraction?

He dug his toes into soft dirt and propelled himself up the slope, signaling her to stay quiet. The first vehicle was just ahead. He could hear their voices, hushed but clear, traveling through the forest. Moving slightly, he caught a brief look at the enemy through the heavy foliage. They were partially hidden by heavy brush, and he'd have to go down a slope and up another to reach them.

"Wait for the spotter, Tony, he's swinging back around," a man standing behind the Jeep advised.

"Where the hell are they?" Tony, the driver, tapped out his impatience while the other three soldiers surrounding the Jeep exchanged a quick, annoyed look. Clearly they were far more experienced than their driver and had more patience.

Sam knew his biggest problem was the eye in the sky. Most likely they could see the heat from their bodies, otherwise the copter would be useless in the thick canopy. Azami must have realized the same thing. She rolled out to the edge of the open, coming up on one knee as she strung an arrow into her bow, aiming up toward the empty sky. She went perfectly still, leaves and twigs caught in her hair and papering her very expensive pin-striped suit so that she nearly blended in with her surroundings.

Sam took advantage of her change of position. All he needed was to get his enemy in clear sight, and he preferred to do so without an audience. He dug his elbows into the soft dirt and leaves, scuttling up the slope like a lizard until he was able to look over a rotting log. Three men, armed with automatic weapons, stood beside a Jeep. They were dressed like hunters, but their weapons were for killing men. The driver sat at the wheel, looking up toward the sky, eager to get on his way.

The wash from the helicopter struck Sam before the overgrown dragonfly came dancing through the sky. The door was open and a man crouched just inside, an automatic weapon cradled in his arms. The pilot was skilled, maneuvering through the heavy canopy to give his gunner the best advantage.

Azami calmly let her arrow fly, sending it on its way and instantly following with a second so fast the two shots were nearly simultaneous. The first arrow went through the throat of the gunner, and the second took the pilot through his eye. At once the helicopter lurched like a giant wounded bird.

Sam wasn't about to look a gift horse in the mouth. Teleportation was something he'd studied and tried to understand on an intellectual level. He had taken part in the research and knew there were several studios under way including at Samurai Telecommunications—that were on the verge of discovering just how it all could be done, but not with a human being. In theory, the person teleporting would be reproduced and then destroyed while his copy ended up somewhere else. He knew how it worked on *things*, transporting particles, but not how he was able to do it so smoothly. He no longer cared about the how—maybe he could really move faster than light and he simply *appeared* to teleport.

Sam projected his body to that spot directly behind the man at the rear of the vehicle. The mercenary's attention was directed to the sky, his eyes wide with shock, his fingers around his gun without a real understanding of what just happened. Sam gripped the mercenary's head in two very large, strong hands and wrenched, dropping him onto the ground, neck broken. Another burst of speed had him behind the man who had stepped out on the passenger side. Sam used a knife, dragging him backward, lowering him to the ground, and moving once more.

To move numerous times with that burst of speed was dangerous, causing his stomach to churn and his mind to go fuzzy around the edges. He'd made two kills before the helicopter had even begun to spin out of control. He came up behind the third soldier fast, grasping his head and giving him a quick, decisive jerk. He had always been abnormally strong, and the enhancements as well as his physical training had added to his natural strength. He dropped the dead man and crouched low just as Azami's third arrow took the driver straight through his neck. The Jeep rocketed forward as the dead man's foot stomped down hard, slamming into the tree ahead.

The chopper came down with the sound of metal grinding and men screaming. Still in a crouch, Sam looked down the slope to Azami. His vision was blurred and his head screaming at him.

"You're damned good with that bow."

She bowed slightly. "A little known fact—samurai were renowned with bows and arrows long before the sword. And there were female samurai, some very famous."

"I have your father to thank," he guessed.

"That you do." Her eyebrow rose slightly. "You're pretty fast. I didn't even see you make your move on them and that's unusual for me."

"You were fairly occupied making certain you took out the helicopter—and thank you for that."

She nodded solemnly. "You're very welcome."

"We're not out of the woods yet," he said. A second vehicle was close.

"That's stating the obvious," Azami flashed a small smile and deliberately looked around at the thick forest of trees.

He found himself smiling to himself with grudging respect in spite of the situation as he crouched down beside the last man he'd killed. She was a woman to stand and fight with a man, not run when there was adversity or danger. And why the hell had *that* thought crossed his mind? Her scent was driving him crazy, even there, out in the open.

"I don't recognize any of them," he said. "No IDs on them, but they look like typical mercs to me. Guns for hire. Have you seen them before?"

Thorn made her way to Sam's side, careful to stay in the brush as much as possible. She studied each face of the fallen men carefully as Sam quickly searched for any means of identification. She noted that he passed the face of his watch over the bodies but also the vehicle and license plate.

"I don't recognize them either. If they were looking to kidnap my brother, they certainly went about it wrong."

"Have there been threats?"

"There are always threats against Daiki and the company," Thorn said.

Each time Sam's eyes met hers, she felt a peculiar brushing of butterfly wings in her stomach. Very light, but the sensation made it difficult to breathe. She loved his dark eyes and the way his gaze drifted over her almost like the lightest touch of fingers. "Nothing stood out lately that made either Eiji or me become more concerned than usual. Perhaps the threat was to you."

She tested him to see his reaction but instantly realized the speculation was a mistake. Those dark eyes jumped to her face with far too much intelligence in them. Worse, he seemed to take her breath away, leaving her feeling as if every last bit of air had rushed from her lungs.

"Why would you think that? I'm a soldier, nothing special. I don't have a reputation for creating the most superior satellite and software in the world. I can imagine dozens of countries as well as drug cartels and terrorist organizations very interested in acquiring your brother, but there isn't anyone who would have a reason to come after me."

Azami followed him away from the fallen mercenaries, noticing they were still moving away from her brothers and the other GhostWalkers. Her mind raced with the possibilities of how the attack had occurred. It was too much of a coincidence to think that Daiki wasn't targeted. The newest satellite software, audio, and lens was light-years ahead of the competition and Daiki was reputed to be the developer. It made perfect sense that he would be in danger. They had discussed that fact at great length, Daiki and Eiji persuading her that because of her past and the job they all knew they would ultimately undertake, it would be better to keep her out of the spotlight. She had agreed.

More than once, there had been attempts to hack into their computers. Thieves had tried breaking into their building and infiltrating their ranks numerous times. This attack on them might not have anything at all to do with Whitney. He had no idea she was alive. He hadn't even bothered with the tracking device she knew he'd placed in many of the other girls. She hadn't been important enough to track. She'd been nothing but garbage to him and he'd thrown her out.

Sam puzzled over Azami. She appeared completely serene in the midst of blood and death, but she wasn't. He couldn't put his finger on what was wrong any more than he could have explained why he was so certain that it was Azami Yoshiie and not either of her brothers who was the most intelligent, the most dangerous, and the leader of the three, but his gut never lied to him.

From the moment she was near him, every nerve ending in his body had gone on alert, every sense seemed heightened. He was very aware of the wind in the trees—the smoke drifting through the canopy and the sound of insects ceasing to their right. A wave of silence suddenly descended once again, spreading around them. He dropped low, signaling to her as he would his men, an automatic reaction before his brain registered that she was a civilian and wouldn't recognize the need for silence and to go to ground. He turned his head and found she was in position, bow and arrow at the ready.

In that one swift glance over his shoulder, he found every detail of her imprinted on his mind. The scent of her drifting with the wind, a fresh, citrusy smell that teased his senses. The way the breeze slipped fingers into her thick, shiny hair, feeding a need to do the same just to feel the silky strands against his bare skin. He knew it was insane to be in the middle of a combat situation and be so completely captivated by the way the light played over her flawless skin and brought attention to the outrageous long lashes surrounding her cat's eyes.

It was just a little bit sick to be so completely taken with her just because she was a warrior woman. She appeared demure and even introverted—not at all the type of woman to appeal to him. Sam wanted a woman with her own opinions, one with complete confidence in herself as a sexy, intelligent female, not some yes-person who agreed with everything he said. He wanted more than a physical attraction and, unfortunately, his relationships never seemed to last beyond the first date. He'd never considered a female soldier—not once—when he'd thought about a partner, but Azami Yoshiie was damned sexy with a bow and arrow in her hands and that composed, serene look on her face.

"What is it?" she asked.

Her voice sang in his veins as if tuned specifically to his body. He turned away from her as a thought crossed his mind. Was he *too* tuned to her? Was there something else at work? He shook his head, thankful his back was to her. His thoughts were too outrageous to be considered—but on the other hand, Whitney had paired male and female soldiers together using pheromones and some sort of a virus that reacted in the brain to create paths bonding mates to one another.

He took his time examining the terrain around them. Something was out there—and coming toward them, not in the vehicle that seemed to be going away from them. An amateur trick. He had been leading Azami toward the next bunker, hidden a good twenty feet beneath the earth, intending to get her out of danger and under wraps where the enemy had no chance to acquire or kill her on his watch. Daiki Yoshiie's sister might be worth secrets to the billionaire. He was certain they were cut off from the bunker he'd been trying to get to.

"What do your names mean? Azami is pretty. Does it have a pretty meaning?" All GhostWalker women, females Whitney had taken from orphanages around the world and experimented on, had been given the names of flowers or seasons. Whitney had dehumanized them, not even allowing them to know their own birth dates. Azami Yoshiie couldn't possibly be one of those girls, but his body was too attracted and she raised such an alert, his radar shrieking at him. Something was off somewhere. He kept his tone very casual and very low, projecting his voice solely to her, as if they were discussing the weather and the topic didn't matter at all.

"My name can be interpreted as heart of the thistle or flower of the thistle. In any case, my father thought the name was pretty." She kept her voice equally hushed. There was affection for her adopted father in her voice.

Sam didn't make the mistake of turning around, but his heart rate jumped, just for a moment at the word "flower." "And your brothers?"

"Eiji can be interpreted as two protectors."

"A good name for a bodyguard," Sam commented. "And Daiki?"

She laughed softly and he did turn, the sound was intriguing and musical. He could listen to that sound forever. She was still ready, the bow and arrow waiting, but her eyes were soft with memories.

"Daiki means great tree. Even as a young boy he was big." She hesitated. "We tease him about being so powerful and great, but his name can also mean noble, and just between the two of us, so he doesn't get a big head, I secretly think his name says who he really is."

The crack of a branch snapping was loud. Something hit a tree trunk with a resounding crash. Sam turned and dove onto Azami, all in one move, taking her down hard, both arms going around her and rolling away from the sound. He did his best to protect her from the worst of the rocks and fallen branches. Azami didn't fight; instead she ducked her head into his chest and held on while he took them as far from that sound as possible.

The explosion rocked the ground, the sound so loud it hurt their ears. Sam put his lips against Azami's ear so she would feel his mouth moving. His words, however, were projected into her mind. *Are you hurt?* His breath caught in his throat—waiting.

Azami shook her head, an almost imperceptible movement.

They have someone waiting ahead of us and on either side. They'll keep blasting, herding us toward their trap. I want you to backtrack . . .

Before he could finish, she shook her head again and

pressed her lips against his ear. "I'm staying with you. Just move."

Azami was telepathic. There was no question in his mind she was psychic. She'd felt those surges of energy when he'd contacted Kadan and Nico and she'd heard him clearly, although he hadn't spoken aloud.

Thorn stiffened, her fingers curling around the dagger hidden beneath her jacket. She'd screwed up. Totally screwed up. The moment Sam's arms had wrapped around her body and she felt him, felt every muscle hard and defined, felt his much larger body imprisoning hers, she went into major meltdown. Never, in all her existence, had such a thing happened. Her world—*she*—was all about control.

Eight years of her life had been spent in torture and she'd never flinched, never once made a mistake. The years with her father had instilled even more discipline, and yet with Sam's scent finding its way into her lungs, invading every one of her heightened senses, she couldn't find her breath. The sensation was so strong, so intrusive, she felt threatened at her most elemental level—and yet more alive than she'd ever felt in her life.

She had been very careful to keep apprised of Whitney's experiments and she knew he paired GhostWalkers with his orphaned female soldiers, but she was gone long before Sam had become a GhostWalker. She *couldn't* be paired with him. Whitney could have perhaps saved something of her DNA to pair her with Sam, but he didn't have access to Sam prior to her being thrown away. It was impossible and yet . . .

Breathe.

That single, velvet-soft enticement filled her mind, rocking her far more than the second explosion did. His voice was a caress, a weapon with more power than a knife or a gun had over her. Instinctively she began to inch the dagger from the sheath. Sam's hand clamped down hard on her wrist.

Our enemies have us surrounded. Do you really want to

go to war with me right now? Let's get out of this first and deal with what's happening between us afterward.

She detested that he knew her reaction to him—but at least she wasn't alone. He'd admitted he was just as shaken as she was. Shame poured through her. Regret. She had dishonored herself and her father by such a disgraceful mistake. Nevertheless, she had to move forward. She relaxed her grip on the dagger and nodded her head to indicate she agreed with him.

We move straight ahead. They're trying to keep us boxed in. We'll have to take out the soldiers in front of us as quietly as possible and slip through their line. I've tried to isolate separate sounds to see what we're looking at, but the concussions messed up my hearing.

Sam's voiced steadied her. He was matter-of-fact, a soldier assessing their situation. She forced air into her lungs. Sharing her mind with him seemed almost more intimate than sharing her body. He was everywhere, his body rock-hard while she had melted into him, becoming part of him. She felt as if she shared his very breath. She was samurai and she could handle this utterly intimate position with a fellow warrior.

My hearing is messed up as well. But there are more than four of them on our left side. I think both vehicles and the helicopter were meant to drive us to the foot soldiers. Oh, God. The moment she opened her mind fully to him to push her thoughts to him, he flooded her mind with—*him.*

He filled her, all those dark lonely places she kept hidden from the world—from the ones she'd come to love. There was no way to hide from him. He was warmth and strength and everything she didn't believe in and distrusted. Loneliness lived and breathed in her. She was careful to keep who she was hidden, especially from Daiki and Eiji. She didn't want them to know the darkness permeating her, and yet she was instantly exposed and vulnerable to this total stranger. Worse, once he flooded her mind with his strength and purpose, with the essence of who and what he was—that brilliant, determined, and very confident warrior—she felt more connection to him than she did with any other human being.

I agree. They're using military tactics on us.

Azami hesitated before venturing her opinion, but she'd thrown her lot in with this man, at least until they were out of the situation. *I think the mercenaries are considered expendable. They had no idea you have a military compound anywhere close to them. They were too relaxed. The real soldiers are in front of us.*

For one heart-stopping moment her breath caught in her throat as his lips seemed to press ever-so-briefly against her ear. *I think you're right. So the real question becomes, who really is after us, because they sure as hell know about the military compound and that they're on a time limit. My people will be coming in hot and fast.*

She turned her head to look at him. The moment their eyes met, his so dark and velvet soft, her stomach reacted with that strange fluttering. She smiled at him. *Then we'd better get to work before someone else gets all the fun.*

A slow grin spread across his face and reached his eyes. Approval was there and in spite of her determination to remain unmoved by anything else this man did, warmth spread through her.

My boss would kick my ass for deliberately taking you into combat.

I'm very proactive when it comes to saving my own life, she assured him. *Or going after someone who endangers my brother. We need to know who is behind this.* Thorn put steel into her voice.

She wasn't going to back down. The attack hadn't been directed at the compound itself. More than likely the threat was to her brother, and she'd been the one to allow him to take her place in the public eye. She moved subtly, telling him to let her go.

Sam nodded and signaled straight ahead. She liked that

in him. They weren't going to waste time and energy on the expendable mercenaries hired basically to get killed—he was going after the real threat. And he didn't waste valuable time trying to argue with her; he recognized that she was no liability to him but rather a seasoned warrior.

They moved slowly, using the sounds of their enemy to cover their presence. Thorn would have preferred the night, but she could be invisible during the day nearly as well. The soldiers would be on high alert, hunting the two of them.

In the trees, she warned. *Three o'clock.*

Another at nine o'clock. Branches are too thick at twelve. Maneuver around and see if you can spot him. Take him out with your bow. I'll handle the other two.

Her stomach muscles protested. The trees were a good thirty to fifty feet high. If he used a gun, the noise would draw the enemy in numbers. She could . . . Thorn stopped abruptly as another thought occurred. Sam was an enhanced GhostWalker. She hadn't seen him cross that slope to get to the mercenaries, but he'd killed three of them before she shot the driver. True, she'd been distracted by the helicopter, but still, he'd moved too fast for anyone normal. Was it possible that he moved the way she did? Faster than the speed of light? A form of teleportation? Could there be two people capable of such a thing?

She slipped past him, careful not to disturb leaves as she used an animal's tunnel to scoot through the heavier brush. She went about three feet before she turned to look over her shoulder. Sam wasn't there anymore. She glanced toward the tree at nine o'clock and then tried to see the one at three o'clock. The view was entirely obscured, and in any case, she had a job to do.

Sam needed privacy to work his skills. Sending her off to find the enemy was a calculated risk. Could he kill both snipers in the trees before she was spotted? He didn't waste time, taking the closest tree, the one at three o'clock. The man was up high, about thirty feet, sitting in the crotch of the tree, his rifle resting on the branch snaking out to provide both cover as well as support.

Trees were extremely dangerous when using teleportation. Too many sharp edges and the potential for missing smaller, hidden twigs made the idea terrifying, but his enemy was sitting up in that tree with a sniper rifle, hunting him and Azami. He wasn't about to let that go. In any case, the foot soldiers had told him nothing about this particular attack. He wanted to find a way to follow the thread back to the snake's head and he had to do it before Azami got hurt.

It was difficult not to think of her as a soldier. She was too well trained and it was easy to see her as a warrior rather than someone he needed to protect. She *felt* capable. She *felt*, gut-deep, like a partner. Still, he had to get into both trees and take out the snipers if they were to hold out until help came.

He studied the tree carefully, taking great care to find the perfect place to insert his body without damaging it and still get to the sniper before the man could alert the others— or kill him. He watched as the wind blew through the leaves and shifted the branches subtly. It was fortunate that the crotch of the tree was fairly bare of snapped-off branches, lessening the chances of making a mistake. He didn't want to end up with a stake stuck through his leg—or any other part of his anatomy.

He picked his retreat, a spot closer to the other sniper, one that should afford him a good enough view to scope out an entry point. Unfortunately, the space was free of cover and he'd have only a moment to slip into the brush before the sniper would spot him. To ensure his chances, he would have to cause a small distraction, buying him just enough time to vanish.

Sam made the jump fast, a blinding, blurring speed that took less time than his thinking process had. His body hit the vee of the tree perfectly, but the momentum nearly threw him off the other side. Something bit hard at his calf and dug into his back, but he dismissed the pain and caught the sniper's head by his hair, jerking it back as the knife bit deep into the throat. He shoved the body from the tree as he made the jump back to his retreat point, hoping the other sniper would look up at the movement of the body and give him those few seconds he needed.

He found himself a little disoriented, but he managed to slip into the brush and lie flat, his heart racing as he checked to make certain he was still all in one piece. Blood seeped from a stab wound on his calf where a broken branch had jabbed him. He couldn't get his hand to his back without disturbing the brush around him to test for blood, but it hurt like a son of a bitch, so he didn't need evidence that trees were not the place to try teleportation. Still—he was going to do it again.

He studied the sniper through the foliage. Dark hair, dark skin, yet not black, the man definitely knew the business end of a rifle. Sam found having enhanced vision was very helpful in just these situations. The sniper was much higher up in the tree, the branches thick and plentiful, making the tree easy to climb but much harder to teleport into. It would take seconds to actually make the jump and kill the sniper, but the hazards were far greater. He sighed. He was going to take a hit with this one.

Sam teleported through those close branches to the spot he'd chosen directly behind the sniper, another thick branch with smaller limbs sprouting in all directions. The sniper was speaking softly into his radio. The language shocked Sam. *Farsi*. What the hell did that mean? What would an Iranian sharpshooter be doing in the Lolo National Forest? How did soldiers from a foreign country make entry into the United States with the weapons they had?

As his feet found purchase on the branch, his weight sent a shiver through the tree, enough that the sniper turned his head while he was still talking. His eyes went wide with shock and he broke off abruptly. Sam lunged forward, kicking hard, driving his foot into the man's chest, sending him tumbling out of the tree as he tried to swing his rifle around.

The man fell, his mouth wide-open but no sound emerging. The rifle fell with him, but not before Sam caught a good glimpse of it. There was no doubt in his mind that the rifle was a Dragunov sniper rifle, produced in Iran on the Nakhjir sniper rifle. He needed that evidence. He materialized beside the body and snatched up the rifle, projecting himself back to his chosen retreat spot before sliding into the brush once again. Bullets hit all around him, zipping into the brush from several directions.

"Surrender," a voice barked out. The command was issued in English, but heavily accented.

Sam scuttled like a crab, his body hugging the ground as he slipped through the small animal trail into heavier brush. Bullets pounded the dirt, spat splinters from the bark on the trees, whipped through leaves, and hummed past his ears. One burned his back and another skimmed his arm, slicing hot and painful, taking a strip of flesh. But he found the depression he'd been looking for and scooted into it, burrowing deep.

The volley of shots ceased as if someone had given an order. "You will die if you don't surrender," the voice warned again.

When Sam made no sound, the hail of bullets seemed to increase their fury.

Where the hell was the cavalry? *Azami? Are you clear?* He was going to have to chance surrendering, because he was definitely going to take a bullet if this kept up.

I'm coming around behind them, taking them out one by one. Are you hit?

He loved how calm her voice was. She could have been strolling through the park. *Not yet. I'm going to give myself up. Hopefully they won't shoot me. Stay out of sight. I'll escape as soon as I'm able.*

They might kill you.

He liked the protest in her voice. *True, but I don't think so. I think they'll want information. They've come a long way for something. If they take me with them, I'm leaving a rifle here. Take it to Ryland, and for God's sake, don't get caught.*

That's not going to happen. Go ahead and surrender, but if they kill you, I'll be following them all the way back to their base, and I don't take prisoners. You know they're after my brother, not you.

Sam was counting on whoever these people were wanting her brother or at least information about him—that and they would know his team would be coming down that mountain any moment after them and they'd want to wrap this up fast and get the hell out of Dodge.

"Stop shooting," he called. "I'm giving myself up."

CHAPTER 4

———⟨∼⟩———

Sam pushed the rifle slowly into deeper brush, careful not to rustle any leaves. He waited until the guns were once again quiet. "I'm standing up now. No one get crazy on me."

His heart drummed out the time in his chest. This was the single moment no one ever wanted to live in. Life or death? There were at least seven to ten of the enemy, not including the second Jeep full of mercenaries. Any one of them could get trigger happy and his life would end in a hail of bullets. He really didn't want to go out that way. Taking a deep breath, he let it out and slowly stood, both hands raised high. His gaze moved fast over the entire area, noting positions of the enemy. There weren't as many as he'd first thought—or Azami was making the most of her time.

Do you need me to create a distraction? I can lead some of them off you.

No, don't do anything yet. When I need you, I'll give you the signal, but don't let them know you're close—not yet.

"Link your fingers behind your head and walk forward," the man in charge ordered.

Sam had six semiautomatics centered on him. He did

what he was told. The occupants of the Jeep were worrisome, and now that they had him, they were going to move fast to keep his team from raining fire down on them. He and Azami had bought a few minutes, but not enough to get his team down the mountain.

The brush was thick and he swore as he deliberately walked through it, swallowing more precious minutes and making a show of stumbling. He didn't want to look like a threat to any of them. He couldn't quite look like a whipped pup, but he tried to project that image. He was about to reveal secrets to Azami, and there would be questions he didn't want to answer, but if he was going to get out of this alive and keep her safe, he had no other choice. She'd be watching him this time and she'd see what he could do. This time, the battle was more like a pool game, all about the angles.

One of the men made a comment, laughing a little at his discomfort, the words in his own language. *Not so tough. They lied to us about these men,* he interpreted.

"Shut up," the commander growled, clearly not wanting them to speak anything but English.

He was more cautious than the others and absolutely the biggest threat—which meant the commander had to go first. Sam chose each target carefully. He could take out five of them for certain, but his energy would be sapped quickly after that. He'd have to be in almost continuous motion, taking only a second for each kill. His body wouldn't have time to catch up to the speed he was moving. He wouldn't feel whole, the sensation of his body tearing apart strong, but he simply had no other viable choice.

Azami, when I give you the word, can you take the two soldiers hanging back in the trees, nearly out of my sight? Can you see them?

No problem.

There it was—that supreme confidence he found sexy as hell in the middle of a firefight. Who knew he was such a fucking pervert that a woman in battle could turn him on with just her soft voice filling his mind with assurance that she could take out the two soldiers. Purring. She purred, the sound of her voice vibrating through his entire body.

Time slowed down like it always did for him when he needed it to. The wind rustled the leaves in the trees and lighter branches swayed gently. The sky overhead was pale blue, a few wispy clouds floating. A perfect day. He noted the faint crackle of leaves as mice scurried away from the intruders. Somewhere a hawk screamed. Life continued with or without Sam Johnson.

The commander signaled the closest man forward. It was now or never. Sam sent Azami the order. *Take them.*

He ran straight at the commander, his fingers gripping the handle of his knife. He crossed thirty feet with blurring speed, so that the commander blinked and Sam stood in front of him, already drawing the blade across his throat. Sam ran for the soldier twenty feet from the commander, banked off a tree and plunged the knife through his throat, twisted and was sprinting toward the third soldier. Racing up the trunk of a tree, slingshotting off, somersaulting in the air, he landed behind the third soldier, cutting his throat as his feet touched ground. Another burst of speed took him directly to the fourth soldier.

He slashed in a figure eight, cutting arteries, feeling the effects of repeated teleportation, his body beginning to shake with overload. He put on another burst of energy, racing from the fourth soldier to the fifth. He zipped around trees, to come up behind the soldier.

The entire thing had taken seconds only, but the fifth soldier had caught the fall of his companions and whirled around in a circle, his finger steady on the trigger. Sam had to turn with him, staying behind the man, praying Azami was clear of the stream of bullets as they cut through leaves and trees and mowed down branches. His body shuddered, legs suddenly rubber. Sam plunged the knife deep into the soldier's kidney, knowing he was going to go down. He had to take the soldier with him to keep him off Azami.

The gunfire would draw the Jeep filled with mercenaries, and he was terribly weak. He might not be able to protect the woman. *Get out of here. Make your way back to your brother. The team is on the way, in the air now. I can feel them getting closer.*

He twisted the knife free and plunged it a second time, determined to take the soldier down with him. His knees gave out and he went down hard, retaining possession of the knife. The semiautomatic continued firing as the soldier sprawled over Sam, the sound deafening.

I don't need protection.

There was just a bit of haughtiness in the soft voice filling his mind. She poured warmth and confidence into him. The gun went silent, but he felt the vibration under him, indicating the Jeep was racing toward the battle. Sam summoned strength and shoved the dying soldier off him. The man rolled, his dark eyes staring at Sam in a kind of a shock. They'd been a far superior force in numbers, but one Ghost-Walker and a woman had destroyed them.

You get your men?

Of course.

Sam pushed down the smile that little haughty note brought out and rolled to get his hands under him. He groaned at the sudden crashing pain and tried to push himself onto his hands and knees. This was more than weakness from teleporting too much. The distances had been relatively short and his body felt nearly settled. He'd taken a couple of deep wounds from the stabbing broken branches in the trees, but really . . . in front of Azami?

"It isn't going to happen," he muttered. "You're a fuckin' GhostWalker. Get on your feet and move, soldier."

He felt a surge of psychic energy, a strong wash surrounding him, and instinctively he twisted, looking for the threat. Azami materialized on his left side, reaching down to slide her arm around his waist. Shock waves rocked him. There was no way she could use teleportation, yet she'd been a great distance from him. How had she managed to cross that space in under a second? As far as he knew, he was the only one in the world who could do such a thing—and yet, she had. He recognized the burst of power, the alarming buildup of energy and the way her body shimmered for a moment, nearly transparent until all molecules caught up with her speed.

He found himself looking into those dark, mysterious eyes. For one moment, he felt as if he was falling forward and he caught himself. He was not about to lean on anyone, let alone a woman. "Who the hell are you?" Because she was no ordinary woman, and more and more his radar told him he was dealing with a fellow GhostWalker. And if that was so, and she hadn't identified herself as such, if she was lying about who she was, they had a major problem.

He did *not* want to kill this woman. Everything in him rebelled against the idea, yet that nagging suspicion refused to go away. He held his breath. The wind seemed to cease.

"I'm the woman who happens to be saving your butt right now. Keep walking. We're about to have more company. If you go down again, you won't be getting back up."

Hell. He knew he'd been hit, it just hadn't registered in his brain yet. He'd been moving too fast, but someone had fired repeatedly and a bullet had clipped him—somewhere. He was used to the aftermath of teleporting, the sheer exhaustion and the pain as bones and tissue realigned, as if somehow, they hadn't all quite found their rightful places back in his body. He accepted the help from her, not wanting to fall on his face in front of her.

Her waist was very small. His hand was so big, he was almost afraid to put it on her—afraid anywhere he touched would be inappropriate. Fucking hell. He should be thinking about guns and bullets and self-preservation, not how perfectly her body felt against his.

They hobbled away from that scene of death and chaos, back into deeper woods. Azami didn't go far. She set him down beside a large tree. He could feel the earth trembling.

"The others are close. My team's about five minutes out."

He blew out his breath and assessed the damage. "I can handle this. Seriously, woman, you're driving me crazy." She was too, but not in the way she should be. He should want her hiding in the bunker with her brothers, Kadan and Nico protecting her, but no, she was here, in danger, and all he could think about was how good she smelled. And how very glad he was that Kadan and Nico had wives they adored.

Azami laughed softly. "I seem to have that effect on men—driving them crazy. Apparently my behavior is not normal."

"You're damned attractive and you're distracting me." The words were out before he could censor them, shocking him and judging by her face, shocking her.

"I think you're a little delirious."

The teasing note in her voice slipped inside his guard and warmed him. Damn it all, she wasn't who she claimed to be and he was responsible for the safety of his team and for Lily's baby. The woman was overpowering his good sense with sheer sex appeal. He turned his head toward the sound of the engine drawing near, more to distract himself than for any other reason. He'd known all along that Jeep was close.

Overhead they could hear an approaching helicopter, the sound of the blades growing loud. Azami sent him another smile and made a move to rise from behind the brush. Alarm rushed over him and Sam caught her wrist, yanking her back to safety. She didn't resist, or even look annoyed. She simply looked down at the fingers shackling her and then back up to him, raising an eyebrow.

Damn, she was calm. He liked that. He also liked that her fingers had settled around the hilt of her knife. His curved around hers, holding her hand still. "You don't trust me."

"I don't know you. But I see you lack trust in me as well."

He flashed a wan grin. "I don't know you either." He indicated above the canopy with his chin. "They aren't ours."

Thorn glanced at the sky, her heart thudding hard in her

chest. *Two* helicopters? That was some serious firepower. Mercenaries and Iranians. What was going on? Someone wanted either Sam Johnson or her—very badly.

Ropes dropped from the helicopter hovering some distance away, and several men began fast-roping down. She assessed the damage to Sam. He'd been shot. It looked like a through and through, but the bullet had entered on his right side and come out the back. He'd lost a lot of blood. It was only his training and iron will that kept the pain at bay and the soldier from passing out.

It was impossible for a woman like Thorn not to admire Sam as he pushed himself up, sliding his weapon forward and going to ground without so much as wincing. The back of his shirt was covered in blood and there was more on his calf. "Stay still," she advised. "And take a breath."

She didn't give him time to think about it, as she pulled a thin, rather large rectangle-shaped bandage from her pack. Shoving up his shirt, she slapped it over the wound. He gasped and turned his head to look at her over his shoulder, suspicion in his eyes. She ignored it and reached for the front of his shirt.

"That feels like some form of a drug called Zenith. My blood vessels are expanding rapidly. My body's going hot and flooding with adrenaline. You get the same reaction from Zenith." There was accusation in his voice. "I had no idea there was a topical form. Before it was banned, it was given via injections."

She slapped another medicated patch over the entry wound. "It's second-generation Zenith. Definitely not going to kill you, so mellow out."

The suspicion didn't ease, she could tell by his eyes, but he turned back toward the enemy. There was nothing he could do either way, the patches had been applied, the Zenith was in his system, and so he turned with a casual shrug of his shoulders, making her admire him all the more.

"How would you know about Zenith if you don't know Dr. Whitney?"

"I didn't say I wasn't acquainted with the man. You never asked me."

Thorn slipped into place beside him, lying on her belly, her eyes watching the enemy force fan out and disappear into the brush. "Military. Trained. I think we're looking at an elite force." She assessed the enemy.

"My team is just minutes out," he reiterated with confidence. "Keep your head down."

She sent him one dark look of pure reprimand. She'd already given away too many secrets, but then—so had he. She respected him for that. He'd taken his job of protecting her quite seriously, even when he saw she could handle herself. And he hadn't tried to relegate her to the background as so many other men would have. He treated her as an equal. He hadn't fought the Zenith patches and he knew the first generation eventually killed its host if one wasn't administered the antidote within the prescribed time frame. That told her he was very seasoned and completely confident in his abilities. She may have underestimated him just a little.

Sam grinned at her, that quick, cocky smile sending shock waves through her. She'd *never* reacted to a man in the way she was reacting to him. One flash of his white teeth, those dark eyes warming with a teasing light, and her body overheated, her blood rushing through her veins with more exhilaration than she'd ever felt. Sam Johnson made her feel alive.

She'd been in countless perilous situations—it was the very nature of her business—and she'd never encountered such a physical and emotional reaction to anyone. "You're a dangerous man, Sam," she accused.

His grin widened into a mischievous smirk. "You have no idea just how dangerous, Ms. Yoshiie."

That grin promised all sorts of things that had nothing to do with enemy warfare and everything to do with male versus female. Why would that softly whispered taunt turn her into pure melted heat? There was something turbulent and stormy and so seductive in his eyes, so appealing to a woman with her nature.

They were surrounded by an unknown enemy force, and yet the man beside her seemed to turn the experience into an exhilarating roller coaster of emotions. She'd never felt so feminine as she did now, there with her guns and knives and bow and arrows, lying beside Sam in the rotting vegetation and brush. And damn it all, she *loved* that he was dangerous.

They began moving in unison, as if dancing, using elbows and toes to take them over the uneven terrain, two lizards propelling themselves forward soundlessly. Not even the whisper of clothing gave them away as they crab-walked their way closer to the enemy. On the right the sound of the Jeep's engine suddenly died and a voice called out in Spanish. Another answered in the same language. As if pulled by strings, they looked at one another, both puzzled. Thorn couldn't believe how in tune they were. Why would mercenaries be in one Jeep and Mexicans in a second along with obviously military-trained Iranian soldiers hunting them?

You really are very popular, aren't you? Thorn asked him, a teasing note creeping into her voice. She slipped her knife out of the scabbard and turned toward a sound in front and to the left of her. Someone was near—too near.

Sam laid a restraining hand on her arm. *Bloodthirsty woman. Leave them be. The cavalry is in the air and we want to be able to track them back to whoever sent them. Someone has to be left alive.*

That's a lot of someones to be left alive when they're determined to kidnap my brother.

What she *should* have said was to quit touching her. *No one* touched her—not without her permission—and she wouldn't give it if they did ask. Sounds increased all around them. They weren't going to have much choice soon. The soldiers moving toward them weren't from the Jeep. These were men who knew what they were doing in the forest. They came in formation, fanned out, covering ground, armed and ready for anything. They were moving swiftly as if they knew they only had minutes to find their quarry.

We're nearly in the open. We won't stand a chance like this. Her hand slipped once again to her gun. She was good in close combat, but there were too many to take down that way. It would have to be loud and that would draw fire. She could smell the coppery flavor of blood, but there was no scent of fear coming off of Sam.

Trust me. I know that's hard when you don't know me, but if you trust me, we'll be fine.

Her heart thudded. The closest she came to trust was her father—maybe Daiki and Eiji—but even then, she preferred to rely on herself. She protected *them*, not the other way around. She swallowed the edge of fear—not from the enemy but from her own strange feelings. In the end, if they tried to take her prisoner, she'd kill as many as she could before they killed her. For one long moment she stared into those dark, fathomless eyes, letting him know silently her intentions. He didn't flinch away but seemed to understand she had no intention of being taken alive. She would never be a prisoner again. Her nod was nearly imperceptible, but he caught it.

He wrapped his arms around her and turned, pushing her smaller body deep into a depression in the ground beneath a fallen tree. His body on top of hers obliterated everything, so that there was nothing but him in her world. He went completely still, his skin color changing subtly. He was wearing jeans and a loose shirt, a casual, almost elegant look on his muscular frame, his good looks drawing attention from the fact that the clothing reflected his surroundings so that he faded into the background. In an environment such as this one, his clothing was another tool of combat.

The soldiers were around them now, two on either side. The trunk of the tree shuddered as one booted foot stepped atop it. She didn't move a muscle. Above her, Sam's body seemed completely relaxed, although she felt the coiled tension in him, much like a snake ready for action. He might give the appearance of relaxed indolence, but he could easily explode into action.

Relax.

They are the enemy. But it wasn't the enemy that had her tense. She was feeling things she shouldn't. For him. Her awareness was frightening. She felt every breath he took, every beat of his heart, the bunching of his stomach muscles. She could almost feel the blood running hot in his veins.

He wouldn't understand. How could he? She'd read his file. He hadn't had it easy, but he still wouldn't understand the demons running her. Her father had worked hard to rid her of them. Demons had no place in a samurai warrior. She admired both Daiki and Eiji. They had overcome their daunting pasts to replace rage with serenity. She had failed to wipe out that terrible anger completely. At the most inconvenient times—like now—anger exploded to the surface.

A dark, black cloud settled over her, and Dr. Whitney with his inhuman, reptilian features stared coldly and dispassionately down at her with absolute, utter distaste. He could take apart a child, dissecting them as he would an insect without so much as noticing they were still alive and suffering—she ought to know, she still had all the scars.

Her heart nearly stopped when Sam's mouth skimmed, featherlight, across her forehead. She was certain it wasn't just warm breath, but the actual touch of his lips. Accident or not, it set her blood rushing hotly. An insect crawled over her hand and she controlled the itch that ran up her skin, but it was impossible to control deep inside where something totally unknown to her—something feminine and all woman—reached for him.

She held her breath, certain in the knowledge that a great storm was coming in her life and that this man was at the center of it. Her fingers dug into the muscle of his arms inadvertently as if she needed to hold on to the only thing solid when everything else around her was spinning out of her control. She'd been waiting all of her life for revenge—or justice; either would work, but now she thought perhaps she'd been completely off course. *This* was what she'd been waiting for—this moment, this man—and he was about to turn her life upside down.

The soldier stepped with both boots onto the tree trunk, rocking it. She felt the pinch across her back, but didn't wince, didn't make a move or sound. She kept her eyes wide-open, observing Sam. His skin was discolored, fading into the leaves and branches scattered thick over the ground. She felt the small movement of his arm, so slow, inch by slow inch so as not to disturb a single leaf. His eyes, those beautiful dark eyes, changed subtly—became almost hypnotic so that she couldn't look away even if she tried.

The soldier stepped down onto the ground a scant inch from where Sam's arm rested against the trunk of the fallen tree. He curled his fingers, his eyes still staring into hers and brushed, ever so gently, against the camo-clad leg as the man took another step. She felt the movements of his arm—an easy uncoiling of the snake before it struck, feather-light and very gentle.

The soldier took three more steps and staggered. He called out in Farsi. Abruptly, to their right and left, two more soldiers rushed to his aid. The one Sam touched sank to the ground, his hand trembling, trying to hold on to his leg—the leg she knew Sam had brushed so casually. What had he done? There had been no sound. No change of expression, but he'd touched that man in that exact spot, she'd felt that subtle movement. *What was different about his eyes?* She swallowed and continued staring into those mesmerizing eyes, half incapable of looking away and half trying to understand what was happening.

The two other soldiers took positions on either side of their fallen comrade, the nearest one with his leg inches from Sam's arm. Again, she felt that slow, stealthy movement. She knew she should have let go of his arm, but she kept her fingers positioned against his strange-colored skin. Sam wasn't finished. Whatever he'd done to the first soldier, he intended to do to another, and she was determined to unlock his secrets.

Sam didn't blink, his eyes shimmering with a fire deep under all that dark cover. His muscles bunched and rippled. His expression didn't change. His gaze didn't shift. He could have been lying in the grass studying the open sky. She knew his heart rate didn't changed at all because she felt each beat. His breathing was slow and steady. The man should have ice water in his veins, but even that wasn't true—she felt the heat of his body.

Thorn couldn't prevent the rising admiration for this man. He was truly dangerous and she wanted to uncover his every secret. That file had meant nothing but data to her. This was a man Dr. Whitney deemed useless to him and yet he could teleport and he had another unseen weapon she was determined to ferret out. Had Whitney miscalculated Sam's psychic abilities as he'd done hers? She knew Sam had been altered genetically, his DNA manipulated, but there was little information on Sam beyond his ties to General Ranier.

The soldiers spoke in hushed tones. She translated in her mind, unsure if Sam knew the language or not.

"Something bit me. A snake perhaps. My leg's on fire and my heart's beating too fast."

Great drops of sweat ran down the soldier's body, covering his clothes with damp, dark splotches. Thorn smelled fear. In the distance, the sound of a helicopter moving toward them grew in volume.

Again she interpreted the soldier's conversation in Farsi. "We have to go now. Get back to the clearing."

"I can't walk."

"We'll help you. We have to hurry." The answer was gruff, as if the soldiers had turned their heads away from their fallen comrade, toward the ominous sound of the helicopter.

She felt the muscles ripple ever so slightly in Sam's arm, the most gentle of flexes. His arm moved with that same infinite slowness, brushing so lightly that she heard the whisper against the material of the soldier's fatigues, just along his calf. Again, his arm moved back with that same unhurried motion to the ground. So, he understood Farsi as well. And he was about to strike at the soldiers.

His eyes glowed with a fiery red bursting like angry starlight through a dark sky. His face never changed expression. He seemed . . . relaxed. She was trained in warfare, skilled in so many arts, and yet tension coiled in her so close to the enemy in preparation for battle. They were virtually hiding in plain sight a scant foot from the soldiers and Sam was clearly attacking them, yet his body was without anxiety or stress of any kind. He was—*magnificent*. Dr. Whitney was a fool to call this man expendable.

She felt that brush, so exquisitely delivered, that same unhurried featherlight bite of . . . what? Death? Poison? If so, how did he administer it? Did he carry a syringe? She was adept at passing an enemy and dispensing of them with no more than the small stinging bite of an insect, yet this was different. The soldier gripped his fallen companion and with the aid of his friend, the two set out at a fast pace toward the clearing where transport waited impatiently.

The second soldier stumbled. This man had taken at least three running steps, perhaps four, before he felt the fire of the attack. He grunted, dropped the now incapacitated soldier, and sat abruptly clutching his calf. "I was bitten too. I felt it. I feel it. Like fire creeping up my leg."

The third soldier looked warily around the ground, his semiautomatic pushed forward, finger on the trigger, his eyes scanning sharply. Thorn realized Sam had known all along it was a possibility the one he couldn't reach might get trigger happy and spray the ground. He had virtually covered her body with his, tucking beneath the added safety of the tree trunk. Still, he remained perfectly relaxed, his eyes smiling down into hers. The soldier backed away from the two fallen men slowly.

"Send Martinez for these two. They can't make it back," he ordered in Farsi into his radio.

He turned and sprinted away from the two fallen soldiers,

racing through the trees to reach the helicopter. Sam rolled away from her.

Now you've got a few minutes to interrogate them. Make it quick. They won't live long.

He was up fast, moving with his blurring speed to kick away the guns. The only way she could tell that he was weak was the slight tremor of his hand as he wiped it over his face. In spite of the application of the topical form of Zenith, promoting fast healing, the blood loss, coupled with the tremendous drain on him from using teleportation, had sapped his energy. In spite of it, he was a soldier through and through, refusing to give in to pain or exhaustion while there was still more to be done.

Thorn slipped from beneath the log and brushed at the insects, casually flicking them off her clothes as she took two steps toward the soldiers. The capricious wind shifted and she caught the smell of sweat. *Sam!*

She didn't hesitate, launching her body at Sam. He caught her in midair, drawing her in, wrapping strong arms around her as he dove back and away from the two fallen soldiers. They hit the ground, Sam rolling under her to protect her. She heard him grunt, the air leaving his lungs in a rush. Angry bullets spat all around them, kicking up leaves, dirt, and splinters. Sam rolled fast, taking her into the area densest with trees.

The moment he let her go, she crawled behind the thickest trunk she could find, making herself small.

We have to move. Follow the coordinates in my head. I know you can teleport. Don't argue with me, just do it.

Sam's voice carried an absolute authority she normally would have taken exception to, but sanity and self-preservation overruled pride. He pushed the coordinates into her head and she recognized the spot he gave her. She didn't hesitate, moving with that gut-wrenching, sickening speed that took her breath and burned her body so that the moment she was once again still, she always had to mentally check herself to assure every piece had arrived safely.

Thorn had the presence of mind to hold completely still, unmoving, waiting for him to arrive beside her. She guessed that would place his body between her and any danger, but she didn't dive for cover, afraid of interfering with Sam's successful arrival. She felt the wash of unbelievably strong psychic energy, the surge so powerful it shook her. Heat burst around her as Sam's body shimmered, nearly transparent, looking like ash more than human, and then he was there, real and solid, his hand settling around her arm to push her toward cover.

The helicopter with the Iranian soldiers had already taken to the air, rocketing fast across the sky, a second helicopter in hot pursuit. The sound of gunfire was loud, bursts of fire streaming between the two mechanical birds.

Sam and Thorn slipped into the dense brush and hugged the ground. It was a little ironic that they'd spent most of their time together in such close proximity. He probably knew her body much more intimately than anyone she'd grown up around—and she knew his. She sent him another grin, her eyes lighting with mischief. She couldn't help it. He made her feel so alive, every nerve ending lighting up and aware.

You alive, Sam?

The voice startled Thorn. She heard it clearly and knew she was still linked to Sam. She knew he'd leave her mind, all that strength and warmth gone to leave her absolutely, utterly alone. She'd never realized she'd felt alone. She loved her adopted father and brothers. They weren't terribly demonstrative—but neither was she. Still, there was no way for them to understand just how truly different she really was. She didn't belong anywhere. She never felt entirely comfortable with anyone until she found herself fighting beside Sam.

Strangely, she seemed to know what he was going to do and she trusted that he'd get it done. He seemed to afford her the same trust. She'd always been a puzzle to everyone around her and even to herself, but with Sam, he'd put all the pieces together, using parts of himself, and they just fit together. She took a breath and saw him look at her—a look of regret. And then he was gone and for one terrible moment, it was unbearable to be Thorn again.

Her entire body shuddered, as if the mental loosing was also physical. Biting ice cold swept through her veins so that she had to grind her teeth to keep them from chattering. The scars on her body and in her mind banded tight, robbing her of breath and reason—but only for a brief moment. She was Thorn. *No one*, *nothing* was going to defeat her. She took a breath and looked away from warmth and happiness. Bleak cold settled over her once again.

Sam glanced at Azami. Ryland's voice was loud in his head and he hadn't yet detached himself from her. He knew he had no choice, but he'd never felt so reluctant to do something of paramount importance to his team. He knew she would see the unhappiness in his eyes, but in that moment he didn't care how vulnerable he was to her. The loss of her would be a terrible blow when she'd filled every empty space with her strength and conviction. With her humor.

He took a deep breath and let go of her. The loss rocked him as he knew it would, leaving him strangely cold and for one bloody second, without hope. He actually experienced grief before he clamped down hard on his strange and entirely inappropriate emotions, turning himself back into stone. He found it odd to feel so completely lonely when he'd never minded being alone. Without her in his mind, he felt he'd lost too much of himself.

Sam shook his head. *We're fine. We've got a Jeep full of mercenaries to drive off, and you've got trained soldiers in that helicopter. Iranian.*

There was a small silence as Ryland digested that shocking bit of information. *You're certain?*

That's affirmative. Are the other two civilians safe?
Yes.

Sam detested what he was about to do. Guilt ate at him, a terrible stone in his gut, but it had to be done. *I don't believe Azami is who they claim she is. She has many of the same gifts I do. She can teleport and she's psychic. Kadan and Nico have to really watch the other two. I've been uneasy from the first, but I don't have an idea what's really going on.*

Roger that.

Ryland's matter-of-fact voice was a comfort. Sam had conveyed uneasiness from the moment he'd approached the trio of visitors from Samurai Telecommunications, but he hadn't actually warned his team something was off. He'd waited for Kadan or Nico to raise the alarm, to at least feel the strange warning that he couldn't shake, but neither had said anything.

I think they're all armed to the teeth, at least for certain she is and she fights like one of us. We've got five Mexicans in a Jeep, everyone else on the ground is dead.

Cleaning crew on the way and Gator's in position to tail them. Let at least one go.

Roger that. But he didn't feel good about hunting with Azami, allowing her to put herself in danger when he'd just betrayed her.

Dr. Whitney was an implacable enemy and he wanted the children. Lily and Ryland had a baby boy in the compound, and more than anything else, he had to be protected. Just a few miles farther up the mountain, Team Two had twin babies and there was a softly whispered rumor that another woman was pregnant. No one spoke of it, to keep the information from reaching Whitney, who seemed to have eyes and ears everywhere. In San Francisco, another Ghost-Walker couple had a baby too, and if Lily purchased this satellite from Samurai Telecommunications, the Yoshiie family would visit both compounds as well to install software.

Sam couldn't take the chance that Azami was involved in a plot to aid Whitney. He couldn't see what she would get out of it, but there was no taking a chance with the children. He found he couldn't look at her. The terrible knots tightened to the point of cramping in his belly. He pushed himself up as the sounds of the helicopter and gunfire faded away.

"We've still got to harass the ones in the Jeep." He kept his face averted, his features expressionless, and his tone gruff.

"Sam."

His name was a whisper of sound. Soft like snowfall or the drop of the leaves in the fall. He took a breath. She didn't continue—just waited for him to face her. Silence stretched between them, but she wouldn't bend, demanding he face her.

"Damn it, Azami." Screw politeness. He'd sold her down the river and she'd probably saved his life with her patches of Zenith, although that was one more condemning mark against her.

Still she stayed silent. The wind persisted blowing through the trees, and he could hear the Jeep moving toward them, heading fast for the trail out.

He turned his head and his heart actually jerked in his chest as his eyes met hers. She smiled at him. She looked so beautiful standing there so still, her expression composed, serene even.

"I would have done exactly the same thing."

Damn her for that. Absolving him of his sins. He shook his head. That didn't make him feel better, although it was probably her intention. "Let's get this done. And one stays alive. We need him."

CHAPTER 5

Sam didn't wait to see if Azami would follow. The Jeep was his problem, not hers. She was a guest and one who would be very thoroughly vetted *again* before this day was done, thanks to him. She'd held up under intense scrutiny by the CIA, Homeland Security, and the GhostWalkers themselves. Other countries around the world purchasing her products for military use also investigated her and she'd come up clean. Yet Sam had doubted she was who she said she was. Maybe he was just going crazy and all Samurai Telecommunications employees were trained in warfare.

He swore as the Jeep topped the small rise, bursting into view, with five dark-haired men, heavily armed, looking wild-eyed and disheveled. Not soldiers, but certainly men used to killing. His brain catalogued the information even as he fired methodically, taking out the two on his side and avoiding shooting the driver. He expected return fire, but the other two soldiers went down in the Jeep, automatic weapons falling from nerveless hands and dropping to the ground as the driver careened out of sight, four dead bodies in his vehicle.

Sam turned his head just as Azami lowered her weapon.

He frowned. He'd seen blowguns before, but like most of her weapons, this one had been modified. The darts were tiny, no larger than an unshelled peanut, the needle so thin and tiny he knew it would be impossible to discover that entry point. He would bet his last dollar that whatever last-acting poison was used was undetectable. The loads were tiny, but in small individual chambers that looked harmless. She could deliver several shots before having to reload.

"I see you have no need of a sword."

"Very difficult, these days, to get them through security," she pointed out without changing expression.

"You're extremely accurate with that weapon."

"With all weapons. My father was an exacting man."

"You're a very dangerous woman, Azami Yoshiie." Sam meant it as an admiring compliment.

One eyebrow raised. Her mouth curved and she flashed a heart-stopping smile. "You have no idea how dangerous." She said his own words right back to him and he believed her.

"And you're just as adept with a sword as you are with your other weapons?" he asked curiously.

"More so," she admitted with no trace of bragging—simply stating a fact. "I said so, didn't I?"

Sam turned on his heel and strode toward her purposefully. "I'm about to kiss you, Ms. Yoshiie. I'm fully aware I'm breaching every single international law of etiquette there is, and you might, rightfully, stick that knife of yours in my gut, but right at this moment I don't particularly give a damn."

Her eyes widened, but she didn't move. He'd known she wouldn't. She was every bit as courageous as any member of his team. She would stand her ground.

Thorn moistened her lips. "It might be your heart," she warned truthfully.

"Still, I have no choice here. I really don't. So pull the damn thing out and be ready."

She felt her body go liquid with heat, a frightening reaction to a woman of absolute control. "If you're going to do it, you'd best make it really good, because it very well might be the last thing you ever do. I have no idea how I'll react. I've never actually kissed anyone before."

Her heart thundered in her ears, drowning out the sounds of the insects coming back to life around them. She was more terrified in that moment than she'd been during the battles with the enemy soldiers. She had no idea how she would react. Self-preservation was strong in her and Sam threatened her on such an elemental level she had no real way of knowing what she might do to defend herself.

With every deliberate step he took, Sam loomed larger and larger. She'd recognized that he was a big man, strong and battle-hardened, but she'd been going into combat at his side, so she hadn't concerned herself with physical attributes. Now, she could see every detail. There was dark purpose in his eyes, a growing desire that left her breathless and weak. She *couldn't* be weak—not now, not in her most important hour.

She should have stepped back. Her fingers did curl around her dagger, but she didn't draw it. She didn't move. She stood captured in those dark eyes, watching his desire growing—for her, for Thorn, the warrior. He knew she was far more than Azami, her brother's bodyguard, and he admired her for it. No, it was more than admiration. He desired her because of it. He desired the warrior in her just as much if not more than the woman.

She found herself lost in his eyes as he stepped right up to her, without hesitation of any kind. His fingers curled in the lapels of her perfectly fitted jacket and he yanked her the scant inches separating them. Or had she leapt toward him in that last split second? She honestly didn't know— only that with the first touch of his aggressive male energy engulfing hers, she felt a hot rush through her entire body. The moment his hands fisted in her lapels, the heat turned to molten lava, an explosion in the pit of her stomach that flushed her skin. Her breasts felt swollen and achy, and dampness invaded between her legs.

His mouth came down on hers and instantly the world shifted. For one second she put the peculiar sensations rushing through her down to loss of breath, but then she couldn't think anymore. Just feel. Her skin went electric, her bones turned to water, her blood to fire. His lips were firm and cool and so demanding. She opened her mouth and allowed him to sweep her away with him.

Thorn had no choice but to wrap her arms around him and hang on as the ground beneath her feet rolled. He poured into her mind, hot and strong and determined to claim her for his. She felt the hilt of the knife digging into her palm and she took a better grip until she felt him giving himself to her. Fully. Everything. He opened to her. Let her into his mind. He was giving every bit as much as he was taking.

The world he opened for her was pure sensation. Pleasure burst through her like a hot firestorm. She felt her body melting into his, felt his heart beat, every breath he took, as if they were one person instead of two. Her mouth seemed to belong to him instead of her, kissing him back with a fiery passion she hadn't known she was capable of.

Sam knew he was in dangerous territory, but he couldn't stop himself. He *had* to taste her. No, if he was being honest, the terrible need to kiss her was far more than simply tasting her. He needed to claim her for his own. The urge had been growing in him from the moment he'd first set eyes on her. The more he was with her in such an extreme situation, the more he admired her. He found himself waiting for her smile, for the way her eyes lit up and the sun set streaks of light playing wildly through all that sleek, black hair.

He found himself needing to drop everything, strip himself bare of all shields to let her inside, no matter how bad the idea was. The moment his mouth came down on hers, he knew he was too aggressive, especially with that soft little admission—*I've never kissed anyone*—making his heart pound and hot blood pool low and vicious. But he couldn't stop. She tasted—like heaven. Everything disap-

peared around him, dropping away until there was only Azami
with her soft skin, silky hair, and that elusive scent that drove
him mad.

He fully expected the woman to stab him through the
heart with her dagger. He could see the fear in her eyes just
before his lips came down on hers, and it would never do to
frighten a woman like Azami Yoshiie. She was a warrior
through and through. Duty and honor were uppermost in
her character. Control mattered, just as it did to him, and he
was taking them both to a place neither could control.

Risking his life didn't matter to him. Only kissing her
did. He merged with her in some undefined way, so that hot
passion pounded through both of them. His hand slipped
into that thick silk and bunched, holding her still for him,
the other finding her slender neck, his fingers splayed wide
to take in her soft skin. He poured himself into her, filling
her, his tongue dueling with hers while they both drowned
in sensual need.

Azami shuddered, her lips trembling, and then she consumed him as aggressively and as honestly as he did her.
He felt her inside of his mind, running like lava through his
veins, wrapping around her heart and filling his very bones
with her.

"This is madness," she whispered against his mouth when
they both came up for air. Her dark eyes searched his face.

Sam didn't have any answers. He knew she was right.
They might be on opposite sides in a deadly war, yet he
couldn't let her go. She fit with him. The world around them
was out of sync, not the two of them.

"I know," he admitted as he rested his forehead against
hers, looking into her eyes.

"What are we going to do now?"

A slow smile curved his mouth. "I really expected you
to kill me so I wouldn't have to figure that part out."

She blinked, her black fan of thick silky lashes fluttering
as wildly as her heart. She moistened her lips. "You're not
getting off that easily."

Sam watched the dawning smile, the way her soft mouth curved and the warmth spread to her dark eyes with absolute fascination. "Well. Damn." He looked around, feeling as though he was coming back from a great distance. "We have a few of dead bodies, a disposal team on the way, and you haven't asked a single question, Azami. Does this happen a lot when you take orders for your satellites?"

"First time. But I always come prepared." There was a teasing, mischievous note in her voice that slipped through every defense and aimed straight at his heart.

He knew he needed to release her, but once he allowed his physical connection to drop away, he was uncertain if he'd ever have a chance to reconnect. Instinctively, he knew Azami was elusive, like water flowing through fingers, or the wind shifting in the trees. He needed a way to seal her to him.

"How does one court a woman in Japan? Do I need your brothers' permission?"

She blinked again. Shocked. A hint of uncertainty crept into her eyes. She frowned, and he bent his head to swallow her protest before she could utter it. Her mouth trembled beneath his, and then she opened to him, like a flower, luring him deeper. Her arms slid around his neck, her body pressing tightly against his. He tightened his fingers in her hair.

He was burning, through and through, from the inside out, a hot melting of bone and tissue. He hadn't known he was lonely or even looking for something. He'd been complete. He loved his life. He was a man with teammates he trusted implicitly. He lived in wild places of beauty he enjoyed. He hadn't considered there would be a woman who could ever fit with him, who would ever turn his insides soft and his body hard.

Feel the same way, Azami. He didn't lift his mouth, kissing her again and again because once he'd made the mistake, he was addicted and what was the use fighting it? Not when it felt so damn right.

Somewhere along the line, his kiss went from sheer

aggression and command, to absolute tenderness. The emotion for her rose like a volcano, encompassing him entirely, drawn from some part of him he'd never known even existed. His mouth was gentle, his hands on her, possessive, yet just as gentle. Another claiming, this coming from that deep unknown well.

Feel the same way, Azami, he whispered into her mind. An enticement. A need. He waited, something in him going still, waiting for her answer.

Tell me how you're feeling?

She hadn't pulled away. If anything, her arms had tightened around his neck. He shared every single breath she took, feeling the slight movement of her rib cage and breasts against him, the warm air they exchanged.

Like I'm burning alive. Drowning. Like I never want this moment to end. He wasn't a man to say flowery things to a woman, nor did he even think them, but he shared the honest truth with her. *Like we belong.*

Once he let her go, the world would slip back into kilter. He wanted her to stay with him, to give him a chance with her.

She didn't hesitate, and he loved that about her as well. She gave herself in truth in the same way he did. *I feel the same, but one of us has to be sane.*

She initiated the kiss when he pulled back slightly, chasing after him with her soft mouth, fingers digging tightly into the heavy muscle at his neck, sighing when his lips settled once more over hers. He took his time, kissing her thoroughly, again and again, all the while slipping deeper into her spell and hoping she was falling under his.

Is this your idea of sanity? He'd make it his reality. He was falling further down the rabbit hole and he'd make her his sanity if she'd fall with him.

Her soft laughter slipped inside his heart, winding there until there was no shaking her loose. *Not really, but you have to be the strong one.*

He kissed her again. And again. *Why is that?*

You started this.

Okay, that was fair enough. He sighed as he lifted his head. She didn't make it easy for him to be a gentleman either, but he'd already blown that big time, so he just steadied her with his hands biting into her waist, holding her, looking into those dark eyes.

"Tell me how to properly court you, Azami. I'm serious. I've never courted a woman before, but you're the one."

A shiver went through her. A shadow crept into her eyes. "Why do you think that so quickly? You just barely met me."

His brain threw on the brake, catching that wariness that was too strong to be a woman naturally wondering why a man found her so attractive so fast. Chemistry sizzled between them, but she . . . *feared* it. *Distrusted* it. His mind spun fast, throwing out answers he wasn't so fond of.

"Have you actually met Dr. Whitney, then? Do you know him?"

Azami swallowed and took a step back, her long lashes veiling her eyes. "Yes, I've met him. He's a monster. High IQ, but not anything like my brother." Her eyes met his. "Or you."

He recognized that she was telling him she'd investigated him thoroughly. Why him? Lily was purchasing the satellite. Did her company routinely investigate others living near or around someone making a buy from them? That made no sense.

"Why would you know anything about me?" He was a member of an elite military team that operated completely under the radar. They were not given credit for any mission. Few knew of their existence. Only those with the very highest security clearance would know anything at all about Sam Johnson. Azami Yoshiie shouldn't know any real particulars on an individual soldier. He expected that she would know about the GhostWalkers because she wouldn't sell a satellite to just any company and she was plugged into the military— she'd sold a few satellites to them. But there was no reason whatsoever to know anything about an individual member of that elite unit.

Thorn shrugged, her breath catching in her lungs. She was in murky waters now. If she'd read Sam wrong, she could blow everything. He was truly a man who could go from totally relaxed to full-out attack in a split second, and she had no doubt that he was an intensely loyal man. She was dismayed to find she wanted him to be loyal to her. She didn't want him to be so suspicious of her, and yet she was immensely pleased that he was.

Thorn had never felt so conflicted. If he didn't have the intelligence he possessed, or the skills as a warrior, she would never be able to respect him—or be attracted to him. He had to be suspicious or she would have dismissed him as she did nearly everyone else.

She spoke the truth, knowing she was deliberately misleading him. "Dr. Whitney attempted to purchase a satellite from our company about two years ago. Of course we don't do business with anyone we don't meet." That much was true—but Whitney had refused the meeting. He'd gone so far as to offer more money and said he could handle the software installation and the training of the technicians to run the software—which made her brothers shake their heads at his enormous ego.

"He has one of your satellites?" Sam asked.

She shook her head. "No, we did not go through with the sale. My brother was not impressed with him. His manner is disrespectful." Again that was strictly the truth, and anyone knowing Dr. Whitney would know he had an ego the size of Europe and was totally rude to anyone he considered inferior—which basically meant everyone.

Sam frowned at her. His expression gave nothing away, and she made a mental note not to try to play poker with him. She could keep her serenity all day and few could ever see what was going on inside of her, but she wasn't going to bet her life—or those of her brothers—that Sam couldn't read her. He'd been suspicious of her from the very moment he'd laid eyes on her.

"Were you ever alone with him?"

Her heart jerked hard in her chest. Memories flooded her mind, the silent screams of a small child, the pain wracking her body, a knife slicing through her chest. Her heart ceasing to beat and then jerking awake, just as it was now. She slammed the mental door shut hard. That way lay madness. She never looked at those memories unless they served a valuable purpose and there was no such reason now.

"We are a traditional family in many ways," she replied enigmatically, avoiding a lie. She wasn't above lying to serve her mission, but not to Sam, not if she could help it.

His eyes warmed. "So we're back to you giving me instructions on how to properly court you. Do I ask your brothers' permission?"

He was stealing her heart with his sincerity. She shook her head. "I am not a woman who would be practical in your life, Sam. You need a home and family . . ."

He laughed, interrupting her carefully chosen words. The sound was pure masculine amusement, sending a curling heat through her and making her forget everything she was going to say.

"I'm a soldier, Azami. That's who I am. What I am. My woman will be my home—my family. Beyond that, who knows? I believe you're that woman."

Thorn swallowed hard. Now her breath was coming too fast, her lungs burning. He shook her like no one else ever had with his stark admissions. His honesty. Who in the world was like him? "You are an intellectual like my brother. What drives you to put your life and your tremendous brain on the line?" She couldn't prevent that little bite in her voice. He was made for great things and yet he chose combat.

"You tell me," he fired back.

"I have a duty to perform that is sacred to me. Perhaps the attraction between us is strong because our values are so very close."

She *wanted* that to be the reason—or that for the first time in her life she'd met a man she truly couldn't resist. Her attraction to Sam Johnson had *nothing* to do with Dr.

Whitney. The idea was simply impossible. She'd been thrown away long before Sam had applied to the Ghost-Walker program. Even had Whitney paired Sam with Thorn, he couldn't have paired Thorn with Sam. The wild churning in her stomach settled a little. Her attraction to Sam *had* to be the real thing, not manufactured by a monster for his own purposes.

"I understand duty," Sam said. He looked around him. One helicopter down. Two Jeeps and many soldiers dead. The cleaning crews would hopefully be able to identify where the threat had come from. "Do you think these soldiers came after your brother?"

Thorn's gaze followed his careful study of the battlefield. Did she believe the soldiers had tried to kidnap her brother? Nothing else made sense. The soldiers hadn't attacked the compound where Lily and her child resided and they'd retreated the moment help had come. It was actually a very well-coordinated attack. They couldn't know that Sam's GhostWalker team had strewn the forest with hidden bunkers or that she and Sam would be able to teleport so skillfully.

"Yes. I think someone with a great deal of money has orchestrated this attack in order to kidnap Daiki. It is the only real possible explanation that fits." She waited a moment and then into the silence breathed his name. "Sam." It was improper to address him by his given name, as he did her, but these were extraordinary circumstances. She waited patiently until his eyes met hers. She needed to look into his soul when he answered her.

"Do you work for Dr. Peter Whitney? Are you affiliated with him in any way?"

His frowned deepened. "Dr. Peter Whitney has committed indescribable crimes against humanity with his experiments. He's operating outside the law. The man is a criminal and needs to be stopped. He's our greatest enemy."

"Then why are you working with his daughter?" Thorn asked, her voice dropping low with accusation.

Sam pushed a hand through his hair. He looked tired, a

great oak tree, swaying in the wind. She'd almost forgotten his wound and loss of blood. The Zenith had helped, stopping the bleeding and providing the adrenaline needed to keep going, but the drug was wearing off and Sam needed medical attention.

"Is that what you think? You're so far off base. You came here thinking she would be just like her father. Lily is as much a victim of Peter Whitney as everyone else he's ever come in contact with. She works harder than anyone else to uncover his location, but he's got powerful friends who help to hide him."

She could see that was all the information she was going to get out of him on the subject. He was fiercely loyal to Lily and despised Peter Whitney. He hadn't bothered to disguise the loathing in his voice.

"You might want to sit down, Sam," she advised softly. "The Zenith kick is fading and you're going to crash hard."

Thorn couldn't prevent herself from stepping forward and slipping her arm around his waist. "If we get to the tree line, your people can find us easier, but we'll still be protected. Do you think you've got enough left to make it to the edge of the road?"

His arm circled her shoulders and he pulled her beneath his arm, but she doubted the gesture had anything to do with weakness. He didn't feel weak at all. His body had no give to it, muscle flowing beneath his skin, almost as if he were made of steel. He didn't lean on her, but she couldn't let go of him. They walked in silence through the forest, avoiding the areas where there were dead bodies. She had no doubt the cleaners wouldn't find anything useful to identify them. If the men in the Jeep had come back to kill the two fallen Mexican soldiers, fingerprints would be useless.

"You know they shot those soldiers to keep us from questioning them," Thorn said.

Sam nodded, concentrating on each step. He wasn't going to appear weak in front of her; after all, he did have some pride.

"The enemy didn't want to leave anyone behind who could help us unravel the conspiracy." The first bullets had gone to kill the dying soldiers, giving Azami and Sam a few seconds to escape. They'd been lucky. "We have dental and faces, even if no fingerprints. We'll get a hit. And no one will lose our tails. We have one on the Jeep and one on the helicopter," Sam assured. "We're pretty good at what we do."

Thorn looked up at his face and his breath caught in his throat. The sun slid through the heavy foliage and kissed her flawless skin. Her lashes fanned down, two thick crescents and her body moved against him in a rhythm that sent the now familiar heat coursing through his veins.

"I'm sure you are," she replied.

With another woman he might consider she was throwing out an innuendo, but Azami didn't flirt. What she'd given of herself to him had been freely given. She was extremely composed and very private. He counted himself very lucky that she'd responded to him at all.

"Daiki is . . ." She hesitated. "Important to the world. His work is unsurpassed by anyone as of yet and many countries would love to get their hands on him. It is virtually impossible to infiltrate our company. Our staff is kept small and is moved from country to country when needed."

"How can your security be that tight? You have to hire . . ."

She was already shaking her head. "Sam, we are our own security. Everyone who works for Samurai Telecommunications is known to us since our childhood. The majority were trained by my father from the time they were children, and after his death, by one of his children. We employ family and family of family—if that makes sense."

Sam knew it was a common business practice in Japan for employees to work for the same company for years and their children and children's children to follow suit. He snuck a peek at the distance to the road. He could just make it if he concentrated and kept putting one foot in front of the other. He'd managed to block out the pain for some time,

but now it was pounding at him hard, demanding acknowledgment. He didn't want anything to interfere in the last
hour or so he had alone with Azami. Once they were back
in the compound, they might very well become enemies.
Certainly, until they had satisfying answers, he would have
to protect his team.

"It makes sense. And it's smart. If Daiki is responsible
for what I understand is groundbreaking software, who
developed the optical lens? From what I understand there is
nothing even coming close to it on the market?"

Azami glance up at his face. "I believe Lily has that information."

"I didn't think to ask her. I only know they were talking
very excitedly about the satellite and what it could do for us."

Azami shrugged. "He's written up in all the magazines.
It isn't a secret. Eiji developed the lens. Between the two of
them, there isn't much they can't do."

"So Eiji is every bit as valuable as Daiki in the making
of the newest satellite system. If he were to fall into the
wrong hands, your company would pay a great deal to get
him back. Or he could be forced to reproduce the lens to
enable another faction to reproduce the satellite."

The trees lining the road seemed to be getting farther
away, not closer, which made absolutely no sense. Every
step was like wading through quicksand, and if he remembered correctly, he was in forest, not swamp.

His mind seemed to stay sharp enough and his focus
remained on Azami—every breath she took, the scent of
her enveloping him, the way her soft hair slid against his
arm and chest. He felt her tighten her arm around his waist.
She was surprisingly strong for such a small woman. He
shook his head. No, something important was eluding him,
slipping through his mind so fast he couldn't grasp it long
enough to discover what it was.

He moistened his lips and looked down at the top of her
silky head. "You're really beautiful, Azami."

Thorn looked up at Sam's unguarded face. He was

crashing fast. He'd lost too much blood and the Zenith had kept him going, but he was going to need medical attention fast. "Sam, call in your people now. Tell them you need a medic and blood." She enunciated each word carefully. "Tell them you're wearing two patches of second-generation Zenith."

"*That's* the important information." He smiled down at her, as though happy she'd helped him remember.

Thorn nearly groaned. He was very far gone. "Sam. Call in your people right now. Tell them to come *now*."

He stumbled to a halt and stood there swaying, rubbing at the frown lines between her eyes with his fingertip as if that was far more important than his wounds. "How would you know about second-generation Zenith being in existence? Only we know about that. And how did you have access to it?"

"*Sam.*" She used her sternest voice. "We need your team now. Call to them."

He went down, a giant oak tree chopped off at the trunk, his legs completely giving out and he was on the ground, staring up through the heavy canopy at the clear blue sky, eyes wide-open. Thorn went down with him, trying to cushion his fall, a thread of desperation running through the calm. He must have lost more blood than she'd first thought. She should have pushed him much earlier to call his team, to let them know he was injured. She hadn't because . . . well . . . she just hadn't been smart.

"Sam, open your mind to mine. All the way, let me in." She used her voice shamelessly, a warm honeyed tone, slipping inside his mind to settle there. He *had* to let her inside. She searched for threads, anything that might lead her to his team. She knew, without a doubt, that he'd communicated telepathically with them. She'd never tried to get inside another mind deep enough to find a path to someone else. If she didn't, help might be too late.

She understood that his team's first obligation would be to rescue Daiki and Eiji, transporting them quickly to safety.

The cleanup team could take its time. And anyone coming to get Sam might think they could drive. They needed a helicopter and a medic fast. Second-generation Zenith didn't break down the body and cause it to bleed out as the first generation had done— Sam wouldn't need an antidote, but that didn't mean the blood loss wouldn't eventually kill him. The drug had forced his system to speed up, not slow down, and any wound inside his body—and he had a hole through him—might continue to bleed internally.

"Sam." She caught his shoulders and put her mouth next to his, so that she felt every warm breath that he took. His skin felt cool, all that wonderful heat slowly dissipating.

His eyes focused on her. "Kiss me."

The whisper was so soft she might not have heard it, but she felt the words formed against her own lips. She crossed those scant inches, settling her mouth on his, opening her mind to his, allowing him to slip into her. She refused to get lost in his kiss, pushing for him to open his mind more fully. The moment the barrier slipped, she poured in fast, afraid even as consciousness slipped away, he would close his mind to her. He was very disciplined, very trained, and she doubted he was a man who would give in to torture, yet his mind was unguarded when he kissed her.

She found that elusive thread to his leader. Captain Ryland Miller—Lily Whitney's husband. She was ashamed of herself for hesitating. Would she allow Sam to die because of her mission? There had to be a line one didn't cross. Letting them know of her abilities would complicate things, but Sam already suspected too much about her. She couldn't live honorably if she allowed him to die just to keep her secrets.

I am Azami Yoshiie. I am with Sam Johnson. He's wounded and needs a medic immediately. He's lost a tremendous amount of blood. You'll need several units. To stop the bleeding and keep him on his feet I administered two second-generation Zenith patches. The surge has worn off and he's crashed from blood loss. His pulse is weak, his skin cooling fast. He hasn't completely lost consciousness.

Her heart pounded in her chest. The small silence seemed like hours when it wasn't more than a few seconds before a deep voice filled her mind.

We'll have a helicopter in the air in three minutes. ETA to you, ten. Medic and blood on board.

She should have been disturbed that he didn't ask her questions about how she had managed to tap into his mind—that meant he was a pro all the way. He didn't even ask her about the Zenith and they had to be both outraged and shocked that not only did she know about it, she actually had some in her possession.

Medic wants to know if there's arterial bleeding.

Not that I can see. I think there might be internal bleeding.

Roger that.

There was another short silence. She realized he was communicating with someone else.

Keep him talking, try to make him stay with you. Has he responded to you verbally?

No. Thorn felt frantic. She could feel him slipping further from her. She knew the pathway to Ryland Miller, so she didn't need to include Sam, but as long as she was in his mind, she could monitor his brain function. *He's slipping in and out.*

He's strong. The voice was utterly calm. *He's a soldier. He'll respond to commands. Talk to him. Force him to stay with you.*

Thorn framed Sam's face with her hands and pressed her forehead against his. "Sam, listen to me. They're coming for us and we won't have much time. I will not show affection to you in public, in the way Westerners do. In my family, courtship means nothing."

His lashes fluttered and she found herself looking into his dark eyes. She was fairly certain Ryland had meant she was supposed to bark commands at Sam to keep him alert, but their connection was far more elemental, far more primal, and he responded to her instinctively—or she liked to think so. In any case, she had his attention.

"Only a proposal of marriage is treated with the utmost respect. If my brother doesn't cut off your head and accepts such an outrageous suggestion, you will be considered family and must treat my brothers in the same manner. Such an arrangement is not taken lightly in our family. You mustn't mention courtship when we are back with the others."

She pressed her mouth against his. "And no more kissing."

For one moment, her heart nearly stood still when she swore his lips curved beneath hers, the lightest of movements, but then he was fading again. Panic welled up. "Don't you *dare* die on me, soldier," she snapped, forcing a crisp, sharp command into her voice. "Open your eyes and look at me, Sam."

His eyelashes fluttered and he gave a wheezing gasp. She was losing him. The helicopter and medic were going to be too late. Thorn swore under her breath and once again leaned into him.

"Don't leave me. I need you." She choked the words out, horrified that they might be true. She barely knew this man and yet she knew him far more intimately than anyone else in the world. She'd been inside his mind. They fit, like two pieces of a puzzle. He accepted who she was, that elusive woman who stood quietly inside the warrior. He treated her with respect—as an equal. He hadn't hesitated to go into battle with her and he hadn't checked to make certain she was doing her part. The world couldn't lose this man. He was something very special.

He's crashing. He's crashing now. She kept the edge of panic from her voice, sending the message with utter calm while inside she felt herself shattering.

There was that small silence and then the voice came— every bit as steady as hers. *Use another Zenith patch if you have it. Just one.*

Her breath caught in her throat and for the first time she hesitated. *That could make him bleed out faster if he's bleeding internally.*

It will force the blood to his brain and keep him from brain damage and buy us the time. Lily will operate when she gets there. Just do it.

Lily Whitney—Peter Whitney's daughter. Did she dare trust her as Sam did? Lily had been the one to develop the second-generation Zenith drug. Was she experimenting with her new drug on Sam? Was she like her father? Did she consider Sam expendable, or was she really trying to save his life?

She ran one caressing finger down his face, took a breath, and made her decision.

CHAPTER 6

Thorn held Sam's hand and brushed the hair from his face as the helicopter approached. She ached inside, the tension growing as the helicopter landed and the occupants spilled out. Several men raced to set up a tent, while two more and a woman approached her. She let go of Sam, slowly getting to her feet, aware of every weapon she carried, most concealed now. One man carried a litter while the other paced alongside of him, hands free, his eyes not on Sam, but on her.

Her stomach fluttered, but her nerves held steady. This man was her guard. Tall, red hair, solidly built, it was nearly impossible to ignore him. First had come Sam's warning and then Ryland Miller, no doubt, had told them all to watch her carefully. She knew the drill. There would be politeness, warm smiles, cold watchful eyes, and guards watching her every move. Every one of these men was a GhostWalker and they recognized one another. She had known, when she'd made the decision to enter their camp, that she'd be at risk, but the end result—to improve her chances of finding Whitney's location—was well worth it. Her brief trip into fantasy—

pretending she could actually have Sam—was gone and her very familiar reality was back.

Lily Miller rushed to Sam's side, nodded at her with a polite murmur, but her entire focus was on Sam. Thorn kept a hand close to her dagger. If Sam Johnson died from Lily's attentions, Lily would follow right after him and damn the consequences. Thorn played out each step in her mind. She would kill Lily swiftly, use teleportation to get into the clearing she and Sam had first jumped to, and then disappear. The GhostWalker team would have home field advantage, but she had confidence, not only in herself but in Daiki and Eiji. They might not be enhanced or have psychic abilities, but they had unbelievable skills, and they would never panic.

Thorn kept her eyes on Lily while the redheaded guard kept his eyes on her. Lily assessed Sam's condition quickly. She handed Thorn a bag of fluids with the briefest of nods.

"Come on, Sam," Lily murmured softly. "Hang in there for me. Give me two more minutes. Just two. That's all I need." Even as she whispered cajolingly, she inserted a needle into his arm, frowning in concentration as she tried for a vein that seemed elusive.

The big soldier kneeling on the other side of the cot steadied Sam's arm for Lily, his face a mask of concern. He was all muscle, and yet the look on his face revealed hints of genuine affection and love—the sort of emotion a man like him would show only when fear ate at the edges of his mind. He sent her a quick reassuring smile in spite of the fact that he was anxious.

"Tucker Addison, ma'am. Sorry about the circumstances." He was deeply afraid for Sam—they all were. That frightened Thorn even more. She should have known something was wrong much earlier.

She inclined her head. "Azami Yoshiie." Sam had used far too much energy teleporting, again and again. She knew from experience how difficult it was on the body, yet he'd done so wounded and unflinching. Was it possible using teleportation had aggravated the wound in his body?

SAMURAI GAME   99

Lily was much easier to read than the man. She was so apprehensive over Sam's condition, she had no time for anything or anyone else—not even a potential enemy or an honored guest. Sam was her only concern. Thorn felt the tight coiling in her body ease just a little. There was no way to take the kind of anxiety Lily was displaying.

Lily found the vein in Sam's arm. With a rapid efficiency Thorn couldn't help but admire, she hooked up an IV and then a second one. Blood and fluids pumped into Sam nearly before Thorn could take a second breath.

"Is he going to make it, Doc?"

Thorn narrowed her gaze to center on the speaker, the man standing at Sam's head.

Lily frowned. "Of course, Kyle. I refuse to allow any other option. It's safe to move him to the tent now."

She glanced at Thorn, as if really seeing her for the first time. Thorn realized that, until now, Lily had viewed her as little more than an inanimate object on which to drape supplies while she saw to her patient.

"Ms. Yoshiie." Lily inclined her head in a slight nod of respect. "I'm sorry we're meeting under such extreme circumstances. We have to move Sam into the tent. Would you mind carrying these?" She held out the bags of fluids. "I need to keep my hands free."

Thorn shook her head and immediately stepped up to take the bags from Lily. Another man hurried to help Tucker lift Sam into the litter. They moved fast toward the tent, Lily running along beside them. Thorn's sense of urgency revived with a vengeance. Lily had declared Sam safe to move, but if they were running, he wasn't out of the woods yet.

Thorn's mouth went dry and her heart began to pound. The scars on her chest throbbed and burned. Blood thundered in her ears. She moistened her lips. "Are you going to operate right here?"

In a tent? Outdoors? *Without anesthesia?* For one horrible moment she was six years old again and out of her mind with pain and fear. She ran along beside the litter, her gaze refusing to focus on the ground or anything else around her. She could hear a child screaming so loud she couldn't focus, the sound high and animalistic. Reality retreated until she could only hear that softly pitched, modulated voice with its perfect elocution that sent chills through her at night and kept her afraid to close her eyes.

Think of the contribution you're making to science, Thorn. Whitney spoke as if she should be grateful that he was operating on her without anesthesia, and because she was a child and one with a rather low IQ, he thought, he felt he needed to speak very distinctly and slowly for her to understand. *When we're finished here, I will be so much closer to knowing how much pain a GhostWalker can sustain without succumbing to death. You should be grateful you can help so many others.*

Whitney stood above her, poised, unflappable, his expression perfectly reasonable and interested as he stood over her writhing body with a scalpel.

Please. The child's pleading voice. Sweat beading on her forehead, dotting her body, the terrible fear permeating the room. *You did this already.*

Of course, Thorn. That same soft, *reasonable* voice. *We have to repeat the experiment again and again to make certain of our facts. I've explained that to you. You're old enough to understand what's expected of you. Lie still and this time, I want you to concentrate on not allowing your heart to stop. You can do that, can't you?*

Thorn pressed her hand over her wildly pounding heart. She felt bruised, her chest so sore she couldn't breathe, the aftermath of Whitney bringing her back to life again and again. Sometimes she woke in the middle of the night to the sound of her heart flatlining and the echo of the burst of shock pulsing through her body.

Her hand slipped to her dagger and she increased her stride to catch up with Lily, moving in behind her, close enough to kill her and slide away right under the watchful eyes of her guard—and he was watching her. Deliberately

she brushed back strands of her hair, allowing concern to
show on her face as she looked down at Sam. Her moment
would come when she entered the tent. Her guard would be
outside. She would have to slip the blade deep twist and
teleport through the narrow opening back to the clearing
she'd need to find.

Thorn risked a glance into the tent. It was much larger
than she'd first thought. They all stopped abruptly in the
first section. Behind a net, she could see two men hastily
setting up covered, sterile trays of instruments. Her stomach
lurched. She couldn't catch her breath, her lungs raw and
burning for air, her vision clouding until . . . Eyes stared
down at that small child, masks covering the lower half of
their face. *Him.* Whitney. So perfectly calm, shaking his
head at how unreasonable and stubborn she was.

Take a deep breath, Thorn. Just like the pool. It isn't any
different. You need to beat your last time. You can do so
much better if you just try. That unshakable, *reasonable*
voice, so completely unflappable, the eyes always so bright
with dispassionate interest. Very slowly they lowered the
transparent plastic wrap that would deprive her of all air.
Her heart thundered through the cold, sterile room. She
could feel her heart pounding so hard, her chest hurt from
the inside out, bruised and battered. Her head had been
shaved because Whitney felt it would get in the way of his
experiment and he needed to stick electrodes on her scalp.

She was so close to Lily she felt the very rhythm of her
breathing as they entered the first small area not netted off
as an operating room. This section was all for preparation.
She swallowed hard and forced sound to come out of her
suddenly blocked throat. "You have anesthesia here?"

"I'm not taking chances on losing him. We'll operate
right here. If he has a nicked artery, he's in trouble. We've
got everything we need in the tent." Lily sounded distracted
again. "Of course we have anesthesia."

Both men inside the netting wore scrubs and even their
shoes were covered. Tucker and his companion passed the

litter through the net to the other two men. Lily took the bags of fluid from Thorn and placed them on the litter at Sam's side. Immediately he was whisked away—taken to the sterile operating table inside the larger section of the tent. Thorn allowed her fingers to slip away from her dagger, fearing, with memories so close, she might make a mistake.

Lily scrubbed her hands and arms with some kind of solution out of a bottle and held out her arms, and Tucker disinfected his own hands before helping Lily into surgical gloves and a full set of scrubs.

It was obvious the surgical field setup had been practiced often. Tucker, Lily, and the others were too efficient and fast for this to have been a one-time thing: the tent going up, everything in sterile packs ready to use, even the smooth way Tucker had gotten Lily into her scrubs. He covered her hair with a netted cap.

The ground shifted beneath Thorn's feet, the memories pouring out so fast she couldn't stop them. Whitney approaching the table and that small child knew—*knew*—what was coming next. *You're seven now. Not a baby, so stop acting like one. I'm tiring of your endless tantrums. Saber stopped your heart multiple times and you were just fine. This is the same thing.*

It isn't. It isn't. This hurts. Electric shock. The terrible pain flashing through her body, making her teeth clamp down so that sometimes she bit herself. She tried to tell him, but nothing fazed Whitney. He never lost control. And he never stopped.

Science matters, Thorn. It is necessary to make certain every experiment is reliable.

Thorn could hear the child screaming, her mind nearly gone, her body and heart so weak now, she knew there would come that day when he couldn't revive her—and she wanted it to come soon. This had to stop. She'd overheard him tell one of his assistants that her heart was weakening fast and the damage would be too great to continue and soon she'd be of no use to them.

"Ms. Yoshiie?" Tucker indicated outside the tent. "Please accompany me."

Thorn found she didn't want to leave Sam, which made no sense. His life was in Lily's hands, and Thorn's presence would have no impact on whether he lived or died. Yet, still, she didn't want to leave. Her reluctance bothered her because it was so deep, almost elemental. She pressed her lips together, grateful for her father's teachings. Her face was composed, even serene. Her hands weren't even shaking, although deep inside, her mind was crumbling into pieces and her body felt shattered. Her childhood was far too close. She shook her head, uncaring what he thought. She wasn't leaving, not yet. Her legs were rubber anyway, so she wasn't at all positive she could leave.

Father. The child called to the one man who had steadied her, thought her worthy enough to save. *Help me. I'm lost again. Help me.* But he was no longer alive to hear her call even if she yelled at the top of her lungs. She was alone and left with no protection in place.

Her eight-year-old heart still echoed in her ears, that shuddering thud that had lost its rhythm as she lay in the box, her nails digging into the lid, breaking off in an effort to get out. Had she been buried alive? No, she could hear voices. She was so cold—ice cold—for so long and finding it nearly impossible to breathe. She was suffocating in that tiny box, curled up on her side, desperate to know if she would ever get out.

Darkness. A car ride through a strange city with strangers. The car had slowed, her door opened, and she'd been shoved out, hitting the ground so hard she was certain every bone was smashed. She was afraid to lift her head, to look around. The scent of garbage and urine was strong. Small red eyes glowed at her from the darkness. She had never been out of the compound where Whitney conducted his experiments, and this place was almost more frightening.

She heard heavy footsteps, smelled a sweet, overpowering odor, increasing her terror. She closed her eyes tightly.

Someone toed her with a boot. Hard hands moved over her body, and the man said something in a language she didn't understand. A man laughed. She smelled the other—the man she would come to know as her father. The man who saved her. She would always recognize that wonderful scent.

He arrived with no sound, like an avenging angel, complete with sword and fierce eyes, so alive, so warm, and he made her feel safe and warm and worth something. And now he was gone. *Father. I'm lost in this nightmare. I can't close the door. Where are you?*

The danger in this mission had always been those nightmare memories that often were more vivid than reality. Daiki had warned her that her memories would surface and try to consume her, but she hadn't considered that they would be so strong that mere memories could affect her physically. She wanted to wrap her arms around her middle and hold herself very still until the earthquake passed.

Azami?

Thorn stepped back, looking wildly around. Her name had sounded soft, and slurred, but very distinct in her mind. Her father? Back from the dead? She tried to fit the sound with her father's distinct voice. The accent was off. No matter how hard she tried to make her name sound as if her father reached out to comfort her—she couldn't make the accent right.

The soldier named Tucker stood a few feet from her, watching her closely, the curiosity in his eyes telling her she was not keeping her countenance as serene as she should. Just to her right lounged the silent redheaded soldier she was certain had been appointed to guard her. She was about to lose reality right in front of these people. She would disgrace herself—live in shame for all time. Her father had taught her to overcome such things. Her mind and body could be divided if need be. She would dishonor her father if she couldn't pull herself back together.

"Ms. Yoshiie?" Tucker stepped closer.

The scent of blood was overpowering. It was so difficult

to breathe, but she made herself stay still. "Please call me Azami." Thank God her voice didn't shake as her insides were. She could feel sweat trickling down the valley between her breasts. "My brothers and I have adopted a more West ᵢᵢ ᵢ ᵢ ᵢₚₚᵣₒₐᵢₕ ᵢₕₐₙ ᵢₒₘₑ ᵒᶠ ᵒᵘᵣ fellow countrymen. It doesn't offend me to have you use my given name."

"I'm Tucker then, ma'am," the large man replied.

Like Sam, he was dark-skinned and brown-eyed. He looked like the kind of man you wanted at your back in a fight. He flashed a smile that didn't quite reach his eyes. Although he didn't appear to be watchful or suspicious, she knew that he was every bit as alert as the soldier in the background. Every bit as alert and on guard as she was.

Thorn needed a few minutes of solitude to push back the memories of a child's terror. She glanced into the tent and knew the moment she'd done so that it was a mistake. Bright lights shone down on Sam. She could smell blood. She could see a bloody scalpel in Lily's blood-covered glove. The lights blinded her eyes until all she saw was that terrible sharp blade coming toward her chest, slicing through her skin, muscle, and tissue, digging for her heart.

She was cold. So cold. Ice had invaded her veins. Everywhere she looked the lights stung her eyes and exaggerated the monstrous features of the masked figures bending over her. The doctor, with his reptilian-cold eyes, reached for a shiny metal instrument with two handles connected by a bar in the middle.

It is nothing to fear, Thorn. Simply an instrument to spread your bones to get to your weakened heart. Surely you want me to fix it for you.

He moved the paddles closer together and leaned over her. She bit back a scream, sweat pouring from her body, her heart hammering so loud it echoed through that cold, sterile room.

Azami. The voice was more slurred than ever. Male. Brushing over the memories of a terrified child. Soothing. Warmth pouring through all that terrible ice-cold.

Thorn stiffened, pressing the back of her hand against her mouth. *Father?* Oh, God, she was truly losing her mind. She couldn't pull back and there was nowhere to run and hide, to be alone in order to gather herself and push those memories back behind that steel door she kept closed in her mind.

"What's wrong with you, Kyle?" Lily's voice snapped out. Imperious. Demanding. "Keep him under. Do you think I can do this when he's awake? We're going to lose him to shock if he doesn't die from blood loss."

"He's fighting it," a man answered. "I swear, I'm afraid to give him more. He might not come back. He won't go under. I've never had a patient react like this before."

Through the netting, Thorn saw Lily bend over Sam. "Don't fight it, Sam. Go to sleep and let me take care of you. Don't fight me."

Azami.

There it was again. Her name. But it was Sam, not her father calling to her. It was Sam, still connected to her mind, reading her memories of childhood. That child who had been used for experiment after evil, bloody, torturous experiment. Her body sliced open—usually without anesthesia so the doctor could gauge her ability to withstand pain. So many experiments from depriving her oxygen, forcing her underwater into a cold pool to see how long she could hold out and if they could bring her back. The enhancements that Whitney believed were complete failures. Her DNA tampered with. Forcing the other girls to use their gifts on her to perfect their abilities.

I will not have you destroying my record, Thorn. You are such a disappointment to me and I've given you every opportunity—far more than anyone else.

She knew even if she clapped her hands over her ears, she would never stop that voice from telling her that her brain was useless to him, but at least he could dissect her body and examine her so he could avoid inadvertently creating other useless subjects like her again. If she would only behave and cooperate, he could test new medicines and procedures before trying them on his more valuable subjects.

He had operated without anesthesia many times to judge the body's ability to withstand pain before it gave out. He'd stopped and restarted her heart just as many times. Her heart had grown so weak Dr. Whitney had believed she would die anyway, so he'd finally thrown her away—into the alley of one of the worst streets where human trafficking and sex traders plied their slaves.

Sam knew too much. He knew who she was. If she could hear Whitney's voice echoing through her mind, so could Sam. He was sharing her mind, her memories, every horrid detail. She swallowed hard, sweat beading on her skin. It never once had occurred to her, when assessing all the risks to her coming to the GhostWalker compound, that someone would share her mind and uncover her childhood shame. Those terrible years of torment and vulnerability.

"You'll have to give him more. I'm going to lose him." This time there was desperation in Lily's voice.

"He's turning his head, Lily, trying to look . . ." The voice trailed off.

Thorn looked up to see both Lily and the other man looking toward her, following that slow head turn Sam made even in his barely conscious state. They knew he was looking at her. To warn them? They'd probably think that, but he was trying to reach out—to help her. He was every bit as selfless as her father had been.

Mamoru Yoshiie simply appeared from the darkness, a small, almost thin man in a gray kimono and wide leg trousers, split-toed socks, and sandals. Behind him were two young boys, one thirteen, the other ten. Yoshiie had stood over her, shaking his head at the small group of thugs who had begun to gather close to see what he would do to her. Later, she learned, the thugs were the feared yakuza, who ran the sex and drugs in this part of the city. They bowed slightly to Yoshiie and slowly gave way as he bent to lift her into his arms.

Thorn had been so frightened. She was tiny, her weight no more than a feather to the older man. He stared into her eyes and peace descended. She had never felt like that again with anyone—until Sam.

She closed her eyes. She should let Sam-go. She should be glad he was slipping away. Her heart slammed hard in her chest. The scars burned like fire. The little girl wouldn't stop screaming. Even her fingernails hurt where she'd torn them off trying to get out of the small box they'd stuffed her into on the trip back to Japan.

She forced air through her lungs. There was no letting Sam go, not even to save her own life. There might be no chance for them, but Sam Johnson needed to be in the world. She rejected Dr. Whitney's assessment that he wasn't worth anything. *She* wouldn't throw him away, not when she'd been inside of him and knew he was worth all the gold in the world. Her father would never have thrown him away. Just as he'd saved Daiki and Eiji and his beloved daughter, Azami, he would have plucked Sam from any danger and raised him to know how to take care of himself.

Don't, Sam. Not for me. It was a long time ago. Let them work on you. Just go to sleep.

I can feel such pain in you.

She took a breath and deep inside, she stilled.

His voice swamped her. Brought her warmth, but she felt that terrible loneliness that echoed through his tone. Sadly she knew how he felt. He'd been in her, all that heat and strength, and when he was gone, she'd been aware of just how alone she'd been for too many years. She didn't know how it would ever be possible to have him in her life—not when she had no choice but to complete what she'd set out to do—but with him alive there was always a chance. In any case, the world needed a man of compassion and strength and duty such as Sam Johnson.

Don't leave me. Please just let the doc take care of you. She couldn't quite stop that small pleading in her voice. He shook her. Crawled inside of her. *Moved* her when few things—or people—did. She had just left herself raw and exposed and more vulnerable than she'd been in years. She guarded her emotions far more than she did her body. She trusted few people. It had taken years to fully trust her father and brothers and yet she'd just given herself to Sam.

Don't leave me. To a woman like Thorn, that was the epitome of weakness. She ducked her head and kept her expression perfectly blank.

Warmth slipped into her mind, filling the cold spaces, and shoved hard at the heavy open door of her childhood memories. He was saving her sanity even as he was slipping away. She kept breathing, in and out, stilling the terrible inner trembling. Whitney was gone. His voice. His eyes staring at her. She was alive and she was whole.

Sam. She whispered his name in her mind. Thankful for him. Afraid for him.

"Put him out," Lily called, fear edging her voice. She sounded almost desperate.

They knew. They all knew about her now. Her gaze jumped to Tucker's. She forced another calming breath. They knew she was telepathic, but that didn't mean they knew about her childhood.

Could she put Sam out? She moved into his mind. He was definitely fighting the anesthesia—for her. Because she was upset and he was worried for her. She soothed him, assured him, and pushed him subtly toward acceptance. She knew the exact moment he succumbed, going out, drifting away from her so that she felt a wrenching separation and once again, she was utterly alone.

"Thank you," Lily called, her voice muffled.

"Just save him," Thorn said, loud enough for the doctor to hear. She forced air to continue breathing. Breathing in. Breathing out. Presenting that absolutely serene countenance to anyone watching her—and they were watching— even more closely now.

This time she initiated leaving the surgical tent. She couldn't breathe in there. Tucker and the redheaded man followed her out. She got as far as the trees on shaking legs and stopped, leaning against a solid trunk and drawing in breath.

"Are you armed?" Tucker asked.

Her eyebrow shot up. "Of course I'm armed. I'm Daiki Yoshiie's bodyguard. He's had more threats against him than your president. I have permits to carry weapons, even in your country." She spoke with great dignity, pitching her voice low, as if his question was totally ludicrous. She wasn't altogether certain what she would do if he commanded her to surrender her weapons. And no way was she going to submit to a search.

"You brought down the helicopter."

Tucker made it more of a statement than a question. She supposed he knew because Sam didn't carry a bow and arrows and he must have received a report from whoever was cleaning up the bodies.

She didn't blink. Didn't show emotion. "It was necessary for our survival."

Tucker pulled a water bottle from his pack. "You must be thirsty."

She regarded the proffered bottle carefully. They were still treating her as a guest, yet her guard, the redheaded soldier, was definitely on alert. His gaze hadn't left her no matter what was going on around him.

"Thank you." She took the bottle and indicated the soldier. "Is he assigned to make certain I don't go crazy and kill everyone here?" She injected a faint note of humor into her voice.

Tucker gave her an easy smile that didn't quite reach his eyes. "This was a very coordinated and well-planned attack on your brother and perhaps you as well. Sam was assigned to keep you safe. Ian McGillicuddy has that honor now."

She turned and smiled at McGillicuddy. He was a big man, his red hair spilling across his forehead and his green eyes piercing and intelligent. He was guarding her all right, but it wasn't necessarily to keep her safe. She saluted him with the water bottle and took a long, cooling drink.

McGillicuddy nodded, but he didn't smile and he didn't take his eyes from her.

"Sam said my brothers are safe. I hope they're under a tight guard."

"Yes, of course. Kadan and Nico have them inside the compound. It's a fortress. No one can get to them there," Tucker said.

The concentrated smell of blood made her stomach lurch—an unusual reaction, so it had to be the aftermath of her memories bombarding her. She hoped that door was firmly closed. Glancing toward the tent, she didn't try to keep the worry from her face.

"I thought it was a through and through and that he'd be fine."

"You couldn't have known. Sam's tough," Tucker added. "Once he went back twice for wounded and no one realized he'd been shot twice himself. We didn't know until he was in the helicopter heading home and he just sort of passed out. That's Sam."

She liked Tucker all the more for the genuine respect and affection in his voice. "He was extremely efficient in the firefight. We were greatly outnumbered. The enemy spoke in English, Spanish, and Farsi. Two of the soldiers were murdered by their own people, presumably to keep them from talking."

"The bullets were concentrated in the mouth, destroying teeth and faces. Soldiers must have mopped up after your kills, making certain to slow down identification. Have there been specific threats against your family?" Tucker asked.

"There are always threats." Thorn looked around for a place to sit. Her legs were beginning to get a little strength in them, but she knew she needed recovery time. "I'd like to sit down if you don't mind." She said it more for McGillicuddy's benefit than for Tucker's. She didn't want to make any sudden moves and have the man shoot her. She forced her legs to work—to glide soundlessly through the vegetation until she found a suitable spot to sink onto the ground gracefully.

"I'm sorry," Tucker said immediately, looking remorseful. "I should have found you somewhere comfortable right away."

"I think we both had other things on our minds," Thorn said truthfully. "The adrenaline's wearing off."

"We can get you back up to the compound if you're anxious to see your brothers." Tucker sounded reluctant but willing.

Thorn didn't blame him. Clearly he wanted to make certain Sam remained alive. She shook her head, sending him a quick smile. "I think I'll stick around. You know how it is. When you're in combat with someone, you get close fast. He was pretty amazing. I want to know firsthand that he's going to make it."

"Are you telepathic?"

The question was so casual, the tone equally so, that for a moment it almost didn't register. Tucker Addison was very smooth at interrogation without seeming to be. He acted as if he was making innocent conversation. Thorn took her time, fussing with the pins in her hair, restoring a semblance of order as she looked up toward the blue sky. Night was still a few hours off, but the wind was picking up, blowing a few clouds overhead.

"Yes. I haven't spoken to another telepath since my childhood." That was strictly honest. "I found it exhilarating, shocking, and a little frightening that Sam had such a strong ability. I could hear him when he spoke to me." She flashed a small smile and reached for a leaf, examining the thin veins running through it. "The gift came in quite handy during the battle."

"Why wouldn't Sam let Lily put him under?" Tucker crouched down opposite her, his gaze intent on her face.

Thorn shrugged. It was always better to stick as close to the truth as possible. "He was worried about me. We fought together, and I think he believed I was his responsibility—at least that's what it felt like to me. He stepped between me and the soldiers several different times. I told him I was fine and that I'd stay close. That seemed to satisfy him."

She was back to the game of wits, and her confidence was coming back. She knew how to be Azami Yoshiie, inside and out. She was samurai through and through. Her father's daughter. That eight-year-old child, with all of her insecurities and terrible memories, was locked behind the door. Azami just had to keep her there.

So far, Tucker was making polite conversation, slipping in a clever question every now and then, but he hadn't asked the significant question—where had she gotten second-generation Zenith. It wasn't on the market as of yet. No one should know about it. So how had she? And how had she acquired it? Good questions that would require real answers. She knew he would wait until she was inside the compound where the GhostWalker teams would easily have the upper hand.

"I think a good cup of tea would be excellent right now," Thorn said. She loved the tea ritual her father had often used to calm her when, as a child, she was unable to find her center. Just the thought of her father comforted her and continued to infuse her with confidence.

Tucker's white teeth flashed at her. "You're the second woman to suggest tea in a situation like this. I have to admit, I drank it with her, but I'm a coffee man myself."

"The tea ritual is always comforting," she said. "It's always nice after a battle."

He raised his eyebrow. "Do you often go into battle?"

"I was trained from the time I was a child in the way of the samurai by my father. It is a way of life, and the use of weapons as well as hand-to-hand combat is part of the lifestyle. Of course along with traditional weapons and fighting technique, we were required to master the modern arts of warfare as well as weapons. So, I guess you can say, I often go into battle. We keep up our skills. Our company provides this training for our employees. My brothers and I often instruct as well as train in order to stay sharp."

"Your father must have been an unusual man."

Thorn nodded. "Most unusual and wonderful. I miss him every day." Her soft voice was infused with the warmth of a million memories.

The thought of her father brought her even more confidence and completely settled the last of the nerves in her stomach. Daiki and Eiji were both men of honor, like her father. She had never thought to meet a man who might live up to what her father and brothers were—until she met Sam. She knew his mind intimately. He would sacrifice his own happiness for the good of his team. He would sacrifice willingly his life for theirs. He knew what duty and honor were and stood for both.

Thorn found it strange that when she had finally set into motion her plan to track down Whitney and serve him justice or at the very least cut off his supporters and put him on the run, she found a man she could believe in—one she could trust.

"Life is very strange," she murmured aloud.

"That it is," Tucker agreed. "We had no idea we'd be cleaning up a full-scale assault on our guests. We don't always use this road. It's a private one we put in ourselves. In the winter it's completely impassable. We use snowmobiles or winter vehicles on the public road. It's odd that they would set up an ambush here. How could they possibly know we would use this route to bring you and your brothers up to the compound?"

Thorn turned the question over in her mind. "There are two routes and you never choose one ahead of time?"

Tucker shook his head. "We deliberately set no pattern when we're traveling."

"Maybe that's why they had the second helicopter and it came late to the party," she speculated. "They might have had a welcoming committee on both roads. A helicopter and two vehicles per road. Once they knew the route they could call for the others to back them up. They weren't that far away. A Jeep could cut through the forest and a helicopter just had to fly like a bird in a straight line."

Tucker nodded. "Not bad."

She sent him a small smile. "A test? Or not bad for a girl? You already knew that, didn't you?"

He grinned at her. "Our women are on the feisty side, just like you. You sit there very demure and look sweet, but you're a tiger in sheep's clothing. If Sam's all worried about you, he's worried about the wrong woman."

Thorn inclined her head. "You might tell him that when he wakes up."

CHAPTER 7

Sam struggled into a sitting position, his lungs screaming for air, sweat dripping down his face into his eyes. He threw an arm over his stinging eyes and took a deep breath, fighting for air. Blood thundered in his ears and his throat felt swollen and raw. He swore and shoved at the damp, springing curls spilling onto his forehead. He was *never* going to sleep again, that much was clear.

He'd seen a lot of really ugly things in his life, but his nightmares of torturing children—little girls—horrified him. He could never get to the child, no matter how hard he tried. He woke exhausted, in a panic, bile rising, every muscle in his body tight with tension and his mind in chaotic horror for the small child.

"What is it, Sam?" Lily Whitney-Miller asked. She handed him a damp washcloth. "You aren't sleeping more than a couple minutes at a time and you wake up like this. Your pulse rate is out of control. Can you tell me what's happening? You've been like this for nearly seventy-two hours."

He swallowed down another curse, took the cool cloth and rubbed his face, breathing in and out to regain some semblance of control. "Nightmares. They're bad, Lily. I've never had anything like this in my life."

"What kinds of things are you dreaming about?"

"Doctors torturing children—little girls." He cleared his throat to manage an intelligent sound. "Operating unnecessarily on them, Lily. Over and over." He was going to keep to himself that the "little girls" was always specifically *one* girl—Azami. He couldn't close his eyes without seeing that child being dissected *without* anesthesia.

Lily frowned, her brows drawing together. "Forgive me for bringing this up, Sam, but prior to the general and his wife fostering you, you lived in a very abusive household. Perhaps you had nightmares as a child and the trauma you suffered is re-creating the memories."

"What trauma?" He was genuinely puzzled. The only trauma he'd suffered was the damn nightmare.

"Sam." Lily's voice dropped low. Her doctor-to-patient voice made him wince. "You were shot. You were forced to kill several men in order to protect our guests. I think that's trauma enough for anyone to produce such nightmares."

He shook his head. "No way. I've been shot, stabbed, and I've killed. Hell, Lily. How many times have you patched me up? You know I've never had anything like this before. I'm afraid to close my eyes."

"Any soldier can start exhibiting PTSD at any time," she reminded, her voice gentle.

Sam shook his head. "It isn't that, Lily. I probably should be more bothered by the things I've had to do than I am. We've talked about it many times. I feel I have the right to defend myself. In any case, I believe in what I'm doing. This isn't PTSD."

"When did the nightmares start?"

He shrugged, reluctant to continue talking on the subject. He wanted to ask where Azami was. She was on his mind every moment, yet he was afraid now that they were back in the real world, she would reject him completely.

"It's important, Sam. I need to know."

He sighed and scrubbed back the hair tumbling on his forehead with both hands. It was nearly impossible to refuse Lily when she used that tone. She'd become like a sister to all the men when she wasn't "mothering" them. "In the operating room. The nightmares started in the operating room."

"Tell me about them."

He shrugged. "They're nightmares, Lily—like a horror movie unfolding. An insane doctor is operating on a little girl over and over without anesthesia. Other terrible experiments as well, all with the same child. I'm not into horror films, but I swear this was a mad scientist taking apart people alive just to see what made them tick." Belligerence had crept into his voice. He felt like a little kid admitting to his mommy he was afraid of the closet monster.

Lily looked even more concerned. "You've been operated on before, Sam. Has this happened before? Nightmares? Anything like this, maybe on a lesser scale?"

"What difference does it make?" He was sick of talking about it, sick of thinking about it, afraid he'd never get those images of horror out of his mind.

"You were given second-generation Zenith. I need to know if it has side effects. And it's important to always document any problems with anesthesia. It helps me to be better in the field. All four GhostWalker teams share information. We want to be able to set up surgery in minutes and give the best possible care right on the spot. Sometimes—such as in your case—minutes count."

That made sense. Lily made perfect sense, and he was all over the place. He needed sleep, but most of all he needed to know that Azami was still close and that she was all right. Lily had just given him the perfect reason to ask about Azami and the second-generation Zenith—why she would have it, how she got it—but he wasn't ready to find out if his betrayal of her abilities to Ryland had led to any harm to her.

"No, Lily, I've never had nightmares like this before in my life." He was careful to keep from looking at her. "Doctors operating on children without anesthesia? No way. I never imagined my mind could go there."

Lily pulled up a chair and sat rather gingerly as if her leg was hurting her. She always walked with a limp, but Sam had never asked her why. Too much time had passed and he thought it would upset her. She always acted as if she didn't notice her limp, but once, someone had mentioned it and for a moment, her confidence had vanished and she looked like a young girl, very unsure of herself. Sam, as well as the others on his team, had felt instantly protective of her when she'd revealed that small vulnerability.

She let out a small sigh of relief. "In some ways, your nightmares make sense, Sam. You were operated on in the field and just before I went into the tent, Azami asked me if we were going to operate on you without anesthesia. I thought it was a strange question, but if she was worried about it, you could have been as well. In any case, you very well could have overheard her comment and it stayed in your subconscious. You fought going under. We had a difficult time with you at first."

Lily's explanation was more than reasonable, but it didn't make the nightmares any less intense. He definitely wasn't going back to sleep, but he nodded to reassure her. Lily mothered all of them, although she was younger than many of them. He always enjoyed his conversations with her—she was extremely intelligent and he appreciated the mental stimulation when they had discussions. He didn't like worrying her.

"You look tired, Lily. Were you up all night with me again or with Daniel?" Her son was a constant source of amusement—and worry—to all of them. He was highly intelligent, active, inquisitive, and able to find clever ways to elude capture when he escaped. He often was most active at night—and impossible to see if he didn't want to be seen.

Still, he was the joy in all of their lives. Daniel represented hope to them. He loved nothing more than spending time with each of his "uncles." Each "uncle" knew the compound had to be secure—that Whitney would do anything to get his hands on one of the babies born to a GhostWalker. More than anything else, the GhostWalkers protected Daniel and his mother.

"My beloved child escaped again last night. I hope you know all of you have contributed to his delinquency—and he's not a year old yet."

Sam tried to look innocent. "False accusations." He pressed his hand over his heart. "How can you say such things?"

"Maybe catching you teaching him to climb and Jonas showing him how to pick a lock might have something to do with it, although I suppose I should be grateful Jonas didn't teach him the art of throwing knives."

"That's next year. Where did he go this time?"

"He found his way into the tunnels. Don't ask me how."

Sam burst out laughing. He loved the baby, as did all the men. They took turns watching him while Lily did research and generally worked her butt off for them. Unfortunately, Daniel was so advanced that they often forgot they were talking to an infant and stimulated his mind into behavior Lily didn't approve of.

"Ryland says if it wasn't so dangerous to do it, he'd microchip him so he'd know where he was at all times," Lily admitted, laughing with him.

Sam rubbed at the bridge of his nose. "I suppose since Whitney put microchips in all the girls he experimented on, no one wants that for the babies, although we'd be able to track them if someone got their hands on one. In San Francisco, it was a very near miss with Kane and Rose's child."

"I know." Lily sighed softly, sobering at the mention of her father. "We're trying to come up with alternatives. The thing is, if we had a way to track any child he kidnaps, it would be safer, but if Whitney manages to put another spy in place and finds out, he conceivably could use a microchip against us."

"When did Whitney start placing microchips in the girls he experimented on? At what age?"

Lily shook her head. "I didn't find any data on that yet. We have to be careful sneaking into his computer. Our Flame here—and now Jaimie out in San Francisco—handles gathering information and then we sort through whatever we managed to get. It's a slow process, because we don't want him to get suspicious. Still . . ." She trailed off shaking her head.

Sam studied her face. "Lily, honey, you can talk to me. You're upset about something. Is it Daniel? I know he's extremely active, but he's really an amazing boy." He patted her hand. "I know cribs and playpens don't hold him and he can get out of anything, but he's loving and sweet and so intelligent."

"I've taught him sign language, as his speech skills won't really develop for another few months—at least they shouldn't. But he signed to me, unless I'm reading him wrong, that he has an imaginary friend who plays with him."

Sam was alarmed at the little hitch in her voice. She sounded close to tears.

"They play games like hide-and-seek. So I guess he thinks he's playing with this friend when he's hiding from us."

She blinked rapidly as if staving off tears and Sam's heart thudded. Lily rarely showed vulnerabilities, and when she did, it was heart-wrenching.

"I don't know that much about children, Sam. It isn't easy having a superchild for a first child. I read and research, but there's no manual. The one thing I do know is that Daniel should be happy and fulfilled by his parents without needing an imaginary friend."

"Lily." His voice dropped into a soothing cadence. "You have to know you're a good mother."

She shook her head. "I didn't exactly have a childhood like other children, Sam. My father is Peter Whitney. The girls I thought were my sisters were taken away and used for experiments. *I* was an experiment. I was isolated a good deal of my childhood. Truthfully, all the parenting classes in the world aren't going to help me. Why would Daniel need an imaginary friend at his age? I provide him with all kinds of stimuli, both mental and physical. Ryland and I hold him all the time and love on him. All of you shower him with attention so it just doesn't make sense."

Sam hated to hear the pain in her voice. If it wasn't for Lily, all of the GhostWalkers would be in terrible trouble. She'd shared her enormous wealth with them. She provided health care and, more important, exercises and ways to help those who were without filters to live in a world without an anchor close to them. She continued to research and work to find ways to help them overcome all the obstacles they faced with their enhancements, as well as learning to perfect using psychic talents. More than all of that, Lily was a genuine, loving person with exceptional values. He loved her like the sister he'd never had.

Along with all of the things Lily did for all four teams of GhostWalkers, she was trying to learn to be a mother of a child with special gifts. Daniel was physically and mentally advanced and yet still really an infant. There were no guides for such a child.

"Have you spoken with Briony about Daniel's 'friend'? Maybe her twins do something similar." Briony was married to Jack Norton, a member of GhostWalker Team Two.

Lily shook her head. "Jeremiah and Noah are a bit younger than Daniel. He's nine months now and already walking and climbing. They aren't far behind him either, from what I've seen. You know we get them together often because they seem to want to be together. Daniel often asks me to visit with them. At least their playdates wear them out."

"Ryland told us a while back that you think they all have a secret language."

Lily frowned again, nodding her head. "I think they're all telepathic and they communicate silently, but they do have some kind of language built on sound. They definitely have a strong bond. When we were in San Francisco for Rose and Kane's wedding, even though their child was just a few weeks old, the boys all were very interested and clearly tried to communicate with him."

"That's reasonable, Lily," Sam pointed out. "You're a strong telepath, Ryland is as well, and Jack and Ken Norton have been communicating telepathically with one another since they were small children, just like Daniel appears to be doing."

She pressed her lips together, clearly still a little worried. "That's true, and it all makes sense, of course. We suspected Daniel and the twins would be extremely gifted, but they're infants. It makes it difficult to know what to do with them."

"The boys are very happy," he said. "I think that's the most important thing. And because they're intelligent, you can explain early why we take so many safety precautions with them." He flashed her a small, teasing grin. "That way, when your husband barks out his orders, Daniel won't want to rebel."

Her return smile was a little reluctant. "Daniel already has that man's number. With our son, he's all bark and no bite."

"Did I hear a rumor that someone else is pregnant?" Sam asked.

Lily glanced toward the door. Sam's heart gave a strange little jerk. Was she worried about strangers overhearing what she might say? Did that mean Azami was still in the compound? She hadn't come to see him yet—at least not that he remembered. He was fairly certain Lily had knocked him out to force him to rest.

"Mari, Ken's wife, is pregnant. She's having complications and I've put her on bed rest. She's definitely carrying twins, which doesn't surprise me. Her husband is a twin and they come from a long line of twins. She's a twin as well.

They're keeping the pregnancy under wraps. They don't need the added stress on her of Whitney trying to acquire her while she's pregnant. She can't fight. She shouldn't get up at all, not if she wants to carry, so if there's an attack on the compound, she'd be in real trouble. I've reinforced her cervix, but carrying the weight of twins, I don't know. Obviously, I'm not an OB, but Ken and Jack thought it important to keep the news in the family for now. If her pregnancy gets any more complicated, we'll bring an OB in. After it turned out Eric was working for Whitney, I just don't trust any outsider now."

"You take on a lot of problems with all of us, Lily," Sam said.

"I never had a family, not a real one. Neither did Mari, or Flame, or any of the girls. You're my family now. I worry about all of you. Flame's cancer is still in remission and I hope we keep it there, but I still haven't fully been able to help Nico's wife, Dahlia, or Tansy, Kadan's wife. She still has to wear gloves when she touches anything, and Dahlia occasionally slips up and starts fires." She pushed both hands through her hair. "My father did a lot of damage to a lot of people."

"It isn't your responsibility to fix everything, Lily," Sam pointed out. "No one blames you. I hope you realize that."

She sent him a wan smile. "I know. It's my nature to fix things." She pushed a hand through her hair. "Jack told me his twins seem to know that something's wrong and they reach for Mari. They like to lie on either side of her, near her tummy. They press very close and both make humming sounds. The thing is, it's the exact same notes in a pattern, over and over. He thinks they're talking to the babies."

"That's amazing."

"They're infants. Most babies their age wouldn't even be aware of a pregnancy, let alone have knowledge that their cousins were in trouble."

"So we tend to have little geniuses. Is that so difficult to believe? You're one. Jack and Ken are extremely intelligent.

I don't know their wives that well, but I can't imagine them falling in love with someone who couldn't keep up with them."

Lily nodded and swept her hand through her hair a third time, looking more agitated than ever. "My father would kill to get his hands on this information. Sooner or later he's going to try to find a way to get to the babies, or at least find out about them. The moment he does, once he actually knows what they're like, he'll move heaven and earth to acquire them. I know he will."

She pressed her lips together. "The thing is, Sam, I think he might leave Jack and Ken's babies with them because from what I've read in his reports, he thinks they're incredibly gifted, but he doesn't necessarily think the same of Ryland. He wasn't happy that Ryland and I—his first real pairing—worked. He didn't think it would. I think he wants to take Daniel from us." She glanced toward the door. "He knows I'd follow Daniel. I'd go back to Whitney just to be with my son."

"Lily." Sam gentled his voice. "Have you spoken to Rye about your concerns? That's why we've moved up here. This compound is defensible. And Team Two is close to us. They'll help us if we're attacked."

"Providing they aren't being attacked at the same time."

"There was already a concentrated assault and we handled it. Remember, honey, I got shot?" Sam tried a little humor.

Lily shook her head. "That wasn't my father. I know it wasn't. Do you really think he'll do an all-out assault and risk harming one of the babies? No, he'll find a way to penetrate, slip in and out without us knowing there's even a threat."

His heart stuttered. Azami and her brothers could just be that threat. She could easily get in and out without anyone knowing.

"We won't let that happen, honey," he said, meaning it. If Azami and her family had come to the compound to steal one of the babies for Whitney—and he very much doubted it—he wouldn't let that happen.

Sam glanced up at the bag of blood hanging on a pole beside his bed. "Why more blood?" He figured it was time to change the subject and give Lily an emotional break. She had it tough and whether she knew it or not, GhostWalker Team One had her back and watched over almost more protectively than anyone else. In any case, he needed to be on his feet and figure out what was going on in his home. He couldn't protect Daniel while he was lying flat on his back— assuming the Yoshiie family was still in the compound.

"It sometimes happens, Sam. You lost a good deal of blood before we operated and even with what I gave you a couple of times, you were still a little low. I really do want you to try to rest. The Zenith is helping you heal faster, but it's possible you're not manufacturing the blood as fast as you should. I'm wondering if it's a side effect."

There it was again—his opening to find out more information—but he kept silent. He didn't want to ask and know one way or the other. If he stayed quiet, there was always hope.

"I want to get up."

"No way, Sam."

He grinned at her. "Haven't you heard about me, Lily? I have this problem with the word 'no.' It just isn't in my vocabulary."

She put on her sternest look, which wasn't nearly as stern as she thought. "I'm the doctor here, Johnson, and that means I know what's best."

His eyebrow shot up. "*Johnson?* Is that all you've got? I bet Ryland thinks you're all cute when you get serious on him. Of course you know what's best. Nevertheless, I'm getting up. My butt's growing to this bed."

Lily burst out laughing. "You're impossible. You've been down less than a week, you nut."

"No way." He sent her another coaxing grin. "Are you sure? It feels more like a month. Where is everyone?"

"They're locked up in the war room. And no, you can't go."

There was that word again, but he wasn't going to point it out to her. If she didn't take the needle out of his arm, he was going to do it himself the moment she left.

As if reading his mind, Lily sighed. "I'll take it out, but I'll shoot my husband if he allows you to do anything but sit in a chair. You got that?"

"Hmm. Shooting Rye. I could get behind that one, Lily. The man is annoying when he's throwing out orders, which, by the way, is all the time."

"Tell me about it. He orders me around as well." But she was laughing again, her eyes soft the moment she spoke about her husband.

Sam had always loved to see that open affection Ryland and Lily had for one another; now he felt a little envious. He had never thought to want a woman to look at him like that until he'd met Azami. Every time he closed his eyes, he could see her face. He could taste her in his mouth. Once, during the night, when he'd woken up in a sweat, close to screaming, the nightmare of that small child being tortured and out of his reach, he felt the brush of her hand and smelled the scent of her.

"Take this thing out of my arm, Lily." He hesitated. "Please." He was getting up and if she didn't cooperate, he was going to leap out of the bed right in front of her, but sometimes one could get a lot more from Lily by being nice—and polite.

"Stop rushing me, Sam," she snipped back, as if he was her brother.

He liked that about Lily. She rarely took offense when the men became bossy with her—which was often—but she still did what she wanted, ignoring them. Lily definitely went her own way and she always had that quiet air of confidence about her.

He deliberately made growling noises under his breath, making her laugh as she fussed over the bags hanging on the stand.

"All right. What a grump," she added, as she took the

needle from his arm. "And stay off your feet. You might heal fast, but trying to heal that hole in your body in a few days is asking just a little too much—even of Zenith."

He couldn't help the wince. He felt as if he might be lying to her by not making inquiries, but he was determined to find out if the Yoshiie family was in the compound and if they were, just what they were up to. He owed Azami the chance to explain the Zenith and anything else she could before he gave her up to Ryland.

Lily left him with one more admonishing look and he breathed a sigh of relief. He didn't want her sticking around to witness him trying to get out of bed. He knew it wasn't going to be a pretty sight. Just changing position took his breath away. He swung his legs over the side of the bed and waited until his vision cleared. His mouth still felt parched, as if he could never again get enough to drink. Breathing deeply, he put a little weight on his feet. The room spun, receded, and righted itself slowly. Gritting his teeth, he stood.

Black swirled in front of his eyes. White stars shot straight at him, great comets soaring and rolling. His stomach lurched. He'd been shot more than once. Knifed twice. He'd even had a brief stint with electric shock, but he'd never felt quite so weak. Was that the loss of blood or the crash after using Zenith? Good question for the doc. He forced more air into his lungs and waited for the world to right itself because there was no way he was crawling back into bed.

It took a few minutes for his legs to gain strength. The pain in his abdomen was easy enough to push aside, but the invading weakness wasn't as cooperative. He took slow steps over to the bathroom, grateful the distance wasn't far. He had to breathe deeply with every step and stop twice. Sam cursed under his breath. By the time he entered the war room with his team, he had to get this under control. It didn't help that his body broke out in a sweat and small beads dotted his skin.

Cold water helped. He took a brief, cool shower, taking

care not to disturb the glue holding him together, sitting on the chair someone had thoughtfully provided for him. They'd all had their share of wounds, so it wasn't hard to try to figure out what a fellow wounded soldier might need. He sank back into the bed and rested before he attempted to dress, but at least the lurching stomach and sweats had receded. His knees weren't nearly as wobbly. He didn't bother with shoes—bending over was too difficult to contemplate. He was a little proud of himself for walking in a straight line down the center of the hall without staggering or even listing to one side.

Sam pushed open the door to the war room. The large table was circled with his team members, who all looked up, various expressions on their faces. Most relieved, some a little shocked, and his captain openly scowled at him. Tucker and Gator, his two best friends, both grinned at him. Tucker jumped up to shadow him back to the table, ensuring he wouldn't fall on his face and humiliate himself. Everyone, including Sam, knew what was coming.

"What the hell do you think you're doing, Sam," Ryland demanded, bringing knowing grins to everyone's face. "If my wife finds you up, she'll skin both of us alive."

Tucker's grin widened.

Sam shrugged. "She knows."

"Didn't you need another blood transfusion this morning?" Tucker asked, a hint of innocence in his question.

Sam knew there was nothing at all innocent about the inquiry. He was deliberately stirring the pot—which meant Ryland.

Sam shot him a look that promised retaliation. "Go to hell, Tucker."

Raul "Gator" Fontenot nudged Kadan. "He looks a bit like a ghost, don' you think?"

Sam tried his famous stare down, but truthfully, his legs felt a little rubbery. He pulled out a chair and allowed himself to drop into it, stretching his legs out in front of him to ease his protesting body. More than anything, he wanted to ask about Azami. How was she? Was she still in the compound? Did they have the Yoshiie family under house arrest? Had anyone questioned her regarding her psychic capabilities? What about the second-generation Zenith?

It was impossible to lie in bed and wonder what was going on with her. He woke up thinking about her, and dreamt about her when he wasn't having nightmares, but he damn well wasn't asking—not them and not Lily. Not anyone who would notice it was entirely out of character for Sam to make inquiries about a woman.

"Sam." Ryland didn't have a "reasonable" voice, not when it came to his men—or his wife's or son's health. "Get your ass back to bed."

"I can't do that, sir. I need to report. If the Yoshiies are still in the compound . . ." That was a blatant fishing trip, and he waited patiently for Ryland to bite.

Ryland's scowl deepened. "If I needed you to report on the Yoshiies, I would have been at your bedside demanding a report. They rested the first day and they've been shown around the compound. Lily's been handling that."

"You showed them around?" Sam's heart jumped and settled into a normal beat. He took a slow, careful look around. There was an overwhelming relief that Azami was still close and that he would see her again. There was also guilt that he felt that way when he was more than certain that something was a little off about the Yoshiie family. More, there was that peculiar rush of adrenaline he got when he knew he was in a battle of wits, which only added to his alarm.

"Ian's been watching them. They've been under guard every moment. In any case, we're purchasing the satellite. They need access to our computers."

"Have they been in this room?" Sam asked.

Ryland got it. He'd always been an intelligent man. He sat up very straight, every bit of casual ease gone from his body language, revealing the dedicated soldier. "They've been working a good portion of this week to set things up. What is it, Sam?"

What could he say? That Ian couldn't possibly guard Azami and keep her under a watchful eye?

"I don't know about the other two, but Azami has skills. Gifts. She's every bit as talented psychically as any one of us in this room—maybe more so."

Ryland nodded, visibly relaxing. "She admitted as much to us. As all of us had natural psychic talents and we know they exist, Lily says it isn't surprising to find such gifts in others who haven't been enhanced."

Sam nodded. It made sense. The members of the team came from different backgrounds, as did the other teams, so of course they couldn't be the only ones in the world with developed psychic gifts. He was a little surprised that Azami had admitted to her abilities. She had fought beside him bravely, revealing extraordinary psychic gifts that she had to know might put the sale of the satellite in jeopardy— might even put her life at risk—yet she hadn't hesitated. He couldn't help but respect and admire her.

And want her. You want her for yourself, Sam. He admitted the truth. He'd never wanted a woman for himself before. He felt tremendous affection for the wives of the various members of the GhostWalker teams, and each was quite different in personality, but none of them would suit him. He was very driven at all times. He needed mental and physical stimulation and there was no doubt Azami was that woman.

But was she his enemy? He just couldn't quite get over that small nagging doubt in his mind that she was one of them—a GhostWalker—which meant she was as enhanced as they were. If she was enhanced, if she had been one of Whitney's experiments, what was she doing in their compound, and why didn't any of the other GhostWalkers recognize her when all of them could feel the subtle differences in energy that identified one another?

He looked around at his teammates. Clearly none of them

were worried about the Yoshiies moving around the compound. He wanted to relax a little, but the tension refused to dissipate. Still, they'd had a day or so to further investigate Azami and her brothers. He had to think about things a little more. Get a few more pieces before he made up his mind one way or the other. He definitely had more of a nagging doubt about the Yoshiies—Azami in particular—than any of the other GhostWalkers, and they were all sharp and gifted. Maybe he didn't trust his strange, almost overwhelming attraction to her.

"So who the hell shot me? What have you found out so far?" he demanded. "And did anyone bother to retaliate for me?"

Ryland laughed. "You bloodthirsty animal. I think you did enough retaliating of your own. Do you have any idea what the body count was?"

"They attacked me," Sam said righteously. "They should have stayed the hell home."

Tucker nudged him. "If anyone made it home, I'd have to say they probably wished they'd never left in the first place. You're a monster, Sam."

"Who?" Sam insisted.

"We're still working on it. The moment we have any IDs or we know the entry points into the country, I'll brief everyone," Ryland said.

"*Two* helicopters, Rye. They had to come from somewhere and they had to land somewhere. Fuel is always a problem," Sam felt compelled to point out. They'd *shot* him.

"They put down at an abandoned airstrip not far from here. It was part of a private estate that's been on the market for several years. We'll find them. We're on their trail and when we do, we'll know who sent them."

Sam knew he had to be content with that much. They'd gather information first. That was always the way, and information took time.

"What are you working on now? Catch me up." He picked

up the file sitting in front of Gator and flipped it open to
study the contents.

Ryland looked around at his men with his steel gray
piercing eyes. "We've got a problem, I'm certain of it. Two
people suspected of being in Whitney's employ dropping
dead might be a coincidence, but three? No way. And the
woman, the witness, Sheila Benet, at two out of the three
accidents? We're missing something here." He turned his
attention to Sam. "These are reports of deaths that have been
ruled accidental. None of them raised an alarm anywhere
else, but my gut tells me something's definitely off. We
flagged two of these people at least two years ago and the
third, Major Art Patterson, we put on our watch list about
three months ago."

Sam's eyebrow shot up. "Patterson worked on the general's watch. They got into a thing a while back and he told
me he was concerned about the man. He actually said he
was keeping 'the enemy' close."

Ryland nodded. "It was the general who put Patterson's
name on the watch list."

"We've got both Flame and Jaimie tracking this woman
Sheila Benet, finding out everything they can about her,"
Kadan added. "It's *way* too much of a coincidence."

Sam scanned the medical reports of the three victims
Ryland mentioned. A woman appeared to have died by slipping on water in a bathroom and hitting her head on the sink
at an infamous nightclub. The second incident was a man
dying in a car accident, his car going off the road on a
remote mountain highway. The third, Major Patterson, lost
his life in a restaurant, apparently dying of anaphylactic
shock in front of a host of witnesses.

"I've studied all the reports," Kadan added. "I went over
both the investigating officer's and coroner's reports meticu-
lously. They look like straight-up accidents, all three of
them, but something is off. My gut doesn't lie and it's
screaming at me."

Nicolas "Nico" Trevane looked up from where he was cleaning weapons. "I'm in agreement." He was a big man, half Native American, half Japanese, and all lethal. "But how could any of these have been anything *but* an accident?"

Sam scanned the report of the army officer a second time, his mouth going dry. He moistened his lips, his pulse beginning to race. He wished he hadn't gotten up after all.

"Sam?" Ryland frowned at him. "Do you need to lie down?"

There it was. His out. Hell, yeah, he needed to lie down. He swallowed down his need to protect Azami and cleared his suddenly clogged throat. "The medical examiner's notes on Major Patterson's throat seemed pretty significant to me." Why the hell did this seem like such a betrayal? His loyalty was *solidly* with his team—his brothers. He would protect Daniel at any cost.

"Spit it out, Sam," Ryland ordered. "Why would you think that bruising was significant when the ME mentions he had a known allergy to peanuts and the bruising is in the shape of a peanut. The death was ruled accidental."

Sam nodded his head, reluctant to continue, but loyalty demanded he do so. "He didn't find a peanut in his body anywhere."

Kadan leaned forward. "But it's possible that when he was choking he coughed it out."

"I'm just speculating that maybe he didn't eat a peanut," Sam persisted, hating himself. This was far more difficult than he'd thought it would be. "The woman who lunched with him said he didn't eat anything with peanuts. He knew he had an allergy. It's just a thought."

"You've got a point," Nico said. "That bothered me as well."

"His airway could have swollen closed," Gator said. "With the bruisin', it would have been natural and there were signs of swellin'. All the witnesses said he was chokin'."

"But the ME said there were inconsistencies. Anaphylactic shock usually isn't quite so fast. His EpiPen was nowhere on his body and his colleagues said he always carried one," Kadan said, his voice thoughtful.

Ryland regarded Sam through half-closed eyes. That sleepy look didn't deceive Sam for a minute. The man was sharp and he knew Sam wasn't finished. He simply wanted for more of an explanation.

Sam had it to do. Give her up. *Azami. I'm sorry.* But that wouldn't cut it. How could she forgive such a thing? Telling his team about her weapons would only force her to answer more questions about herself.

He shook his head, tossed the medical report back in front of Gator, and looked around the room. "It's possible that someone, using a blowgun, shot a tiny dart into the major's mouth, poisoning him. The delivery system, no more than peanut-size, could have dissolved. If he wasn't looking for it, the ME may have missed a very fine needle mark." He drummed on the table with restless fingers. "If I were an assassin, I would have learned everything about my targets and I would have found out Patterson had a severe allergy to peanuts. If I could deliver the toxin to him, no one would ever know it was anything but an accident, just like the other two."

There. It was done. He looked around for a glass of water. Tucker had a water bottle unopened in front of him. He snagged it and chugged nearly half of it.

"A delivery system that dissolves?" Ryland echoed. "It's possible."

Kadan and Nico exchanged a long look. Finally Kadan shook his head. "Do you have any idea how accurate one would have to be to use a blowgun in full view of the public and hit someone in the mouth when they were talking? The chances of anyone having that kind of skill are nearly impossible."

He'd given her up. He damn well wasn't going any further until he had a chance to talk to her. Sam remained silent. He felt like hell, both mentally and physically. He was beginning to sweat again. He tried not to move, the pain from his wound just waiting for the smallest shift of his body to assert itself.

"You make impossible shots in high winds," Gator pointed out. "It's not like it couldn't be done."

Nico shook his head. "It's not the same thing. You're talking about hitting *inside* the mouth. I could put a bullet in the mouth, but it wouldn't matter if it was opened or closed. You'd have to time it perfectly. And this was done in a crowded restaurant."

"Impossible," Kyle "Ratchet" Forbes agreed. Slightly under six feet, with blue eyes and a medium build, his looks were deceptive. He was abnormally strong and a genius with explosives as well as being a doctor. "No one would try it in a crowded room in a public situation. If they missed . . ."

"But maybe they don' miss," Gator said, reluctant to give up on the mystery theory. He looked toward Sam for confirmation.

Sam couldn't say another word. The room shifted a little, the floor rolling. He was grateful for the chair he was sitting in.

"If you're assassinating someone, you don't want a maybe," Kadan pointed out.

Kyle grinned and gave a little shrug. "There's that, of course. You'd have to be absolutely confident in yourself to try something like that."

"Maybe a tribesmen from the lost tribes in the Amazon came a-visitin'," Gator said with a small laugh.

"I could do it with a knife," Jonas "Smoke" Harper said into the silence. Lithe, medium height with blond hair and Florentine gold eyes, he was a quiet, highly intelligent man who could have been a master thief. He was an undisputed master with knives. "It would be difficult, but with enough practice, and studying my mark, I'd be able to know his mannerism's, the way he moves, the little things that give people away when they're talking."

"You could hit a man from across the room *inside* his

mouth with a knife?" Kyle asked, half skeptic, half awed believer.

Jonas nodded. "I know I could." Jonas had grown up throwing knives with a circus family, he'd practically been born with a knife in his hand.

"Really?" Kyle's eyebrow went up. He leapt up and raced out of the room.

"He's up to somethin', Smoke, you'd better watch out," Gator advised Jonas in his slow Cajun drawl.

The men erupted into laughter. Jonas shrugged and took out one of the many knives he carried most of the time. Around the room on various walls hung well-used targets, testimony to the fact that when idle, Jonas threw knives and was *very* accurate.

Nico held up his hand. "Let's think about this. If we're really going with the assassination theory, the bathroom and the car accidents are very doable. Any assassin worth his salt could rig a car, or make the hit in a secluded bathroom. It's just the major's death that's harder to figure out, right?"

Kadan nodded. "And yet, of all three, his death seems the least likely to be an accident."

Kyle slipped back into the room, a huge grin on his face. He plopped a can of peanuts down on the table in front of Jonas. "Let's see."

Gator nearly leapt over the table. "I want to try. Hand a few peanuts to me." He didn't wait but scooped a handful out of the can.

"I said I could hit the target with a knife," Jonas said, holding up a wicked-looking two-inch throwing knife. "Start talking and let's see if I can time it just right."

Kyle threw a peanut at Jonas's mouth as he spoke. The peanut hit him on the bridge of Jonas's nose. War erupted. Team members scooped up peanuts and flicked, threw, and chewed the nuts, laughing uproariously. Through it all, Sam was very aware that Ryland remained silent. Hard knots formed in Sam's belly. He knew Ryland. The man didn't lead the team because he was stupid. Those piercing gray eyes were locked onto his face. Steady. Unblinking. Sam remained stubbornly silent, making him ask if he wanted any more information.

The room spun a little and he almost hoped he'd just faint and get it over with. He'd never live down an actual faint if it happened. For the rest of his life, Gator and Tucker would dramatically fall to the floor in an adaptation, swooning at every opportunity to remind him, but it might be worth avoiding Ryland's questions. Sam gripped the table hard to keep from swaying. He became aware of the throbbing, pulsing pain in the region of his gut every time he moved. He'd been able to block it before, keeping the pain to a nagging ache, but now his pulse seem to keep time with that lurching, pounding wound in his abdomen.

Ryland heaved a sigh. "You're one obstinate son of a bitch, Sam. Is there a reason why you're not coughing up all the information?"

The other men stopped their antics, although Gator stuffed another handful of peanuts into his mouth, crunching while they all waited for his answer.

Sam shrugged. "I saw Ms. Yoshiie use a blowgun in combat. It was very small and I realized, when I read the report, that a small blowgun would fit into a man's hand easily and if he was good enough, he might be able to deliver poison to the back of a throat."

Now he couldn't gracefully exit. He had to hear what that revelation brought. Just because Azami had a blowgun didn't mean anything. Hell, he was probably going to faint if he stood up and made an exit anyway.

"You don' look so good." Gator's voice was suddenly concerned. "Tucker, let's get him out of here."

"I'm fine." If they were going to discuss reasons for Azami to have a blowgun, he wanted to hear every word. Sadly, even sounds were fading in and out. He looked around the room, saw mouths moving, but he couldn't hear a word.

Ryland suddenly stood, as did most of his teammates.

Tucker and Gator reached him first, supporting his large frame with strength.

"You're done, Knight," Ryland said. "Take him back to his room. I'll send for Lily."

He didn't have the strength to protest and in any case, when Ryland spoke in that tone, no one disobeyed him.

CHAPTER 8

———— ∾ ————

Screams pierced Sam's ears, jerking him out of a deep sleep. The sound of a mindless animal in excruciating pain. Long, dreadful wails. Pleading, incoherent cries. He leapt up and sprinted down the long hallway. The stark white hall was narrow and stretched out before him for seemingly miles. The screams grew loud, more agonized, the begging unintelligible, but clearly pleas, the voice taking on the pitch of a child.

His heart pounded as he passed great glass windows. He peered in as he ran and his blood went ice cold. Room after room was empty, but the aftermath of the butchery was everywhere. Blood was splattered up the walls and dripped steadily from steel tables to form dark puddles on the floor. White hospital coats had been carelessly tossed aside along with trays of surgical instruments, all stained a murky wine red.

His mouth was dry and he pushed himself to greater speed, using blurring speed, but still the hallway extended on and on. The screams began to wane, trailing off into a gasping hoarse plea that wrenched at his heart. He found the last room, still filled with men in bloodstained coats and small masks bending over a cold surgical table. Great drops of blood dripped steadily from a patient he couldn't see. The child writhed and moaned and pleaded, the tone filled with horror and pain.

A guard posted at the door leapt at him, coming out of the shadows fast. The blade of a knife glittered bright, caught in the light from the surgery room. He slapped the knife hand down, controlling the wrist with his palm while he slammed his fist hard into the guard's throat. Choking, the man fell backward and Sam kept moving, rushing forward, kicking open the door to the surgery. Glass shattered around him, exploding into the room, showering the nearest bloodstained coats with long splinters and lethal shards.

He threw the nearest man into the wall, wading through them as if they were nothing more than paper dolls. He shoved them out of his way, reaching the stainless steel table and the child strapped to that cold metal. Blood ran from her body, her chest ripped open. Her eyes were wide open, staring at him, filled with horror, with terror and pain. She had Asian features, but her hair was as white as snow, a thick cap of cornsilk.

"It's all right now, baby," he whispered, his throat closing on a terrible lump. He'd never seen such a thing, a mere child dissected like an insect. "I've got you. I won't let them hurt you ever again." Tears burned in his eyes as he reached for her. "I'll take you to someone who can help you."

He found the ties binding her to the table. The ties bit into her soft skin, digging deep so her wrists and ankles bled as well. Cursing, he turned to face the faceless monsters who had done such a thing.

"Why?" he demanded, taking a threatening step toward them. For the first time in his life he *wanted* to kill another human being.

"Science of course." The disembodied voice sounded reasonable and not in the least afraid of him. The surgeon removed the bloody gloves and tossed them carelessly into the sink. "She's a throwaway. I've given her a useful purpose for her life. She understands."

Sam took a step toward the surgeon, his fingers itching to wrap around that neck and strangle until there was no more breath in the body. The surgical mask was removed with that same careless precision, and Sam found himself looking at Dr. Peter Whitney. With an oath, he took a step toward the monster. The child's breath rattled in her chest and Sam swung quickly around to see her cat-shaped eyes glazing.

"No, baby," he whispered. "Stay with me," he coaxed. "Stay with me."

He stared down at that baby face. She looked so familiar. That silky white hair that made no sense, the dark eyes fringed heavily with black lashes, the soft skin. He recognized her face and yet her name eluded him.

"Please," he pleaded, afraid to lift her into his arms. She was like a broken doll, and anywhere he touched her would hurt. "Stay with me," he repeated.

"Open your eyes," she answered softly. "I'm not going anywhere."

Sam blinked. Above him, that same face swam into view, older now, no longer ravaged, but serene and composed. He blinked again, trying to understand. The child had white hair, this woman had hair as black as midnight.

"Sam, look at me. Wake up. You're having another nightmare."

"Azami." He breathed her name, more breath than sound. His heart jumped at the sight of her. "You're so damn beautiful."

She brushed at his hair with gentle fingers, barely a touch, just that whisper of movement against his skin, but he felt it right through to his bones. "You were having a nightmare."

He caught her hand. She instantly curled her fingers into a fist and took a step back, shaking her head. He pried open her fingers one by one and pressed her palm over his heart. His gaze searched hers. Her eyes didn't drop. She let him

see who she was. His breath caught in his throat and he
lifted a hand to her cap of black silk.

"Your hair was white," he whispered. "The child in my
nightmares was you, but your hair was white."

Azami pressed her lips together and then slowly nodded.
"I prefer to allow you to believe that I'm beautiful. I suppose
sooner or later you'll have to know that isn't true at all." Her
smile was brief and a little wistful. "You made me feel
beautiful."

Sam sat up, and then waited a moment for the room to
right itself and the flash of pain moving through his abdomen to fade. He tugged on her hand to pull her close to the
bed until she either had to tip over or sit on the bed. "You
are beautiful, Azami."

She raised a tentative hand to her hair. It was the first
time she looked truly vulnerable. "It isn't real."

He sank his fingers into the thick mass of hair, his fingers
curling into a fist, crushing strands in his palm. "This is no
wig, honey. I can tell the difference between real hair and
a wig." Her hair felt like pure silk.

A faint smile curved her mouth even as she swallowed
hard. Sam kept one anchored in her hair, the other pressing
her palm to his chest.

"Tell me." Clearly she didn't want to. Her revelation had
to be a matter of pride with her. A woman's pride, not a
samurai warrior's pride. He understood that very clearly just
by the way her gaze wavered for just a split second. She was
Azami Yoshiie, a trained samurai, and she didn't falter long,
but he caught the tiny hesitation just before her chin lifted
and her eyes locked on his.

"The color, I dye it. I've already gone gray, or at least, in
my case, white. My hair turned white when I was a child—
around three."

Rage burst through him, hot and bright, a volcanic emotion that shook him as nothing else ever had. Three years old.

"How long did that monster have you?" he asked, his
voice low because it was the only way he could control it.

Azami didn't deny the obvious. She shrugged. "I was eight when my heart gave out and he threw me out. He put me in a box and shipped me to Japan. His men took me to an alley in a part of the city where the sex trades were and they tossed me out like a piece of garbage. I suppose to Whitney I was. He always said I was useless, and eventually my body just refused to hold up to his experiments."

He wanted to drag her into his arms and shelter her, just as he had the small child she'd been. "I'm sorry I wasn't there." He meant it too. "Is that when your father found you?"

She nodded. "I was skinny, my body a mass of ugly scars and my heart trying to decide if it would function or give up." A tiny smile broke through, an affectionate memory she found amusing. "My father shaved my head in the hopes my hair would come back black. It came back streaked. I look a bit like a skunk unless I dye it."

He found the memory more heartbreaking than entertaining, but he smiled just the same because he could see she needed him to feel that same delight in her reminiscence of her father. "I've always found skunks to be quite beautiful," he admitted, sincerity lending his voice a solemn tone. He inhaled. "And you smell amazing, unlike a skunk."

Genuine laughter reached her eyes. "I don't know, Sam. I think a skunk's smell might be pretty amazing."

He ran a finger down her face, lingering on her soft lips. "Why didn't you tell me about Whitney?"

"Lily. I wasn't certain if she was working with her father."

"Did you come to kill her?"

She pulled back, frowning at him.

"I could understand if that had been your intention, Azami," he admitted. She hadn't tried to lie about being that child to him and he was fairly certain she wouldn't lie about this.

"No, she wanted to purchase one of our satellites. I had turned down her father. I had to meet her and decide whose side she was on."

Sam believed her. "Has Whitney contacted you since

he . . ." He trailed off, not wanting to say the words. It had to hurt, being discarded, even though Whitney was a monster. He was the only parent the orphan girls had known. He'd collected them from orphanages when they were mere infants.

"Threw me into the streets?" she finished for him. There was no bitterness in her voice. "It was the best thing that could have happened to me. My father loved me and taught me how to believe in myself—and believe in the world again. He gave me an honorable code and a way to make a difference. I had nearly fifteen years with a man who respected life and fought evil. He gave me every opportunity and showed me that, although many doors might be closed to me, there were other honorable paths for me to follow."

Sam frowned. He heard that hurt, wistful note in her voice when she'd said, "many doors might be closed to me." What did she long for?

The pad of his thumb slid over her lips. "How can any door be closed to you, Azami?"

That threw her—just for a moment he saw that sudden insecurity and it shocked him. Azami was a woman of confidence. She was intelligent and a skilled warrior. What could she long for that could be unattainable to her? Every protective instinct he had welled up. His hand curled tighter in her hair. White hair? What would that be like for a child of Asian descent? To be so traumatized that even the hair on her head betrayed her?

"Azami, I want to know. Show me the worst you have." He could only hope his expression stood for him, the sincerity of his voice. He leaned forward to press his forehead against hers. "I don't know your world or your cultures. I know this is too fast and you don't trust it, but we fit. You and me. We fit together perfectly. When you're in my mind, there's no loneliness, only warmth and security. We have this one chance and everything around us doesn't matter. Together we can do anything at all. Accomplish anything. I know it. I can't explain it, but I know it to be truth. Show me. Let me be the one to show you that you can have everything you want with me."

"You don't know me, Sam. I'm not the woman you think I am."

He lifted her head with his fingers beneath her chin and looked her in the eyes. "I attended a meeting today with my team. There were three people connected to Whitney's pipeline to the White House who supposedly died in accidents. I don't think they were accidents. You have every reason, just as we do, to try to stop Whitney. You can teleport, you're highly skilled with weapons, including a blowgun, and if someone told me to take a shot in the dark as to who might be responsible for those deaths . . . Well, honey, my money would be on you."

She didn't blink, and he admired her all the more for that expressionless serenity she faced adversity with. She reached out with both hands and framed his face, all the while looking him in the eyes. "Do you wish to know the truth for yourself or for your team?"

"My team will figure things out without my help. They're already close. You have to make the decision whether or not we're your enemy. We're not and have never been your enemy, but you need to know that for yourself. You have to know that I'm with you all the way, Azami. I don't give my word lightly and I know you're the one. The only one for me."

"Is it possible that Whitney somehow paired me to you?" she asked.

He could hear the underlying horror and fear in her voice. He shook his head. "I don't see how he could have. In any case, maybe his gift is in the knowing which couples belong. I belong to you and it has little to do with sex. I'm attracted to you, yes, that drive is there and I think that's very obvious to you. But it's so much more than that. I think about you, Azami, and you make me smile. You're everything I've ever wanted in a woman, and I've spent a hell of a long time looking. Give me this chance."

She regarded him for what seemed an eternity, her serene demeanor hiding her thoughts, but he could feel the tension in her. She moistened her lips and his heart stuttered. She'd come to a decision and for one moment he wanted to stop her. If she crushed every chance, he'd have to abide by her decision—but he wasn't certain he could. He *knew* with absolute certainty that they should go through life together, and if he couldn't have her, no other woman would measure up in his mind.

"I was useless to him, remember?" This time she let the hurt show in her voice. The child was still there. "I wasn't worth stitching up properly. There was no way to correct the damage he did to my body." *Or my mind.*

She poured into his mind, filling him with her warmth and her emotions. She was every bit as afraid to end what they had as he was.

Sam knew he was using a delaying tactic, but it was still important. "When you have so many amazing gifts, why didn't Whitney value you more?"

Regret and guilt flashed in her eyes. "I hid everything from him. I suppose I didn't really understand that if I showed him a psychic gift he wouldn't use me for experiments. I could hear the other girls screaming sometimes and he knew what they could do. He *felt* sick to me, and it grew each time I was around him. I think I instinctively hid any talent and he couldn't detect one. That must have made him crazy because he prided himself on knowing who was psychically gifted and who wasn't."

"You were just a toddler." He reached to pull her across his lap and fire took his breath as he stretched his abdomen, reminding him he wasn't 100 percent. He breathed away the pain and held her to him, wanting to comfort the child as much as the woman.

"I knew when he touched me that something was wrong. I knew he didn't love any of us and never would. I hid my talents instinctively and then later, when he was using my body for experiments, I thought that was what he wanted from me. I probably was half crazy with fear all the time. A child doesn't think the way adults do."

"Surely you don't blame yourself for what Whitney did to you," he said, nuzzling the top of her hair. He couldn't detect any white hairs, but she'd probably dyed her hair right before visiting the compound so there would be no roots for anyone to see.

Azami turned her head to look at him. "I was a child. Of course I blamed myself. He was so cold toward me. I never once got a smile from him like some of the other girls. I never felt worthy. It was almost a relief that I was used for experiments because at least then he told me I was useful. That was part of his brilliance—to withhold love and approval so we would do anything to try to please him. A part of me knew he was completely mad, but the child just wanted his love and approval."

Again Sam experienced that tremendous flare of rage. It roared through him bright and hot, shaking him with the savage intensity. He was a thinking man, not a primal warrior, but he felt like one in that instant. He *needed* to kill Whitney, to wipe him from the face of the earth and out of Azami's memories. How could any human being traumatize an infant to the point that her hair would actually go white when it was naturally black?

He brushed a kiss on top of her head, helpless to do anything but try to silently comfort her. He couldn't imagine what her father had found in that alley, a child so torn and weak with a mop of white hair and skin over bones.

"I watch Lily and Ryland with their son, and the way they treat him is so different—the complete opposite," Azami said. "He's a happy boy. I can feel the love they have for him and the way he responds."

Of course that would be important to her. He should have known she would check on the condition of an infant in the care of Whitney's daughter.

"We protect the compound so that there's no chance of

Whitney getting his hands on one of the babies. He's tried, and we know he'll try again."

"He won't stop," Azami said. She shifted away from him. "Sam, you know we won't work. I think about it all the time and there are far too many complications. I have a company, my brothers, you have your team and your family."

"That's logistics, Azami, and you know it," he said. "If we want this, we'll find a way. There's always a way. You're afraid, and it's not of my team, or what I do, or even me."

She slipped off his lap, back onto the floor, the movement graceful, flowing water over stone. There wasn't even a whisper of sound, reminding him what she was in that beautiful package—a lethal weapon. She didn't need guns or arrows; her father had trained her to be a woman to be reckoned with and given her the honor and code of the samurai. In his way, her father had ensured that Whitney could never again torture her.

Yet Whitney still lived in her head. Sam could feel the man as sure as if he was standing in the room with them. He colored everything in Azami's life whether she knew it or not. She stood, her head up, the woman her father had taught her to be, facing him, eyes steady, mouth firm, shoulders straight, unapologetic for who she was, yet she was reluctant to let him all the way into her life. And that was all Whitney.

Sam waited, his pulse pounding in his ears. He could taste her in his mouth, feel her rushing through his veins, and yet she was so far from him.

"Azami Yoshiie is an illusion," she finally whispered, her voice filled with sorrow and despair. "From my dyed hair to my seemingly perfect body. Azami doesn't really exist."

She was telling him something so difficult she trembled in the telling, but still, she held that firm, upright stance, with that serene expression on her face even though her eyes were alive with pain. She swallowed once, a hard lump he could clearly tell, but she didn't waver. He almost stopped her. Azami was a woman of courage, and yet telling him this dark secret took a terrible toll on her. It was all he could do to sit on the bed silently and wait for her to reveal the one thing she knew would keep them apart.

Very slowly her hand went to the hem of her shirt. His breath caught in his throat as she lifted it, revealing her flat, defined abdomen and the soft skin there. He knew the moment he saw the spiderweb tattoo attempting to cover the scars running up her waist in all directions, circling around her narrow rib cage and traveling up higher to under and between her breasts, spreading completely over the left breast and partially over the right. The scars continued, peeking out from under the tattoo with its intricate web, dissecting her flesh from front to back.

She turned slowly. The tattoo on her back was even more detailed, not the lines of a spiderweb, but a triumphant bird—a phoenix rising from the ashes flowing from the top of her shoulders, spreading across her delicate back, the wings intricate and lacy, slowly narrowing to a curving tail of wispy feathers hugging the small of her back and curving over her right buttock. The scars were more rigid, jagged and raised so that the flowing tattoo held hundreds of images and scrolls. Both the bird and spider were done in shades of color, mostly dark, but the phoenix had gold and red outlines that only served to heighten the dramatic effect. He found the tattoos fascinating rather than repugnant. She'd turned all those scars, those badges of courage, into pure artwork and he admired her all the more for it.

Sam slipped out of his bed and again had that strange fading in and out moment, but it passed much more quickly than the first time. He padded over to her, towering over her much smaller figure. She didn't flinch or give ground when his fingers slid over the ridges on her back, tracing the myriad of images, feeling the thick scar tissue beneath the impressive tattoo. Very gently he turned her around to face him, allowing him to view the spiderweb crawling across her body, rippling with every movement of her defined muscles.

He could see why a woman would look at the scars on her body and think she was destroyed. Clearly she'd had multiple surgeries and at least one heart surgery. Her soft, flawless skin made the scarring almost obscene. One breast was larger than the other, and a little lopsided, and a part had been carelessly cut away. Tattooed over the shiny scar, right beside her nipple, was a female red-backed spider. Sam leaned forward before he could stop himself and brushed a kiss over that spider. His lips skimmed her nipple, tongue curling for just one breathtaking moment along the dark peak before he lifted his head and looked into her eyes.

Azami stood very still, holding her shirt above her breasts, her eyes wide with shock. "You can't possibly want me."

Her voice was so low, so shocked, so incredulous, Sam couldn't help but smile. He bent his head to hers. Lips inches from hers, he curved his hand around the back of her neck. "Honey, I'm totally naked, in case you hadn't noticed. I think my wanting you can't possibly be in question."

Her gaze left his eyes, dropped low, and she inhaled audibly. His erection was long and thick and made no apologies for his desire for her. Her image as a woman was wrapped up in how she viewed her body. She didn't realize that every inch of her scarred body, now covered in artwork, was testimony to her strength and spirit.

Sam tipped her face up with his thumb. It took a few seconds for her gaze to follow the lift of her face. Her eyes were wide, her long lashes fluttering a little, reminding him of feathery fans. "I'm going to kiss you, Azami, so if you have that dagger of yours handy, now might be a good time to use it if you're so inclined," he whispered, his lips brushing hers as he reminded her of their first kiss.

He captured her answering smile, and warm breath, as his mouth settled over hers. The world tilted and righted itself. Sam urged her closer to him. His body was naked and shamelessly demanding toward hers. She had forgotten to let go of the hem of her shirt, holding it across the top of her breasts while she melted into him, suddenly boneless.

His chest crushed the soft cushion of her breasts as he pulled her into him, his erection lodging just above her belly button. She felt fragile, and yet all muscle beneath her skin. The scars rasped against his cock, creating a friction he hadn't expected. His breath exploded out of his lungs and he tightened his hold on her, afraid she'd try to escape when all around him the earth was shifting under his feet.

She tasted like a combination of flame and sex, a deadly mixture, a volatile cocktail rushing through his bloodstream and melting his mind. He knew he had dropped too far too fast and there was so much unresolved between them. They barely knew one another, but he was certain of the woman who had gone so courageously into battle with him. Kissing her over and over, his body as hard as a rock, need so urgent he could barely think, Sam allowed himself to just fall over the edge with her.

Azami gasped and pulled away from him, her hands finally letting loose of her hem to clutch at his neck for support. "I can't breathe. You've made me so weak I can't stand up," she confided in a shy voice.

Sam took a deep breath, knowing his belly would protest, but he needed to reassure her. He lifted her, cradling her against his chest, a little surprised at how light she was when she was all firm muscle. "I've got you, honey. You're safe with me." He wanted her to feel safe with him. It was necessary to go slow, to get himself under control. "You've never been with a man, have you?" Kissing her had already told him she was untutored, an innocent in the ways between a man and a woman, and that meant he had to go slow, be very careful of her. She had a poor body image and doubts about her ability to be a woman.

Her father had been wonderful to her, loving and kind, and he made certain to give her the skills to survive in the world. He'd given her a sense of family, but inadvertently, he'd fostered the belief that no man would want her scarred body and freakishly white hair, by telling her she would live an honorable life as a warrior without her own man, and

Azami believed that meant, once again, she wasn't good enough.

Her long eyelashes fluttered again. "Did I do something wrong?" Her voice was filled with trepidation, but once again, she met his gaze squarely.

He let himself smile. "No, honey, you did everything right. I just have to take a breath myself here and do the right thing."

"Which would be?" she prompted.

"Get in bed alone or get some clothes on. I have to talk to your brothers before we get into trouble."

A slow smile teased the corners of her mouth and warmed her eyes. "Talking to my brothers could get you in trouble."

"Maybe, but risking my life to tell them I want your hand in marriage is well worth it to me." He set her on the bed and looked around for his jeans. His mind was still a little scattered and his body didn't want to cooperate with his intellect. It took a moment to pull up his jeans and button a few buttons. The material felt stretched and uncomfortable, but at least she was safe—for the moment.

"Does it bother you that I don't have a clue what I'm doing?" Azami asked, as candid as ever.

"Men tend to be very proprietary over their women, Azami. I'm quite happy being the only man you ever know intimately. In any case, I know enough for both of us. Trust me, honey, we have nothing to worry about in that department."

She gave him a lopsided smile. "You're so certain, Sam."

He leaned into her, framing her face with his hands. Her face looked so small against the largeness of his hands. "Once in a great while, Azami, believe me, not very often, a miracle happens, a gift comes along. I'm a man who deals in death on a nearly daily basis. I put my life on the line and don't expect to come back every time I go out. You're my gift, Azami, my personal miracle. Maybe it happened too fast for you and you need time to catch your breath, and I'll give you whatever time you need; just don't say no and shut the door on us."

It was as much of a plea as a man like him could manage. She had the face of an angel with her eyes and full lips and all that soft skin.

"I should, Sam. For you, I should; but I won't."

The relief was tremendous. He hadn't realized just how tense he'd grown. He knew the intense physical attraction wasn't one-sided, he could see her desire growing in her eyes and feel it in her kiss and melting body. Still, she was extremely disciplined and slow to trust. He felt privileged that, through their mind link, she'd given that trust to him.

Sam brushed his mouth over hers and straightened, smiling. "I just have to figure out a way to keep your brothers from taking off my head when I ask for your hand. It's not like a soldier has a lot of prospects. They might think I'm after you for your money."

"They would be more understanding of that reason for such an offer—a business transaction. They will have far less ability to understand you wanting me as a wife for other reasons."

Again he couldn't detect bitterness or even a bid for sympathy; Azami was simply stating a fact as she saw it. "They'll have to get used to it," Sam said.

"We do not ever show affection in public," Azami cautioned. "I don't want you to be offended if I don't show how I feel."

His eyebrow rose. "Are you afraid I might grab you in front of the world and kiss you like crazy?"

She nodded solemnly. "It isn't done."

His grin went wider. "It's done. We just have to pick our spots. We both have the ability to transport from one area to another. I think if I'm desperate, I'll just give you the sign and we'll exit fast and return before they notice we're gone."

Azami looked at him as if she didn't quite know what to think. His fingers curled around the nape of her neck, drawing her closer to him. He found that bemused, confused look adorable, but he was fairly certain a warrior woman wouldn't find that description appealing, so he wisely kissed her instead of commenting out loud.

She gave herself up to his kiss, her tongue dancing with his, her slender arms creeping up around his neck.

Open your mind to mine he whispered in the much more intimate form of communication. *I need to feel you inside of me, and I need to be inside of you.*

He might not be able to have her physically, not yet. Instinctively he knew she wasn't ready to give him her body. The intimacy of telepathic communication would have to be enough. He prayed it would be enough and give him the strength to do right by her.

There was a moment of hesitation and his heart went still. His mouth moved coaxingly against hers, a gentle, tender assault to entice her. Her mind opened and warmth poured into him. Her strength, the vulnerability she hid from the world. She filled all the cold, dark places in him, lighting him, illuminating the darker shadows and instantly removing every vestige of loneliness.

When we're like this, Azami, welded together, you can know more about me than any other human being will know living a lifetime with me. He caressed the silk of her hair, his palm cradling her head. *I won't ever go anywhere. I'll be with you, just like this. See who I really am inside. Judge me on my character, not on whether or not Whitney has done something to pair us.*

He knew that was her primary worry. When she entered into his mind, strong and courageous, that doubt was there as well. Azami didn't try to hide it from him, nor did she pretend she felt comfortable with her body or with him seeing her flaws. To him they weren't flaws, nor would they ever be.

Sam . . .

She kissed him with exquisite gentleness until his heart stuttered and his body threatened to burst through the material of his jeans. She brushed the pads of her fingers so lightly over his skin, shaping his shoulders and the muscles of his arms. The touch was barely there, yet he felt it as if she was branded into his bones.

How could it possibly work? You're here. I'm in Japan. We both have a job.

But she wanted him. She wanted to give herself to him and in a way, she already had. It was impossible to be in her mind and not know her. She had committed to him the moment she'd revealed her body to him. She'd allowed him to share her mind and memories. He hadn't betrayed her trust by searching her mind for how she'd assassinated Whitney's three flunkies, although she didn't try to hide anything from him. He knew she was going after Whitney and how could he blame her?

Sam folded her closer. *It's going to work because there is no one else for me. I never thought I'd have a woman of my own.* He really hadn't.

He lifted his head slowly, waiting for her long lashes to lift. He loved those soft twin crescents, impossibly long and feathery, fluttering against her high cheekbones right before she opened her dark eyes to meet his gaze. He loved the sensation of his heart dropping the moment their gazes met and knew she would always affect him like this—just this way—his body so aware of her, his mind filled with her so there would never be room for anyone else.

Okay, then. You can risk your life and ask my brothers' permission.

She didn't sound quite as positive as he would have liked. He nuzzled her nose, kissed both eyes and the corner of her mouth.

"Tell me, Azami," he coaxed. "I don't believe in secrets. My woman will know what's happening in my life and I need to know about hers. I don't want hurt feelings between us. If you have concerns, we need to address them."

She lifted her chin. "I have a mission to accomplish. It's a matter of honor. I can't stop until it's done. I'm not unrealistic. I'm aware I probably will not be the one to kill him, but I have made it my duty to cut him off from the aid that lends him legitimacy."

"I understand, Azami. I do. I'm a soldier. In any case, if you're trying to bring down Whitney, you've got allies right here. Four teams of GhostWalkers are dedicated to finding him and destroying him."

"He's got powerful friends," she warned.

"Believe me, honey, we're very aware of that."

She suddenly smiled. "You call me by your American name. Honey. We do not use this term in my country. I like it, but it seems strange."

"It's a term of endearment meant for a girlfriend or spouse," he explained.

She took a breath, stepped back, and spread her hands. "He called me Thorn. Whitney. He said I wasn't a flower, but only a thorn and there was nothing he could do to change that, no matter how hard he tried."

Another revelation. She was very still. Holding herself. Waiting. Sam took a breath, wanting to make certain he said the right thing. When they'd met, he'd asked her what her name meant. He smiled at her, taking one step to close the gap she'd put between them, his hand cupping her chin, forcing her head up.

His heart did a curious somersault looking into the courage in her eyes. He would always see her this way, his Azami, facing the worst, expecting the worst, yet not flinching, but looking him right in the eye. He was a man who lived a life of duty, choosing honor and danger, although he had many choices. He had degrees and offers, but he was driven to be a soldier, to defend his country and the people in it. He had never thought to find a woman who could understand him, or admire his choices. He could see both in her eyes.

"You are Azami, the very heart of the thistle. The flower of the thistle. Whitney has no place here, nor can he stand between us. He's nothing to us, honey. Do you have any idea what we are together? What kind of strength we'll have united? Whitney can never defeat us, or break us. He wanted to create pairs of soldiers to be dropped into enemy territory, carry out missions without aid from the outside, and escape unseen before anyone ever knew they were there. We're that perfect pair and he never even saw it. He is *not* invincible. He created the GhostWalkers—and you're one of us, whether he knew it or not. And we'll be his downfall."

He knew she loved her family, but how could she ever feel she belonged, with her strange psychic gifts, her tortured past, scarred body, and white hair? Just as he never quite belonged anywhere until he became a GhostWalker.

"You belong with me, Azami. Your family will be my family. My family—the GhostWalkers—will be yours."

"You're a very dangerous man, Sam Johnson," she whispered. "You stand there, tempting me with your pretty words of a future together, the devil in his blue jeans, so good-looking you're impossible to resist. I don't know why I can't say no to you."

His grin widened. His arms slid around her, pulling her tight against him. He didn't want so much as a breath between them. "That will stand me in good stead in the future." He bent his head once more to the temptation of her angelic mouth.

CHAPTER 9

Kissing Azami was as close to paradise as he was ever going to get, and Sam allowed himself to get lost in her, but he was a soldier—a GhostWalker—and there was always that part of him that never rested. He felt the whisper of energy rather than heard footsteps, but he knew they were about to have company. Reluctantly he lifted his head and saw the same regretful knowledge in her eyes. He would never have to worry that his woman wouldn't see danger coming. Her hand had already dropped to the dagger she carried inside the loop of her intricate belt. It was unseen, but he'd felt it the moment he'd pulled her tight against him.

Sam stepped slightly in front of Azami, an instinctive move, not to protect her from danger—he knew by the energy field that Ian McGillicuddy was coming down the hall to check on him. All the members of his team had taken turns dropping in, but he wasn't certain if she wanted to be seen with him or if she wanted the chance to disappear.

Her hand slid over his bare back, the lightest of touches as she tended to do, but he felt the wave of warmth she poured into his mind.

I am not ashamed of being with you, Sam.

Sam found himself smiling like an idiot as Ian pushed open the door. The Irishman stopped abruptly when he saw Sam standing, his jeans carelessly buttoned, shirt off, exposing his wounded abdomen and bare chest. Sam knew instantly that Ian was aware of Azami by the way he inhaled and frowned, confusion in his eyes.

"You can't be in here." Ian stated it as a fact.

Sam sank back onto the bed. He was definitely growing stronger, but standing could be troublesome on shaky legs. The pain of his wound had definitely receded. "Why not?" he asked a little belligerently.

"She can't; it's impossible. I was standing guard at her door." Ian's gaze met Azami's. "To protect you of course."

"Of course, because there are so many enemies creeping around your halls," Azami said, her voice soft and pleasant, a musical quality lending innocence and sweetness.

Ian's frown deepened as if he was puzzled. She certainly couldn't have meant that the way it came out, anyone listening would be certain of it. "Just what are you two doing in here anyway?" he asked, suspicion lending his tone a dark melodrama. He even wiggled his eyebrows like a villain.

Sam kept a straight face with difficulty. Ian was a large man with red hair and freckles. He didn't look in the least bit mean or threatening, even when he tried.

"Azami was just telling me how when she left her room to inquire after my health, there was a giant man with carroty hair snoring in the hallway beside her door."

"There was no way to get past me," Ian insisted.

Sam grinned at him. "Are you saying you *did* fall asleep on the job, then?"

"Hell no." Ian scowled at him. "I was wide awake and she didn't slip past me."

"You say," Sam pointed out, his tone mocking as he folded his arms across his chest and leaned back casually, pleased he could tease his friend. "Still, she's here and that proves you were looking the other way or sleeping, just like that time in Indonesia when we parachuted in and you fell asleep on the way down. I believe that time you got tangled in a very large tree right in the center of the enemies' camp."

Azami's lashes fluttered, drawing Sam's attention. He almost reached out to her, wanting to hold her hand, but she'd mentioned a couple of times she didn't show affection in public.

"You fell asleep while parachuting?" she asked, clearly uncertain whether or not they were joking.

Ian shook his head. "I did not. A gust of heavy wind came along and pushed me right into that tree. Gator told everyone I was snoring when he shoved me out of the plane. The entire episode is all vicious fabrication. On the other hand, Sam here, actually did fall asleep while he was driving as we were escaping a very angry drug lord in Brazil."

Azami raised her eyebrow as she turned to Sam for an explanation. Her eyes laughed at him and again he had a wild urge to pull her to him and hold her tight. Primitive urges had never been a part of his makeup until she'd come along; now he figured he was becoming a caveman. Her gaze slid to his face as if she knew what he was thinking—which was probably the case. He flashed a grin at her.

"It is true. I did fall asleep at the wheel. We nearly went right off a cliff down into a gorge. But there were extenuating circumstances."

Ian snickered. "Are you going to pull out the cry-baby card? He had a little bitty wound he forgot to tell us about, that's how small it was. Ever since he fell asleep he's been trying to make us believe that contributed."

"It wasn't little. I have a scar. A knife fight." Sam was righteous about it.

"He barely nicked you," Ian sneered. "A tiny little slice that looked like a paper cut."

Sam extended his arm to Azami so she could see the evidence of the two-inch line of white marring his darker skin. "I bled profusely. I was weak and we hadn't slept in days."

"Profusely?" Ian echoed. "Ha! Two drops of blood is not profuse bleeding, Knight. We hadn't slept in days, that much is true, but the rest . . ." He trailed off, shaking his head and rolling his eyes at Azami.

Azami examined the barely there scar. The knife hadn't inflicted much damage, and Sam knew she'd seen evidence of much worse wounds. "Had you been drinking?" she asked, her eyes wide with innocence. Those long lashes fanned her cheeks as she gazed at him until his heart tripped all over itself.

Sam groaned. "Don't listen to him. I wasn't drinking, but once we were pretty much in the middle of a hurricane in the South Pacific on a rescue mission and Ian here decides he *has* to go into this bar . . ."

"Oh, no." Ian burst out laughing. "You're *not* telling her that story."

"You did, man. He made us all go in there, with the dirtbag we'd rescued, by the way," Sam told Azami. "We had to climb out the windows and get on the roof at one point when the place flooded. I swear there was a crocodile as big as a house coming right at us. We were running for our lives, laughing and trying to keep that idiot Frenchman alive."

"You said to throw him to the crocs," Ian reminded.

"What was in the bar that you had to go in?" Azami asked, clearly puzzled.

"Crocodiles," Sam and Ian said simultaneously. They both burst out laughing.

Azami shook her head. "You two could be crazy. Are you making these stories up?"

"Ryland wishes we made them up," Sam said. "Seriously, we're sneaking past this bar right in the middle of an enemy-occupied village and there's this sign on the bar that says swim with the crocs and if you survive, free drinks forever. The wind is howling and trees are bent almost double and we're carrying the sack of shit . . . er . . . our prize because the dirtbag refuses to run even to save his own life—"

"The man is seriously heavy," Ian interrupted. "He was

kidnapped and held for ransom for two years. I guess he decided to cook for his captors so they wouldn't treat him bad. He tried to hide in the closet when we came for him. He didn't want to go out in the rain."

"He was the biggest pain in the ass you could imagine," Sam continued, laughing at the memory. "He squealed every time we slipped in the mud and went down."

"The river had flooded the village," Sam added. "We were walking through a couple of feet of water. We're all muddy and he's wiggling and squeaking in a high-pitched voice and Ian spots this sign hanging on the bar."

Both men turned toward the door and Azami moved back into the shadows as another man entered. Tucker Addison regarded them all gravely from just inside the doorway.

"What's going on in here?" he demanded. "You sound like a pack of hyenas and there're only two of you."

Sam's belly knotted and the laughter faded. The others couldn't detect Azami's energy any more than Whitney had been able to, although she clearly was a GhostWalker.

"Sam got the big idea to tell Ms. Yoshiie all about the time we 'rescued' the Frenchman and swam with the crocodiles," Ian explained. "Of course he's blaming the entire thing on me and he was just as curious."

Tucker's gaze jumped to the shadows, scanning the room. Sam resisted the urge to reach out to Azami protectively. Tucker, like every GhostWalker, was a predator, highly skilled and dangerous. Azami didn't need his protection any more than Tucker did, but still, the need was there.

She shifted, a deliberate movement to draw Tucker's eye to her, her long lashes at half-mast, giving her a deceptive, innocent, and very demure look. "These men are telling me a tale that is very difficult to believe."

Her voice was soft and musical, pleasant to listen to, a tribute to her heritage. Long strands of hair were artfully loose from her carefully pinned hair. It suddenly occurred to Sam that those beautiful, long, decorative pins holding her hair in place were really lethal weapons. Her thick bangs brought attention to her incredible eyes and delicate features. She looked so fragile, not at all the samurai warrior he knew her to be—and there lay her greatest strength.

Tucker visibly relaxed, his mouth curving into a smile as he took up the conversation. "Actually, the story is very true. Sam and Ian really are that crazy. Well, they weren't the only ones. Gator wanted to go in as well, but everyone knows he's completely insane. He spent too much time in the swamp where he grew up."

"You went in too," Sam pointed out. "And I didn't want to go; I had no choice. I couldn't let Ian go alone."

Tucker shook his head. "You were damned sick of the Frenchman and you wanted to throw his ass in the croc pit. He was really fighting going out in that storm. We thought he was just chickenshit."

Sam shrugged. "Later we found out he'd betrayed his country and fed the terrorist cell intel, helping them set off three simultaneous bombs in Paris, so there was a good reason for him slowing us down. Unbeknownst to us, we were returning him to France for trial with the proof. We thought we were risking our lives to bring him out and he was fighting us. We should have known then, by his behavior, that he didn't want to be rescued. We just thought he was a pain in the ass."

"If you were having such a difficult time with him, why would you stop to go into a bar?" Azami asked, clearly puzzled.

Tucker snorted. "Ian said to see the crocs, and Gator said it was to get free drinks. Sam wanted to feed the crocs the Frenchman. In any case, I look back and they're climbing in through the window. It was broken out and water covered a good two feet of the floor. I couldn't just let them go in there without having their backs. And I sure didn't want to face Ryland and tell him the 'prisoner' we rescued got fed to the crocodiles."

Ian burst out laughing. "As I recall, you pushed me through

that window and it was a bit small for you so you kicked out the windowsill."

Sam nodded. "Oh, yeah, that's the way it happened and I shoved Mr. 'Fraidy Cat through and climbed in after you both."

Azami started laughing. "I can't imagine what Mr. Miller had to say to you when he found out."

The three men exchanged looks and began laughing uproariously. "He said, 'Pass me a bottle of scotch,' when he came back and stuck his head through the window."

Azami stared at them incredulously. "So *all* of you decided, in the middle of a rescue mission, during a flood, with hurricane winds, that it was necessary to go into a bar with crocodiles?"

"Well . . ." Tucker hedged.

Azami's gaze flicked toward the door and she moved, a tiny subtle movement that once again had her fading into the shadows. It seemed more a trick of the light than any real desire to disappear, but Sam couldn't help but admire her skill. She was in a room filled with GhostWalkers, yet she disappeared right before their eyes without even a whisper of cloth brushing the walls. There was no footfall, no rustle of clothing, nothing at all. One moment she was there and then she was gone.

"There was 'Smoke,'" Sam said, his gaze lifting to the door and the man filling it. "He wasn't having any of those crocodiles."

Jonas Harper entered. "Always the voice of reason, ma'am. Someone has to be with the number of crazies in this outfit."

Before the words were out of his mouth, the other men began laughing again. Sam noted that Jonas was looking right into the shadows where Azami had disappeared. It wasn't just that he'd heard her voice, he knew where she was. For some reason the fact that Jonas could see her set his heart tripping. He hadn't expected that tiny surge of jealousy that another man might be able to detect her. He had grown used to the idea that he was the only one who saw what a truly lethal weapon she was.

Azami's warmth poured into his mind, filled with a soothing amusement. *He sees in the dark and I am part of the dark. His eyes glow like those of an animal on the hunt.*

Whitney screwed with our DNA. It's more than probable that he has large cat or wolf DNA somehow.

"Someone must be the voice of reason," Azami said aloud, "but from the snickers of your fellow teammates, I am uncertain that person is you, sir."

Jonas gave the others a long, slow, reprimanding glare. "I told every single one of you that you were nuts to go into that bar. The trees surrounding it were bent over, almost in half. I told you they looked like praying mantises about to swoop in on prey. And was I right?"

Tucker laughed. "Damn right, you were." He nudged Sam. "Those trees came right down on top of that building and took out the wall and part of the roof with us in it."

"I dropped the Frenchman," Sam confirmed, laughing. "Right on his ass."

"The tree smashed the croc barrier and these big mothers come swimming right through the middle of that bar right at us," Tucker said. "I never saw such big crocodiles. Sam and I were swept underwater by the tree branches and those crocs were loose in the water with all of us."

"Jonas there," Ian continued, "he pulls himself inside and sits up top of the windowsill with his knife in his teeth and then does some kind of circus maneuver and the next thing we know he's hanging upside down from the ceiling and telling us to get the hell out of there, that he's got us covered."

"Of course he looked like a chimp swinging on the chandelier, which, by the way, was hanging by one bolt and was nothing more than a couple of lights strung together by a chain," Sam added, doubling over with laughter. "I'm looking up through the water, this heavy branch across my chest, and I could see Jonas swinging like a madman right over the water."

"So the damn thing snapped." Jonas took up the story, as Ian was laughing too hard to continue. "I landed on the Frenchman, who was screaming his guts out. Sam was no help. The crocs were swimming around like they were confused, sort of circling the room. They looked like prehistoric dinosaurs and pretty damn scary."

Sam felt the energy that could only prelude a Ghost-Walker. He took up the story quickly, laughing as he did. "Then Gator lets loose and starts yelling like a banshee. He was doing some kind of Cajun ceremonial rain dance or something . . ."

"I knew you were in here swappin' lies about me," Gator said. "I could hear you laughin' two houses over. You're gonna wake the dead. And, ma'am, don' believe a single lie these jokers tell you. I saved 'em all that day. It was our darkest hour, with giant crocodiles swimmin' around the room, water pourin' in from every direction, trees fallin' on us, and the bunch of them grabbin' at the liquor bottles and splashin' around, bait for the crocs."

Azami's low laughter was pure music. Sam was fairly certain he was already addicted to the sound of her voice. That low, alluring tone, so pleasant he could listen to it forever.

"I don't know what a ceremonial Cajun rain dance is, but why would you perform such a ceremony if it was already raining?" she asked.

"*Exactly,*" Tucker said. "We all asked him that later and he just insists he saved us by dancing on the bar and performing weird gyrations."

"I've told you all a *million* times that bar was wet and I was slippin', not performin' some rain dance in the middle of a hurricane," Gator protested. "I don' even know a rain dance."

Gator's statement drew more laughter. Sam wrapped his arm around his stomach, afraid if he didn't stop soon, his wounds were going to rip open just from pure amusement.

Azami shook her head as she slipped closer to the bed, leaning one slim hip against the frame closest to Sam. "Your mission sounds much more fun than anything I've ever done."

"Fun?" Ian's eyebrows nearly met his hairline. "Ma'am. You don't seem to understand the deadly peril I was in there at that bar. The Frenchman was trying to drown me and the crocodiles were circling me, thinking I was their next meal."

"Didn't you say you wanted to swim with the crocs?" Sam asked. "We all heard it. And as I recall, Tucker and I were the ones stuck underwater and you were clinging to the side of the wall like a lizard."

"I wanted to *see* them," Ian corrected solemnly, "*not* swim with them. But you know," he added, brightening significantly, "the sign did say if you swam with them and survived, you get free drinks for the rest of your life. Technically, that bar owes me free drinks, because I swam with the crocs and survived."

"Technically, Ian, you didn't swim with the crocodiles. You barely got your big toe wet once they were loose. That was Sam and me," Tucker snickered.

"How?" Azami asked. "How in the world did you all make it out of there?"

The men exchanged glances and then laughed again.

"Tom Delaney," Sam said.

"Tom Delaney," Tucker and Ian agreed simultaneously.

"We call him Shark," Gator confided.

"The new guy. We had a new addition to our team and he'd come along to learn the ropes, so to speak," Sam explained. "He'd been a GhostWalker for some time and had an impressive record, but none of us had worked with him before. We thought it was a get in and get out, no problem mission."

"Never been on one yet," Tucker said, "but I'm always hopeful."

"If it can go wrong," Jonas added, "it does."

"So we've got this new guy none of us are sure of," Sam continued. "He's leery. We're leery. We all think we just grab this Frenchman and get out of there fast, right? Except the Frenchman starts yelling and fighting. He kicked me. And he bit Tucker."

Instantly laughter erupted again.

Tucker looked wounded. "Seriously, ma'am, that bite hurt. He was truly vicious. Lily insisted on giving me a tetanus shot or something. With a needle." He shuddered dramatically.

"Poor baby," Sam soothed. Tucker had been wounded several times and he'd never made so much as a whimper. The idea of him whining over a needle was ludicrous—but funny. "Quit interrupting. We'd gotten into the house without anyone knowing and the idea was to get out the same way—like ghosts. That's what we do. But that Frenchman—and the weather—had other ideas. Apparently he'd been recruited in high school and once he'd gained a position in the government allowing him to feed the terrorists intel on the movement of money and weapons, he began to work in earnest. From what I understand, someone became suspicious and cut off his line of communication. Immediately the terrorists 'kidnapped' him, hoping that by doing so, they'd throw the government off the scent and they could use him if France ransomed him. Of course, we didn't know any of that; we just were sent to get him out."

"Freaky little bastard," Gator commented.

"The next thing we know, we've stirred up a hornet's nest and we've got everyone and their mothers shooting at us," Sam continued.

Azami raised her long lashes and looked at Sam, her eyes laughing and a little challenging. "So why did you really go into that bar?" she asked. "Because I don't believe you would do so unless you had no other choice."

There was a brief moment of silence. The men exchanged long, knowing grins.

"She's not so easy to put one over on, is she, Sam?" Ian asked.

Azami smiled at him, looking as serene and composed as ever. "You may joke all you like, but clearly you are professionals, and in the middle of a rescue mission during a hurricane, something very compelling would have to drive you to stop what you're doing and get trapped in a bar that was being decimated by the storm."

"True," Sam agreed, "but Ian really did notice the sign and we'd stopped for a second because the river had flooded and our escape route was cut off."

"The Frenchman made a run for it," Ian took up the story. "Straight into that bar. Bullets were flying, the river rising, and we had to make a quick decision—let him go or get him back."

"Hell no, he wasn't getting away," Sam said emphatically. "I thought about shooting him in the leg. But that little bastard was coming back with us, even if I had to carry him every step of the way."

"I can see you have a stubborn streak," Azami observed.

"Ha!" Ian agreed. "You don't know the half of it. He was going in after the Frenchman no matter what anyone said. I sure wasn't going to let him go alone."

Gator flashed a cocky grin. "Sam really did nearly shoot our runaway, but Ian jumped through that window after him and then it was on."

"And you all followed him, of course," Azami said.

"Well, ma'am," Jonas said. "There was liquor in there and no one was minding the bar. Ian is Irish. We had to make certain there was something left."

"We all had a mighty thirst after all that runnin' from those bullets, ma'am," Gator added.

"How did you get away from the crocodiles, or is that part of your embellishments?" Azami asked.

"*Embellishments?*" Ian said, astounded. "She's casting aspersions on our story, gentlemen. There were crocodiles swimming around inside and Gator was gyrating on the bar.

Jonas managed to fall on the Frenchman, and I was in the water, my life in *deadly* peril. I hadn't even managed to grab hold of a bottle of good Irish whiskey and there I was about to die. No self-respecting Irishman would die without at least one drink."

"How terrible," Azami murmured in sympathy.

Ian nodded, much more pleased with her reaction. "Now you're beginning to understand the seriousness of the situation." He glared at his fellow teammates as they burst into laughter again.

"Tell me who this Shark is that came to your rescue," Azami prompted.

Sam started to reach out to take her hand and stopped himself. He had not asked for permission from her brothers and she'd told him a couple of times about public displays of affection. He sighed. He was going to have to find it in himself to keep his hands off of her, even when he seemed to need to touch her.

His eyes met hers and she smiled at him. Just for him. Her eyes warmed slowly, going from that cool darkness to molten heat.

I want to touch you. Skin to skin. The admitting of his secret need, even if it was only a whisper in his mind, made him feel closer to her.

Azami shifted again, a slight, subtle movement that put her even closer to the bed where he sat. Her bare arm slid against his, the merest of brushes, yet he felt her touch all the way to his bones, branding him hers.

"We call him Shark because he's good in water, ma'am," Tucker said.

Azami smiled at them, leaning against the bed, making the movement so natural Sam was certain no one would think twice about it. "Enough addressing me as *ma'am*. My brothers and I are quite fine with using the more personal first name. We don't find it insulting. Please call me Azami; I will consider it an honor."

Sam couldn't help but stare at her. She sounded so

demure and sweet, her long lashes veiling her eyes, her lips both fascinating and alluring as she spoke.

Tucker nodded. "Azami, then. Shark's name is Tom. He recently joined our team and like we said, it was his first mission with us. We were still feeling our way with him. He didn't hesitate at all. He was in that water, swimming under the water to Sam and me. Ian was splashing like crazy and Gator was doing his wild Cajun thing to keep the crocodiles' attention focused on him while Shark worked to move that tree off of them."

"He had to breathe for us underwater. I'm good in the water and can stay down a long time, but not like Tom. He was all over it. Give us air, work on the tree, and give us more air until he had that sucker off of us. Ian kept splashing around and Gator kept up his crazy antics as bait and Jonas and Rye worked above the water to help lift the tree."

Azami pressed her lips together tightly, regarding Sam without speaking. She knew, in spite of all the joking and laughter, just how dangerous the situation had really been and how close Sam and Tucker had come to losing their lives.

This is the kind of work you like?

Sam nodded slowly. *Does it bother you?*

"What happened to the Frenchman? Did he get away?" Azami asked aloud.

I am samurai. I have chosen a life of honor. It's only fitting that the man I am considering sharing my life with would do so as well. I do not fear death and clearly you do not either. My father taught me never to fear death, but to live my life to the fullest, to embrace every moment as if it might be my last. My choice for a partner is one who lives his life in this way.

"*Hell* no, he didn't get away," Ian said. "We dragged him back with us and handed him over to the French. They were very glad to get him, and I believe they put him on trial for treason. He deserved whatever they threw at him."

There is no doubt in my mind, Azami, we belong. He no

longer needed to touch her to know she was committed to him. Her warmth was in his mind, filling the lonely places.

He had lived on the streets, scrounging his way, one step ahead of the gangs and the pedophiles until he'd tried to steal a car with the idea of getting out of the city. He had no plan at the time, only a desperate need to get away from where he was. General Ranier told him it was providence that he had tried to steal Ranier's car, allowing them to meet. Secretly, Sam didn't care what it was, only that they had met and the general had given him an education and a direction. Now there was Azami. She was his direction and the path seemed very clear to him.

"Uh-oh," Ian whispered, overly loud. "We're about to get busted."

Azami moved even closer to Sam, protectively, her body shielding his from the door. He had to smile. His woman wasn't going to sit peacefully in a corner in the face of a threat.

"It's Ryland," he said softly.

She glanced at him over her shoulder. The movement was graceful, a whisper of silk and sin, temptation in the form of long lashes and serenity masking fiery passion. His heart jumped toward hers. Azami smiled at him. Intimate. Only for him. Such a brief exchange, but it was enough to know she was his. All that she was, was his.

Ryland filled the doorway, his broad shoulders so wide they nearly took up the space entirely. In his arms, Daniel snuggled against him, alert, bright, ready to join in the fun with all of his uncles.

"Do you think you're making enough noise?" Ryland demanded. "It's the middle of the night, in case no one's noticed."

"Did we wake Daniel?" Ian asked, instantly concerned. He held out his arms to the boy. "Come here, my little man."

Daniel looked past Ian, his gaze clearly settling on Azami. He broke into a smile and instantly took his index fingers and hooked them together, signing "friend." He held out his arms toward her and nearly launched himself from Ryland's arms.

Azami took the boy and hugged him to her. "Hello, my little friend. Did we wake you up? Your uncles were just telling me some exciting stories about things they've done." She spoke to him as if he were an adult, not a toddler, looking into his eyes as she held him close.

Sam could imagine her with their child, a protective mother for certain, he could see it in the way she held Daniel.

"You've met?" Ryland asked.

His tone put Sam on edge. He sat up straighter and swung his legs over the edge of the bed in preparation—for what, he wasn't certain. Ryland had sounded more than suspicious— he'd sounded accusing as well. More so, his team had gone onto alert. This was Daniel—the most protected member of their family—and a stranger had gotten to him right in their midst.

"Daniel has been telling us all about his new friend. We thought he had made up an imaginary friend to play with." Ryland's gaze shifted to Ian's face. Ian—Azami's guard. If she'd met Daniel, where had that meeting taken place, and how?

Ian squirmed uncomfortably. It didn't matter that they'd all been laughing with Azami moments earlier; every man was looking at her as if she was the enemy. Sam slid to his feet, steadying himself against the bed for a brief moment before he found his footing again.

This time there was no mistaking Ryland's accusation, and Sam understood. Lily had been upset over the idea that Daniel would have to have an imaginary playmate. More than that, Daniel was to be protected at all times from outsiders and yet the child had greeted Azami as an old friend, which implied multiple meetings. He was always naturally suspicious of strangers.

"He's a wonderful boy, and so very bright," Azami said, as Daniel snuggled against her. She rocked him gently. "He came into my room on the first night. I heard a small noise in the fan and a screw dropped out onto the floor. I looked up and he was looking down at me, laughing. He was quite curious that you had company and didn't introduce him. I explained that not all strangers were good people and some could be dangerous to him and that you were protecting him. He signs quite well."

Azami never raised her voice, or appeared in any way as if she recognized the heightened tension in the room. She seemed relaxed, her attention focused on the toddler, but Sam wasn't deceived in the least. She was a force to be reckoned with and for some reason, his teammates didn't feel her energy as he did. That continued to worry him.

There was a long silence. No one expected that explanation, but they shouldn't have been surprised. Daniel was definitely an escape artist. He liked small spaces and already he was using tools like a pro.

Ryland glared at his son. "You went to our guest's *bedroom*, Daniel? Do you think that's appropriate behavior?" He signed as he spoke.

Daniel shook his head and pressed closer to Azami. He signed back to his father.

"I don't care if she didn't mind," Ryland sounded gruff. "She is our guest. Her bedroom is a sacred place, a sanctuary for her. We don't intrude. Do you understand?"

Daniel nodded his head.

"More than that, it isn't safe for you to go meet a stranger without our knowledge. You have to have time-out for that." Now Ryland sounded sterner than ever and Daniel's face began to crumble, tears swimming in his eyes.

The men exchanged uneasy glances. None of them liked it when Daniel cried and he definitely knew it, playing them easily when he sat in his little chair sobbing.

Azami's subtle move put her under the shelter of Sam's arm. Daniel looked up at him, his lip quivering. Sam leaned down and brushed a kiss over the boy's mop of hair.

"What does one do on time-out?" Azami asked. Her

voice was softer than ever, but Sam felt the hair on the back of his neck raise. Clearly she didn't like the idea of the boy being punished.

"Daniel sits in a chair for two minutes," Sam explained hastily.

Daniel knew by the way she held him so protectively that he had an ally in Azami. He gave a little sob and pressed his face into her shoulder.

"You tie him to a chair?" Azami glared up at Sam.

Ian burst out laughing. "If you tried tying that boy to a chair, momma bear would come at you with teeth and claws."

"And a very big gun," Ryland added. "I don't know what they do in Japan, but we don't tie our children to chairs. He sits in it because we tell him to. It's safe and doesn't hurt. He doesn't like the isolation and understands there are consequences for naughty behavior. In this case, he also violated a safety rule."

"What happens if he gets out of the chair?" Azami asked. "Before the two minutes are up?"

"He is placed back in the chair and we go at it all day if necessary," Ryland said. "Raising Daniel requires patience as well as love." He looked around the room. "I think it requires all of us. We work together. Clearly we dropped the ball. I'm sorry he disturbed you on your first night with us. Thank you for being so gracious about it."

"I rarely sleep at night. I needed to make certain my brothers were safe and had all they required. I felt better seeing they were assigned guards as well."

Ian regarded her with a clear frown. "Are you saying you left your room last night?"

"Well, of course. The baby had to be put back to bed. I wasn't going to shove him back up into the vent and hope he made his way back to his room safely," Azami said.

"That's impossible," Ian denied. "I didn't leave the door. I didn't, Rye. I didn't fall asleep tonight, or last night."

Ryland turned piercing eyes on Azami, waiting for an explanation.

"Your son is an extremely intelligent and curious child," Azami said. "And very gifted. Perhaps too gifted for his age."

Ryland reached out and plucked Daniel from her arms. "What do you mean by that?"

Sam bristled at the belligerence in Ryland's tone. "She didn't mean anything," he snapped before he could stop himself.

Ryland's gaze jumped to his face.

"Sir," Azami said calmly. "Your son is in the greatest danger possible and not from anyone outside this compound. From himself. Like Sam, like me, he is a teleporter."

CHAPTER 10

A stunned silence followed Azami's quiet revelation. The members of GhostWalker Team One exchanged uneasy, shocked looks.

Ryland rubbed his chin over his son's thick cap of hair, his eyes closed briefly. Sam couldn't imagine what was going through his mind.

"Are you certain?" Ryland finally asked. "I've seen no evidence of Daniel teleporting."

Azami slowly nodded her head. "I'm very sure. He's young and there's an art to it, but learning can be both painful and dangerous, as Sam knows well. The gift didn't really begin to manifest in me until around the age of ten. I would feel broken apart inside and find I'd moved from one corner of a room to another and couldn't remember walking across the room. It was frightening. For a while I was afraid to tell my father, afraid I was losing my mind. Your son is a mere baby and he's already experiencing that same sensation."

Ryland buried his face against the baby's neck, his arms tightening until Daniel squirmed and he was forced to ease up. He raised his head, his steel gray eyes meeting Sam's. "Did you know?"

"I never even suspected, Rye," Sam said. "Now that Azami pointed out the possibility, I can see that a few times, Daniel was in one spot and then he was a few feet away playing with my tools, but I didn't feel the 'broken apart' effect until I was about eighteen. Neither you nor Lily has the ability to teleport, so it didn't occur to me that Daniel would have it. But then, I don't think my parents could do it, or they would have been all over television and selling their story for their drug money. Hell, Rye." Sam rubbed the bridge of his nose, not knowing how to comfort his friend.

Daniel could very well teleport right into the middle of a wall before he ever fully understood the danger. Ryland and Lily had a difficult time as it was, let alone knowing their child could put himself in the middle of the forest, the mines, or up on the roof. The psychic gifts they had been born with, and then enhanced by Whitney, were both a blessing and a curse. Each talent could be extremely dangerous, especially in one young and inexperienced.

"You snuck past me, didn't you?" Ian accused. "I knew I hadn't gone to sleep."

Sam understood what Ian was doing: giving Ryland time to assimilate the danger to his son and come to terms with it. He deliberately drew attention away from their leader.

"Many times, as a matter of fact," Azami said, willing to sacrifice herself so that Ryland could take a moment to recover and hold his child close. "I tweaked your chin once."

Ian rubbed his chin, glaring at her. "You did. I felt it. A draft hit me and it felt like someone pulled a hair from my chin."

"It was red and I couldn't resist. You really need to shave," Azami pointed out. "What's with that little red fuzz on your chin anyway? Is it some sort of statement I don't understand?"

"Statement?" Ian flared, stroking the tiny little red vee on his chin. "This is manly, woman. Don't you know that?"

Azami gave a slight bow, lowering her lashes and chin demurely, but not before Sam caught the sparkle in her eyes. "Forgive me, Ian, I did not know a man of your stature needed fuzz to be manly. I can only plead ignorance of this custom."

The men snickered and nudged Ian, Tucker reaching out to touch the red fuzz. Ian punched his arm away.

"Tucker," Ryland said, his voice once more commanding. "Take Daniel to his mother. Make certain she understands the danger. We'll figure out how best to help my son comprehend the danger he's facing. Please give her that reassurance." *Stay with her at all times. Be ready. If Azami can slip past our guards, it's possible her brothers can as well.* He added the command telepathically, uncaring if his guest felt the surge of energy accompanying the psychic gift. Aloud he continued. "We'll be in the war room. I think Ms. Yoshiie has a little explaining to do before we go any further."

Tucker nodded in understanding. He took the boy into his arms, looking larger than ever with such a small toddler clinging to him.

Sam had known it was coming, but he still had hoped for a little more time to cement his relationship with Azami. He didn't want her taking offense to the grilling Ryland was certain to give her. Ryland wasn't privy to her mind. He couldn't know she wasn't a threat to Daniel or their team. He would have to find reassurance his own way.

Sam glanced at Azami. She was impossible to fathom, her expression as serene as ever, and that could either mean she'd been expecting Ryland's interrogation after her revelation, or that she was fully prepared to fight her way out of the compound.

"Ms. Yoshiie." Ryland gestured toward the door after handing off his son to Tucker. "After you."

Again her lashes fluttered, two crescent-shaped fans, feathery and beautiful, hiding her expression and making her appear fragile and feminine when Sam knew she was made of steel. Sam took a step after her and Ryland shook his head.

"Not you, Sam. You stay here."

It was a clear command. Sam was a soldier first and foremost and he'd never disobeyed an order from Ryland in his life. Every muscle in his body tightened. Ryland turned on his heel to follow Azami out, but Sam used his speed to cut him off. The effect on his body robbed him of breath, but it didn't matter. If Azami was facing a firing squad so to speak, she wasn't doing it alone.

"With all due respect, sir, I can't do that."

The room went silent. Everyone turned to stare at him. He didn't take his eyes from Ryland's.

"That wasn't a request, soldier," Ryland said.

"I'm aware of that, sir, but in this instance, I feel I have no choice but to attend this meeting and request that you rescind that order."

"And if I don't, you intend to disobey?"

Before Sam could answer, Ryland stepped close to him, nearly nose to nose. Sam didn't give ground. They stared at one another a long time in silence.

Tell me what she is to you.

She's my Lily. I believe in her, Rye. Sam answered his friend and commander the only way he knew how—honestly. *She's one of us whether she admits it or not. I've been in her head, and she could never hide a threat to us from me. She isn't here for Daniel.*

Ryland continued to stare at him a few minutes longer before he nodded his head and spun around to stalk out of the room.

"Are you crazy?" Ian hissed. "You're lucky you're wounded. Has anyone *ever* disobeyed an order?"

"He understands I have no choice," Sam said and dragged a shirt off the nightstand. He didn't bother with shoes, padding barefoot after Ryland and Azami.

His teammates circled him almost protectively and he

found himself grateful for their camaraderie. They might not understand, but they were showing support, hoping Ryland wouldn't take his head off, or confine him to quarters for the rest of his life.

Sam waited until Azami sank gracefully into a chair before he chose the one beside her. He caught the men exchanging quick glances, but he didn't care. Azami wasn't going to be alone when Ryland questioned her. Sam was absolutely convinced she wasn't Whitney's ally and that she was no threat to Daniel. If anything, she wanted to help the child.

"Perhaps a cup of tea," Azami suggested. "If that's possible."

She appeared absolutely calm—much calmer than he was feeling. Sam wanted to gather her close and protect her from what was to come, but she clearly didn't need him to shield her. There was no fluttering of nervous hands; she folded them neatly in her lap and simply waited while everyone took a chair. Ryland nodded toward Gator, who quickly leapt up to make a cup of tea for Azami.

"Ms. Yoshiie," Ryland began.

She inclined her head in that graceful, demure way she had. "Please call me Azami. I would prefer to learn American ways."

"Azami then," Ryland said, in no way deceived by her delicate features. "I think it's time for an explanation, don't you?"

"You certainly deserve one," she agreed. "You've been more than patient. Dr. Whitney called me Thorn. He gave the girls names of flowers and seasons, a careless acknowledgment that we had to be called something other than the numbers he gave us in his files. He thought me quite useless as anything other than for experiments, so instead of a Lily, or a Rose, I was a Thorn to him, a constant pain that nagged at him until he threw me away—back onto the streets in Japan. I was eight years old."

Silence greeted her matter-of-fact revelation. Ryland put

both hands on the table and leaned toward her, his piercing steel gaze fixing steadily on her face.

"GhostWalkers recognize one another by the energy surrounding us. I don't feel it when you walk into a room," Ryland made it a statement. He looked to Kadan for confirmation.

Sam shoved down anger. He rarely got angry, but Ryland was all but calling her a liar.

Kadan shook his head. "I don't feel anything at all," he agreed, "but Sam did. From the very beginning he felt something was off about the Yoshiie family, in particular Azami. He went so far as to scan their faces and send them to Lily to run the facial recognition program." Kadan too leaned toward Azami, a slight frown on his face. "Why would Whitney find you useless to him and the program when you're obviously gifted?"

"Whitney is able to recognize those with psychic talents, even when they are mere infants. Unfortunately he isn't a terribly patient man with children. My ability to teleport didn't appear until I was ten."

"There was a mention of a child named Thorn," Kadan told Ryland. "Jesse, from Team Two, his wife, Saber, talked about her a few times."

Azami remained quiet, and she held herself away from Sam. He knew what she was doing. If Ryland didn't accept the things she told him—if this meeting turned bad—she didn't want him in trouble with his unit or to have to make a choice between them.

Don't worry about me, Azami. I'm a grown man. I make my choices and I live with them. I know exactly what I'm doing and why.

Ryland's head snapped around. "Speak out loud for everyone to hear if you have something to say, Sam. That's why you're here, isn't it?"

Sam had rarely heard Ryland use that voice and more than anything else, as low and as stern as it was, the tone told him he was on treacherous ground.

"I told her not to worry about me, that I make my own choices and I know exactly what I'm doing and why." Sam wasn't about to dodge the truth.

"I hope you do," Ryland said.

"I had reservations about the Yoshiie family from the moment I met them, especially Azami. From the beginning I thought it was possible she was one of us—a GhostWalker. It wasn't that I felt the familiar energy, I can't put my finger on what it was exactly, but I was very uneasy and indicated that to Nico and Kadan as well as sending Lily pictures," Sam reported. He resisted the need to put his hand over Azami's folded hands beneath the table. "Of course my first worry was for Daniel."

It was important Azami knew that he would fight with his last breath for the boy against anyone who tried to harm him. She had to know his loyalty to his team whom he considered family ran deep, as would his commitment to her—and any children they had.

"She fought beside me, Rye. I've been in her mind. She saved me out there. I put my life in her hands and I would never have allowed her to come here if I thought for one moment she was a threat to Daniel or that she was working with Whitney." Sam looked him right in the eye. "If you don't know that much about me, what the hell am I doing here?"

Ryland didn't flinch. "If I didn't know that much about you, Knight, you wouldn't be sitting at this table. Wounded or not, you'd be on your ass in the brig."

"Mr. Miller . . ." Azami began.

"*Captain*. Captain Miller," Ryland corrected.

Sam ducked his head. Ryland was royally pissed. It was difficult to get the man riled, but once he was, there was very little backup in him.

"Forgive me," Azami said in her demure tone, those long lashes lowering as she bowed her head gracefully. "This is my fault. When I was young, my father asked only a couple of things of me. He asked that I live a life of honor and that

I throw hatred and anger away as useless. I hated Whitney with the passion only a child could have. My father taught me that he is a monster, yes, but my hatred of him gave him great power over me. Bringing a man like Whitney to justice is impossible, but someone has to try."

"How?" Ryland asked. "You must have a plan."

Azami looked around the table. "You are asking me to trust all of you when you don't trust me."

"You came to our home on false pretenses," Ryland pointed out.

She shook her head, her eyes steady on his. "That is not so, Captain Miller. I insist on visiting all corporations or countries who wish to purchase one of my satellites. Our company is legitimate and I know you didn't choose us blindly. We deliver the best in the world. There is no competition as of yet. Our lens is superior, as is our software, to any other on the market. *You* reached out to us."

Gator placed a cup of tea in front of Azami. "I noticed you took milk in your tea earlier."

She smiled up at him. "Thank you."

"Can I get you anything else, ma'am . . . Azami?" Gator asked.

Sam shifted in his chair. He was happy someone was being polite to her, but of all the men, Gator was the most charming with women. He was totally enamored of his wife, but that didn't stop women from falling for him.

Azami raised her long lashes and looked at him directly. The impact struck like an arrow straight through his heart. How did she know? How were they so connected? He wouldn't betray his family or team, but he'd fight with every breath in his body for her. Her eyes seemed like the midnight sky, dark and yet sparkling with stars, embracing him with heat, with something very close to desire. Then her lashes came down and she was once again focusing on Gator.

"No, thank you," Azami said politely. She took a very ladylike sip of tea and put the cup back in the saucer before she looked once more at Ryland. "It is our policy to vet everyone who wishes to purchase from us—that is well known throughout the world. Three weeks after we turned down Dr. Whitney, his daughter Lily made inquiries. Was that coincidence or was he using her to acquire our satellite another way? I think that question is very legitimate, and as a responsible company, we had to get the answer."

Sam knew he was falling fast. She was so composed under fire, so perfect in every way for a man like him. He loved the way she looked: regal, a Japanese princess with etiquette ingrained in her, with such grace and poise, and yet any moment she could erupt into a lethal killing machine if circumstances called for her to do so.

Ryland nodded. "I suppose you have a point. I would do the same thing."

"I knew Whitney would eventually try to get his hands on one of our satellites, and it was the perfect opportunity to get to him. He would have to meet with us. His location is well hidden and he moves often. He can utilize any U.S. military base in the world and has friends in very high places helping him. He's a ghost, elusive and impossible to track at this point. Our satellites were the perfect bait."

"What went wrong?"

Azami shrugged. "He refused to meet with us personally. He wanted his representatives to stand in for him, so of course we refused. He offered much more money, but we reiterated we had a policy in place we never deviated from. He still refused a face-to-face. Three times he tried bribing one of my people and once he tried blackmail, in the hopes of being able to duplicate our software and lens."

"He would try to get a spy in your camp."

"It is impossible."

"Nothing is impossible, Azami," Ryland disagreed, using her first name as a sign of peace between them. "Not with his money. He'll keep coming at you."

"He won't succeed. Those working for me were helped in some way by my father and owe him allegiance. They were trained as samurai and they will not dishonor themselves."

"If he found something to blackmail one person with, he will find another."

Azami sent Ryland a serene smile and a small shake of her head. "The man he tried to blackmail immediately came to me and confessed what he thought was shameful. It was not and he remains fine, but had he felt he could not live with the shame, he would have ended his own life with honor. That is our code. Whitney cannot conceive of such loyalty, and that, ultimately, will be his downfall."

Sam knew Ryland couldn't dispute her statement. The GhostWalkers many times had said exactly the same thing. Whitney had wanted a strong unit that could operate independently under the radar, men and women completely loyal to their cause and to one another. In that, he had succeeded far more than he had ever expected.

"You have to admit, after such persistence, to get an order from Whitney's daughter, it would be natural to think perhaps he was behind the request for a satellite," Azami continued.

Ryland also couldn't dispute that statement either. He would have been suspicious himself had the scenario played out that way. Whitney was a cunning opponent and he never stopped trying once he made up his mind to something.

"There's no doubt a high-resolution satellite would give him the capability to track our children more easily," Ryland admitted. "I can't say that I wouldn't have done the same thing."

"I would do anything to keep such an instrument out of his hands," Azami admitted.

"Why wouldn't you come to us the moment you realized Daniel was out of his room and getting into things that might be dangerous?" Ryland asked.

Azami took another sip of tea, unhurried and composed, her mind racing as she tried to decide just how far she could safely go without endangering anyone else. It was one thing to take a chance with her own life, but she had someone in Whitney's camp she had to protect. She set the teacup down with delicate precision and looked up at Ryland, carefully meeting his eyes.

"Your wife is Whitney's only acknowledged daughter and she's a scientist who carried on his work. She inherited his wealth and his laboratories. It wasn't completely unreasonable to wonder just what she was doing with her child. When I learned she had a baby here, I was determined to see that the child was well loved and not used for experiments."

There was no apology in her voice at all. She had done what she believed to be right—and she wanted to make it clear to everyone at the table that she would have done the exact same thing if she had to do it over. She wouldn't aid Whitney in any way—especially not for money.

"And what did you find?" Ryland asked, his voice dropping an octave.

Sam inwardly winced. Ryland speaking low was never a good thing. Anything to do with Lily and Daniel made him extremely protective. Azami was treading on thin ground without a hint of apology.

Azami had no hesitation in answering. "I found Daniel to be a delightful, amazing child, well loved and protected by his parents and all of his 'uncles.' He's very happy. You provide him with support, and stimulation, yet you give him balance so that he's not pushing himself before he should. I couldn't imagine better parents."

"And yet we didn't catch that he could teleport."

As a father, Ryland seemed vulnerable to Azami. She hated that she caused him worry. "Well, he can't actually teleport yet, thankfully; not more than about a foot or less," she pointed out. "But it will be soon and he needs instruction and firm rules or he'll have very bad accidents. I learned the hard way as I suspect Sam did. Daniel's too young to find himself inside a wall." She leaned toward Ryland. "Why would you think you could recognize the signs so early in him? I almost missed them and I practice daily."

"I can work with him," Sam offered. "I enjoy spending time with him, Rye."

Ryland's gaze shifted to Sam's face. Azami could see that Ryland was definitely worried about his son attempting to teleport, and she knew he should be. It was an extremely dangerous gift, and in a child—an infant, really—the gift could be lethal.

"Thanks, Sam. Lily isn't going to take this well. We have to strike such a balance with Daniel and we're always guessing on how much to let him do and his ability to understand the things we try to teach him. I suspect this is going to be difficult. If his natural inclination is to teleport when he suddenly wants to sneak a cookie, we're going to be reprimanding him constantly."

Azami flashed a small smile. "He loves his life. He's quite good at communicating. He already understands that he's loved and you put down rules to keep him safe."

"He's a sponge," Ryland said. "He soaks up information at a rapid rate. I have no doubt that he'll speak multiple languages, and his motor skills are already amazing." A small grin escaped. "I guess every parent thinks that."

Azami leaned toward him again, making up her mind. She was going to throw in with the GhostWalkers. She had no doubts about this particular unit; she'd spent the last few days spying on them. She even had tiny cameras in various locations throughout the house. Eiji and Daiki were adept at fitting the cameras in places no one would ever find them. They could walk through a room and place one in mere seconds. She just had to strike a balance to protect her informant. She wouldn't risk his life, not even for credibility.

"You have a much bigger problem than me, Captain, or your son teleporting. We have stumbled across some information suggesting you will be getting orders to go into the Congo to assassinate General Armine, who is in a fight with Ezekial Ekabela to take over the rebel army. Ezekial's brother, General Eudes Ekabela, was killed by a Ghost-Walker, and Armine took over before Ezekial could step into power. Whitney needs Armine out of the way to allow Ezekial back into power. Ezekial has control of the diamond mines and there is a particular size diamond that Whitney needs for a new weapon he's working on. The price Ezekial Ekabela is demanding is Armine's assassination and a GhostWalker to pay for his brother's death. Whitney agreed to the terms. Since Jack Norton, whom the rebels are desperate to get their hands on, has twins, Whitney is giving them someone from your team."

Azami took a breath and avoided looking at Sam. Her stomach muscles tightened, her breath refusing to leave her lungs. She didn't want to see condemnation in his eyes. She hadn't warned him, not even when she was kissing him, committing to him in her heart. She forced the words out. "Whitney believes that Sam is useless to his program and he's willing to sacrifice him in exchange for the diamond."

Sam raised his eyebrow, but didn't say a word. Gator nudged Tucker, but one look from Ryland stopped any teasing they might have done.

"Any orders coming to us would be classified," Ryland said, his voice dropping another octave. "And then there's the matter of the second-generation Zenith that my wife has been working on, and no one should have even a whisper of it, let alone an actual patch.

She'd known that was coming. Azami recognized the instant suspicion and she couldn't blame him. If he'd come to her with classified information on a team that didn't exist to the outside world, where they were going and what was in store for them, she'd be extremely wary of just how that information had come into an outsider's hands. She had known the moment she disclosed what she knew, Ryland would really begin his interrogation.

She kept her hands folded in her lap beneath the table. Her stomach was jittery, not because she feared these people—she knew she could kill several of them before they got to her—but because she wanted to choose each word carefully and make them understand she was on their side without taking a chance on risking lives. "Whitney has several people working for him giving and passing along information, as well as helping forward his agenda. Clearly those helping him are people in positions of power. They do his bidding. I've intercepted his commands to a woman named Sheila Benet. She's his number one courier."

Beneath the table, Sam's fingers wrapped very gently around her wrist, cautioning her. He didn't want her to go any further. She had eyes and ears in the war room and knew the GhostWalker unit as a whole didn't believe the three deaths associated with Sheila Benet were accidental, and it was obvious Sam didn't want her confessing to murder. From the moment he had recognized that someone could have used a blowgun to kill Major Patterson, she was certain he would figure out who had done so. She had known the moment she met him that he was too intelligent to fool for long and had she been able to, she wouldn't have looked at him twice.

"The same Sheila Benet that witnessed two accidents? One in a bathroom of a night club and one in a restaurant?"

"I read about the accidents," Azami said truthfully. Her computers certainly searched for certain names that might come up in any news article or report. "I found it interesting that she was at both accident sites."

The pad of Sam's thumb slid back and forth over the inside of her wrist in a caress she wasn't certain he was aware of—yet she was all too aware. She was rarely distracted by anything, but that small movement sent a shiver of heat down her spine. She should move her wrist away from him—she couldn't afford any distractions—but she couldn't bring herself to do it.

"We found it equally interesting," Ryland said. "We don't believe either of those deaths was an accident. And there was a third—a car accident as well that is suspect."

She didn't blink. "I have to agree with your suspicion. With Benet involved, I am certain those people had to be in

Whitney's employ. It would be too much of a coincidence to think they both died within weeks of each other—although stranger things have happened."

Ryland studied her face with those piercing, steel gray eyes. She couldn't imagine his son at sixteen lying to his father. She hadn't lied, but she was definitely omitting facts. Ryland Miller seemed to see into one's soul.

"You had nothing to do with those deaths?" he asked outright.

Inwardly she winced. There it was. If she told the truth, they could have her arrested. If she lied . . . Well, she wasn't a liar. She widened her eyes and allowed a little frown, tipping her head back to look at him directly. "Why would you think that? How could you even consider such a thing?" Those were fair questions and she had sidestepped answering truthfully.

If Ryland cared enough to check, and he might, he would find she was in the United States at the time of all three "accidents," but until he had that fact, she was going to dodge every single incriminating question to the best of her ability.

Ryland frowned, studying her face. She knew she looked innocent. That was one of her best gifts, that ability, a natural one that her adopted father had helped her to perfect. Her diminutive size and delicate, almost fragile appearance was an asset. People always underestimated her abilities. She deliberately gave the appearance of a shy, demure woman who spent most of her life indoors.

These men were dominant and protective by nature. She read them easily. They made no attempt to hide what and who they were—warriors, every one of them—and yet they had a soft spot for women and children. To them, women and children represented what they were fighting for. The women and children were the reason they put their lives on the line for the freedom of their country, to keep those they loved safe and protected. That creed was bred into their very bones. As a samurai, she was trained to use every advantage, and her innocent looks aided her in unexpected ways.

Ryland suddenly snapped his head around and his eyes met Sam's. "Is she full of shit? Or is she for real?"

Her stomach did an unexpected somersault. If there was one person sitting in the room who saw right through her, it was Sam. Ryland was his friend and the leader of his unit, a man Sam respected and felt great affection for. Azami had to suppress a growl. Sam wasn't going to lie to Ryland, not even for her, and she wouldn't respect him if he did. It was a lose-lose situation.

For the first time, true tension crept into her. She forced herself to breathe normally, to look as calm and serene as ever. Those strong fingers stroking her bare, inner wrist ceased moving and settled around her arm like a shackle.

"I *know* she's the real deal, Ryland," Sam said, his voice equally low.

Which could mean anything. Azami didn't dare glance at him. Her heart had begun a strange pounding, the rhythm new to her. She had an unexpected urge to lean over and lift her face to his. His voice was absolutely honest. His simple sentence meant nothing to Ryland, but everything to her.

Her eyes burned for a moment, forcing her to lower her lashes. Her father had stood for her. Her brothers were in another room right at this moment listening so that if necessary, they could fly to her aid and all three might have a chance to fight their way out. Never had anyone else stood up for her, and Sam was not only standing but placing himself in front of her. He believed in her to the point that, although he wasn't being deceptive, he was still deflecting.

Ryland evidently knew Sam very well. Those steely eyes narrowed. "You're a damn big help, Knight. If anything, *you're* full of shit."

"I'm telling the absolute truth, Rye," Sam confirmed.

"I'm sure you are. What the hell's going on between you two?"

Sam shrugged. "I plan on asking her brothers' permission to marry her."

Azami gasped, swinging her head around to look up at

him. It was one thing to fight quietly for her, but he was openly aligning himself with her.

Sam's fingers tightened on her arm, but his gaze was locked with Ryland's. "Azami is a GhostWalker. She's one of us and more than that, she's the one for me. I want you to know that up front. That's how certain I am of her."

"And you don't think that there's a possibility that you're blinded by your feelings for her? You just met her. Don't you think that happened just a little too fast?"

Azami winced. She knew what Ryland was implying. Whitney had somehow managed to pair them together. She kept her head down, long lashes covering her eyes to prevent anyone from seeing distress that might show.

"So how did that work out for you, Ryland?" Sam demanded. He looked around the table. "For any of you with a wife?" He shrugged his broad shoulders. "I don't much care if Whitney paired me with Azami or not, although I don't see how he could have, but I know she fits with me. There isn't a doubt in my mind."

Azami shook her head. As much as she wanted Sam for herself, she couldn't let him sacrifice. "Let's slow down. There's something else you should know, something that may be very pertinent to how you're feeling right now, Sam." Her lungs felt squeezed for air, but she had to be fair to him.

"I don't need to know anything else, Azami," Sam assured.

The tears burned again and she blinked rapidly, her throat clogging for a moment.

"You might not need to know anything else," Ryland said. "But I do. Please continue, Azami."

It was a major concession that he'd used her first name again. His voice had been filled with warning to Sam. She rested her hand over his, a very light measure of caution beneath the table. She didn't want him to get into trouble with his unit, at least not before he heard what she had to say.

"Whitney's pairings so far have seemed to fit. I specu-lated that perhaps that was part of his psychic gift and he clearly has one. Those of you I've tried to study a bit seem very grounded by one another, but none of you have been placed in a position that might cause you to do something you don't want to do."

"What do you mean?" Ryland asked.

"Suppose you had to make a choice between your wife and your son?"

"There would be no question. My wife would expect me to choose my son. He's a child who needs help and guidance and love right now. If she suddenly went crazy and wanted to get rid of him, which is what you seem to be implying, then of course I would protect my child."

Azami didn't try to hide her relief. "Violet Smythe-Freeman didn't."

"She has a child?" Ryland looked around the table at his men. "Are you certain?"

"She aborted the child at Whitney's demand. And she killed Senator Freeman. He was scheduled for the operation. They had taken him to do the surgery at the hospital and Whitney insisted on seeing Violet. They met at a small private airport. He was alone with her for several hours in a hangar. There appeared to be some sort of field surgery set up in the hangar, but my informant only caught a glimpse of the inside. When she emerged, she appeared different, very submissive toward Whitney, yet flirtatious. She boarded her plane and went straight to the hospital and pulled the plug on the senator, and then insisted on an abortion."

Ryland frowned. "You believe he paired her with a second man and she immediately killed the senator and his unborn child? She was completely loyal to Freeman. She betrayed all the women in the compound in order to secure an alliance with Whitney."

"Senator Freeman had no psychic ability. His child would be worthless to Whitney," Azami pointed out. "Violet is well entrenched in the political arena. She's intelligent and personable if a bit cold. The camera loves her and there's talk of her running in the senator's place. A weeping widow who valiantly fought for her brain-dead husband, trying to find a way to save him, would definitely look good in front of a camera. And her voice is enhanced."

"Who was she paired with?" Ryland asked.

Azami shook her head. "My informant doesn't know. Violet was groomed to take a political position in Washington. Whitney wanted her in the White House. The senator was supposed to be the vice president. Violet would have continued to have a great deal of influence. If she is elected to a senatorial position and her loyalty is to Whitney, can you imagine how he could use her to influence his programs?"

Ryland sat up straight, comprehension dawning. "You think Violet Freeman is paired to Whitney himself."

CHAPTER 11

———⌒∿⌒———

There was a small silence while the men seated at the table absorbed the idea. Whitney paired, perhaps married to a U.S. senator. What kind of carte blanche would he have for his experiments? The idea was daunting.

"Who is your informant?"

Sam threaded his fingers through Azami's and held her hand under the table. He wanted to brush his mouth across her knuckles just to show her none of the things she said mattered. He wasn't afraid of anything Whitney might have done to pair them together. He didn't see how the man could have, not when Azami hadn't seen Whitney since she was eight and he had joined the GhostWalker program a few years ago.

"You know I can't give you that information any more than you'd give it to me," Azami told Ryland. "You can choose to believe me or not, but the point is, once Whitney got his hands on Violet again, she ceased to be loyal to Freeman."

Ryland sat back in his chair, assessing Azami for a long time. Sam knew that look. The man respected her, even liked her and was beginning to believe her. "I don't believe

Violet was ever loyal to Freeman. She might have been paired physically with him, but she wants power. She craves it like a drug. Freeman was a means to that power and she obviously controlled him. From all accounts, Violet was different from the other women from your childhood. She wanted status with Whitney and did whatever it took to get it. The more she climbed that ladder, the more power she wanted. Freeman wasn't a man she fell in love with. The power was what she loved. For a while there she believed she could break away from Whitney and get the things she wanted. If he paired her with him, that allegiance is all about what she can get and the status she can achieve. If you're right, Azami, she believes she'll eventually end up in the White House."

Azami's breath left her lungs in a little rush. Sam resisted pulling her into his arms to hold her close to him when he heard that soft sound of relief. Ryland had given her the reassurance that Sam couldn't. The GhostWalkers, paired by Whitney or not, loved one another and still, under even extreme circumstances, would choose to take the honorable path.

"Thank you," Azami said with a graceful head bow toward Ryland. "I do not want to think that if Whitney gets his hands on one of us, he could turn us against each other."

"He may think he can," Ryland said, "but I seriously doubt it."

The tension drained from Azami. Sam was aware that to his teammates she seemed at ease. He was the only one in the room who knew she was anxious. He wasn't in her mind, but he could still feel that slight disturbance of her energy. Her gaze lifted to his face, drifting over the hard edges, taking him in. He was no prize, certainly not the handsomest man in the room, but he knew without a doubt, no one else would understand or be as loyal to her as he would.

Azami pressed her lips together and then switched her gaze back to Ryland. "That's good to know."

"If this information you've given us is true," Ryland said, "Whitney's probably been pumping arms and money into the rebel camp for some time in order to gain control of the diamond mines. Tens of thousands of people have lost their lives and still it isn't enough. Whitney must be determined to gain control, through the rebel forces, of that specific area—that particular diamond mine."

"Can that diamond be so important to him?" Sam murmured aloud. "Back when Jack and Ken Norton went in with a team to rescue a senator, we believed that senator was part of a coalition trying to get rid of the GhostWalkers. Suppose we were right, but the senator double-crossed Whitney? Suppose Whitney and the senator were originally acting together to get a diamond or diamonds Whitney wanted and the negotiations didn't go as planned because the senator had other ideas?"

Azami shrugged. "That's entirely possible. Senator Freeman was being used as Whitney's way into the White House. He paired him with Violet, thinking she would influence Freeman to do Whitney's bidding. I know that Whitney provided money to back Freeman's campaign using several corporations to donate."

"Senator Freeman's father and Whitney went to school together," Sam told her. "He's a powerful man in banking."

Azami nodded. "He communicates with Whitney often. I think the idea, eventually, was to take control of the presidency. They groomed Freeman's son for the position, paired him with Violet, and helped his political career."

"But Violet got greedy," Sam said. "Or maybe it was the senator. They broke with Whitney and aligned themselves with whoever it is in the White House that wants to get rid of the GhostWalkers. He would have to have access to classified information, so someone . . ."

"Like the chief of staff, Bernard Scheffield?" Azami suggested. "He was also in Whitney's class, but was his archenemy."

Ryland swung around to pin her with a stare. "Where the hell do you get this information? I knew they went to college together, but archenemy? I never heard that."

Azami shrugged, looking smug. "They despise one another. Whitney often speaks of him in disparaging terms. He's even gone so far as to say he's working with foreign nationals to bring down the U.S. Whitney believes in a strong military and that every U.S. citizen should be protected, much like the Romans. If harm comes to a U.S. citizen, the retaliation should be swift and brutal."

"Does he want us to go to war with everyone?" Ryland asked.

Azami shrugged again. "Whitney believes that Scheffield is advising the president against building up the military—that he wants to cut funds to the military and always, always chooses a diplomatic path. Whitney was so furious when American tourists were taken prisoner after hiking near the Iranian border that he actually discussed assassinating the chief of staff. Whitney told his private army that everyone knew those taken were just kids. He claimed the Iranian government was using them to try to force the U.S. into giving them what they wanted, all of which was probably true, but it didn't warrant the military intervention that Whitney believed should have been taken immediately."

"How long has this feud been going on?" Sam asked. "Not since they were in school?"

"Apparently Bernard Scheffield comes from money. Big money. He was considered a big deal in school. Not only did he have money and relatives in high places, he was the smartest kid in the school—until Whitney showed up."

"So egos, then. We know Whitney has a massive ego." Sam said.

"You have someone providing you with good intel," Ryland said. "Are you absolutely certain you can trust him? Or her?"

Azami looked at him with cool eyes. If he was fishing, she wasn't biting. "Yes. Absolutely."

"You have no objections to Sam asking permission to marry you?" Ryland asked, suddenly changing the subject.

Sam swore under his breath at that deceptively mild tone. Ryland wasn't finished.

Azami lowered her lashes so that they feathered across her high cheekbones like two fans. "It is the custom in my family and a matter of respect."

"Before you go that far, Sam," Ryland continued, "perhaps Azami might explain how she came to know about second-generation Zenith and how she came to have those patches."

Her heart rate jumped. She didn't so much as blink, but the pad of his finger was over her pulse, and Sam felt that jump.

"I told you, I have an informant. The work was stolen, but I don't know how they got it. I checked your wife's computer myself and then had Daiki recheck it. That computer is clean, but Whitney has her work. He bragged to some of his researchers how smart his daughter is."

"He has Lily's work on Zenith?" Ryland pounced on that. "She only puts research notes on her personal computer. How the hell did Whitney get into her computer without any of us knowing?" He glared at Gator. "I thought Flame put alarms or something on her computer for this very reason."

Gator shrugged. "You'll have to talk to my wife about that, Rye, not me. I don' know a thin' about computers. She talks a foreign language when she gets goin'."

"If Whitney has found a way to get into our computers again . . ." Ryland trailed off.

"We sweep the computers before we install software, and Daiki has written an excellent virus and Trojan protector program we install routinely with the software. I'm telling you, her computer is absolutely clean. He didn't get her work from here," Azami said. "Someone else has her work or you have a traitor here."

Ryland sighed and swept both hands through his hair,

clearly wondering how Whitney had managed to get his hands on Lily's research. As far as he knew, the only other person they'd shared with was their boss, General Ranier.

"So your informant told you about Lily's discovery," Ryland prompted, giving up, for the moment, trying to figure out the modern technology warfare. "How did you get it?"

"I took it from his computer, of course," Azami admitted. "Crossing computer swords with Daiki will get one cut down. Whitney sent us an inquiry about purchasing the satellite and in the email, there was a very clever virus, one that without Daiki's new software program, we probably wouldn't have been able to detect. To Daiki, that was a declaration of war. We replied and were in his computer just like that."

"Does Whitney know?"

"He might eventually, but he won't be able to trace it back to us." She shrugged. "He's got a brilliant mind, that brother of mine, and he can come up with incredible ways to protect our systems that would take years to unravel."

"So what did you do with my wife's research?"

"No one else has seen it. I took the formula from Whitney's computer and ran it through my labs myself. It showed great promise, so when I was certain she believed she had the kinks worked out, I tested it on myself of course."

Sam's breath caught in his throat. The first generation Zenith killed the user unless they were given the antidote within a matter of hours. *You should never have taken such a chance.* It was impossible to remain silent. He allowed his anger to pour into her mind.

Those dark, exotic eyes shifted to his face. Melted. Turned hot. Not with answering anger but with desire. Everything inside him shifted to let her in. She didn't change expression when she looked at him, only there in her eyes, but she didn't need to. He felt her, flowing into his mind, filling him up, wrapping herself tightly around his mind and heart.

He wanted her. Not just that all-consuming urgent lust pounding in his blood, but with something softer and deeper and much more intense than the physical passion making such harsh demands on his body. He could hear his blood thundering in his ears and roaring through his veins, filling his cock so that he pulsed with need, but still, that hot, bright passion flowed with sheer tenderness he hadn't known even existed in him until Azami had come along.

"You tested an unknown drug on yourself, knowing the first generation could kill the user?" Ryland sounded almost as outraged as Sam had been.

"I do not ask others to do what I wouldn't," Azami said. "I studied the first drug's compound as well as your wife's version. I spent months going over the data. Your wife definitely felt she'd made a breakthrough and everything that Whitney had on his computer regarding her work was first class. Her notes are detailed and easy to follow, where his are cryptic and difficult. He encodes everything. The man is paranoid."

"Don't try to lead me off the subject. That was sheer lunacy testing an unknown drug on yourself and you damn well know it."

She leaned toward Ryland. "Fortunately, I don't have anyone else to answer to," she replied mildly, letting him know she wasn't under his command.

"Your brothers didn't object?"

"We don't boss one another. I told them what I was doing and what to do if anything should go wrong. They didn't like it any more than you did, but the second-generation Zenith proved to be a miracle drug when one needs it."

"You own a satellite company; why would you need a drug like Zenith?" Ryland asked. Sam very carefully slid his thumb across her inner wrist in a caress, warning her at the same time. Ryland was no one's dummy. His carefully worded questions were designed to trip her up, casually asked or not.

"We go into dangerous countries and often must protect ourselves. Other governments use different methods to get what they want—and they want my brother's software and the high-resolution satellite with Eiji's lens. Our work is very unpredictable, especially if we decide against selling to a corporation or country who believes they have a right to our equipment."

Sam was astonished at her absolute composure. He knew he shouldn't be; she'd shown nerves of steel during the fight in the forest, and from the moment Ryland had begun interrogating her, she had been poised and collected. She even flashed her serene smile at Ryland, as if he wasn't quite bright and he should have figured out the answer without bothering her with such an obvious question.

"You always act as your brother's bodyguard?" Ryland asked.

"Yes. Eiji insists as well, although, like Daiki, he's far too valuable to the company. I like to think I'm as important as my two partners, but sadly, I don't contribute the way they do. I'm the most expendable."

Sam's fingers tightened around her wrist in protest. Her tone told him she was telling him the absolute truth as she saw it.

"Our company is small, but the people working for us are ours. They depend on us for their livelihood. That means Daiki and Eiji must continue to keep moving us forward. Both are innovative and they have amazing ideas for the future."

Ryland leaned back in his seat and regarded her steadily. "How do you know that your people can be trusted? You believe in them, I can see that, but it would be impossible to ensure that more than a tight circle of people would be loyal."

Azami shook her head. "None of my people would betray us. I would trust them with my life."

"Would you trust them with your brother's lives?"

For the first time she hesitated. "I don't trust anyone with the lives of my brothers," she whispered. "They are all I have."

Sam felt rather than heard that uncertain note in her voice—Thorn's voice. The child who had been so carelessly thrown away by Whitney.

That is no longer the truth. You have me whether or not you have accepted me. I will always come for you, honey. I will be your family. Sam found it strange that things he'd *never* say out loud, he was perfectly fine with sending into her mind. There was an intimacy that transcended embarrassment when sharing the same mind. *I mean what I say, Azami. You will always be able to count on me.*

Sure, it was too fast. He knew Ryland was trying to keep him from falling, tumbling off a high cliff into a deep abyss, but Sam had already willingly stepped off the cliff and he had no desire to go back. She was worth the fall. If, in the end, she couldn't make that commitment to him and she shattered his heart—well, he knew the cost before he'd made the jump.

Azami shook her head. Even that slight movement was graceful, all that silky hair sliding around her like a halo while long strands fell artfully down the back of her slender neck.

Ryland sighed loudly. "This is getting us nowhere. No orders have come down to the effect of our unit—and specifically Sam—heading to the Congo. The general gives me leeway to pick my own team best suited for a mission. I know their specific psychic skills. We no longer document when a skill shows itself. Lily develops exercises to strengthen them and as a team we practice drills, but even the general doesn't have specific knowledge of what we do. It would be extremely unusual for the general to order an individual into the field. Especially . . ." He broke off.

"Sam," Azami finished for him. "I'm aware that the general was responsible for Sam's education."

"He gave me a home just as your father gave you one," Sam clarified.

She pressed her lips together and ducked her head, her mind closing off to him abruptly. Sam glanced at her sharply. There was something wrong, something she wasn't willing to share with him. Azami had been honest with him almost from the beginning.

"Our orders don't work like that," Ryland reaffirmed. "I pick my own team."

"It is easy enough to wait and see just how the orders come in," Azami murmured.

Ryland glanced around the table at his men. "Have any of you heard that Senator Freeman died? Or that his life support was pulled?"

"You'll hear it soon," Azami assured, her voice confident. "They'll put a great spin on it, one sure to gain the grieving widow the most sympathy possible. If Whitney's grooming her for the White House, you can bet he'll use his friends and those who owe him to position her for election. That has to be his plan. He wants that kind of power."

"He wants to continue his experiments in peace," Ryland said. "He doesn't give a damn about the White House."

Kadan suddenly leaned back in his chair, the creaking of the chair drawing Ryland's attention. He had remained quiet, as they all had throughout the interrogation. Kadan rarely spoke, but when he did, everyone—including Ryland—listened. "She's right, Rye; we know he was grooming Senator Freeman for the presidency. He threw money and his friends behind the man and gave up one of his gifted women in order to control the man. He wants the military backing. In a way, it would be good for us, because whoever our enemy in the White House is at present—and remember, Violet had thrown in with them—wants us out. Whitney having a friend there ensures we don't get sent on suicide missions."

Azami stirred, but Sam gently tightened his fingers.

"Whitney has to be stopped," Kadan added. "He's out of control. Any man willing to do the kind of experiments he does on human beings is a butcher. He's lost all contact with reality and humanity. If he pairs up with Violet, we're in real trouble."

"I think it's happened," Azami said. "According to my informant, she went into that hangar cold and distant and came out flirtatious and animated with Whitney. I've studied the woman. She despised Whitney and all he did. She saw Freeman as a way out of the GhostWalkers and she took it and protected her husband as best she could. She tried to move heaven and earth to keep him alive and find a way to bring him back. The last thing she would want to do was to crawl in bed with Whitney again, yet there's no doubt, that's exactly what happened."

"Figuratively," Ryland said. "I don't think he likes females or males."

"But he'd sleep with Violet if that cemented the relationship and gave him power over her," Kadan pointed out. "Rye, as much as I hate to admit it, I think Azami is right about this. It's what Whitney would do."

Ryland rubbed the bridge of his nose. "Seriously, we had enough problems when Violet and Whitney were opposed to one another. If they get together, we're in for a rough ride."

"And what about the men who shot me?" Sam wanted to know. "Did Whitney send them after all?"

Kadan sighed. "That gets a little complicated, Sam. I don't believe they were after you. I think, again, Azami was correct when she said they were after her brothers." He drummed his fingers on the table. "The Iranian soldiers came in via Mexico. The word we got was they were led into the United States through the drug tunnels the cartel has. These tunnels are elaborate and even heated in places. The mercenaries acquired the helicopters and Jeeps. The soldiers were taken to small planes and we tracked them to a small private airport."

"The cartel was used before," Azami said, "in an assassination plot against the Saudi ambassador to the U.S. Is there some faction in Iran working with the cartel and now they're making a grab for Daiki and Eiji?"

"I doubt if it's some faction," Kadan said. "But anything's possible. At least we know how they got in to the country and how they got out again."

"It isn't the first time the cartel has been in bed with Iran," Ryland said. "There are rumors that they're training the cartel's hit squads in terrorist tactics, but so far we don't have anything concrete on that."

Azami smiled. "A high-resolution satellite would change that for you. I've got pictures of camps."

Ryland leaned toward her. "Have you shared that information with anyone?"

"Who would I share it with? I have a mission, and that's to try to cut Whitney off from those who enable him in his brutal experiments."

"How do you plan to go about doing that?" Ryland asked, his tone almost gentle.

Again, Sam tightened his fingers around Azami's in warning, although he shouldn't have worried. She shrugged her slender shoulders. "There is no clear path," she said, her statement as much of an enigma as she appeared to be. "But I will find one."

Kadan burst out laughing. "You're not going to get anything out of that woman, Rye, so short of torturing her, you may as well throw in the towel. She beat you at your own game."

Azami continued to look innocent as if she had no idea why all the men were smirking.

"If we're finished here," Sam said. "I have to go talk to Azami's brothers."

"Tonight?" Ryland asked. "Sam, you need rest."

"That's all I've been doing lately and I'm asking before she changes her mind."

Ryland looked straight into Azami's eyes. "Do you plan on changing your mind?"

"That is to be seen, isn't it?" she said softly. "If we're done here, I must return to my room and rest for a little while."

"Will your brothers be awake?" Sam asked.

She smiled her mysterious smile. "Of course, they would not sleep while I am being asked questions by Captain Miller. They are as protective of me as I am them."

Sam's head came up. *They've been listening this entire time?*

Do you think they would leave me unprotected? Had your captain deemed me dangerous and attempted to arrest me, we would have fought our way to freedom, or died trying. Her eyes met his. *Be very certain I am the kind of woman you wish to spend your life with.*

Sam looked into those dark, liquid eyes. She possessed a kind of magic no other woman held for him. *You're exactly the kind of woman I want. Don't think you're getting out of this by trying to warn me off.*

Her mouth turned up at the corners, a soft smile meant only for him, and then she very gracefully rose from the table, gave a slight bow to Ryland and the others, and slipped from the war room without a whisper of movement.

"Holy cow, Sam." Gator fanned himself. "You're goin' to be in more trouble than I am if you marry that girl."

"Do you have any idea what you're getting yourself into?" Ryland demanded. "She gives nothing away. She doesn't show emotion at all. How can you know she feels the same way about you? Feels anything at all for you? Because I didn't see it."

"Public displays of affection are against her nature," Sam said. "Believe me, she feels."

"What's not to like, Rye?" Kyle demanded. "She's beautiful, exotic, and wealthy."

"How's it going to work, Knight?" Ryland asked Sam, ignoring Kyle. "She owns a company in Japan. Her family is there. You're a soldier, sworn to protect your country. You're a GhostWalker, and you damn well belong here—with us. Do you really think she'll be happy living up in the mountains? It snows here and we can barely make it out. We have money to make life a little easier, yes, but she's used to a different way of life altogether."

"Is she?" Sam asked. He pushed himself to his feet, wanting to end the discussion. He'd already considered everything Ryland was telling him and he didn't want to go over it again. What did a soldier have to give a woman like Azami? Why had she even looked at him twice?

"I'm not finished. Do me the courtesy of listening, since you can't obey a damn order," Ryland snapped.

Sam tightened his jaw, but dropped back into his chair. He'd been lucky that Ryland had backed off from the order. He rubbed his jaw, regarding his friend carefully. "I'm in love with her, Rye. I know all the objections. Do you think I haven't thought of all of them myself? Yes, it happened too fast. I've been in her mind. I know what she's like . . ."

"You know what she wants you to know. All of us have the ability to open up or close off and without a doubt, she's that good." Ryland sighed and got up to pace across the floor, picked up a mug, and poured hot coffee into it. "You and I both know she took Whitney's pipeline out. She assassinated three people."

Sam shrugged, careful now, on shifting, dangerous ground. "Maybe. I've assassinated a hell of a lot more than that. I don't exactly have room to throw stones. None of us do."

He studied Ryland's face. They were more than friends. They'd gone to battle together and watched each other's back. They had complete trust in each other. Ryland was concerned for him, that much was obvious, and Sam couldn't blame him. It wasn't that Ryland didn't want to see him happy; hell, he hadn't known he was unhappy. He'd been just fine until Azami had come along. No wonder Rye thought he was crazy.

Sam looked around the table at his silent companions. Normally they were all heckling one another and playing juvenile pranks on each other. They were all just as concerned as Ryland. He didn't know what to say to reassure them. There wasn't a single part of him that had a doubt that Azami was the woman for him—yet what could he give her? He couldn't argue with Ryland, not because he wasn't certain of his choice, but he wasn't certain how he could be her choice.

"You aren't going to be reasonable about this, are you?" Ryland asked.

"No. I made up my mind. I'm asking her brothers for permission. I don't want to wait. I want her with me. She knows I'm a soldier and that I belong here. I know I can help her in her work just as she'll be an asset in mine."

Ryland's frown deepened. "She isn't part of this team."

"Not any more than the other women, Rye, but she's a GhostWalker and she belongs with us. She fits with me."

"Are we going to talk about what she said? About the orders coming down to us?"

Again Sam shrugged. "It won't be the first or last time one of us has been targeted. If she's right, we'll handle it."

"Sam . . ." Ryland started to say something and abruptly cut himself short.

"Say it." Anger welled up. He looked around the room. "I know exactly what you're thinking. I knew it the moment Azami mentioned those orders and you made such a big deal out of telling her you pick your own team. This isn't the first time anyone's implicated the general in wrongdoing. Yes, he was Colonel Higgens's friend. He knew Whitney. He knows a lot of people. He wouldn't sell me down the river because a madman asked him to. Even if he specifically names me to go, Rye, that doesn't mean the orders come from him."

"I'm not saying you should suspect the general of being in league with Whitney," Ryland hedged. "It just makes good sense to watch your back. People aren't always what they seem, Sam. The people we can trust are the ones in this room, not out there." He pointed out the window. "And just for good measure, the general is the one person we shared Lily's work on second-generation Zenith with."

Sam pushed down anger. "The general has been a father to me. I joined the service to be like him. Don't stand there and tell me you're not suspicious of him, because you've been suspicious from the day everything went to hell. You're a paranoid son of a bitch, Rye. And now you're suspicious of Azami. You think everything's a conspiracy and everyone is involved."

Ryland's eyebrow shot up. "Aren't they? Isn't everything a conspiracy?"

Sam didn't smile as he knew Ryland wanted him to. General Ranier had fallen under suspicion several times and each time he'd come back clean, yet his unit didn't altogether trust him. Sam loved the general. He'd given up a lucrative job in the civilian world to follow the general into the service. He loved and respected the general more than anyone else in the world.

Sam ducked his head. That wasn't entirely the truth. Ryland had come to take that place, and somehow, the general had slipped down a few notches, which was why Sam was so belligerent and defensive when the subject was brought up. He felt guilty. Plain and simple he felt guilty because more than once, he'd had the hairs on the back of his neck stand up around the general and he hadn't said a word to anyone else. He was guilty either way. Not telling his team his strange feelings, and not believing in the man who had taken him off the streets.

What had made him worry? Sam shook his head to clear it. Little things. Shadows. Whispers. The general had always had a schedule, a fixed routine, and he stuck to it. The last year, there had been phone calls, meetings at odd hours. Ranier was responsible for national security, so a clandestine meeting shouldn't have raised an alarm, but Sam had sensed something different in the general and twice, when he'd asked, Ranier had avoided meeting his eyes. That was *entirely* wrong.

"What is it, Sam?" Ryland asked.

Sam detested the quiet sympathy in Rye's tone, as if he'd already tried and condemned the general. "Nothing," Sam said. "Nothing at all."

"She is beautiful," Ryland finally admitted.

"She's a hell of a fighter," Sam said with a small smile, willing to allow the subject to be changed. "She'll be a big help working with Daniel, Rye. She learned to teleport at an earlier age than I did. She made more mistakes and is probably more aware of the dangers to a child."

Ryland nodded, not quite assenting. Sam knew it would take a lot for both Ryland and Lily to trust an outsider with their child. Right now, he didn't want to stop and reassure Ryland. His heart was pounding and his mouth was dry. He was going to put his neck under the blade of a samurai sword tonight.

He pushed himself up again and held on to the table until his protesting wound stopped the persistent throbbing. He wouldn't have minded a glass of whiskey right now, but he wasn't backing out. If asking her brothers permission to marry her was what it took to get into their family, he was all for it. He started out of the room and then hesitated, turning back. He couldn't just leave them all exposed.

"When we teleport, we need to know exactly where we're projecting our body to. We can't just arrive in the middle of the room where a table might be. We have to have eyes at least and sometimes ears. I use cameras. Very small cameras when I'm going to teleport in a crowded area. I study the terrain ahead of time. And in case you've forgotten, I always have backup. Azami as good as told you she did as well."

Comprehension dawned immediately. Ryland swore under his breath. "The room is bugged."

"She had to have had eyes in here," Sam said. "And if you were her brother and she was about to sit on a hot seat, what would you do?"

"Find the bugs," Ryland said, sounding tired. "I hope to hell you're right about that woman, Sam. Gator, go wake up that woman of yours. I need some answers. We need her to run the computers for us."

"Tonight, Boss?" Gator complained. "I had other ideas." He wiggled his eyebrows suggestively.

"We all did. Hop to it."

"What about Sam?" Tucker asked. "His woman is the one who got us into this."

"I'm wounded." Sam clutched his abdomen dramatically and staggered with quick, long strides so that he made it to the doorway in three quick steps.

Jonas coughed, sounding suspiciously like he'd muttered "bullshit" under his breath. Kyle threw a peanut at him and Jeff surfed across the table in his bare socks to try to catch him before he bolted.

"He's in *love*, boys, let him go. He'll probably just get laughed at," Tucker said. "Do you really think Azami's brothers are going to allow her to hook up with Sam? She's fine and he's . . . well . . . *klutzy.*"

"That hurt," Sam said, turning back.

"Did you get a good look at those boys? I thought Japanese men were supposed to be on the short side, but Daiki was tall and all muscle. His brother moves like a fucking fighter," Tucker added. "They might just decide to give you a good beating for having the audacity to even *think* you could date their sister, let alone marry her."

"Fat help you are," Sam accused. "I could use a little confidence here."

Kyle snorted. "You don't have a chance, buddy."

"Goin' to meet your maker," Gator added solemnly.

Jeff crossed himself as he hung five toes off the edge of the table. "Sorry, old son, you don't have a prayer. You're about to meet up with a couple of hungry sharks."

"Have you ever actually used a sword before?" Kadan asked, all innocent.

Jonas drew his knife and began to sharpen it. "Funny thing about blade men, they always like to go for the throat." He grinned up at Sam. "Just a little tip. Keep your chin down."

"You're all a big help," Sam said and stepped out into the hall.

This was the biggest moment of his life. If they turned him down, he was lost. Azami wouldn't go against her brothers. She might go her own way in battle, but she would never defy her family over something so important as a spouse. He wished he'd asked her a few more questions about the customs. He had no idea what would be an insult and what wouldn't.

Sam moved through the house to the second wing. Lily and Ryland's home contained all the offices and a maze of halls that led to Lily's laboratories. The guest wing adjoined the meeting rooms, giving guests and the resident family plenty of privacy. Each of the members of Team One had their own home, built in the forest but protected by the main compound. The training center was on the other side of the laboratories, a large complex where the team could practice on a daily basis. There was a large indoor pool to work out in as well as an armory, although each home contained a separate armory.

The small hospital was connected to the laboratories. Sam was grateful that Lily had chosen to have him in her small guest bedroom sometimes used as an infirmary for a team member recovering from a wound that didn't need around the clock care. Sam disliked hospitals on principle. Staying in Lily's house was always warm and friendly. All the men stopped by and visited and even baby Daniel came to see him.

He stopped in front of the largest guest room. It had a large sitting room and private bathroom for important business guests such as Daiki and Eiji Yoshiie. There was no sound, but he knew they were in there waiting for him. They had bugged the war room in order to better protect their sister. He had no doubt that in spite of the fact that they weren't psychic, both men were skillful warriors.

He couldn't believe that his hands were clammy and his heart pounding. He'd gone into full-scale battle with less apprehension. Both men spoke excellent English, so there was no language barrier, and if truth be told, he spoke fluent Japanese. Standing in front of the door, he took a moment to inspect his clothing. He was barefoot, wore jeans and a carelessly buttoned shirt that had a few bloodstains clinging to it. Damn. He should have changed.

What the *hell* was he doing? He should have carried her off like a caveman. He could persuade her to marry him. Wine. Sex. Candlelight. Yeah, he could manage that. But asking stone-face swordsmen for permission? They were probably laughing at his predicament. He would be if Azami was his sister.

Sam took a breath and knocked on the door before he talked himself out of it—a polite knock when he wanted to pound until the door broke down and he just demanded they hand her over to him. He wasn't going away without her. If she thought about it too long, she'd change her mind. What sane woman wouldn't?

The door swung open slowly and Eiji's broad frame filled the doorway. He stared at Sam without expression, his dark eyes thoughtful. "May I help you?"

If the man was a team member, Sam would have told him to can the crap; after all, they knew *exactly* why he'd come. He gave a slight bow instead and tried a tentative smile.

"Please excuse my attire; I had no other clothes with me." He nearly groaned. That had been a little reminder that he'd gone into battle, but maybe not such a good idea. He'd been wounded. They might think he wasn't a good enough soldier to protect their sister. "The matter is urgent or I wouldn't have disturbed you so late. I wish to speak to you and your brother."

Eiji studied him a moment longer and then stepped back, his robes flowing around him as he did, using that same fluid motion Sam recognized in Azami. The apartment was lit with candles rather than the harsher lights overhead. A Go game was laid out between two chairs on the smaller coffee table, and clearly they'd been playing. He couldn't help but notice that a long samurai sword lay inches from Daiki's fingertips, enclosed in the ornate scabbard.

Daiki rose and gave that studied, perfect bow that made the two men seem as if they were traditional warriors of old.

"I had hoped that your wounds were not so bad," he greeted. "Thank you for looking after Azami."

Sam breathed a sigh of relief and allowed himself a smile. "I think it was mutual."

Daiki waved him toward a chair. Sam nearly groaned. Not another chair. He could get in and out of one, but he looked like an old man doing it. He took a deep breath and took the plunge.

"I don't know how this is done in your family, so I'm just going to get right to the point. I would like your permission to marry Azami. I know I'm not much to look at and I'm in a high-risk job, but we're . . . we . . . *fit*. I'll make her happy. I know I will."

"Her happiness is not of paramount importance," Daiki said. "Her safety is our first priority. Azami would throw herself in front of a bullet for the ones she loves."

Sam heard the dark warning in Azami's brother's voice. Daiki Yoshiie was definitely a man of confidence. He talked with great intelligence, his voice cultured and smooth, yet he moved like the whisper of the wind. The man would hold his own in any fight—if you ever saw him. Their father had trained them in the way of the samurai and it had become their way of life. They chose to put the principles into business, but nevertheless, they could use them just as easily if needed to defend themselves.

"As would I," Sam said. He didn't know what else to say. Daiki told him the truth about Azami and Sam knew it was true. There would be no stopping what he knew was central to her character any more than they could stop the need to protect those he loved in him. He was certain that simple statement was a test to see his reaction. Azami was Azami and there was no changing her, nor would he want to do so.

"She is her own woman. I will protect her with my life and love and value her for all my days." He felt silly saying the truth aloud to strangers even if the men were Azami's brothers.

Daiki studied his face for a long time before he stepped

forward and opened his palm. "This ring was made by our father for the man who would see beyond the past and bring her happiness. You are her choice."

The ring was small, delicate like Azami, but intricate, just as her personality was. The blossom of a thistle nestled in the middle, surrounded by thorns. Along the band was etched a detailed samurai sword. The work had been done by a master craftsman. Sam stared down at that tiny symbol of a man's commitment to a woman and knew that the artist had been equally gifted and detailed when it came to making weapons.

"I would have liked to have met your father," he murmured.

Daiki bowed as he placed the ring in Sam's hand. "He would have liked to have met you."

Sam closed his fingers around the ring, a strange soaring sensation in his heart.

"My father found my brother and me in the street just as he did Azami. Several nights a week would we walk on those streets with him. When he found her, she was surrounded by those who would have used her for the child sex trade. They knew him and knew he would have fought to the death for her. He saw her bravery, right there in that horrible alley, the light in her eyes, the courage she possessed. She has a spirit no monster could slay. That's what my father saw in her, and he knew a man would come along who would see that same spirit. I'm glad it is you."

Sam bowed slightly. "Where is she?" He could barely get the words out. He needed to see her. Right then. Right now. He had expected her to be there, but he knew little of the traditions of her family.

"I believe she has gone to your home to welcome you," Daiki answered.

Sam's stomach did a slow somersault while his heart lifted.

CHAPTER 12

Sam had chosen a spot in the forest of trees near a running stream with water tumbling over a series of small boulders to build his home. His porch overlooked the stream, with his bedroom situated so he could open his windows and listen to the water as it made its way down the tumbling rocks to the cool pond below. Lacy ferns scattered along the narrow bank grew in every shade of green. Homemade paper lanterns floated down the stream, glowing softly, lighting the water so that it sparkled like jewels in the night and illuminated the delicate night fronds.

"Magic," he murmured aloud. "Azami magic."

She was welcoming him home in her own way. If his heart hadn't been soaring before, it was now. He paused to watch the lanterns floating gracefully down the small series of falls toward the swirling pool of water several yards away. In the darkness of the forest, the warm radiance lent the water a luminosity that added to the magical illusion of the world around him shifting and changing. The rest of the world dropped away until there was only this moment, this place—and Azami waiting for him.

His childhood had been one of drugs and apathy, his mother, unable and unwilling to give up her habits to look after him. He'd been hungry most of the time, dodging blows from whatever men she brought home and walking through needles and filth barefoot as she rarely bothered to find him a pair of shoes. Later, when he was a bit older, he fended for himself, learning to steal food, all the while trying to get an education. He stole textbooks from thrift stores, desperate to feed a mind always seeking more knowledge. Fate had intervened in the form of General Ranier when he'd boosted Ranier's car. The general, instead of having him arrested, took him home.

Ranier and his wife had been good to Sam, much more than he deserved, paying for his education, sending him to boarding schools and giving him money to buy decent clothes. But, and he felt a little guilty—okay, a *lot* guilty that he'd never felt at home there. The old man wanted to be addressed as sir. He was gone all over the world, busy with his career, too busy to be home for holidays. His wife often accompanied him and when she wasn't, her charitable organizations kept her too busy to see him often. They were good to him, and he loved them for it, but their house had never been his home.

He'd built his house with loving hands. He knew he wanted to stay here in this wilderness, surrounded by men he trusted and had come to let into his world, but each time he came back from a mission, the house was empty and cold. No matter what he did to it, there was no life in it. Azami had already made just approaching the house seem more of a coming home than he'd ever had.

He took his time walking up the stone path to his door. Insects rustled leaves. An owl fluttered its wings while it watched for a meal. Frogs took up a chorus of love songs, each trying to outdo the other. This was his world with Azami, closed to everyone else. She was his and only his. No one else knew the woman behind that perfect mask of serenity. No one felt her passion and fire smoldering beneath the surface. They had no idea of this . . . He turned to look at the sheer magic she'd created there in the forest for him. Forever wasn't long enough to spend with a woman like her.

Still, he stayed outside the door, holding his breath, half afraid his miracle wasn't reality. The paper lanterns floating down the stream and bobbing up and down in the pond created a beauty he'd never had in his life—and had never expected to have. There wasn't a doubt in his mind that Azami had been created for him—sent to him—and yet he was half afraid that if he actually opened the door to his home, he would be alone and he'd discover everything was an illusion. He'd been wounded; perhaps he was dreaming the entire thing up.

"You don't have that vivid an imagination, knucklehead," he whispered and dropped his hand to the doorknob. He couldn't have conjured up the images in the forest, let alone a woman like Azami. He turned the knob and pushed open the door.

He smelled exotic flowers the moment he crossed the threshold. The room was warm and bathed in soft candlelight. He hardly recognized his front room, yet it was the same. She came to him with a whisper of silk, to stand directly in front of him. Her hands went to his shirt and he bent his head, allowing her to slip it off. She folded the material unhurriedly and set it aside. Her hands dropped to the zipper of his jeans. There was possession in her touch, and a deference he hadn't expected.

He said nothing, aware of everything about her as she pushed his jeans down the columns of his thighs. He stepped free of them. She folded the jeans just as carefully. When he was completely naked, she picked up a man's silk robe obviously brand-new, probably intended for her brother judging by the size of it. She held the robe open for him to slip his arms into. Her eyes were very dark, twin black pools of hot liquid, her long lashes veiling much of her expression, but for the first time, there was some shyness in her gaze.

She took his hand, her fingers tugging at his wrist. "Come with me."

He followed her silently through his home to the bathroom. Again, candles were her choice of light. The softer glow threw dancing shadows on the wall. He had designed the bathroom to be a very large, tiled shower, with a showerhead above and a handheld nozzle. His tub was large and deep. He was a big man and enjoyed soaking in his tub and looking out the large window into the deep forest.

Steam filled the bathroom, evidence of a very hot bath being drawn, and the room smelled of cherry blossoms and spice. She had set a small wooden stool in the middle of the open shower for him to sit on. He allowed her to tug off the silken robe and lead him to the stool. Azami removed her own robe, folded both, and set them out of harm's way.

His breath caught in his throat as she moved to his side. Her body was small and delicate, but extremely firm, muscles sliding beneath that delicate frame. Her hair was up in that strangely elegant style, thick, with her dark bangs falling, drawing attention to her eyes. Long strands of hair fell from the upswept do past her shoulders, hinting at a dark silky waterfall when he pulled those long ornate pins from her hair.

"The bath is more than cleaning your body, Sammy," she explained.

Her voice, so soft and expressive, sent a shiver of awareness down his spine. Heat coiled around his heart and snaked into his belly. Just her voice affected him, so gentle, a whisper of sound that he felt all the way to his bones. No one had ever called him Sammy before, and he would have punched them if they had, but with her caressing voice, the name suited him just fine. Were other men so enamored of their woman? She'd crept into his mind and buried herself there, so deep there was no getting her out.

"You must also cleanse your spirit. At the end of a day, body, mind, and spirit must all come together. It is necessary for harmony, especially in the life of a warrior. I would show you my way, if you wish."

Her lashes lifted and he found himself staring into those

dark pools of midnight velvet. The impact was like a hard punch, low and wicked. No one should have those eyes. She didn't need much else to bring him to his knees.

He reached down to frame her upturned face with his hands. "I can't imagine denying you anything, let alone something so obviously important to you."

He couldn't stop himself from leaning down and brushing her mouth gently with his. His heart fluttered, and as naked as he was, his body responded, his erection fierce and urgent. Her gaze dropped to the evidence of his desire for her and a whisper of a smile curved her mouth as she waved him to the stool.

Sam sank onto the little wooden stool, allowing her whatever she wanted. Azami reached for the handheld nozzle and what appeared to be some kind of sea sponge. Her body brushed against his shoulder. So close to her, he could see the fine lines of the spiderweb tattoo valiantly trying to hide the scars crisscrossing her body. Her small breasts tempted him, two handfuls of soft, firm flesh. He couldn't stop from touching that small spider residing so cleverly just south of her nipple in that small crater created by the hack job Whitney had done on her body.

Still, he remained unmoving as she circled around behind him, cascading hot water over his shoulders and back with the sprayer. Somehow she'd managed to get the exact temperature to find and remove every knot from his muscles. The heat felt amazing, but it was her hands, soaping him so gently, fingers kneading into his skin, that sent him to a different place. The aroma wafting up to surround him was exotic and smelled fresh, yet very soothing. The hot water, scented soap, and her hands sent him to a place of magic. *Azami magic.*

Sam closed his eyes and savored the feeling of a woman—*his* woman caring for him. She built up a feeling in him of total contentment, humming softly as she became totally immersed in the task of washing him thoroughly. The sponge slid over his skin, massaging lovingly. She urged him to lift his arms above his head. He felt the brush of her breasts as she reached to soap and scrub his arms and armpits, sliding over his muscles to reach even his fingers and hands, massaging thoroughly until his body felt nearly boneless.

The feeling was both erotic and yet gave such a sense of well-being, of being taken care of. In a very short time, Azami had created a home and brought love and warmth into it, and he knew that no matter what happened, he would never forget this night.

Her hands, tugging on his hips, urged him to slide back on the stool, giving her better access to wash his buttocks. She was very thorough about that as well and the sensation was unlike anything he'd ever known.

When she came around to the front of him, he caught her hands. "You don't have to do this. I don't expect you . . ."

Azami lifted her long lashes so those dark eyes regarded him soberly. "I *wish* to do this for you. You did not ask it of me. The ritual gives me great joy. I hope that you come to love it, Sammy, because caring for you gives me great happiness."

How could any man not love being treated with such tenderness? He watched her face as she soaped his chest and scrubbed with the sponge, taking great care to remove all traces of antiseptic. Her face held that same serenity he was used to, but now emotion shone through—tenderness, rapt attention and concern. There was no denying she enjoyed taking care of him. She appeared nearly spellbound as she urged him to stand. With one foot she moved the stool and proceeded to soap his hips.

Still, he knew this ritual, for Azami, was much more. She was giving herself to him, declaring herself, in her own way, to be his. That *he* was her choice. However she treated him in public, without expression, no hand holding, no kissing, there would be *this* behind closed doors. To the rest of the world, she was samurai, to Sam, she was love.

Sam closed his eyes as her soapy hands slid over his bare

abdomen, careful of his glued, healing wound. He sent a silent thanks to Lily for her second-generation Zenith that allowed his body to heal with such speed. Azami traced his defined muscles with soapy fingers and gave him that same thorough attentiveness she'd displayed when washing his back and chest. She never rushed, although he knew she was as aroused as he was. She luxuriated in the pleasure of caring for him, allowing the passion between them to build slowly into a roaring fire, yet she continued at that same unhurried pace to give him a priceless gift.

Her hands slipped lower to cup his balls. His cock jerked hard, so swollen he felt he might burst. He waited, his breath caught in his lungs until her hands slipped up and over him, her fist tight as she washed him thoroughly. When he could find his breath, he looked down at the top of her bent head. The candlelight swirled through all that black silky hair and before he could stop himself, he leaned down to press a kiss in the exact middle of her upswept do. The action had his cock shifting in her hands. Instinctively she tightened her hold, her lashes lifting so that he found himself looking into her eyes again.

He pushed his hips forward, savoring the exquisite feeling her tight fist produced, feeling on the edge of paradise. She smiled and moved the sea sponge under his balls and down the column of his thigh. He let out his breath.

"Am I going to get a turn?"

"If you wish it," she replied without looking up. "Otherwise you can soak in the tub while I wash myself."

No way was he going to deny himself the pleasure of knowing her as intimately as she knew him. She had paid particular attention to his every reaction to her touch. She knew his body very well and he intended to have that same knowledge of her.

"I wish it very much," he replied and caught the back of her neck, waiting until she looked up at him again. "Kiss me right now, Azami." The command came out more of a growl than actual words. He had never been so aroused and yet so content at the same time. He hadn't even known it was possible to feel both sensations.

She didn't hesitate, lifting her face so his mouth could come down on hers. He kissed her with the same thoroughness she'd shown washing him. He wanted to kiss her forever, to gather her close, but her small hand pressed delicately against his chest.

"I am almost finished, Sam," she whispered.

He straightened, waiting to see what she would do. She sank gracefully to her knees in front of him on the tiled floor and his heart nearly stopped and then began to pound. His cock was a fierce ache, hot blood pounding so hard he could count the beats along the prominent vein. She ignored the urgent demand and soaped and washed his legs with that same unhurried movement. The silk of her hair brushed the sensitive head of his cock, sending ripples of pleasure surging through him.

When she tapped his calf, he put a gentle hand on her shoulder to steady himself and lifted his foot up so she could wash the sole. She looked so beautiful, there at his feet, steam rising around them, so engrossed in her self-appointed task.

"A man could get used to this very fast, Azami," he said.

He was not a man who'd known care—not even as a child. Neither had she. Maybe that was why it was so important to her. And he could see that it was. She moved around behind him. Any other woman might have appeared subservient in the same position, but not Azami. She just looked beautiful and exotic and a miracle to him.

"I hope you enjoy this ritual, Sammy," she said, again with that slight shy note in her voice. "This is one I wish to perform nightly."

Nightly? She planned to wash him every night? "Like this?" He might have died in that battle and somehow made his way to heaven. He looked over his shoulder at her. She was working diligently down the column of his thighs.

Her head lifted to look up at him, those lashes covering

her expression for just one moment, and then he was looking into her eyes. "*Exactly* like this. In your home, you must be cared for, Sam. It is important to me."

"Baby, you know that I'll need to take just as good care of you," he said gently, warning her that their relationship wasn't going to be one-sided. He planned to lavish attention on her and she needed to be willing to accept what he had to give. "That's important to me."

She smiled at him, that soft, mysterious smile that had his body as hard as a rock. Wordlessly, he held out his hand for the soap and sponge. She placed both carefully in his hand and turned her back to stand in front of him. Sam closed his eyes again, just to savor the moment. She was so small and delicate, a deceptive package of soft skin, silky hair, and absolute steel. He didn't urge her to sit on the stool. She was quite a bit shorter than he was; instead, he stood behind and checked the temperature of the water before he allowed it to cascade down her back and over her shoulders.

He washed her with that same slow, unhurried attention she'd given him, realizing why she had enjoyed the ritual so much. The connection he felt toward her deepened with every stroke of the sponge over her skin. He grew to know the contours of her back, the sweeping curve of her buttocks, and the details of her phoenix rising from the ashes. He scrubbed at the delicate feathers that made up the long curving tail. He took care with her slender neck, massaging the muscle of her shoulders as he washed her, just as she had done for him.

She sighed softly and when he reached his arms around in front of her, she obediently leaned against his chest. He made certain the water didn't spray her in the face as he let the water spray over her breasts. He took his time soaping her breasts, lifting each one carefully to thoroughly soap underneath before rinsing her off. Her nipples fit perfectly into the center of his palms. He couldn't resist leaning down and biting her neck gently, while he cupped her breasts and teased those taut nipples into hard peaks. He felt her breath leave her body, her breasts rise and fall with the same heated need coursing through her veins.

He understood the slow, sensual dance now, the worshiping of each other's body, that slow tender care that showed the other that not only were they desired, but they were loved, appreciated, and thoroughly cared for. He *wanted* to serve her in just the way she'd served him. He'd always known he'd never be happy with anything less than a full partnership from a woman. He was intelligent and he was a warrior. Who would have thought he would find the perfect woman? How had he come to be so lucky?

His hands followed the gossamer lines of her spiderweb. He could feel the ridges of the scars beneath his fingertips. He turned his head so that his mouth was against her ear. "I'm going to take my time eating you like candy."

Her breath hitched again as his fingers danced over the spider and rolled her nipples, tugging and teasing as he briefly indulged himself in the body she'd so generously offered him. Reluctantly he left her enticing breasts to slip his hands over her flat belly. She had a washboard stomach beneath her soft woman's skin. He soaped the tiny little curls guarding her treasures before he urged her thighs apart.

His hands were big and her thighs small. A surge of male pride shook him. She had given herself to him, put herself into his hands and willingly cast her fate with his. She was an extraordinary woman and yet she had chosen to trust her heart, mind, and body to him. His hand cupped the vee between her legs, a deliberate sensual touch, a brand of ownership in his own way. He didn't dare linger too long. Small pearly drops beaded the head of his cock, and with every breath he drew, he wanted her more.

She was definitely as aroused as he was, her breasts rising and falling and her inner thighs slick with her welcoming cream. He soaped her slender legs carefully, memorizing the shape and feel of her. He wasn't surprised that under all that soft, glorious skin were muscles of steel. Yeah, that was his woman, beautiful, sensual, and as lethal as hell.

He took his time just as she had done, careful with her small feet, noting every single scar on her body and inwardly cursing Dr. Whitney for treating her like a lab rat. She'd been less than human to him, and yet, to Sam, she was everything. He turned off the shower and carefully set aside the sponge and wand.

"Now we must cleanse our spirits, Sammy," she said softly, again almost shyly. She took his hand and tugged him toward the steaming water in the deep, two-person tub.

He had bought the large bathtub to accommodate his size, but now he was very grateful it would hold both of them. She climbed in, giving him an excellent view of the perfection of her butt. He didn't try to stop himself from cupping her buttocks, his thumb sliding possessively over one smooth cheek. She didn't protest, but instead, smiled at him over her shoulder as she stepped into the very hot water and scooted to the far side to give him room. She drew up her knees and waited, her dark gaze on his body.

Sam settled into the hot water with a soft sigh. His body instantly surrendered to the heat, steam, and soothing aroma. He stretched out his legs and rested his head against the high end of the back, allowing peace and tranquillity to settle over him. He lay quietly, her legs over his, small feet resting on his thighs. He watched her through narrowed eyes. She allowed her head to loll back as well, her eyes closed, peace surrounding her.

"Open your mind to mine," he ordered softly.

Her lashes fluttered, but she didn't open her eyes, merely complied, pouring into him to fill him up with sweet serenity. They drifted together in a slow tangle of heat, sensuality, and tranquillity. The sensation sent him to a place he'd never been, melded together with her, entwined in spirit rather than in body. The water lapped softly at his skin and he felt every knot unravel until he was boneless. Neither spoke;

they didn't need to, not with their minds so tightly welded together in peaceful oblivion.

Her mind moved in his and he opened his eyes to find her looking at him with slumberous, sexy eyes.

He smiled at her. "Is there more to this ritual of yours? I think this will be my favorite part of the day." There was more, he could see it in her eyes. He didn't think, he knew. She had given him the best evening of his life and he hadn't even made love to her yet.

She nodded her head in the unhurried way she had and drew up her knees to allow him out of the tub. She'd left two large bath towels lying folded neatly on the shelves beside the tub. He climbed out first, caught up a towel and then swung back to her, his gaze hot as he rubbed the towel over his wet skin.

"If I forget to tell you later, thank you for this night. You've made me feel as if I truly have a home." He wrapped the towel low on his hips.

She looked around the spacious bathroom and then back to him. "I feel as if this is my home," she admitted. "The moment I entered, I felt safe and secure. I felt as if I belonged. I'm glad you enjoy the things that are important to me. I wish to make my rituals yours and yours mine."

How could pleasing her not be important to him? He crooked his finger at her and she rose gracefully from the water, a beautiful mythical phoenix rising from the ashes of her past to embrace the future. She walked to him unafraid, unashamed of the small, fractured body tattooed to cover the scars. When she moved, the tattoos moved with her, rippling as if alive. Those fine gossamer threads shimmered in the soft candlelight, playing across her skin and accenting her small waist and small breasts. That little spider moved, as if challenging him to catch it.

When she stood in front of him, he wrapped a thick towel around her body and dried her body gently. "Show me the next step, Azami," he encouraged, nuzzling her slender neck.

She took his hand and tugged him toward the bedroom. His heart tripped a little. He loved her confidence, the way her body moved sensuously beneath the towel, and he couldn't wait to take those pins from her hair and let it fall around her face. She looked all woman, yet she walked without a whisper of movement, placing her foot automatically and lightly on the floor. He could tell it was a reflex with her to test her footing and memorize floor plans. He would bet his life that she could describe in detail everything in his house and exactly where it was placed. How many men had a woman like that?

She turned to look at him over her shoulder, a small smile on her face. "No one but you wants a woman like me, Sam. Most men don't like that a woman is dangerous."

"You'd be surprised," he countered, "although let's not try finding out."

Her eyes laughed at him for that possessive streak he hadn't known he'd had until Azami had come along. He found himself laughing with her.

His bedroom was spacious. He liked room—lots of room. And he enjoyed being surrounded by nature. He knew it wasn't the best idea to have trees close to his house; they could always come down in a storm —or worse, an enemy could use them both for cover to creep up onto his house, or to gain the roof via one of the branches. He didn't care. He loved fresh air and detested the city. He wanted as much forest around and as close to him as possible. A bank of windows overlooked the stream and surrounding trees, with a verandah just outside where he could sit and watch the deer come in close to drink.

Only three candles spilled light around the room. One was much smaller than the other, and a small pot sat over it, warming whatever was inside. Azami lowered the pot so that the flame was close to the bottom and could heat the contents faster. She waved him to a mat on the floor, tugging on his towel. He obligingly handed it over to her and, following her silent direction, lay facedown on the mat.

She slipped out of her towel, folding both neatly and setting them aside before going to the obviously old pot and lifting it away from the candle. He inhaled her exotic fragrance as she straddled him, her warm body sending heat rushing through his veins. He closed his eyes and prayed for strength to endure—to allow her to finish whatever she felt needed to be done before he claimed her wholly for his own.

"This is very ancient and sacred oil," Azami explained as she lifted the lid on the old pot. The scent drifted to him, surrounded him, and seemed to enfold him, all before she ever laid her slick, oiled hands on his shoulders and began a slow, methodical massage. "Each generation has added to the formula. The oil is hand pressed and will absorb quickly into your body, invigorating you even as it soothes tired muscles."

Already he could feel the tingling heat invading and spreading like a wildfire even as, for the second time that night, he felt absolutely boneless. He drifted in a haze of love and lust, of complete contentment. Her hands moved down his back to his buttocks, kneading and working out every kink, but the ritual gave them much more than relief from sore muscles. The more she worked on his body with her small, sure hands, the stronger the connection between them grew, as if that ancient oil created a bond that cemented them together. She massaged all the way down his legs and each foot, with that same easy, slow pace.

"You must turn over, Sammy," she whispered.

He opened his eyes as he rolled over. She had placed both feet flat on the floor on either side of his hips and lifted herself just enough to allow him to turn over. Immediately she lowered her body over his, straddling his lap, her hot, damp center sliding intimately over his heavy erection. Her hands immediately went to his shoulders.

Sam held up his hands. He was aching to touch her and this wasn't going much further, not without him taking her. "Share, Azami."

She smiled at him and swiveled slightly, causing a wealth of sensations to course through his groin. The candlelight played over her skin, the swell of her breast and narrow rib cage. The spider moved, showing itself briefly before she turned again to give him a full frontal view. She held the pot of oil in her cupped hands as if it was precious to her. Her gaze locked with his, she offered him the oil.

Sam coated his hands in the warm, slick oil and waited until she placed the pot carefully on the floor just within reach. When she would have bent forward to resume massaging his chest, he shook his head and lifted his hands to her shoulders. She sat back a little, watching him from under those long, luxurious lashes. He took his time massaging her shoulders before sliding his hands to cup her breasts. The oil disappeared quite fast, just as she'd said it would, leaving her skin softer and silkier than ever.

Watching her face, he brushed his thumbs over her nipples, saw the flush creeping under her skin and her heightened breathing. "Are you afraid, Azami?" he asked. It was a legitimate question. He wasn't a small man, and she was quite diminutive by comparison.

"A little nervous," she admitted, "but I want you quite badly."

He expected nothing less than her honesty. Azami didn't have it in her to play personal games with him. She would tell him what she wanted and provide for his needs as best she could. He knew the ritual bath had helped to calm her nerves and allow her to familiarize herself with his body while allowing him to see hers.

"I love this spider," he whispered and lifted his head so he could taste the oil.

As he expected, some previous ancestor had considered that a husband and wife would be anointed with the oil and want to consummate their marriage bed. Her skin was more than just pleasant, it held a hint of cinnamon, citrus, and maybe apple. He would never forget the smell of her skin or the way she looked with the flickering light dancing over her. He took possession of her breast, drawing the soft flesh into the heat of his mouth.

She let out a soft sigh and bunched her fist in his hair. He teased her nipple gently, his mouth moving over that intriguing spider guarding his woman. "I'm going to roll us over, baby," he said softly.

He wanted her under him. She'd shown him her world and now he was going to introduce her to his. She nodded and straightened her legs as he caught her around the waist and rolled, pulling her small frame beneath his. The oil on their bodies made them both so silky smooth their skin seemed to caress one another as they shifted and moved. He caught the quick nervousness in her eyes and immediately lowered his head, kissing her mouth over and over until she went boneless and pliant beneath him.

"Would you feel safer with a dagger in your hand?" he asked as he kissed his way to the tip of her breast.

"I'm safe with you," she said. "This is new to me, just as the ritual bath was new to you."

"I'll make your experience every bit as wonderful as you did for me," he promised. She was nervous, yes, and maybe, just maybe, there was that little hint of fear for the unknown, but she trusted him.

Sam bent his head to her flat belly and began tracing the delicate lines of the spiderweb with his tongue and lips the way he'd wanted to from the first moment he'd laid eyes on her tattoo. His tongue swirled in her intriguing belly button and moved again to trace her ribs.

"You need another spider right here by your belly button for me to tease," he whispered against her skin.

His body wanted to go fast and take her, burying himself deep over and over, but another part of him wanted to savor her in that same unhurried way she'd built such anticipation. He wanted her soft, breathless cries pleading with him. He wanted her so ready for him there would be little discomfort to her.

Her stomach muscles bunched and rippled beneath his

exploring hand and mouth, her breasts rising and falling as his mouth moved closer. His heart nearly exploded when her mind slipped into his, a little hesitant at first, as if she needed reassurance that he wanted the added intimacy. She would know then—he wouldn't be able to hide what she meant to him. He wanted her with every breath in his body. He needed her just as he needed air to breathe, and he didn't even know how it happened.

Something had happened when their minds connected, out there on the battlefield, and when she'd left his mind, she'd taken a part of him with her. The slow ritual bath had only deepened that bond, pushing his desire so far, creating a hunger so endless for her that it clawed and raked at him. He caught her hands and drew them around his neck, lifting his head to look down at her face. Her eyes were wide-open, and he could see the passion and desire shining back at him. The same hunger clawed at her. He lowered his head to kiss her again, sharing her breath, sharing his mind, one hand sliding down all that smooth skin to find the vee between her legs.

She was all heat and dampness. A private sanctuary for him to get lost in—and he didn't give a damn about trying to find a way out. As his palm covered her mound, his thumb sliding deep into her sheath, she flushed, her body growing hotter. Her eyes went wide with shock and her breath turned ragged, but she parted her thighs wider for him.

"It's all right," he soothed. "You're safe with me, Azami. We'll do this together."

He didn't think he'd survive that long. His body had never raged at him like this, never made such demands. The candlelight made her skin glow and the threads of the spiderweb actually appeared luminous, a trick of the ink. Watching her, mesmerized by her reaction, he slid his finger into that slick heat. She was tight and hot, and with her small body writhing under his, all that silky skin rubbing against him, he feared he might lose his mind.

He talked to her to keep sane, to keep from being a

primitive idiot when she needed to be introduced into the world of lovemaking gently. "I dreamt of you when I was young, back on the streets. So long ago, Azami. I would spend the night huddled in a doorway, afraid I'd have to kill someone to stay alive, hungry, alone, and when I'd be so tired I couldn't stay awake, I'd be with you. You were so beautiful and exotic and unattainable, and at the same time, the only solace I had."

"I dreamt of you too," she admitted softly, her voice barely above a whisper. "I never thought to find a man I would want to share my body with." She lifted her head and waited until their eyes met. "A man who would see me in spite of my flaws." She brought her hand up a little self-consciously to her misshapen breast. The scars zigzagged across the soft mound and just to the side of the nipple, where the spider resided, in that small nook where a small part of her breast was missing. The scar was shiny white beneath the spider.

Sam bent his head to brush kisses across that spider. "The only flaw you have, my beautiful Azami, is that you didn't find me sooner."

Azami laughed softly, but her eyes were overbright and tears shimmered on her long lashes. "Only you could say that. Even my father did not think that. He said I would have to learn to curb my temper. I spent many hours scrubbing the floor of our dojo for losing my temper and nearly taking off the head of my brother when practicing."

Sam nibbled his way up to her chin. "Did you chase him around with your sword?" He moved his finger deep inside her, stretching her enough to add a second finger.

He took possession of her mouth, catching that breathy little moan. He kissed her over and over, savoring the sweet taste of her and the way her lips were soft and firm and her tongue danced with his. He lifted his head enough to kiss the corners of her eyes, removing those tiny, sparkling tears.

"Did you? Did you chase your brother with a sword?"

"Yes." Azami lowered her gaze, clearly ashamed.

Sam laughed. "I knew it. What did he do?"

"He teased me about my white hair and I wanted to chop all of his hair from his head. Father made me scrub the dojo from top to bottom."

"That seems fair to me, shaving his head, I mean."

She shook her head. "My Father was right. I was learning to be quite lethal and I needed to hold my temper over silly matters. Although, I have to say, I was quite secretly pleased when the next time I saw Daiki, his hair was chopped off. He did it himself when he saw me punished."

Sam kissed her neck and then branded her there before kissing his way down to her tempting breasts again and tracing his way along her ribs back to her belly button. His teeth nipped occasionally, his tongue swirling, dancing over her bunching muscles. Her soft moans were like music to him, playing through his body and stroking caresses in his mind. He kissed her belly button and slid lower, inhaling her exotic fragrance. His dreams hadn't been this good. Nothing was this good. He parted her thighs and bent his head to lap at her slick crease.

Azami cried out and clutched at his hair, tossing her head back and forth on the pillow. She tasted as good as he knew she would, an addicting, exciting blend of spice. He took his time, indulging himself, bringing her to a fever pitch of need.

CHAPTER 13

Tears burned behind Azami's eyes. She had never thought to feel this kind of passion—or this kind of love. Her breath came in long, ragged, labored rushes. Her body was no longer her own but Sam's, and she gave herself willingly, yet there was a small part of her that kept protesting. Useless. Not worthy. He was bringing her to paradise, offering her something so precious, a miracle really, and yet what could she give him in return? A lump in her throat threatened to choke her. She should have told him everything, and she'd withheld vital information, fearing he would reject her.

I am Azami. I am samurai, my father's daughter. I am strong. I shaped myself into a being worthy of Sam.

Thorn was gone. Long gone. That malnourished child with horrible white hair, a freak of nature, so useless she couldn't even be used as a rat in a laboratory. It was Azami Sam was taking to paradise, Azami who felt every wonderful sensation burning like a fireball through her body. She hadn't known it was possible to feel like this. To want someone until you almost felt insane with need. To desire another's touch. To writhe beneath them, skin to skin, seeing acceptance in his eyes. Even her beloved father had not thought that she could find such a man and yet she had. A sob escaped and she shoved her fist in her mouth to choke it back.

"What is it, baby?" Sam asked softly, lifting his head to look at her.

She couldn't meet his eyes. His voice, so incredibly loving, soft and sexy, was everything a man's voice should be. How could he talk to her like that? How could he look at her like that? As if she was the only woman in the world? She shook her head, another small sob escaping, further humiliating her. She had stopped crying the terrible night Whitney had thrown her like garbage into the street. She wasn't that girl anymore. That useless child. She was Azami Yoshiie, samurai. But if she was, why hadn't she told him everything?

"Stop it right now."

Sam's voice startled her. Shocked her. His tone was hard with authority and his eyes had gone from loving, consuming her with desire, to commanding.

Azami shook her head and twisted away from him. "I can't do this. I'm sorry, Sam."

She was sorry for both of them. She'd done the unforgivable, allowing him to think she could commit to him, to have a life with him. More, she'd convinced herself, but even her father had known the truth. Thorn was still inside of her, that small, ugly child who would never go away. She'd been born flawed and no matter what she did, she would always remain flawed, useless to a man such as Sam. He just couldn't see it yet, blinded by his infatuation. She hadn't been able to bring herself to a tell him the things he deserved to know *before* he chose her. Where was her honor? She was definitely that miserable child.

Sam moved faster than she thought a big man could, up and over her, catching her wrists, pinning them to the floor on either side of her head. His face was a hard mask, all edges and tight control.

"Don't you ever, *ever*, do that to yourself again."

She'd grown so used to Sam being in her mind that she hadn't considered he could read her thoughts.

"Thorn is as much you as Azami is. It was Thorn's courage I saw in the forest battling with the enemy. It may have been Azami's skill and craft, but she's not whole without Thorn—without Thorn's absolute determination and courage. I *love* Thorn. That's who you are. You're a fucking miracle to me, and right now, all you're doing is pissing me off. You don't want to do that, Azami."

Her heart thundered in her ears, a terrible storm of emotion she'd choked back for years—for a lifetime. "I hate her. I hate Thorn. She won't go away. She's curled up in the fetal position, huddling there inside of me and no matter what I do, she won't go away."

"She is you."

"Stop saying that." She tried to bring her knee up, to get leverage against him to get him off of her. "I'm my father's daughter."

"Stop fighting me. You're not going to win in a physical battle with me, babe. All you're going to do is hurt yourself."

She hissed, grateful that her temper, long suppressed, was beginning to eat through her grief and shame. She needed anger to push him away. She wanted to touch his beloved face, to memorize every detail with her fingers. She'd never have the opportunity again, not once she left him. He wouldn't forgive desertion. She'd seen his file, seen his mother's treachery. He would forever brand her with that same label—no loyalty.

"Stop it," he snapped again. "I'm in your mind. Have you forgotten that? You aren't disloyal. You don't have it in you. You *chose* me. There's no going back on that choice. If you want to talk, then we'll talk this out, but you aren't going to push me away because you haven't quite been able to reconcile your past with your future."

"I have no future," she snapped. "That's what you refuse to understand. I have no future, not with you. Not with any man. I'm damaged. Broken. There's no fixing me. I didn't want to accept it, but . . ."

"Damn it, Azami, I'm not going to listen to this bullshit. There's nothing broken about you," He rolled off of her, getting to his feet and pulling her up all in one motion, wincing a little as his gut protested.

He took her breath away with his grace. He moved like no other man she'd encountered, not even in the dojo where she trained. She tried to remember where she'd left her clothes. Her mind was in terrible chaos. She looked around her a little helplessly.

"Where is this coming from?" Sam asked.

He opened and closed his fist, a gesture she was certain he wasn't aware of, but his eyes had dropped from her face to drift over her body. He didn't look disgusted, if anything he looked tender and loving. His erection wasn't quite as hard as it had been, but it was still there, still attracted to her in spite of . . . What? What was she doing? Why was she determined to shove him away from her? To throw happiness away?

"I need something to wear." *He* didn't mind her body, the evidence of her shame, but she couldn't stand him looking at her, not now when she was so panic-stricken.

Sam glanced around the room, found her a shirt, and tossed it to her while he pulled on a pair of jeans, half buttoning them. Azami pulled his shirt around her body, hastily buttoning it up the front to cover herself and found his scent surrounding her, comforting her.

"Azami." He whispered her name, an ache in his voice. "Talk to me, baby. Just say it out loud. Give us a shot at this. We're both fighters. Fight for us. Am I so easy to throw away?"

Her head snapped up, her stomach sinking. Was that what she was doing? She shook her head. "This isn't about you,

Sam, it's me. I don't know how to do this. I don't know how to get rid of her. My father said . . ." She trailed off, choking back her greatest shame.

She couldn't look at him, she didn't dare. She was being a coward. Running. So she wouldn't have to tell him the rest.

Sam took a step forward and caught her chin in his hand, forcing her head up. "Tell me, Azami. No one else is here, just the two of us. What is this about?"

She took a deep breath and lifted her lashes, allowing herself to meet his eyes. She knew it would be a mistake. She wouldn't be able to resist him, resist that look of such tenderness. He was offering her a world she was terrified to walk into. She knew her worth where she was. She could never go back to being useless, to feel as if she was nothing but garbage, deserving of being thrown out.

"Sam, I'm not meant for this kind of thing. You. Me. I wanted it—I still want it—but even my father believed I could not please a man." The words came out in a little rush, but she got them out. The truth. Her shame. The one man she loved and respected above all others had decreed her useless as a wife and mother. There was only the battle for her, the protection of her brothers and their genius. Her father wouldn't lie to her. He'd seen the damage done to her body and he knew the minds and hearts of men.

"You were meant for me."

"You may feel that you want me now, but . . ."

He put his finger over her mouth. "You're so wrong, Azami. So wrong about so many things. Wrong about your father. About your past. And especially about me." He bent his head and brushed a kiss on top of her head. "Wait right here. Don't move. And I mean don't move. No leaping out the window and running away. Just wait here."

He was gone before she could protest. The window did look inviting, but she wasn't that big of a coward as much as she'd like to be. What did Sam know about her father? How could he know more than she? He made no sense at all. She should have ignored his order but she had some pride left and refused to take the coward's way out. She stood *exactly* where he left her as if the soles of her feet were rooted in the floor. Her heart pounded and her mouth went dry. Even the palms of her hands felt clammy.

She was in full-blown panic mode. She hadn't had a panic attack in years. She'd had them all the time when her father had first found her, but samurai didn't panic. Lungs didn't burn for air and one didn't claw and fight inside where no one else could see. She wanted Sam to just walk away from her and let her sort the entire thing out. She just needed space. Distance. Somewhere safe.

You are safe with me.

He stood in front of her, holding out his hand, palm up, his dark eyes locked on her face. She studied his face, so still he could have been carved of stone, but for his eyes. So alive. So tender. This man stood before her, offering her everything, offering her paradise, and she'd thrown it back in his face because she was still that white-haired child a brutal, inhuman monster had declared useless. She'd allowed her own fears to overcome what she knew of him. He was a man of honor, and yet she dishonored him by not believing he could handle the things she needed to tell him. In truth, it was Thorn who couldn't handle them.

"Not Whitney, Azami," Sam disagreed, obviously still reading her thoughts. "You are considering rejecting me, not because of Whitney, but because you mistook what your father said to you because you believed in a monster and that was the only way you could make sense of everything."

Her gaze dropped to the object in Sam's open palm. Her heart jumped. She'd recognize her father's work anywhere. He was as famous for his intricate jewelry as he was for his swords. She didn't touch that very small ring, but actually stepped back to look up at Sam.

It took a moment to find her voice. "Where did you get that?"

"Your brother gave it to me. He said your father made it

for the man who would bring you happiness. He knew the right man would come along and fall like a ton of bricks for you. You're so easy to want, Azami, so easy to love, but you still reject who and what you are. You are Thorn, that incredibly brave girl who has grown into a remarkable woman. Look at the ring and tell me your father didn't see the true Azami for everything she is and everything she stands for. He loved Azami *because* she's Thorn."

She didn't want to look at the ring. She wanted to look at his face. This man who believed in her when she'd momentarily lost herself. This was a man who would always find that small child huddled in a corner and he'd lift her up, shelter and protect her.

"How blind could I be? How reckless?" she murmured in wonder.

"Your father knows how brave that child is, he always knew. He took you home because he knew your worth. He saw it even as you lay in that street. He put his life on the line to take you from those men. That's Thorn, Azami. That courage of spirit. That will to survive. Whitney couldn't break you as a child. Don't let him do it to the woman."

Still, she didn't take the ring. Instead, she looked at the man holding her father's gift out to her. Sam was really the gift. The sun would always rise in his eyes. He would always be the man who saw her. Almost from the first moment he laid eyes on her, he had looked past her physical body and really embraced her—who she was as a person. She hadn't done the same to him. Had she looked carefully into his mind, she would have seen unconditional acceptance, but she'd been so certain he wouldn't want Thorn. Little Thorn with her misshapen body, carved up by a butcher, with her freakish white hair, useless and thrown away like garbage.

Sam had given himself fully to her, everything he was, right from the moment their minds connected. He didn't try to hide the loyalty he had to his team, or the struggle he felt knowing he had to tell them about her, but he'd stayed true to his character. He let her see who he was while she tried to hide herself from him.

"I'm sorry, Sam. I really am. I don't know why I can't seem to let go of Whitney's evaluation of me."

"Because every child wants their father's approval, and for all intents and purposes, Whitney was your parent," Sam said.

She noted that he spoke the truth. She'd had no one else but Whitney for so long. "He kept me away from the other girls for the most part. There was one girl he called Winter. She was able to stop a heart from beating just with a touch. He made her practice on me, and she would cry and tell me she was sorry. She tried to protect me, but he'd punish her, terrible punishments if she didn't do what he said. She snuck food to me sometimes, and once she gave me a blanket. Whitney took it away from me when he said I was bad."

Sam curled his hand around the nape of her neck. He had a big hand and instead of feeling trapped, she felt safe.

"I should be over it, Sam. I'm a grown woman."

He laughed softly. "Do you really think that the past doesn't shape who we are? Everyone has moments of weakness. You didn't believe you would ever be with a man who would love you, which by the way, makes no sense to me. You have a view of yourself skewed by the things Whitney drilled into you as a child. He was wrong about your gifts, Azami. Totally wrong. If he was wrong about that, then he can be wrong about other things as well. Whitney makes mistakes. And he made a big mistake about you."

"He destroyed my body," Azami said, clutching the shirt-tails, her hands two tight fists. "Not just my scars on the outside. My heart was destroyed by him as well." She raised her eyes to his. "It isn't normal." The truth was going to come out whether she wanted it to or not. She *had* to tell him. It was only fair if she wanted a life with him. No lies between them, not even the sin of omission.

Sam stepped closer to her. "Azami, do you think that would drive me away from you? I want you, just the way you are. If your heart is weak, we can . . ."

She pressed her lips together and shook her head. "Not weak. He thought I'd die from his experiment, but I didn't." She was going to have to tell him. If she was going to truly give them a chance together, he had to know how much of a mutant being Whitney had made.

"What did he do to you?"

She tried a smile, but knew by the expression on his face she hadn't quite pulled it off. "I'm kind of like the modern-day Frankenstein monster. Whitney loved his little experiments. When my heart gave out from all the experiments, he decided to make a synthetic heart—one that would prove stronger than a human heart. Well, not exactly synthetic in the normal sense of the word. I wasn't the first person he tried it on, and the others apparently died. I was a child and the heart he used would 'power' an adult. My body tried to reject it, and he didn't think it was worth it to keep me around long enough to see if the heart worked and my body eventually accepted it."

Sam frowned, studying her face. She could feel him move through her mind, a soft warm force that made her feel safe. With him filling her mind the way he was, she couldn't possibly feel alone. In some ways, the sensation was foreign, but already familiar. He was already becoming so dear to her. She felt as if she'd known him forever. He waited her out, knowing there was more—there had to be. How could she teleport with a synthetic heart? It would be impossible for the molecules to break down and then restore themselves—unless they really did move faster than light . . . He shook his head and waited.

"What do you know about nanotechnology?"

He shrugged. "I studied it of course. It's fascinating and has the potential for changing the world in a number of ways. Basically, it's engineering functional systems at a molecular scale." He paused, his breath catching in his lungs.

She nodded slowly. "Whitney is wild about nanotechnology. He's working on perfecting a way for a device that would travel through the body on a seek and destroy mission of cancerous cells."

"But he uses humans for his experiments."

She nodded. "I read one file where he'd deliberately infected one woman several times with cancer."

"Flame, Irin, who's married to Gator."

Azami's dark eyes regarded him steadily. "Whitney considers that a great waste. He believes she can't have children, so she rendered Gator useless to him other than as a soldier to prevent the deaths of other soldiers. Basically, Sam, he said the same thing about you. And you're attracted to me."

"Even if he could have somehow paired you with me, after you were long gone, how could he have paired me with you? He didn't know me then. He didn't have access to you. And you're attracted, Azami, no matter what you say. Both mentally and physically, you're attracted."

A small smile escaped. "I am not arguing that fact, Sam. I'm merely trying to get you to see the big picture before you leap with both feet and your eyes closed."

"Are you saying he gave you cancer?"

"You know what I'm saying. Nanotechnology doesn't defy the principles of physics. The possibility of moving or maneuvering something atom by atom in theory can be done. Just as teleportation is not against the laws of physics. Already, nanosystems are being developed with thousands of interactive components, and Whitney is going a step further, developing integrated systems functioning like our own cells with systems inside systems."

"Are you saying he found a way to construct a heart using carbon nanotube scaffolding?" Sam tried not to sound excited, but who wouldn't be? "That's impossible. Bone reconstruction is barely beginning and bones are linear. Carbon nanotubes are one-dimensional. No one has figured out how to shape them." His gaze locked with hers. "Have they?"

She didn't answer and his mind was racing with the possibilities. He shook his head, wondering aloud. "One would have to solve toxicity and rejection problems. They'd have to grow the cellular and noncellular components outside the body before replacing the damaged heart with a fully functioning nano heart. How the hell could they do that before transplanting it?" He caught her arms. "It would be a miracle, Azami. It can't be possible. How the hell would Whitney manage to construct a heart from carbon nanotubes?"

"A heart would only have to function like a human heart, not necessarily be shaped like an organic one," Azami pointed out.

"No, but the heart still has to perform the same function as a human heart," Sam argued. "It still has to beat in a cardiac cycle, which puts constraints on the shape. Right now scientists are just beginning to think in terms of using carbon nanotubes for bones because they can't shape them. A heart can't be linear."

"No, even a nano heart would have to go through a pumping cycle that alternates between bringing in the deoxygenated blood and pumping the newly oxygenated blood out to the rest of the body," she agreed.

"*Exactly.*" Sam watched her closely. She was telling him she had a nano heart and his mind couldn't wrap around the possibility. "That particular aspect of the heart's functioning can't really be changed, as the entire rest of the body is set up around it." But it was possible. Every scientist working with nanotechnology had specific goals in mind, and replacing a damaged heart was on the list. No one could figure out how to shape the carbon nanotubes. The heart would be far stronger if all problems surrounding the growth and transplant could be solved. Whitney had experimented on little Thorn for years. He would have access to cells and anything else he would want or need from her body. But was it possible he'd done what others were just imagining?

"If he managed to give you a nano heart, Azami, the world would . . ."

"No one else survived. And the world would treat me just as he treated me. I'd be a freak and an experiment." She crossed her arms over her chest and stepped back, her eyes dark with pain. "I have no idea how long the heart will last. I can't go to a mainstream doctor, not for any reason. What would people call me? Some would go so far as to say I'm not human."

Sam stepped close to her, covering that small distance with one easy step. He caught the nape of her neck and pressed his forehead against hers. "Listen to me, Azami. Whatever you are, wherever you are, that's where I want to be. People don't get chances like this often. I'm no kid, and I never expected to find a woman I would cherish." He straightened, dropped his hands, and paced away from her and then back to stand in front of her. "I don't need much, Azami. I built this house because I wanted a home. It didn't feel like one until you were in it. I want your body just the way it is. And as for your heart, as long as it's beating, I swear you could have a cyborg's heart and I'd be happy. Stay with me. The hell with Whitney or anyone else who wants to step on our happiness. When those doors close, it's just you and me. No one else."

Sam took both of her hands and pulled them to his chest, holding them tight against him. "I can make you happy. I know I can. Whatever it takes. Whatever you need. Give yourself to me, all of you. Thorn, Azami, good and bad, let me have you."

"Sammy." She whispered his name in the stillness of the night. Azami's heart twisted inside her chest. The mutant organ might not be all human, but it didn't stop her from falling in love with this man. How could she not? "Are you so certain that you really want me? Have you considered that if he gave me such a heart and the DNA of an animal, that any child we have might be . . . different?"

Sam studied her face. There it was. Her real fear. The number one fear. She'd let him see the truth of her and now she'd just exposed the one thing that made her most vulnerable. This was the reason she thought her father didn't feel she was fit to become a wife. Not the scars. Not the white hair. A child. Her child. *Their* child.

"Damn it all to hell, Azami," he said, between his teeth. "Don't you ever fucking protect me like this again. Hell, woman, I could have had a heart attack at the thought of you leaving me."

And wasn't she good to keep it all out of her mind, hiding her true fear from him, masking it with red herrings. She did feel vulnerable. She did feel all those things she'd told him, but combined, they weren't enough to send her running, especially when he was making love to her without protection. He hadn't even considered protection. He planned to marry her as soon as it was possible and having children was part of the program. But he hadn't asked. He hadn't discussed it with her.

Azami moistened her lips, her gaze still locked with his. "You're angry now."

"Damn right, I am. At you. At me for being so dense that I didn't even discuss children or protection with you." He shoved a hand through his hair and regarded her flushed face. "Why would you think you couldn't have a child?"

She took a breath and let it out. "Whitney said I was useless, a throwaway. What does he want most, Sam? Children. Superbabies. He conducted all sorts of experiments on me and then he threw me away. Doesn't it stand to reason that he believes I either can't have a child or that it would be defective?"

Sam opened his mouth to protest but snapped it closed before anything could escape. This was a big deal to her. A huge deal. Whitney had colored her entire image of herself. He'd parented her in her formative years, those vital years, and he'd treated her as if she wasn't human. He took away her self-esteem, her worth as a human being. To a woman, at least to Azami, having a child obviously meant something important.

He took a deep breath, let it out, and pushed away the rage that churned in his gut. Fury at Whitney, that monster who would dehumanize a child so he could use her for experiments, and even more at himself for pushing her so fast because she'd turned his body into a fucking walking hard-on. What he needed to do was defuse the situation and let both of them calm down a little bit and think things through. To Azami, the subject was obviously very emotional and frightening as well as being significant to her. He was sexually frustrated as well as feeling like a complete selfish idiot.

"Let's discuss this over tea. I'm not going to be great at it, but you can teach me. I'd like to learn how to properly prepare you a good cup of tea. You drank the tea in the war room, but you didn't enjoy it. This is an important issue to you, Azami. We need to get it hashed out. Let's do it over a cup of tea."

"It would be your baby too," she declared. "It should be an important issue to you as well. You're so willing to be with me and you don't fully know all the risks." She ducked her head. "I should have disclosed everything right away, as soon as I knew you were serious."

He had said the right thing. The tension drained from her face, and her desperate, vulnerable expression was gone. She had a point. A baby would be his. His child. He had just assumed it wouldn't matter to her about children, because, although he wanted some, she would always be his first priority. If she couldn't have them, or didn't want them, so be it. He turned to lead her out of the room where their combined scents with the oil weren't so potent. He needed a little relief himself.

He didn't want to enjoy the fact that she was there with him, a soft whisper of silk moving through the house he'd built with his own two hands, but he couldn't deny that just knowing she was with him, arguing or not, gave him great pleasure. He felt her fingers push into the back pocket of his jeans as she followed him down the hall to the spacious kitchen. He didn't turn around, but his gut settled a little. At least she still wanted that physical connection between them. She hadn't entirely abandoned the idea that they would spend their lives together.

Once in the kitchen, he filled the kettle and set it to heat on the stove before turning to face her. "I don't have the best tea, just some teabags. I don't drink it that often." As in never, but once in a while Ryland and Lily came to visit and he liked to have tea for Lily.

"I brought tea with me," she confessed. "I always bring tea with me wherever I go." She disappeared into the large living room where she'd left a small bag with her things in it.

He loved the sight and scent of her moving around his house. He did have a terrible urge to take those pins from her hair and let it fall around her face naturally, push the shirt from her shoulders, and just put her up on the kitchen table. Dessert would be especially nice.

Sammy!

He laughed, joy flooding him. She was calling him Sammy. That was something. And she sounded as if she was laughing rather than being angry. He'd been broadcasting a little too loud there. At least she couldn't have any doubts that he found her attractive.

"I like that you came prepared," he said as she entered the kitchen. "I'm sorry I didn't think about protection, Azami. I should have."

Her lashes fluttered. Damn. He loved her lashes, and just that little movement sent heat spiraling through his body. It didn't take much to get him going around her.

"Teach me to make the tea the way you like it."

She smiled. "It isn't about liking the tea, Sam. It is about the preparation. One pours oneself into the tea. You make the bowl of tea from your heart. Each movement is defined, and even the setting of the table is about the one you're making the tea for. You must give the preparation your complete attention."

"Show me." He moved up behind her as she went to the counter, choosing to be just a little closer than necessary, crowding her body just a bit until he felt every breath she took. He lowered his voice and put his lips next to her ear. "Show me how you give the tea preparation your complete attention. What would you do if you were making tea for me?"

"Tea for you, at home, when we are alone, is a private tea. I have only a few things with me to make our tea special, but it will be made with all my heart."

She looked over her shoulder, the shoulder he was leaning over, to look up at him from beneath her long lashes. His heart—and body—reacted instantly. Electricity crackled between them, little sparks leaping from his skin to hers and back.

"I have given you my heart, Sammy. I don't know about the rest of me, we must talk first, but my heart you have, such as it is. This is my mistake, not yours. I'm pleased you want me so much. It makes me feel . . . beautiful. I've never felt beautiful before. It is a great gift you've given me."

Her lips were a mere inch from his and he'd be a fool if he ignored that temptation. No one had ever called him a fool. He caught the back of her head in the palm of his hand and lowered his mouth that scant inch to kiss her. She tasted like heaven. His shirt on her was long enough to go down to her knees, adequately covering her, but she wore nothing under it and he was familiar with her body now. He'd tasted nearly every inch of her.

Sam kissed her over and over, losing himself in her, indulging his need, afraid he might never get the chance again to persuade her to stay with him. He wanted her—no, needed her. He'd been perfectly content until they'd shared a mind connection, until she had poured herself into him. She was samurai through and through. Until the doors were

closed and they were alone and then she was all woman—
his woman.

When he lifted his head, her eyes had gone liquid. She
smiled at him that little mysterious smile that made his
stomach do a slow flip.

"Go sit down, Sam, and let me do this. I will show you
another time, when I have all my things with me."

He liked the idea that there would be another time, so he
didn't argue. Toeing around a chair from the table, he straddled it and rested his chin on his hands on the back of the
chair, watching her intently.

She placed a wooden box on the table with a small bow
and opened it quite reverently. Inside the box were tea utensils mostly made of ceramic or bamboo. He could tell the
instruments were quite old and beautiful. Every movement
was precise and graceful as she rinsed and laid utensils onto
a small ornate tray Lily had given him when his house had
been completed. He liked watching her graceful movements.
She was naturally restful to be around, but he knew from
experience, many warriors often were still and quiet but
extremely capable of exploding into action.

She rinsed the two tea bowls with equal care, the flowing
motion of her hands mesmerizing. Powdered green tea was
placed in each of the bowls with a bamboo dipper. She
poured the water from the kettle and proceeded to whip the
tea with a bamboo whisk until it appeared slightly frothy.
Very gently she placed the bowl in front of him and added
two sweets on a small ceramic dish.

She bowed slightly as she placed the dish beside him.
"The tea is bitter and the sweets will balance the taste."

"The bowls are beautiful."

"They belonged to my father's father. This is his traveling
set. It's very old and I always try to give it honor, even when
I don't have all the correct equipment."

"You'll have to tell me what we need," Sam said, making
it casual. There was no harm in believing she would be
spending her life with him.

Her gaze jumped to his face. "There are many complications, Sam. More than just whether or not we can have a child and whether or not it would be normal. You know it's true. What of my brothers? Who will protect them? That duty lies with me."

Sam bought some time by drinking the tea. He'd been in Japan many times and was used to the bitter green tea. He found solace in the ceremony itself and the graceful, fluid motion of hands while preparing the beverage.

"Your brothers both approved of our match. This has nothing to do with them. We can build a lab for them here, or extend Lily's laboratory. You can fly with them when they travel. You know this isn't about your brothers. This is about our child and your heart."

"And the strain of animal DNA Whitney gave me. My brothers have run extensive tests for me. I have a healthy dose of cat in me, which is what allows me to run faster, leap, and land so easily. That's separate from teleportation, Sam. He never knew about that."

"Hmm," he murmured, noting her distress level was rising again. "I have that same strain in me. He used that on several of the GhostWalkers, Azami. He believed it would allow us to be better soldiers."

"So what would that do to a child?"

"You've seen Daniel. Daniel's probably a good part of the reason you agreed to come here in the first place," Sam guessed.

"But not because I considered having a child. I wanted to make certain his mother wasn't like his grandfather. If she'd been experimenting on him and all of you knew it . . ." She left the sentence hanging.

He studied her face, the absolute serenity there. "You and your brothers came prepared to wipe us out and take the boy."

"If need be. He is never going to live the childhood I did."

"At least there, we're all on the same page. Daniel is well loved and looked after. Every man and woman in this compound and the one next to ours would protect him with their life."

She nodded in agreement. "And Lily is a very good mother. She is a great scientist, but she respects life."

Sam leaned back, his hand curling around the back of his chair until his knuckles were nearly white. "Do you want children, Azami?"

She paled a little. He felt like he might have just delivered a punch to her gut. All the air seemed to rush from her lungs and she looked vulnerable, so much so that he had to fight the desire to kick the chair aside and pull her into his arms. He wasn't nearly as civilized as she was.

"I never thought it was a possibility, Sam," she answered, her voice very low. She sipped at her tea, taking her time. "I never thought I would find a man I could respect and love, let alone that he would find me attractive. There was never a question about children. And then I met you . . . and Daniel." She ducked her head. "He's so amazing, isn't he? I rocked him back to sleep the other night."

Her voice had gone all soft and dreamy. He could picture her with their child nestled in her arms. She'd make a fierce, protective mother.

"Do you believe your heart could stand up to carrying a baby, because I'd do it for you, honey, but I'm just not built right." He meant it too. If she wanted a child, he'd move heaven and earth for her to have her wish.

"I have no idea. I would think so. It stands up to me teleporting, so I can't see that it would give out just because I'm carrying a baby, but what with both of us having a strain of cat DNA and both able to teleport, we could be in real trouble."

"Jack Norton has twins, Azami, beautiful babies, and he's got the same strain of cat DNA. Whitney seemed very fond of large cats."

"I tried to find out if Lily was working on the effects on our children," Azami admitted, "but she's very careful with that research if she is."

"Anything to do with Daniel, or any of the babies, she would be extra careful of." She kept that research locked up and out of a computer Whitney might find a way to hack, but there was no reason to disclose that to Azami. Not yet. She was either with them—one of them—or she was walking away.

Her head came up and she looked him in the eyes. "I'm the least human of all with my strange heart and weird DNA strands, but if you really want me and you believe that you can love me, and you're willing to take a chance with me, I want to be with you, Sam."

"Willing to take a chance with you? Love you? Want you? Are you out of your mind, woman?" Sam stood up fast, kicking the chair away from him so he had a clear path to her.

CHAPTER 14

Azami found herself laughing as she fended him off. "You're so impetuous, Sammy. Let me wash my tea things and put them away before you carry me off."

"Carry you off?" he echoed. "I thought the kitchen table looked good right about now."

When he kept coming, she put up her hand to stop him. "Really, it's a matter of respect to honor my father and his father. It's important to me."

He crossed his arms over his chest and tapped his foot to signal great impatience as she began to methodically wash the tea utensils and bowls. She didn't look at him, but kept her back to him, concentrating on the task at hand. He realized she really did pour herself into whatever task she was doing at the time. He waited in silence, secretly enjoying the flowing grace of her hands as she worked.

When she closed the wooden box and turned to him, leaning her back against the table, she smiled up at him. "Do you really want me so much?"

He reached past her to take the box from harm's way and place it gently on the counter. "You have no idea, woman, but I'm about to show you." He didn't even care if he sounded as if he was threatening her. He needed some control here, and not in the way she was controlled.

He didn't like the idea of her thinking of leaving him. He knew he could tie her to him if she just gave him a chance. He couldn't be this sure and not be right.

"I don't know the first thing about this," she confided.

Sam stepped close to her, towering over her. "I do, Azami. Be sure this time because I won't be able to take stopping in the middle of everything again. If you want me to use protection, we'll do that. I have no worries about having a child with you, unless you're afraid of your heart giving out. With or without children, I want to spend my life with you. So you tell me what you want."

She looked up at him from under all those long, feathery lashes, sending his heart rate accelerating. "I held Daniel in my arms and rocked him to sleep and cried the entire time," she admitted softly. "I want to try, but I'm afraid."

He drew her into the shelter of his arms. "We'll talk to Lily about this, Azami. She knows what it's like to be afraid for her child. And Jack and Briony can help set your mind at ease as well."

She bit her lip and nodded. "I had no idea I would have the choice to have a husband and perhaps a baby. My brothers told me of course it was possible and I should consider such a thing, but I won't be with someone who doesn't know what—and who—I am. I make no apologies for my need to stop Whitney. Experimenting on adults is monstrous enough, but children?" She shook her head. "I can't let him continue."

Sam lifted her, cradling her against his chest. She was featherlight, warm and soft. "I know you inside and out and I want every inch of you. I've made my mind up, Azami. I've thrown myself into the ring completely, and I'm in it for the duration."

Azami lifted her fingers to his strong jaw. That beloved face. Those dark, serious eyes. All that curly hair. *Hers.* Was it possible? How had it even happened? She'd done such a terrible thing, going to bed with him and stopping him right in the middle of things. No one had ever made her feel as he did. Out of control—but in a good way. She hadn't even known it was possible. Sam Johnson. She'd read everything she could about him in his files. Right from the moment she'd read his impressive education and his equally impressive missions, she'd been intrigued. She just hadn't admitted it to herself.

"I am usually very good at making up my mind and sticking to my decisions," she said.

Sam laughed, the sound slipping beneath whatever guard she might have left and teasing her senses into complete compliance. This man, behind closed doors, would always be hers. He opened up his mind and his heart to her. He made her feel beautiful and worthwhile. Even more, he treated her as a complete equal on the battlefield. He would always have protective instincts, but she liked that about him.

The house was dark other than the candles she'd lit in the bedroom, and Sam carried her close to him as he made his way unerringly through the house. The doorways were wide and ceilings high to accommodate his frame, but he moved in silence, reminding her he was as skilled as she was.

"We'd better never get into a huge fight," she teased.

"That could be bad," Sam agreed as he set her on the floor beside his bed. "I'm taking these pins out of your hair. Am I going to stab my finger on something and die from instant poisoning, because I need to see your hair down?"

He grasped an intricately painted porcelain hair pin and tugged. The long pin was a slender round cylinder, and when he pulled it loose, strands of hair fell like a waterfall down her back. The pin looked innocent enough, but he didn't trust it. Azami looked innocent and she was a dangerous woman. He would bet his last dollar this work of art was very lethal.

Azami smiled at him and held out her hand. "The pins with cherry blossoms are used in up close fighting or perhaps a quick jab as one passes the enemy on the street. Just press twice and the needle is here." She pointed to the end of the pin. "It would feel much like the sting of a tiny insect if felt at all and they are dead."

"Woman." Sam grinned at her, blood heating at the mere idea of her abilities. She was everything he'd ever dreamt of. "I think I'm just becoming obsessed with you. What about this one?" He pulled a dark red pin from her hair. The porcelain was decorated with lacy leaves winding up the cylinder. "Dark red is for . . . ?"

"Blowgun. It works quite well up to about twenty-five feet. After that, no real accuracy, but handy in a pinch." She placed the dark red pin carefully on the nightstand beside the cherry blossom pin.

He pulled another pin loose and more hair snaked down over her shoulder. This one was black with a golden dragon curling around it. "And this one?"

She shrugged one shoulder. "Arrows. For my mini cross-bow."

Her casual answer, given in that low, husky voice sent another rush of heat spreading through his veins. His blood turned to magma, hot and thick with need.

There was one red pin, three dragon and three cherry blossom pins. Sam pulled each one out slowly, watching the way her hair cascaded down her back in a silky waterfall. He found her incredibly sexy, a mixture of lethal and fragile. Her hair snaked down her back to her waist in another glorious miracle of womanly wiles. He'd had no idea her hair was so long. However she managed to pin it up with seven ornate weapons was simply another mystery.

His hands dropped to the buttons of the shirt she wore. His knuckles brushed bare skin, that soft swell of her breast he found as fascinating as her weapons. He kept his gaze locked with hers. He needed to stroke all that silken skin. His need had continued to grow with every moment in her company until his erection was a continual aching need. She wanted him, he could see it in the way she ate him up with her dark eyes. A slight flush crept up her neck to her face and her breath left her lungs in a ragged rush.

"I'm starving for the taste of you," he admitted aloud, craving her. He'd waited so long. A lifetime. She'd been under his body, in his arms, his face buried between her legs, and he still hadn't managed to have her. Nothing could go wrong this time. He *had* to have her.

He pushed the edges of the shirt over her shoulders and let it drop to the floor. A little slip of a woman, yet she'd captured his heart so completely. He hadn't known he craved a wife and family, a place to call home. Hell. He'd refused to acknowledge that he was lonely. He'd set himself on a path of duty and told himself he would never have those things, so why long for them? And then she'd calmly gone into battle with him, no hysterics, no drama, just getting the job done with as much skill as—or more than—any soldier he'd gone into battle with.

Her hands trembled as she ran them up his belly to his chest. He captured both and pressed a kiss into each palm as desire punched low and hard, taking his breath. He'd never known need to be so urgent, or lust to be laced with such tenderness.

"I won't survive this night if I can't have you," he admitted, drawing her closer to him, so that her body melted against his. "I want you that much."

Her eyes met his. "I want you that much too," she confessed. "I wanted you from the moment I felt your mind in mine. I knew it was you. I just didn't trust the future."

"But you trust me," he coached.

She bit her bottom lip and nodded slowly, her eyes enormous.

His hands went to her hair, that thick mass of silky black as he bent his head, his mouth taking possession of hers to catch that soft, breathy sigh. He kissed her over and over, savoring the taste of her, the velvet sweetness, the fiery spice that caught his blood on fire. His cock pressed hard against her belly as her hands caught at his shoulders for support.

He moved his hips, thrusting gently, rhythmically, while small rockets roared in his brain at the sensation. Her tongue tangled with his, her nails sinking into the muscle of his shoulders while her body trembled.

He didn't want to wait this time. Nothing could go wrong. Kissing her senseless was the only answer, but the soft musical moans and the way her body rubbed against his threatened a loss of control he couldn't afford. He lowered her to the mattress, unbuttoning his jeans with one hand and tugging at them to get them the hell off.

He followed her down, not wanting to lose contact, not wanting to give her too much time to think—or panic. He could see the need burning, but also a little apprehension. He covered her body with his, careful to keep most of his weight off of her as he kissed her. The feel of her small, soft body, all feminine curves and soft, melting skin, only added to the fever raging in him.

He stared down at her body, those sweet curves emphasized by the delicate spiderweb stretched across her narrow rib cage, riding up and over her breasts and down the slope of her belly to stop just above the temptation of dark curls at the junction of her legs. He found that spiderweb sexy, permanent lacy lingerie drawing attention to her silky skin and soft curves. Her flushed breasts rose and fell with her ragged breathing, her nipples, twin hard peaks. That little red-backed spider moved with every breath she drew in and let out.

He bent his head slowly and swiped his tongue over her nipple, just to watch the spider jump in anticipation. She sucked in her breath and beneath his hand, her stomach muscles bunched and her hips jumped beneath his, sending heat spiraling through his body.

"Sammy." She whispered his name, desire drenching her voice. Her body shuddered with pleasure, her eyes glazing.

He lowered his head and suckled, drawing her nipple into the heat of his mouth, ravenous for her. Her husky little whimper destroyed his control and he simply indulged himself, his tongue flicking her nipple while he sucked, his hand tugging and rolling at the nipple of her other breast. Her hands fisted in his hair, her body arching, pushing her breasts closer, deeper into his hungry mouth.

He wanted to devour her. The writhing of her body, her head tossing on the pillow and her bucking hips, drove him deeper under her spell. She was so responsive, so soft, her skin hot silk, rubbing across his near-bursting cock until he could barely think or breathe with his need of her. A growl escaped, a primitive sound rumbling from somewhere deep inside of him.

His hand slipped across her stomach, feeling her muscles, edging lower until he found her slender thigh. His hand could nearly wrap around her leg and he took in as much territory as possible, gripping hard for a moment, pinning her restless leg to the sheets while his tongue and teeth ravaged her breast.

Azami stilled, her eyes widening in a kind of dazed shock. He continued to suckle, his eyes wide-open, staring into hers. She was so beautiful, her silky hair everywhere, her skin flushed, and her breasts heaving.

Mine. He pushed the word into her mind, needing her to acknowledge his possession.

Completely. She didn't hesitate.

His gaze holding hers, his hand slipped between her thighs, sliding through damp silk. She cried out, a soft, broken sound, her body jerking with shock as his fingers dipped shallowly. Her eyes went liquid dark, her head tossing on the pillow again as the tension in her body grew with his every movement.

That little spider moved enticingly again and he licked at it, stroking the spot with his tongue as his fingers slid deeper into hot, slick cream. She was so beautiful, writhing beneath him, her skin flushed and her breath ragged. He couldn't wait another minute. She'd given herself to him, said she was his, and he intended to indulge himself. He wanted all that hot cream for himself. He was losing his mind a little, the fever of need so great, his hunger wild now. Truthfully, he wasn't certain he could have stopped had she asked him a second time.

He kissed his way along that spiderweb, all those delicate threads mapping her body for him. He would know every strand intimately, Lapping at her skin, teeth nipping, he circled her clit with a long, thick finger.

Sammy! Her voice slipped into his mind. Hungry. Shocked. Breathless. She repeated it again and again, a musical chant as he made his way down her body, taking in every inch of her.

I've got you, baby. He wanted to bind her with more than sex, with love, with tenderness. He just had to hold on to his wild cravings and go slow, make certain her body was ready for him. He was absolutely determined to make her first time with him the same paradise as it would be for him.

He sank a finger into her damp depth, shocked at how small and tight she was. The clenching of her muscles only added to the raging need radiating through his body. Her eyes were wide-open again, glittering with a fever of desire to match his own.

Azami stared up at Sam's face, at the sensuality carved so deep in every line. His eyes were pure hunger, predatory almost, and it should have scared her, the intensity of his desire. She was nervous, yes, but only because she didn't want to disappoint him. She was thrilled that he looked at her that way. His desire had to be real, no one could fake that expression. She was amazed and gratified that the sight of her scarred body and misshapen breast didn't repulse him. The need in him was apparent, stamped into his face, alive in his eyes. He was hanging on to his control by a mere thread. It was impossible not to respond to that need.

He shifted his body and a rush of heat flared like a sunburst. She tightened her hold on his shoulders, feeling his muscles bunch beneath her fingers. Against her thigh she could feel the white-hot brand of his heavy erection. Curls sprang around his head, his hair disheveled and sexy from her fists. His eyes were so dark, held so much love, and his face so much torment she had no defenses at all.

I've fallen in love with you, she admitted shyly.

A slow, satisfied smile curved his hard mouth. His fingers moved over her lips, down her breasts to trace a thread across her stomach and back up to her breasts. She drew in her breath sharply as he sucked on her nipple, licked, and then kissed his way up to her lips. She opened her mouth to his at his silent insistence, her tongue twining with his. He moved, his chest rubbing along her nipples, sensitive from his attention. His hard shaft pulsed and jerked against her thigh in urgent need, adding to her growing excitement.

Love is a terrible word to describe the way I feel about you. But I'm going to try to show you. He sounded so tormented she moved her body against his, giving herself to him in the only way she knew how.

He kissed his way to her breasts, her belly button, spreading small kisses and bites and then licking away the sting all along the threads of the web and down to her thighs. Each nip of those strong teeth and rasping of his tongue over the sting sent spirals of heat curling through her body and rushes of hot liquid spilling between her legs. Everywhere he touched, kissed, and nipped, thousands of tiny sparks burst under her skin, creating a terrible fire that refused to be quenched. She couldn't keep her body still, writhing beneath him, her hips lifting to reach him, her breasts pushing hard against his chest. She wanted. Plain and simple, she wanted.

His lips teased the bunching muscles along her belly, his tongue dipping into her belly button. *I need a spider right here, baby.* His teeth bit gently at the top of the vee of curls. *I really want another spider here as well.* He licked at the spot over and over, before catching her thighs in her large hands and drawing them apart. *I've been starving for you, Azami. I was planning to get your body ready for me, but this is all for me. I just need this, so you'll have to be patient will I indulge myself.*

She couldn't catch her breath. His sexy words, his sensual tone, and the demand in his dark tone sent fingers of arousal teasing her thighs. He lifted her bottom up with his two hands, his palms hot and possessive. He sent her one last look from his dark eyes and lowered his head. His tongue swiped through her curls and she gasped, a soft, broken cry escaping.

Azami couldn't think, could hardly breathe as he ate her, licking and sucking and sending sensation after sensation crashing through her. She was mindless with arousal, gripping his hair with her fists as he pushed his tongue deep, stabbing into her over and over. She couldn't stay still, even though he ordered her to twice in a gravelly, warning tone. It was impossible to obey, not with his teeth teasing her clit, his tongue laving and then suckling again.

Tension built fast and sharp, a firestorm raged, and she writhed insanely, bucking, near sobbing with pleas for more. Her body began to spin out of control, winding tighter and tighter, climbing higher and higher until, when his finger sank deep and his tongue flicked, she flew apart, her body fragmenting, rockets going off in her head.

Sam reached for the drawer beside his bed and dragged the small pack out, ripping it open with his teeth. Nothing was going to interfere with her pleasure, not this time. He would make certain she was protected until after they'd talked to the others and her mind was at ease, or they decided permanently against having children. He rolled the condom on and moved up and over her, lifting her hips with one hand and positioning the head of his shaft at her slick entrance. She felt the burning tip enter her, and he pushed no more than an inch or two inside her, but she felt the stretch, the fiery heat. Her body moved of its own accord, muscles grasping him, trying to draw him in further. She felt as if she might not survive unless he was all the way inside of her.

Slow, baby.

The sound of his voice, his harsh panting as he tried to control his actions only aroused her more.

I don't want to hurt you, Azami, and you're so damned tight.

She sobbed his name, pleaded with him to fill her. He bent his head toward hers and licked at her neck, holding himself still as her body stretched to accommodate his size.

She felt him share her breath and then he pushed into her gently, feeling his way. She was slick and her hips wouldn't stay still, even when he gripped her hard to control her runaway body. She gasped and held him to her, fingers digging into his hard, tense muscles.

He gave another small push and she felt the first hint of unease rippling through her body. Sam instantly kissed her, over and over, long, drugging kisses while her body pulsed around his.

Relax for me, sweetheart.

He retracted his hips and plunged deep, taking her breath and her innocence as he buried himself deep. Again he stopped moving, holding her close to him, murmuring reassurances.

I think you're too big for me.

She burned, and not in a good way, as if he was far too large and he'd torn her. She drew up her hands to press against his chest.

You were made for me. Let yourself relax. Already the pain is easing up and you're going to feel so good. You're just in new territory. Trust me.

His mouth found hers again, and she forgot all about pushing him away. Fear slipped to the back of her mind as her body began to respond to his. He moved slowly, experimentally, as if she was a fragile flower he was afraid of crushing. The sensation went from uncomfortable to pleasure very quickly. She lay still, absorbing the way arousal swept through her like a wildfire.

He shifted again, retracting his hips, and she cried out

in dismay. He plunged into her hard and fast, sending streaks of fire racing through her. She heard her own sobbing moan as she tightened around him, an involuntary response, her hips lifting to meet his of their accord.

Are you good now?

He was back to rough panting, forcing control when he was on the very edge. Again that little thrill went through her at the idea that she was the one he wanted so much—her not-so-perfect body.

Yes. Please, Sammy.

He bent his head to nip her chin. *Please what?*

His hips moved again, surging forward, burying himself even deeper. Sensations burst around her, fire seemed to arch over her skin.

Make me yours. All the way. I want to belong to you.

Hell, baby, there's no question.

He moved again, the action making her cry out as fiery heat stroked and caressed. He lifted her hips with his hands, holding her still, watching her eyes. Her heart began pounding in nervous anticipation. He plunged deep into her, the stroke filling her, stretching and burning, pleasure bursting through her. He began thrusting hard and rhythmic, over and over, deeper and deeper, never stopping, driving her up higher than she believed possible.

She felt feverish with urgent need, the tension winding tighter and tighter. She couldn't catch her breath, not with the pounding heat between her thighs, so hard, so thick, invading her senses until there was only Sam and his body welding with hers through pure fire. She could hear the sounds of their flesh coming together, her loud, ragged panting and his harsh breathing. She began to feel the edge of her consciousness fading as fire raged through her, growing into a storm she couldn't stop.

That's it, baby, stay with me, let go. Just give yourself to me.

She gasped, arching closer to him, gripping him hard, her body not her own, wild and out of control, lifting to meet the frenzied thrusting. She heard her own cry as his shaft dragged over her most sensitive spot, pressing hard as he plunged again deep into her. He seemed to grow even larger, stretching her until she thought she couldn't stand the pleasure. A tidal wave ripped through her, her body clamping down hard around his thick shaft, taking him with her. Wave after wave tore through her, the strength of the release shocking, jerking her small body, burning through her body with a force she hadn't conceived of.

She could feel his body reacting to her muscles gripping him so tightly, milking him dry. She fell back, gasping for air, shocked at the almost violent way she'd reacted to his possession.

Sam, struggling for breath, rolled off of Azami, afraid his weight would crush her, since he was as limp as a dishrag. He lay beside her, one arm slung across his eyes as he fought his burning lungs. He wasn't certain he would ever move again. The best he could manage was his fingers, sliding across the sheet to find Azami's hand.

Are you okay, baby?

I don't know. She sounded dazed. *Am I alive?*

I'm not certain either of us are. Give me a minute and we'll go for round two.

He felt movement and managed to turn his head toward her and pry open one eye. She lifted her head and looked pointedly at his soft cock with a small smile.

"You're feeling optimistic, aren't you?" she said aloud, laughter in her voice.

His fingers found her hair, wrapping a length around his fist. He gave a gentle tug and made an effort to find his voice. "That's a challenge, woman, and all good soldiers find a way to meet a challenge."

He felt her laughter in his mind, that soft, melting molasses that just poured in and filled him with happiness. How had he ever managed without her?

"I wasn't challenging you, Sammy. I'm not certain I'll

ever be able to walk again," she pointed out. "I think I have skid marks inside."

Alarm spread instantly. "Did I hurt you?"

"You know you didn't, but we were a little on the wild side. I'm definitely going to be a little sore, but I'm perfectly willing to give up walking."

Again her laughter poured into his mind. That soft, sensual sound could bring a man to his knees.

"I don't think we have to go that far," Sam said, careful not to let his voice shake with emotion. She was a dream he feared he might wake up from all too soon.

"Thank you for remembering to protect me, Sam," Azami said. "I do want a child, but I want to go into it with both of us knowing what we're getting into. I can go on birth control. It's just that I never thought I would need it."

He turned toward her, elbow on the bed, his head propped in his hand. "Didn't you think you'd eventually sleep with someone?" Even as he said it, his mind rejected the idea. He put his free hand on her bare stomach, fingers splayed wide. He nearly covered her entire abdomen with his large hand.

Her long lashes swept down, veiling her expression. "I am never around men long enough to get to know them. You and I had an unusual and unexpected connection."

Her suspicious tone irritated him. "*Don't* say one word about Whitney. He doesn't belong in our bedroom," he warned sharply.

"I wasn't going to."

"But you were thinking it. My connection with you is not purely on a physical level. Whitney can manipulate pheromones, but he can't make a man fall in love with a woman. He can't make him want to protect her." He caught her chin and lifted it, forcing her gaze up to his. "I want to wake up every morning with you beside me. I want to laugh with you. Fight with you. Grow old with you. This—you and me—isn't about lust, Azami."

"I know that," she admitted, reaching to stroke a caress

down his face. "I do, Sam. It's just so—unexpected. When I flew out here, a man was the last thing on my mind."

"Should I expect one of your brothers to try to take my head off with his sword tomorrow?"

"Why would you think that?"

"You're in my bed, Azami," he pointed out.

"You asked permission."

"To marry you. To court you. Not to sleep with you."

"I make my own decisions, Sam. They know that." She smiled at him, that mysterious smile that said so many things. "They know better than to try to tell me what to do."

"That's a relief." He smirked a little. "I wouldn't want to have to fight a relative." He forced himself to sit up. "I'm going to run you a bath. I don't want you sore."

"You don't have to do that."

"Yes, I do." He leaned over to brush a kiss across her mouth. "We're not done. I have a lot more to show you. You need to soak and get some sleep first though." Already he could feel the first stirrings of need moving through his mind.

Azami stayed on the bed, staring up at the ceiling, a bemused expression on her face while he dealt with the condom and started the bathwater running. She turned her head toward him as he came back to stand in the doorway. She looked beautiful, sprawled out on his bed, her long hair everywhere, a little drowsy, her lashes long and her mouth sinful. He was having fantasies about that mouth.

"You know that your friends will try to talk you out of marrying me once they realize you're serious," she said. Her voice was very quiet, very matter-of-fact.

He stiffened. "They know you're not working against them, Azami. They accept that you're a GhostWalker. Anything you've done to take down Whitney is no different from what we do. We're in a fight for our lives, for the lives of our children. They'll not only accept you but welcome you. You're an amazing weapon."

She smiled at him, serenity on her face. "That has

nothing to do with what I'm saying. I'm certain they'll all get used to having me provide information, support, and even tactical help when needed."

"Why would you believe they would have an objection to you?"

"They love you. That was very evident to me when you were hurt. All of them hovered around the room these past few days, continually checking on you. I heard them asking Lily if you needed blood, anything at all to help. They will try to talk you out of marriage to me out of love for you."

He went to her, lifting her off the bed to hold her close to him. "You make me happy, Azami. I'm happier than I ever thought I could be. That's all they're going to care about." He carried her to the bathroom.

She brushed her hand over his face. Her fingers trailed over his jaw and the stubble there, conveying tenderness in that small touch. "Silly man. They will not understand why I don't show you affection publicly. And I cannot. It's against my nature."

"I put a little of that oil in the water. It seemed to have some kind of healing agent in it and I thought it might help," he said as he let her feet drop into the water.

Azami wrapped her hair up, tying the thick mass into a knot on top of her head before sinking gratefully into the hot, scented bath. "Thank you, Sam, this feels wonderful."

"Two things, woman," Sam said, watching as she leaned her head against the taller backrest, relaxing completely. "First, I have no doubt that if I ever *needed* a public display of affection, you would provide for me. I can't see that happening. I have every confidence in your feelings for me. Secondly, we have telepathy. I intend to use that shamelessly when we're out in public. Our relationship is ours. I like it that way."

"You're a remarkable man, Sam," she said, her lashes drifting down. "You really are. When I'm in your mind, I feel your strength and confidence. Your intelligence. I fell in love with that immediately." Her lashes lifted, her eyes meeting his. "I didn't think I would find a man as good as my father. He was a fierce warrior, yet gentle and kind. He was gifted and yet humble. He raised my brothers to be the same."

"And you, Azami, he raised you to be the same."

She smiled. "That's a huge compliment, Sammy. I'm not always as kind and gentle as I would like to be. I have tried to put my anger at Whitney aside and go after him for the right reasons, but it isn't always easy." Her eyes darkened. "It didn't help that he was willing to sacrifice you to an enemy for his own gain. He claimed he would have a man in place to kill you the moment the diamond is in his hand, but you know he wouldn't. You would suffer torture the moment you are in the hands of Ezekial Ekabela. Whitney wouldn't chance sending one of the men in his private army. He can't afford to lose too many more. They're enhanced, but they all have failed the psyche tests and eventually they're going to short-circuit."

"I've run into a couple," Sam said.

"I feel sorry for them," Azami conceded. "They give up their lives, thinking they're going to get something extraordinary. He gives them good salaries, far more than they can ever make in the military, but they have to 'die' on a military mission and give up their lives with family and friends to serve him. In the end, they lose everything."

"He promises them a woman," Sam told her.

She nodded. "I know. I've studied his tactics. I've been trying to find his connections to the military and the White House and sever them, but as fast as I cut one tentacle, he seems to grow another."

"You have to remember Peter Whitney is a billionaire. He is considered by many to be the world's most renowned scientist. Few people are aware of his experiments. He has political connections everywhere. He supported candidates and charities, and has research facilities all over the world. His connection to the military goes way back. He went to school with many of the people now running things."

"His daughter has his money, doesn't she?" Azami asked. "She inherited it when he supposedly died. He never came out of hiding to claim he was alive."

"No, but he'd already siphoned off hundreds of millions to untraceable accounts. Believe me, he has no money problems. And he's so entrenched in the military, he can still land his planes at any military base around the world."

"I couldn't draw him out, not even to meet with us about the satellite," Azami said with a small sigh. She yawned, covering the gesture with her hand. "Every single time I get a fix on his location, he's gone by the time I get there."

"He moves between his facilities and he's got several that are nearly impenetrable. That doesn't mean we won't stop him, Azami. We'll get him." He crooked his finger at her. "Stand up, honey. You're going to fall asleep in the tub."

She complied, pulling the stopper to allow the water to flow out. Sam wrapped her in a towel and lifted her out, drying her thoroughly before working the knot out of her hair so it could fall free down her back. He buried his face in the silky mass.

"I love your hair."

She smiled up at him. "You always make me feel beautiful, Sam."

He hugged her tight. "You *are* beautiful. Hell, woman, get a clue."

She snuggled against his chest. "I'm glad you think so." She put her arms around him and held him tight. "You know I can't help being protective of you, Sam."

He laughed and scooped her up. "I feel the same way toward you." But he heard that little caution in her voice. She was serious about something and didn't think he was going to like it—which meant he probably wouldn't.

He carried her to the bed and tossed her onto the mattress, coming down beside her and dragging up the covers. "Just say it."

"Do you think General Ranier is working with Whitney?" When he remained silent, she lifted her hand to his face. "I ask because he appears to be some of the time, but I can't be certain. Would he betray you to serve Whitney?"

Sam swore to himself, detesting that he couldn't give her a straight answer. "General Ranier is a patriot. He loves his country and has dedicated his life to serving it."

She continued to look at him, not saying a word, yet answering him very eloquently with her silence.

Sam pulled her close, kissing her hard. "Go to sleep, baby. I'm waking you up in an hour or so." He kissed her again, his throat aching. "Just go to sleep."

CHAPTER 15

$\sim$

Sam kept his eyes closed, afraid if he opened them, he would know everything had been a drug induced illusion. His hand reached out and beside him, the bed was empty. His heart skipped a beat and his mind rejected the idea that making love with Azami had all been a dream. For a moment, he was the young boy in the darkened doorway, terrified of moving, of breathing even, because the world would come crashing down.

He inhaled, and her fragrance still lingered in the room mixed with their combined scents. He'd made love to her three times, waking her again and again and still, it wasn't enough to sate him. He wanted her again with every bit as much intensity and passion as he had the first time. There was no doubt in his mind, he would always feel that way about her.

Be real, baby, he murmured in his mind, reaching for her. Needing her to be real.

Silly man. I'm fixing your coffee.

He let his breath out slowly and opened his eyes. *You're a goddess.*

Her soft laughter warmed him, and he lay there a moment just savoring the feeling of being cared for—of love and laughter.

Morning light poured through the window, glowing through a light mist. Outside, tree branches swayed gently, the leaves rustling to add to the music of the running water. The rays of the sun streamed through the tree branches, golden spotlights playing over the rippling stream. The fine layer of mist added a feeling of being cocooned in his own world. He picked up the pillow beside him and took Azami's scent deep into his lungs before stroking a caress over the pillowcase as he replaced it neatly beside his own. Throwing off the covers, he stretched lazily before padding barefoot and naked to the window to look out into the forest.

A small herd of deer moved along the trail leading to the stream. Dipping their muzzles, some drank while others served as guards. His world. He'd never really seen and appreciated it before. The forest and outdoors had always brought him a semblance of peace, but having Azami in his life had changed his perspective on things. He found himself smiling for no reason at all as he turned back to pad across the room to the bathroom.

When he emerged from his shower, a towel riding low on his hips, she was there, looking so beautiful he couldn't breathe for a moment. She carried a mug of fresh coffee. The aroma blended with her scent, a welcoming start to any morning. He found himself smiling like an idiot as he took the mug and bent to kiss her.

"You look beautiful this morning."

Her hair was back up in that twisty thing she liked, each ornate pin in place, with those few artful long strands hanging down around her neck and shoulders making her look sexier than ever to him. He wanted to remove those pins slowly all over again. She wore her silken robe, and clearly nothing else beneath it, but she smelled like heaven, so she'd had her bath. Even her hair had a fresh, citrus fragrance he couldn't quite place but he found alluring. His free hand curled around the nape of her neck. She looked serene, demure even, yet her eyes, when she looked at him, held liquid heat, bumping his pulse rate up.

"How can you look so innocent after last night?"

She gave him her mysterious smile. "A woman must have her secrets, Sammy." Her smile widened and she walked on bare feet over to the neatly folded clothing on top of the dresser.

Sam took a slow sip of coffee, watching her intently. She moved like water, a flowing, fluid motion so effortless she seemed not to displace the air around her. He had a difficult time detecting any surge of energy whatsoever around her. She was at such harmony with her surroundings, she blended in, rather than stood out.

The silk slid from her shoulders inch by inch, slowly revealing the rising phoenix, the long intriguing tail feathers, so lacy, curling along the curve of her buttocks. He nearly choked on his coffee, and his body reacted instantly to the sight of her naked body.

"I'm going to have a hell of a hard-on all day, thanks to you," he accused.

She turned her head, a graceful movement, her long lashes fluttering as she observed him with her dark eyes. "I am glad, Sam. I want you to think of me throughout the day. That will please me, knowing you are looking forward to our bath tonight."

His cock jerked hard at the memory of the way she'd cared for him. He groaned. "You're killing me, honey."

She took a scrap of lace in her hands and slowly pulled it up over her legs, lace shaping her buttocks lovingly while a single lacy strap disappeared between her rounded cheeks. Sam groaned again and stepped close to grasp one firm cheek in the palm of his hand. She smiled at him and moved her bottom more snugly into his hand. Both her hands went to the back of her head, lacing her fingers together, and her lashes lowered, her lips parting slightly.

Sam closed his eyes for a moment, praying for strength.

Hot blood rushed to his groin and the memory of the taste of her filled his mouth. She was naturally sensual, every movement as precise and flowing as when she was in battle or pouring tea. His body had gone so hard he was afraid to take a step, afraid he might shatter. He swallowed hard and dropped the towel from around his hips, one hand closing around his aching erection briefly before reaching around her with both hands to cup the slight weight of her breasts.

He bent his head to her inviting neck, kissing his way down to her shoulder while his fingers plucked and teased at her nipples. Her small body shifted back against him, her skin rubbing along his like a cat.

I am picturing you at my feet right about now, with that pretty mouth of yours filled with my cock.

Really? Her head went back against his chest. Her arm came up around his neck to draw his head down to her lips. She kissed him, drawing his tongue into her mouth until he was groaning at the simulation of what he wanted. *You had only to say so. It will be my pleasure.*

The joy in her voice, in her mind, made his body all the hotter. He hadn't known until that moment that his enjoyment was off the map because of her enjoyment. That was the reason his body responded to her the way it did. Crazy hard. Hot and pounding with urgent need. So close to loss of control. Mind-blowing.

Azami turned in his arms, her breasts brushing enticingly against his chest. She pressed a kiss over his heart and then on various scars along his ribs and down to his belly. His breath caught in his throat as her hands cupped his balls, rolling and squeezing gently before sliding up to circle the girth of his cock. His breath left his lungs in a rush.

She took her time, just the way she did everything. Careful. Fully engaged. Complete concentration. And so damned loving he felt he'd died and gone to heaven. Her soft lips brushed over the sensitive velvet head, small kisses, her tongue swirling around to catch the pearl droplets. He put his hand on her shoulder, and she went to her knees in front of him, her gaze locking with his. The sight of her sent his heart pounding and his hips rocking. She was the most beautiful woman—the most beautiful sight he'd ever seen.

One hand slipped between his legs, massaging along his inner thigh, her fingers moving progressively higher as her mouth slid over the head of his cock. Hot. Wet, Tight. Her tongue danced over and under, hitting that sweet spot that sent a shudder of pleasure down his spine. Fire raced through his veins and raged in his groin, roaring like a firestorm in his belly. Her mouth tightened around him and her fingers found that spot right behind his balls, caressing and massaging while her mouth worked over him.

This moment was for him—all for him; he could see it in her eyes. The giving. The gift of her body to him. The selfless act of passion. The joy in her vibrated through her mouth straight to his hard flesh. The small hand at the base of his cock began to squeeze and release in time to the pull of her mouth and the massaging of her fingers. The suction was hard and tight, and then slow and easy, shallow and then deep with that clever little tongue teasing at the one spot that kept his body shuddering with pleasure.

Sam couldn't take his eyes from her even as his hips began to take over the rhythm, his cock on fire in that silken, wet tunnel. *Take a breath.* Because he needed this now. He couldn't stop the small thrust that took him deeper and damn it all, he'd been proud of being long and thick, but he was pushing her to the limit and he couldn't stop the need building in him—*raging* in him. *Another.* He pushed deeper each time, holding there for just a moment while she squeezed and massaged his cock, while the fire burned out of control in his cock.

She gave herself up to him, coughing a little, but following his command each time he told her to take a breath. The heat built and built, the pressure never ending, never letting up. He could feel the fiery storm in his balls, and those clever fingers never stopped massaging, pressing deeper just as she took him deeper, her mouth so tight, so silky, he couldn't stop the hard thrust of his body as she took him over the edge.

Her long lashes fluttered as her throat worked, but she was valiant and determined, her mouth loving him as he poured into her. He stayed for as long as possible in pure ecstasy before slowly softening while her tongue washed him the way her hands had done, with meticulous care and total commitment.

Sam's knees threatened to give out. He stood on shaky legs waiting for his brain to work again. Azami stood up gracefully, a small pleased smile on her face as she leaned over him, her hands cupping him gently so she could place a kiss on the head of his cock.

"Thank you, Sammy. I love pleasing you."

Before he could find his voice, she padded barefoot into the bathroom, and he could hear her rinsing out her mouth with the unhurried, fluid movements he had come to expect from her. He stood in the middle of the bedroom, breathing deep, shocked that his life had changed in the blink of an eye, shocked that a woman such as Azami could possibly give herself to him the way she did—so completely.

She reentered the room, looking just as innocent and demure as she had earlier, as if she hadn't just taken him to heaven. She reached for the small lacy bra that matched her underwear. "The garrote is such a thin wire it doesn't show up on airport security. And if it did, it simply appears to be an underwire. It's very comfortable, so much so, I forget it's there most of the time."

The moment she began to talk weapons in that sweet, soft voice, heat curled in the pit of his stomach. He sank down onto the bed to prevent himself from making a total fool of himself and falling at her feet. "Nice. I have mine sewn into the seams of my jeans."

She nodded. "I do that as well." She drew a pair of soft, straight-legged black trousers up her slender legs. The material was deceiving, stretching, easily moving with her body.

She added a red silk blouse and picked up an intricate belt. She smiled and handed it to him.

Sam took the belt into his palm, lifting it carefully to weigh it. The belt was made of several strands of woven rope. The weave was artwork, decorative and attractive. The belt buckle was small to fit her size, a flat silver, sturdy, with what appeared to be a sunburst carved into it. "Very lightweight.

"And handy. The rope can hold up to a thousand pounds and yet is easily shot from a crossbow to be used as an anchor to reach another building. The belt buckle is actually a throwing star, or, in a pinch, a grappling hook, reinforced titanium."

"Very handy. That's my woman, the walking arsenal."

She laughed softly. "That's not the half of it." The belt went around her narrow waist and she bent to pull on socks.

"Are those made of explosives?"

Her dark eyes regarded him soberly. "I thought of that, but no, too difficult to get to." She straightened and took a ring from the nightstand, slipping it on her finger. The ruby stone was small, yet it sparkled when she moved her hand. "A tiny amount of powder that can render temporary blindness."

Sam shook his head and caught up his clothes. She really was a walking arsenal and, God help him, all the sexier for it. He watched her reach for her ruby earrings. They dangled delicately from her ears, twin fiery stones at her lobe and several rounded pearls on the end of five braided chains. He raised his eyebrow. No way did he believe the simple jewelry was just that.

She sent him another smile. She touched the white balls at the end of the chains. "These are not real pearls, just shells to house the ammunition for my blow gun. It gives me ten extra needles in a fight."

"I'm getting another hard-on just thinking about you with all those weapons." His hand snaked out, fingers settling around her wrist. He tugged until she was between his legs. "How am I going to get through the day knowing you're so damned sexy, woman?"

Her eyes, heavy-lidded, drifted over his face and down his body, clearly marking him as her territory. "The same way I will. I look forward to our evening together."

"I know there's no public displays of affection," Sam said as he buttoned his jeans, "but if it gets too bad, don't be surprised if I drag you into a closet and tug those trousers down."

Her eyes jumped to his face. "You are a very brave man, Sammy."

"You have no idea what I'm willing to sacrifice if it means more sex with you."

Laughter danced in her eyes as she secured a necklace around her neck. A single pendant hung from the slender chain. "I will look forward to an adventure in the closet," she said with a demure sweep of her lashes.

"That has to be a knife of some kind." The pendant was short, no more than an inch and a half, shaped like a very slender heart. "Is it made of ceramic?"

"Every lady needs one."

He stepped close to examine each piece of jewelry. The craftsmanship was amazing, the details simplistic but appealing. He raised his eyebrow. "You?"

"My father was renowned and I learned from him." She pushed a bracelet made of thin spirals of twisted hemp onto her wrist. The bracelet was quite unique but attractive. She held up her arm. "For my bow or crossbow. I can assemble one in under a minute." She reached for a second bracelet, which she pushed close to the first, a wrap of strands of beads.

Sam didn't have to be told that was a weapon, he'd seen warrior beads before, but hers looked ornate, very beautiful with carved beads. No one would ever suspect that the bracelet was lethal.

Azami added a slim, beautifully crafted watch to her left wrist. He raised his eyebrows.

She laughed. "A lady has to have some secrets."

On top of everything, she looked beautiful in her red silk blouse and black suit trousers. He could see how she could move fast and easily dressed as she was. The blouse was loose-fitting enough that she could have a few knives placed strategically if she was going into battle.

She reached for her shoes. Boots, he corrected himself. Stylish. Low heels with fancy grills going up the front of the pair. He studied the eyelets made of strong metal—titanium? Definitely more than boots, but he had no idea what—only that in Azami's hands, they would be lethal.

Azami swung around as a soft vibration accompanied the flash of a strobe light throughout the room. Sam, who had looked lazy and content, leapt off the bed and dragged on clothes fast. She didn't ask questions but hurried into her jacket, shoving knives into the specially made sheaths. Jamming a gun down into one boot, she added a knife to the second.

Sam shoved the floor rug aside and yanked open a trapdoor in the floor. "Move it, Azami, now." He stepped back to allow her to precede him.

Azami didn't hesitate. She went down the stairs fast, using the rail to slide into the basement, Sam right behind her. She waited in the darkness. She could see, another "gift" from Whitney's enhancements, probably the cat DNA. The basement looked like any man's basement: tools, pegboards, and workbenches. She remained absolutely still—waiting.

Sam went to the side wall closest to them and ran his palm over what appeared to be a light switch. She would bet it actually turned on a light too. A door built into the wall swung open without a sound. Small trace lights ran along a tunnel. This time Sam went in first. Azami followed him in silence. She flexed her fingers and ran a checklist over her body, ensuring every muscle was stretched and limber, ready for anything.

Sam halted in a small alcove, once again using his palm and then his eye on a retinal scan to open another door. Azami's breath caught in her throat.

"Sexy," she commented, peering around him. "I'm impressed."

"We've got them scattered through the tunnels. You'll have to be programmed in to open them. We have maps in our heads to all the various weapons caches," he said as he shoved guns and ammunition into belts and harnesses as well as his boot. "Need anything?"

"Another gun. My crossbow's in my room. I have a mini, but it's not terribly effective at great distances."

She saw his eyes flick to her face, assessing her capability with a gun. She grinned at him, sheer audacity. His features relaxed and he gestured toward the armory.

Azami had already spotted the small automatic she was most familiar with. It fit in her hands easily. She had small hands, and often a weapon just didn't sit right in her palm, but she liked the little automatic. She caught up the belt and ammunition and stepped back, indicating she was ready to go. She didn't like taking an unproven weapon into combat, so she would rely mainly on her speed and up-close fighting if there was need, but the weapon might come in handy.

The moment Sam closed the doors, they began to jog through the tunnel, heading, Azami could tell, straight back to the main compound.

My brothers?

They'll be in the tunnels with Daniel and Lily. No one will take chances with them, Sam assured.

I'm not worried about them. They are samurai. They'll be an asset to you. They fight with great skill and can handle multiple weapons.

Azami was unconcerned for their safety as he seemed to think she would be. She knew both Daiki and Eiji would protect Daniel and Lily if anything went wrong. Sam didn't know them as she did. She'd trained with them and had no doubts about their skills. They weren't afraid to die any more than she was, but the world would lose two incredible and intelligent human beings if they were killed.

What are we facing?

I have no idea. The signal is just for preparation. Some one is approaching the compound. We don't take chances, and it's good practice to stay alert. Most of the time, it's some lost hiker or a group of hunters, but we've had a couple of suspicious vehicles that turn around the moment they realize they're under surveillance.

She *loved* that Sam believed so much in her. They'd made love over and over. She could feel his love and support surrounding her, yet he still saw her as she was: a woman who would never go into the tunnels and wait to be told it was all clear. He understood—without her having to explain— that she would have his back no matter what.

Tunnels run completely underground from our compound to Team Two's compound and between each of the houses. Each section of tunnel every twenty feet has an activation switch and we can blow precise direction blasts.

She noted every turn they made and where each overhead opening to escape was. There were no ladders, but she could feel the difference in the air and just make out a black painted hand grip above her head. There was a way to the surface in five places that she'd counted. She didn't yet know how to use them, but she was grateful they were there. Tunnels could be used to a great advantage, but they could also be terrible traps.

Are those grips trapdoors to the surface?

Yes. You have to jump to them. You catch the grip, invert, plant your feet on either side of the trapdoor, and using the rings to brace your body, heave upward.

So only someone with enhanced strength can open the doors?

He glanced over his shoulder at her, obviously assessing her size and strength. *That's it. And they have to know they're there.* He didn't break stride, jogging at a fast pace down the long tunnel toward the main compound.

I can do it. Remember, I have cat DNA in me, she assured.

I was fairly certain you wouldn't have trouble. There was approval, even pride, in his voice. *This branch takes you to Jack and Ken Norton's compound. It's farther up the mountain, so you're running uphill. It's quite a distance, but if you ever need to get there without being seen, this is your best way. The ground and trees above us keep anyone from finding the tunnels from the sky. You can move freely down here. The passageway may come in handy if we have a houseful of kids.*

The laughter in his voice warmed her. Sam Johnson was no throwaway, and if General Ranier had agreed to trade his life because Whitney needed a diamond, the general was going to die very fast.

Sam stopped abruptly, so fast she actually bumped into him. His head snapped around and he gripped her upper arms with bruising strength. "You won't touch the general. Not for any reason." He actually gave her a little shake.

A shiver went through her at the tone of his voice. She didn't struggle against his hold but looked up at him steadily. "I would protect you with my life, even from yourself, Sam. If this man is betraying you . . ."

"*That* man is the only father I've known."

"*Whitney* is the only father Lily has ever known," she pointed out, refusing to flinch or hedge the truth. "I hope your father is everything you believe him to be, but, Sam, there have been little indications over the course of our investigation that've pointed toward him working with Whitney."

"You *investigated* the general? Do you have any idea who he really is? What he's given to this country?" Sam demanded.

"Sam, that really isn't the point, is it?" She kept very

calm on the outside, but inside, for the first time, she was aware she had a great deal to lose. "You know I'm after Whitney and I'm attempting to cut his ties to legitimacy—especially the military. What would you want done if you find he's betraying not only you but your entire team?"

"You're telling me that if Daiki or Eiji was betraying you, you'd want me to kill them?"

"I would hope you would want to spare me that great sorrow," she admitted.

Sam opened his mouth to speak, but closed it, slowly letting go of her arms, as if he was only just aware he was gripping her tightly. "I don't want to think he's capable of betraying the men in his command," he admitted reluctantly. "I shouldn't be taking out my anger on you. I do believe in him, but once in a while, some little thing will cause me to doubt him and then I get angry at myself. It isn't you, Azami."

She put her arms around him and held him for a brief moment. "I know that."

He dropped a kiss on top of her head. "We've got to hustle."

"Then go, I'm right behind you." Relief was overwhelming. Their first argument and he hadn't told her to get out of his life.

She was still that white-haired child expecting to be thrown away. Her father had always told her that her past would haunt her and she'd have to fight it. The past shaped the future. How many times had he said that to her? She hoped it didn't shame him that she still needed reassurance she was worth something.

She sprinted behind Sam, moving faster now, mapping the tunnel automatically should she ever need to use it. The ground sloped downward, but gently, so that it was easy enough to run. The curving walls were thick and made of concrete and steel. Lily had spared no expense in the building of escape routes.

The tunnel came out at the main house, where the team had already gathered, all armed and spreading out to defend their homes.

"Helicopter approaching," Ryland said as they entered. He didn't even blink twice when he saw Azami armed.

"I'll get my bow," she said and ran for her room.

"It appears to be General Ranier, although he didn't schedule a visit with us and always has in the past," Ryland said, looking at Sam.

Sam shook his head. "He hasn't contacted me."

Azami rushed back to her room, noting the halls were empty and Lily and Daniel were gone. All computers were shut down and the building was eerily quiet in spite of the fact that ten men were ready for combat. She snatched up her bow and arrows, shouldering them along with her crossbow, and raced back to the war room.

Sam was already gone, guarding some part of the compound. "What can I do? I'm telepathic, so you can convey your orders to me as well without a radio," she told Ryland.

"You're a respected guest in this house."

"I'm a GhostWalker," she said. "And Sam's woman. Let me help. I'm better outside than in." For the first time she actually felt as if she did belong and she was ready to fight for that right.

"Take the east side of the roof. I'll let the others know you'll be there."

Azami didn't wait to see if he changed his mind, she sprinted for the roof. She simply poured herself into Sam's mind and she could hear Ryland giving orders and relaying the fact that she would be defending the property with them.

Helicopter landed.

That was the one they called Nico.

General Ranier and the pilot only. No one else in sight. He's come in without even his aide. No gunners. He's alone, Rye.

Kadan, escort him in. Nico, keep an eye on the pilot.

Azami made her way to the roof in spite of the fact that everything looked as if it was all right. She wanted to see the layout of the compound and how much cover was available. Clearly even the roof had been built with combat in mind. There were numerous places for a soldier to stay in cover yet defend the roof and grounds around him. She could see the helicopter on the helicopter pad several yards from the main grounds. Kadan was running beside the man she'd only seen in pictures. General Ranier. She really hoped he was as good a man as Sam believed.

All clear. Assemble in the war room. Nico, keep your eye on the pilot.

The command came several minutes after the general disappeared into the house. Azami wasn't certain if she was included in the command, but she made her way to the war room. If they threw her out, she'd find another way to listen in. Daiki had planted a tiny camera and transmitter when they'd first been shown around the building. The cameras enabled her to move around without fear of getting hurt when she teleported. She didn't need them for most of the rooms, she had the coordinates in her mind now, but they hadn't yet retrieved their equipment, although two of the cameras had been found by the GhostWalkers.

She entered the room in the samurai way, quietly but with absolute confidence. The general glanced up, frowned, and turned to Ryland.

"This is Azami Yoshiie. She's a GhostWalker, sir," Ryland said. "She's one of us."

"And engaged to me," Sam added. "We're going to marry as soon as it can be arranged."

The general looked as if Sam had hit him with a two-by-four. "What the hell are you talking about? We're in a big enough mess without you losing your mind, boy."

"I'm a man, sir," Sam corrected. "I grew up a long time ago. Azami and I want to get married soon. I thought you should know. She'll be an asset to us. She's a skilled fighter."

"She owns one of the biggest satellite companies in the world," Ranier corrected. "She's corporate, not one of us." He sounded brusque, bordering on rude.

Azami continued to watch him, her demeanor demure and serene. It mattered little to her what he said about her, only what he had come to do here. His visit was obviously unusual. The men, although they knew him and had settled into seats around the table, were still very much on alert, ready for anything.

"Sir, what brings you out to our compound?" Ryland asked.

The general glared at Sam for a few more minutes before he sighed. "It's classified. You know I can't discuss it in front of a civilian."

Sam opened his mouth to protest, but Azami inclined her head and left the room immediately. There was no point in arguing. She put on a burst of speed and made it back to her room, quickly turning on the small video screen to watch what transpired.

The general pulled a sheaf of papers from his jacket. "This is why I came." His voice was grim as he tossed the papers down in front of Ryland.

Ryland picked them up slowly, scanned them quickly, and passed them to Kadan. "I pick my own team on any mission, General. You know that."

Azami was surprised Ryland could keep suspicion from his voice. Her heart sank for Sam. The orders had come down to go to the Congo, she was certain of it, and from what Ryland had just said, the general had specified Sam go, just as she'd predicted. Her heart might ache for Sam, but her determination to protect him didn't falter.

"Exactly." The general roared the word. "Why do you think I'm here? I tried to follow this order up the chain, but suddenly, no one is talking. I can see taking a team into the Congo and destroying vehicles and artillery as well as taking out the present leader, that idiot who calls himself General Armine, and the one fighting him for the rebel force, Eudes

Ekabela's brother, Ezekial. Both have got to go if the president in that country is ever going to stabilize it."

"They want *both* men taken out?" Ryland asked.

The general nodded. "They want this genocide stopped there, and the ragtag army of rebels just seems to smash and run. They're good at disappearing. They're keeping the UN from delivering food to the people who need it most, although, if you ask me, the rebels also are holding the diamond mines hostage and the president wants them back, which is probably more of a motivating factor for him asking for help."

"And the bit about retrieval?" Ryland asked.

"Ekabela has a package he's protecting—a large diamond. He claims he would hand it over if Armine is assassinated, giving him control of the rebels. He negotiated a time and place where you'll meet him and retrieve the package. They want Sam to meet with him."

Ryland let out his breath in a long hiss of disapproval. "Sam is the sniper who killed his brother, Eudes."

The general nodded. "He shouldn't know that. Shouldn't have that information, but why specifically Sam, if he doesn't know?"

"That's a good question, sir," Ryland said. "Nico does most of the sniper missions for us. It doesn't make any sense that anyone would specifically ask for Sam."

The general took another piece of paper from his inside pocket and pushed it across the table to Ryland. "That's the name of the man I believe generated these orders. I was stonewalled everywhere I asked, but this man has been in my office, and both times, after he left, when we did the sweep for bugs, we found them. I know this sounds crazy, but I met him twice at charity events Whitney held. I think he's an old crony of Whitney's and they're still in touch. I don't know what these orders mean, but I know we're expected to carry them out."

Azami could see Ryland frowning over the name, but he didn't say it aloud. There were several people she suspected of aiding Whitney and she had them under surveillance.

"Who is he?" Ryland asked.

"He works for the CIA and operates out of Kinshasa. He's in tight with the president there, so it makes sense that the order would come from him, but I couldn't get confirmation, which doesn't make sense. No one keeps me out of the loop. Something doesn't smell right, Rye." He took a breath and avoided eye contact with Sam. "I want you to keep Sam here. I'll take the responsibility for overruling the order."

Relief flooded Azami. The general could have tried throwing suspicion onto someone else if he was still friends with Whitney, but he, for certain, loved his foster son.

"Sir," Sam began.

Ryland shot him a warning glance. "That isn't necessary, sir. Sam was wounded in the battle with the men trying to grab the Yoshiie family. He's in no shape to go on a mission."

The general sat back in his seat, both hands flat on the table. "You didn't think this was information I would have wanted to know?"

"I've been concerned that your office may be . . ." Ryland hesitated. "Compromised," he settled for. "Certainly someone is watching you. We didn't want it known that Sam was injured. Had he not responded to surgery, we would certainly have sent for you."

"Azami saved his life, sir," Kadan added.

"The next time my boy receives so much as a scratch, you send for me," the general hissed.

Azami found herself smiling. He couldn't fake that. He was genuinely angry.

"So what are we going to do about this, Rye?" General Ranier asked.

"We follow orders, sir. We go to the Congo," Ryland said.

"It's a damned ambush," Ranier declared. "There's no doubt in my mind. Take a look at Ken Norton and see what those rebels do to prisoners."

"I guess the trick will be not to get caught," Ryland said.

The general looked as if he might argue for a moment,

but instead, he turned his glare to Sam, his bushy eyebrows drawn together in a frown. "So what's this nonsense about marriage?"

Sam grinned at his foster father, his face brightening. "I'm going to marry her fast, before she has time to think about how crazy it is to marry a soldier, sir."

"You don't even know the girl."

"I know her better than most men know the woman they've been with for twenty years."

Azami knew it was true. He'd been in her mind, saw her character, just as she'd seen his. It wasn't always comfortable because as they became closer, sharing minds more, they slipped in and out without the other knowing. But, once they'd shared minds, it was impossible not to be lonely without him.

The general made a noise. "Do you have any idea how wealthy that woman is? You're a soldier."

Sam just smiled at him.

The general pushed himself away from the table. "I can see I'm not going to do any good trying to stop you. In any case, you need to bring her around to see your mother." His voice was very gruff. "And you're not to move from this compound while your team is in the Congo." He turned to Ryland. "I want you to take your team and follow this directive to the letter. Take that rebel band down. Remove their leaders, pick up the package, take away their vehicles and their guns, and bring back *every* single one of your men. That's a direct order from me. Are we understood?"

"Yes, sir," Ryland agreed, saluting.

CHAPTER 16

"With respect, sir," Sam said, standing, "I would like to talk to you and Ryland about this."

Azami's heart sank. She had known all along Sam wouldn't stay home quietly while his fellow soldiers took his risk for him.

"We're done here, son," the general said and pushed back his chair.

"You would never allow a fellow teammate to go in your place and put his life on the line, possibly blow a mission. You just wouldn't, sir. Are you really expecting me to do less? I'm a soldier first and always. These men are mine, my family, my friends, my team. You know exactly what that means." Sam shook his head. "You know I can't live with myself if someone takes my place and dies."

The general suddenly looked old. "You're all we have, Sam," he said quietly.

"Tucker Addison is not a sacrificial lamb just because he's not your son," Sam pointed out. "He's every bit as valuable to this team as I am. This one is mine. You know I have to go."

Did he have to be so eloquent? A part of Azami was bursting with pride. She would have done exactly the same thing. He wasn't about to allow Tucker Addison to take his place and put his life in jeopardy. Sam was a soldier. He wouldn't hide behind a powerful foster father. She had to be honest with herself. She couldn't have respected Sam if he hadn't acted with honor, at least trying to state his case. She loved him all the more for his insistence, even though she was frightened for him. She had no qualms about death; it was merely a part of life. But now she had Sam to lose, and that wasn't quite so easy to live with.

"You're wounded, Sam. I can't, in good conscience, send you out in the field."

She knew the general was going to capitulate. He wouldn't have even discussed the issue with Sam, he simply would have given the order firmly and left. No, he was listening and admiring Sam, understanding who and what he was, just as she was—and both of them might lose him.

"I had a couple of second-generation Zenith patches slapped on my wounds immediately and I'm nearly completely healed," Sam continued in that same low, persuasive tone. "I'm in no way impaired and certain Lily will approve me for work. I know you received the report on the second-generation drug and have read the miracle reports on it."

Azami's heart jumped. That was it, the link to Whitney. All along she'd suspected Whitney had tapped into Lily's private computer, but there was no other evidence of it other than that study on second-generation Zenith. It wasn't Lily's compound or computers compromised, it was the general's. Her mind instantly connected the dots. General Ranier had gone to school with the senior Freeman, Scheffield, and Whitney. He'd been friends with all of them.

She wanted to reach out to Sam with her revelation, but she needed to wait. Ranier had gone into the military and served with distinction, moving him up the ranks fast. He was a brilliant strategist. Whitney would admire him and count on his support. Scheffield had become an advocate of diplomacy.

She'd been so wrong about Whitney's reasons for choosing Sam. Completely, utterly wrong. She'd thought it had something to do with her—with pairing them in some way, but Whitney hadn't thought about her after he dumped her. She was garbage to him and he'd gotten rid of her. *She* was the one obsessed with Whitney. Whitney truly didn't even know—or care—if she lived. As far as he was concerned, she was dead. Useless and therefore not worth thinking about.

She let her breath out slowly. There was another reason he chose Sam and that reason was in the war room. General Ranier had remained loyal to the president and his chief of staff. He hadn't cooperated with Whitney. He hadn't fed him information nor done his bidding to try to work behind the scenes to forward Whitney's agenda. Peter Whitney would consider Ranier's conduct the worst betrayal of all. The general was in charge of a team of GhostWalkers. They were highly skilled, elite men and women with special psychic gifts the rest of the world knew nothing about.

Azami knew Whitney inside and out. She'd made it her mission in life to study everything about him. His genius was undisputed, but there was no doubt in her mind that over the years, too many privileges and his very genius had eaten away at his sanity. Somewhere along the line he'd lost all perspective and believed himself to be omnipotent. Anyone not agreeing with him or siding with him was his enemy. Ranier would be despised for not adhering to Whitney's code of conduct— complete servitude to him and his ideology.

Sam was not a pawn or a sacrifice; he was Whitney's hand of justice. Sam would be murdered to punish Ranier. That would make perfect sense to Whitney. He would feel as if Ranier deserved the pain and suffering of losing a child. Sam meant nothing to Whitney. He'd already dismissed him.

Azami took a deep breath and let it out slowly between her teeth, turning her attention back to the war room and Sam. Before she could stop herself, her hand went to the screen, fingers drifting over his face. Her pulse hammered hard in her temples, and her throat threatened to close. Sam, her beloved Sam was nothing more than garbage to Whitney, just as she had been. He didn't see Sam's brilliance—or maybe he did and he feared it. Whitney wouldn't want anyone with an IQ to rival his enormous ego.

For the very first time, it occurred to her that if Whitney could devalue a man like Sam, he made a huge mistake by getting rid of her. Whitney wasn't quite as smart as he thought he was. One didn't throw away valuable pieces of experiments to get back at other people. The other mistake he'd clearly made was in not keeping an eye on what happened to her. He had no idea that little useless Thorn was in fact the brilliant Azami Yoshiie and that she was coming after him.

She kept her hand over Sam's face on the screen as the general replied gruffly, shoving his emotion away with a quick, impatient shrug as he gripped Sam's shoulder.

"If Ryland wants you on that team, it's his decision."

"Transport?" Ryland asked.

"It's all in there," General Ranier said, his tone dripping with disgust. "But I wouldn't trust any of it. Not a single person involved in this. And Ryland, don't trust your transport out if things go to hell. Not even your escape route."

"I understand, sir."

Azami closed her eyes briefly. It was easy enough for the general to *say* "don't trust your escape route," but the team needed not only a pickup point but an alternate in case things did go to hell. What would they do if neither route was open to them? Her mind began to race with possibilities. She might not be able to go to the Congo with them—it would be ridiculous to go into battle with a team already set and knowing one another's every move—but that didn't mean there weren't dozens of other ways she could give aid. And she had the equipment and technology to do it.

"Be ready to leave at oh-five-hundred. We'll have an unmarked Learjet standing by to take you. Did you read the directive, Ryland?" General Ranier asked. "They're questioning why a captain is going into the field with his team on a mission like this. They'd like you to sit this one out."

"You know the reason, sir. Not all the members of my team are anchors. We're not like other covert forces and you know that. Some of my men wouldn't survive without an anchor. Lily's working with those that aren't, but the psychic overload is still too much." His eyes met the general's. "We count on you to keep them off of us, sir, and allow us to operate in the way that we can. We can't live with other people, and our unit is tight-knit because it has to be. I think the good we do outweighs any negative. We have never failed in a mission."

"I'll keep them off of you," the general replied, a bulldog expression settling on his face. "And I'll find out who's behind these orders."

"I think we both know who's behind the order," Ryland said.

The general shrugged. "I need to find who his puppet is and bring him down."

Azami smiled with satisfaction. At last. Someone thought the way she did. Cut Whitney off from his power source. He was bound to grow desperate and make a mistake. His ego was far too large to go long without wanting to lead the military and country in the direction he believed it should go.

Sam, it's someone in his office who has been casting suspicion on the general. Someone there he trusts is supplying Whitney with information on all of you. Whitney must have gotten the second-generation Zenith study from the general's office, not from Lily's computer. That's why nothing has shown up in her computer. It's clean.

Azami couldn't allow Sam to continue to have his foster father under suspicion. They had to find the traitor and cut him off from Whitney. She could at least take care of that problem.

Sam cleared his throat. "Whitney has the study Lily did on second-generation Zenith. We've gone over her computer with experts and it's clean. The only other person who had that information was you. We've known for some time that there's been someone feeding Whitney information, and we suspected that information was coming from your office. He knew too much about our orders, things that could only come from a source close to you."

Ranier's head snapped up. Azami sucked in her breath. He knew they had suspected him. One didn't get to his position without being sharp. His gray eyebrows drew together and for the first time, she thought he looked terribly impressive. He glared at his son, and then at Ryland.

"You suspected I was in bed with that despicable lunatic? After what he did to my son? To all of you? To soldiers? Women? You thought I would send you out into combat to be slaughtered?"

"No, sir," Sam said. The ring of truth was in his voice. "I thought you would be loyal to your staff. You trust them. Like Colonel Higgens, you would have a difficult time suspecting one of them of betraying you."

Ranier winced at the mention of Colonel Higgens, a man who had worked against the GhostWalker program by trying to have them murdered. "You should have told me."

"Would you have believed us, sir?" Sam asked.

"That's beside the point. At least I would have been more careful. I've had the same aide and secretary for years. Neither would betray their country or me. Perhaps my computer is compromised. Although . . . Art Patterson worked a couple of offices down. He wasn't privy to that study but he may have managed to get into the computer . . ."

"Lily's research was never sent via computer for that reason," Ryland reminded.

Azami went over what she knew of the two suspects. Lt. Col. Andrew Chapman was a bachelor and a strict military man. He'd served with General Ranier in more than one war and in fact, had saved his life on one occasion. They were reputed to be close friends as well as working together.

Melanie Freesha was a civilian with a high security clearance who had, at one time, actually worked in the White

House before she'd gone to work for Ranier several years earlier. She too had an impeccable reputation. Azami understood loyalty, almost more than any other character trait. She was loyal to her father, Daiki, and Eiji and she'd defend them to the death. Now, Sam was included in that small circle of people she trusted enough to give her loyalty to.

"Andy and Melanie have been with me for years. Andy and I came up through the ranks together. He's a good soldier. I wouldn't be standing here if it wasn't for him. More than once, we fought our way out of some dicey situations. He's a steady, reliable man with a good mind and extremely loyal to his country. He's a career man and doesn't have a dishonest bone in his body. He would no more turn traitor than take a gun out and shoot the president."

The general's brows managed to come together even tighter, his frown fierce. Thunder could have boomed through the room and Azami wouldn't have been surprised. The general believed in what he was telling them. "Melanie Freesha has worked for years in numerous high-security-clearance jobs, and she's performed each with absolute propriety. She may not be military, but she understands it and she knows the value of silence. There has never been so much as a whisper or rumor connected to her. Did you think I didn't consider that there was a leak? I sweep my office twice a day. I don't trust the computer. The GhostWalkers are classified. The entire program is kept secret. No one wants to know it exists. They leave us alone and don't ask questions, so there's really no reason to talk about it—and I don't and neither does my aide or my secretary."

The general was very persuasive, but Azami wasn't buying it. He didn't want to believe that the people he'd worked with for years would betray him. Both were patriotic, but Whitney believed himself a patriot. His descent into madness was not without brilliance, and those loyal to him would only see the brilliance, the drive to protect his country. Certainly many people believed in a strong military nation, and the continual attempts at diplomacy in the face of terrorists or acts of aggression from some countries might be enough to persuade them that Whitney had the answers.

She didn't really understand how the general could pass orders on to his team when he knew they would be walking into an ambush. She wished she was in the room with him. She was much better at getting a feel for someone when she was face-to-face with them. Perhaps it had something to do with their energy, she didn't really know, but it was rare for her to be deceived by someone. It just didn't make sense . . .

He knows what we're capable of. Sam's voice moved in her mind with complete confidence. She had forgotten she'd reached out to him and was still in his mind. They were too connected now, making it impossible to know where one started and the other left off.

That was true, now that she really studied the general's face. He didn't like having to be the delivery man, but he'd flown all the way out to their compound to ensure no one else would overhear the conversation and he had made it more than clear what his team would be facing. Still, aside from not wanting his foster son to be among those going, he had never once acted as if they wouldn't come home alive. If anything, she could see the smoldering anger underneath. He meant what he said when he ordered them to carry out the orders to the letter. He planned on turning the tables on Whitney. His GhostWalkers were going to destroy the rebel army, take out the two men wreaking havoc and committing genocide in the region, get the diamond Whitney wanted, and all come home safe. He believed his men not only could but *would* do just that.

Breathe, Azami. You're holding your breath. This is what we do.

I know. I've seen you in action, but I won't be there with you this time. She was a little shocked at just how upsetting that was. She believed in Sam, but he would be going into a firestorm. If Whitney actually had enough clout to shut down their primary and secondary extractions, they would really be in trouble. The idea was to get in and get out without anyone ever knowing they were there.

"Sir," Ryland said, clearing his throat. "It would be best if you didn't act in any way as if you suspect someone is relaying information to anyone on your staff."

The general drew himself up, an impressive man who had earned the right to be called a four-star general. He squared his shoulders and looked down his nose at Ryland. "I assure you, *Captain*, I'm quite capable of taking care of myself. You just bring my team home safely. Every damn soldier comes home alive, you understand me?"

"Yes, sir."

"Sam, with me." The general indicated with a jerk of his chin.

Sam followed his foster father from the war room, as all the men rose and saluted. The general walked with his measured steps, his bearing absolutely erect, his posture perfect. He waited until they were a good distance away from the others before he turned to face his foster son. Sam could see the lines of age settling into his face, the gray of his hair, the signs that the man, in spite of his excellent physical condition and diet, was growing old and maybe a little tired of the weight of responsibility he'd assumed for so many years.

He put his hand on Sam's shoulder, indicating they were speaking as father and son. "How are you really, Sam? I don't like that you've been targeted once and now you're being sent into the Congo to get ambushed. Worse, I'm being used to send my own boy into a firefight. I want a medical report from your doctor giving you full clearance or I can't sign off on this, regardless of how proud I am that you're choosing to go."

"I'm really fine, sir. I know I'll get full medical clearance. I hope you understand why I have to do this. I could never look any of the others in the eye if I didn't. If someone is out to get me, I'd rather have my chance at them."

"They're using a ragtag army of ruthless, brutal rebels who care nothing for anyone. Not women, children, their country, or anything else. They love to torture and kill. And if they get their hands on you . . ." The general trailed off to shake his head. "You saw what they did to Ken Norton. That wouldn't be anything if they got their hands on you."

"Then I'll be certain not to let that happen," Sam assured.

General Ranier sighed and rubbed his jaw. "Sam, I don't play favorites, I never have, not even with you. This is different. Whitney's behind these orders and he's targeted you specifically for whatever purpose."

Ranier had never really discussed Peter Whitney with him before, and Sam was astounded. The general really had to be worried to talk so openly when he was used to playing things close to his chest. He never talked at home about his work, not even with his wife.

"I'm aware of that, sir. He won't succeed."

"This girl you think you've fallen in love with . . ."

"I have fallen in love with her." Sam looked him directly in the eye. "I'm no kid, long past the age of looking for a woman because I'm joining the service and want someone waiting for me. You know I don't work that way. She's the one. We just fit. We make sense. And she makes me happy, just having her around. This is it for me."

"And you're certain there is no tie between her and Whitney? Do you really think it's a coincidence that she shows up and you get attacked by Iranian soldiers, mercenaries, and known members of the Mexican cartel?"

"She saved my life and helped me kill most of them."

The general stood there for several moments in silence. "Do you have any idea who she is? Azami Yoshiie is part owner of one of the biggest companies in the world. Countries, governments would kill for their satellites. She's amassed a fortune, and it's said that every person working for her is loyal and can't be bribed. Believe me, there isn't a government that hasn't tried to get their hands on that software through every means possible."

"Are you trying to warn me that if I marry her, my government may come to me and ask me to steal documents for them? I will have nothing to do with her company. I'm a soldier, sir, like you, and I'll always be a soldier, certainly not a corporate spy."

"You have the brains to work with her," General Ranier pointed out. "You do. You always have. You could do anything at all, Sam."

Sam realized that the general was telling him it was okay with him if he left the military and went into the private sector. For the first time, he was aware that the general, as gruff and incapable of showing affection as he was, really cared for him. He worried like any other father might.

"Thank you, sir. I appreciate you thinking that I could. I'm happy doing what I do. I'm good at it. I fit in here with this team. And I fit with Azami. We'll find a way to make it work."

"Some women are content with part of a man. They understand that we're just as married to our unit and our buddies as we are to them. They know they won't know where we are or what we're doing half the time, only that it's dangerous work. Other women have to be a full partner. You have to know which kind you're thinking of marrying, Sam. If it's the wrong kind, you'll never make it."

"She's a GhostWalker, sir," Sam said. "She's a soldier, just like I am. She understands what and who I am, and I understand her."

"She's a citizen of Japan, and that's where her loyalties lie," General Ranier pointed out.

Sam opened his mouth to protest and then closed it. He knew what his foster father was implying—that Azami couldn't be trusted with the knowledge of such a highly controversial program as the GhostWalkers. "Sir, you aren't hearing what I'm saying. She isn't just a woman trained for combat. She's literally a GhostWalker. She's one of Whitney's experiments."

General Ranier studied Sam's face as if he might be trying to tell a bad joke. "That's impossible. That girl's been
investigated by everyone who could possibly investigate her.
She has a family in Japan. A father, two brothers . . ."

"She was adopted just as her two brothers were."

"I know that," Ranier snapped impatiently. "But she was
a child when she was adopted."

"Briony, Jack Norton's wife, was adopted. So was Tansy,
Kadan's wife. That's not unusual for Whitney, is it? We don't
know how many others are out there."

"Is she an anchor?"

"She has to be. She has no trouble at all with the overload
of psychic energy. She lived in the middle of a martial arts
school and a sword-making shop. She meets with people all
over the world for Samurai Telecommunications without a
problem."

"This is a problem, Sam," General Ranier said. "If she's
an experiment of Whitney's, she could be a plant."

Sam shook his head. "No, I'd know. She wouldn't be able
to hide it from me. When I say we fit together, I mean our
minds, not just our bodies. She's in me and I'm just as deep
inside of her. For a short period of time we might be able to
hide things from one another, but not for long. It just couldn't
happen."

"You're so sure of her, then?"

"Yes, sir. Absolutely sure of her. I know she's right
for me."

"What of this pairing Whitney seems to do with the
GhostWalkers? Is there a possibility that he's managed to
do that to you?"

"Maybe it's possible he paired her with me—he certainly
could have when he enhanced me—but she was already
gone when he got his hands on me. He couldn't possibly
have paired me to her. What she feels is genuine and I don't
think he can manipulate emotion. Physical attraction, yes,
but not emotion. And I definitely feel emotion for her."

The general nodded. "Then bring her home to your mother. And do it when I can get home." The last was said quite gruffly, as if it was stiff and awkward to admit that he cared enough to meet his future daughter-in-law as well.

"I'll do that, sir," Sam assured.

General Ranier gripped Sam's shoulder hard and then turned and walked out, hurrying back to his helicopter.

Azami waited in the hall for Sam. He was never one to miss an opportunity when they were alone. He caught the nape of her neck in a firm grip and leaned in to kiss her. She melted into him without a hesitation. The taste of her was even better than he remembered.

"A man could get lost in you far too fast, woman," he accused.

She smiled at him, that soft, mysterious smile. "Tell Ryland I can help."

"He'll never take you with us."

"I don't want to go with you." She frowned. "Okay, that's not exactly the truth, I'd like to be at your side, but I think I can be of more help here. Just tell him we can snag a satellite or two and give him unbelievable data while you're all in the field. We'll be able to tell him how many players, where they are, and if you're running into a trap. We have audio capability . . ."

"They'll be scanning for radio traffic," Sam said.

"Of course, but all they're going to hear are the sound of insects and maybe the flutter of wings. If there's rain, they'll hear that."

"How is that possible?"

Her smile widened and her lashes fluttered just that little bit, enough to tell him she had fascinating secrets he would spend a lifetime learning. "Eiji handles the lens. Daiki loves code. I prefer everything auditory."

He should have known. She had an enormous IQ, just as her brothers did. She'd attended the best schools and graduated with honors. Of course she was more than the bodyguard.

"You can communicate in fifteen second bursts. Anyone listening in will hear the exact same sounds they normally hear in their surroundings. Basically the audio is being recorded and played back for anyone listening in during those fifteen seconds of communication. I had to find a way to keep human voices off the loop, and you can't go beyond those fifteen seconds or the natural sounds begin to deteriorate." She shrugged. "I'm still working with it, but I'll perfect it eventually. For now, it will give us the ability to assist you from here."

"Rye will need a demo. He's not going to take a chance on anything," Sam said.

"We came here to give you a demo, so all to the good. I'll need Daiki and Eiji. I also need to set it up as quickly as possible. I know they've probably given you a couple of extraction points, but just in case, I'd like to have another backup plan. I'll need to leave for a short period of time to make certain everything is in place."

Sam frowned. She was telling him the truth—yet not the whole truth. "I need you here to help protect Lily and Daniel. Once our team leaves, there will only be a couple of men here in the compound. Team Two is close and they'll come if there's trouble, but I'll feel better knowing you and your brothers are here." He knew he was being presumptuous to expect the Yoshiies to stay in the compound with most of the team gone.

"My brothers will be here and I'll return as quickly as possible."

Both turned as the rush of energy heralded a Ghost-Walker coming down the hallway. "Ryland needs you in the war room now," Tucker said.

Sam stepped back from Azami, allowing his fingers to brush across her shoulder as he turned away from her. *I love you, woman*. The words felt right to say, although not nearly enough to describe the emotion he felt. *We need to get a license immediately, because I'd like to marry you as soon as I get back.*

He heard her laughter in his mind, filling him with warmth as he walked away from her. That was what he found the most amazing—how she made him feel so complete. He wasn't looking at her, but she was there with him, sharing an intimate moment no one else even saw.

Do you think if we don't marry immediately I'm going to run?

If you had any sense, you would, and unfortunately for me, I'm fairly certain you'll come to your senses sooner or later and run like a rabbit.

You wish, but you're stuck with me now.

He'd like to lock her up somewhere, just to be certain she'd stay where he would know what she was up to. Azami would always go her own way, make her own decisions; he understood that and admired her for it. He would never respect a woman who didn't know what she wanted and went for it. That didn't mean he wasn't going to worry about her.

Ryland had maps spread out on the table and up on the screens on the walls. He glanced up as Sam came in. "The general okay with you going?"

"I didn't give him much choice. What have we got?" Sam said.

"We'll deploy in two teams," Ryland replied. "Team One will be tasked as 'pathfinder' team. Nico, Kadan, Sam, and Jonas, that's you."

The four men nodded.

"You'll make a HALO insertion from a CIA Gulfstream C-11. The crew as usual will be squawking a Yemen business jet transponder code to cover us."

A HALO was a high altitude, low opening jump.

"Normal businessmen you are," Gator said with a little snicker. He sobered up when Ryland shot him a glance.

"They'll drop you at twenty-five thousand AGL, so you'll need your oxygen kit."

Sam nodded his head. The air to ground distance was a long one. They'd better have oxygen.

"For all of you, no dog tags, no ID card, and use sterile British fatigues. TOT will be oh-three-hundred zulu."

The time over the target was called out in universal time.

"Snipers will take Dragunov SVD sniper rigs, and SR-2 submachine guns. Sam, you and Jonas take an AKM assault rifle." He looked around the room. "Each of you will have a Pya Yariggi nine-millimeter pistol. If you're not familiar with any of these, get that way and fast. Believe me, gentlemen, you'll need them."

"No problem," Kadan answered for the others.

"You will get eyes on the objective location to confirm intel reports if at all possible. You'll be responsible for the recon of and establishing of a DZ for the second team."

The drop zone was all-important going in this time, as the area was entirely overrun with rebels and most of the roads were blown to hell.

"You will be setting up a primary and secondary RP to link up with us after we insert. You will also need to set up a primary and secondary PZ, for the extractions of both teams."

It was always necessary to establish two rally points as well as two pickup zones in case anything went wrong. Sam was well aware they expected things to go wrong this time.

"You will recon the rendezvous point, set up shop, and cover Sam and me when we go meet this joker. You have thirty-six hours to complete these objectives." Ryland pinned all four men with his steely eyes. "Any questions?"

"No, sir," Kadan answered.

Ryland tapped his finger on the table as if he itched to say more, but he shook his head and turned his attention back to his plan. "Team Two will stage at an air base in Turkey. We will insert via the same aircraft."

Gator nudged Tucker. "More businessmen. I'm wearin' my suit. The ladies love that."

Ryland suppressed a grin. "Yeah, they will, Gator; we'll let you drop first."

"Thanks, Captain, I'll let Flame know she needs to pick up a little more life insurance."

Ryland shook his head and returned to the instructions. "We'll insert by HAHO from twenty-seven thousand feet AGL," he said, referring to air to ground level.

HAHO was a high altitude, high opening jump. Never fun over a jungle in the dark in hostile territory. They would glide for thirty-five miles using compass and map to reference land features for directional reference.

"We'll be dropped thirty-eight miles east of the objective. We'll soar into the DZ Team One established, approximately two miles from the objective. Four of us will have AKMs and the fifth will have an RPK light machine gun. All of us will carry the Pya Yariggi pistol."

He looked around the room. "Each one of you will carry the following . . ." He waited until his men were ready for the list.

"Four claymore mines, four pounds of C-4, eight blasting caps, eight time-delay igniters, thirty feet of det cord explosive, ten minutes' worth of fuse time, six Mk II frag grenades, four M18 smoke grenades. One red, one green, and two white. I want each of you to also have two M-14 thermite incendiary grenades, three hundred and thirty-five rounds rifle, three magazines pistol, the snipers bring seventy rounds for the SVDs. Everyone," he continued, "two extra battery sets for each radio issued you, UV water purification device, and trauma kit."

Ryland waited again until his men were all finished listing the necessities. "Our objective is to secure and transport a political package. We will take out two rebel combatant leaders and destroy as much rebel equipment and munitions as we can. If we are compromised, we are on our own."

"Wow. How new is that?" Gator asked, looking around with a grin. "I don' think any of us has ever been in that situation."

Tucker nudged him hard enough to make him nearly

topple over. "They've been trying to lose you for years, Cajun man."

"I grew up wrestlin' gators; a little romp in the jungle isn't goin' to get me lost," Gator assured. "Try as they might to get it done."

Ryland held up his hand to return attention on him. "Extraction is scheduled to be provided by the 160th SOAR, special operations aviation regiment. They will be flying an MH-53D Pave Low with two AH-6 'Little Bird' gunships for cover. If both PZs are compromised, then we secure our own transport and try to get to a friendly country." He looked around at the men he'd gone into combat with hundreds of times.

Nico Trevane was Lakota Indian and Japanese, with bronze skin, long black hair, and flat, cold eyes. He was tall, with obvious muscles, yet he could walk silently and slide through any terrain without a sound. He was not only a renowned marksman but he spoke many languages. His psychic abilities were an asset at any time. He was an anchor, drawing unwanted psychic overload away from the other members of his team. He seemed to always know where the enemy was by the emotions and energy surrounding the individual.

Kadan Montague was a broad-shouldered man with strong arms, very muscular, with dark blue, almost black eyes. A thin white scar ran the length of his face. Known for his coolness under fire, at home in any environment, very calm in any crisis, he was Ryland's second in command. He could do what few other GhostWalkers could. He enhanced other psychic gifts, could see images in sound, could be nearly invisible, and was able to shield an entire team from detection. Kadan could cling to any surface like a lizard and change his skin color to match his background. Ryland always knew he could rely on his judgment.

Jonas Harper did his job with the minimum amount of fuss. Blond, medium build with hard, sinewy muscles that allowed him to fold himself into small spaces, Jonas had Florentine gold eyes that could look right through a building. Expert with knives, he'd grown up in the circus and was a high wire specialist, spoke multiple languages, was a master of disguise, a master thief and pickpocket, and could disappear into fog, shadow, or anything available to him. Like Nico, he was a quiet man, but could always be counted on.

Sam Johnson was an undisputed genius, had dark eyes and curly hair, and quiet laughter. He was another who spoke multiple languages and who could do extraordinary things such as teleport. He was also a marksman and incredible at hand-to-hand.

Ryland looked at the four men he called family. He was sending them into hell with no backup.

"Team One is wheels up in six hours."

Sam waited until the others had filed out. "Rye, I want you to talk with Azami. I think she can help."

Ryland scowled at him. "Am I supposed to tell a civilian what we're doing?"

Sam shook his head. "She's a GhostWalker. One of us. And she can make sure we have a chance at getting out of there alive."

CHAPTER 17

Sheila Benet smiled at the maître d' and murmured her name, resisting the urge to glance around the popular restaurant. She was dressed impeccably, as always. Her red power suit had always given her confidence and she needed it more than ever tonight. She clutched her Gucci bag tightly as she followed him to the small table in a very private corner, just as she'd requested. Melanie Freesha waited with that amused superior look on her face she'd worn since they'd first met in kindergarten. Sheila always enjoyed watching her when Melanie wasn't aware she was being observed.

The moment Melanie spotted Sheila, her face lit up. "There you are." She leaned in and brushed a kiss on Sheila's cheek. "It's been far too long. We need to find a way to get together more often."

Melanie was one of the few people Sheila really enjoyed. They'd been friends for a long time, long before Sheila had become Sheila Benet, back when she was merely hungry and afraid all the time. Melanie knew everything there was to know about her.

"I wish we could too," Sheila said, genuinely meaning it. "I miss you, but Dr. Whitney thinks spending too much time together is risky."

Melanie rolled her eyes and poured Sheila her favorite red wine. Melanie always remembered small details. "He likes to dictate to everyone. How are you?" She frowned, observing her friend in the flickering candlelight. "You look tired, Sheila. Is he running you ragged?"

Some of the terrible tension eased. It was nice to have a real friend. Melanie had "saved" her so many years ago, introducing her to Whitney and giving her a purpose and essentially a life. She'd been smart but had no chances, not with her drunken prostitute mother who was willing to sell her to any man for a drink. Melanie always left her window open at night, giving Sheila a place to hide when things got too bad. It was Melanie who came up with her new name and Whitney who provided her identity.

"It's a difficult time right now," Sheila admitted. She allowed herself a slow sweep of the restaurant. She recognized the look of three of Whitney's private soldiers scattered throughout the room. She knew there were more. Her heart began to pound and her mouth went dry. She took another sip of wine. "We're losing people and Whitney thinks someone may come after you."

Melanie blinked. Very slowly she put down her wineglass. "That's impossible. No one can connect me to Whitney. We took pains to make certain there was no link back to him. I've worked my way up to a great position to help him, and my reputation is spotless."

"Still, this is a bad idea, meeting like this. I tried to tell you, but you were so insistent."

Melanie nodded and lowered her voice, glancing warily around. "General Ranier was furious over the orders and he flew out to the GhostWalker compound to talk with them personally. He only brought his pilot with him. I've made it my business to be very close friends with his pilot, and Hank told me the general ordered him to stay with the helicopter. He went in alone and was gone for some time. He didn't say a word to Hank and was obviously upset. I think he believes the orders are a setup of some kind."

Her eyes met Sheila's directly. Sheila tried hard not to flinch. Her nod was nearly imperceptible.

Melanie frowned at her took another slow sip of wine before putting the glass down. Her fingers toyed restlessly with the wine stem. "Who is the sacrifice?"

Sheila shook her head. "Sam Johnson, the general's foster son."

Melanie choked. "Are you kidding me? The general will go ballistic. That's crazy. Did you try to talk Whitney out of it?"

"There's no talking to him right now. He's got an entire agenda and he's determined to carry it out. He's in tight with Violet Freeman again, and they've got some new plan that he hasn't discussed with me. He's very focused and driven right now." Sheila took another look around the room.

This was Melanie's favorite restaurant. The lights were low, the food exquisite, and the waiters handsome. Sheila couldn't fault it, but she couldn't quite relax as she normally did when she managed the rare outing with her best and only true friend. These were dangerous times, whether Melanie recognized it or not.

"I wish he hadn't chosen the general's foster son. General Ranier is a good man, a patriot, and he'll be very upset." She shrugged her shoulders. "I guess it isn't as if Sam Johnson is his *real* son."

"No, he was just some punk kid the general rescued from the streets and gave a life he didn't even deserve," Sheila added to the argument.

Melanie sighed. "Well, Whitney made these soldiers. I guess he has the right to sacrifice one or two if it helps our country to be stronger. Nobody gives a damn about them because they don't know about them. And honestly"—she leaned in close—"if people did know, they'd be creeped out. Seriously, they aren't really human anymore. Peter once told me, they're like animals and it's up to their keepers to watch over them and decide when to euthanize them."

Sheila laughed. "Mel, you're so terrible."

"Not really, just practical. I'm all about our soldiers, you know that. The GhostWalkers are weapons created to aid our country and human soldiers in any way possible. If the destruction of one of them is necessary . . ." She trailed off shrugging as the waiter came over with a slight bow and a sexy, flirtatious smile to take their order.

Sheila took another look around the room, assuring herself everyone was in place while Melanie flirted. She spotted two more of Whitney's men. Directly across from her table was a small Asian woman, obviously a very high priced call girl with a man who was clearly one of Whitney's soldiers stuffed uncomfortably into a suit. The call girl wore a clingy dress that covered her too large breasts and clung to her tiny waist. Her hair was in a short, sexy bob, and she gave her companion her full attention, staring into his eyes.

Two tables over a man with graying hair sat between two larger men. Satisfaction helped take the edge from her tension. Everyone was in place, like the pieces on a chessboard. Whitney was a master player and a master manipulator. If anyone was targeting Melanie and had followed her, they would soon know.

Sheila breathed a sigh of relief and took another drink of her wine, settling back in her chair. Of course Whitney had everything well in hand. She'd argued with him when Melanie had indicated she wanted a meeting, terrified of putting her friend in danger, but she should have trusted him. They'd rented out the restaurant, and just about everyone dining there was connected to Whitney. No substitutes had been made in waiters, bartenders, or kitchen staff. She'd made certain of that herself. And Whitney had provided a much better target than Melanie. He protected his assets and without a doubt, Melanie Freesha was one of his best.

Azami smiled up at the man who had hired an escort for the evening. Twice his hand had slid up her thigh, making her stomach lurch. The tiny receiver in her ear allowed her to pick up the conversation at Sheila Benet's table. She'd managed to plant the microphone when her "date" led her to their table. It was just good luck that he was assigned as a frontline guard to the two women and had chosen the table closest to theirs and even better luck that she'd gotten that tiny dot in place as Melanie was being seated, so she wasn't noticed near the table.

Her date obviously thought he would get very lucky after their dinner, his hands straying often and his gaze drifting to the bulging front of her dress. It never failed to surprise her how men could barely see beyond breasts. Her poor date, Frankie, he'd said, would be shocked to know the things he was drooling over weren't real. She giggled in all the right places and batted eyelashes, keeping his attention on her by touching him occasionally when he appeared to be looking around the room.

She had trained for this, but it wasn't a role she relished. She used broken English and a Japanese accent, playing her part, but it was annoying. She turned her head and everything in her went absolutely still. The breath rushed from her lungs. *Whitney.* He was seated a few tables away, back in the shadows, with two obvious bodyguards on either side of him. For a moment she was totally paralyzed. She couldn't even lower her gaze, she could only stare in shock and a kind of horror.

She'd been eight when he'd thrown her away, but she wouldn't forget that face. How could she? He'd stood over her trembling body a million times, a scalpel in his hand and annoyance on his face. Her body actually hurt. She wanted to press her hand over her heart, but she forced air into her lungs and smiled vacuously up at her "date."

Her target had changed. The deck was stacked against her. Whitney had the place nailed down with his army, but she was fast and she could take him out and maybe make it out alive. In any case, this was the opportunity of a lifetime and one she thought she'd never get. The most she'd hoped for was to cut his pipeline to legitimacy, but this . . . *this* was a miracle and she had no choice but to grab the chance with both hands.

The waiter put a delicate salad in front of her, giving her another opportunity to let her gaze wander around the room. The three tables flanking Whitney's were definitely bodyguards. Behind him was a tall divider with plants on top of it. There were tables on the other side of it, no doubt more of his enhanced army. Killers. Not real GhostWalkers, but men who failed their psych tests and traded honor for money—just as Melanie had done.

Success was always determined by careful preparation. She couldn't let her emotions dictate panic or rushing what had to be a certain kill. She nibbled at her salad, giggled and flirted with Frankie, and planned each move carefully. She would only get one chance. Everyone was armed and shots would be fired, but she had the advantage in that she would be weaving in and out of the soldiers at blurring speed, and if they fired, they'd be killing their own companions. That would help create chaos.

Melanie and Sheila continued to chatter about their lives and the men they took home and got rid of just as fast, comparing notes on lovers and laughing together. Their laughter offended Azami, when they had just dismissed Sam's death—and any of the other GhostWalkers—as if he were no more than a tool to be disposed of. That kind of thinking was Whitney's fault. The men and women in his employ took on his attitude toward the one's he experimented on. They were disposable lab rats. He believed that premise and he taught it to those he surrounded himself with. Since their true motivation was money, it was easy enough to persuade them those he experimented on weren't human and didn't deserve to be treated as if they were.

She drew another deep breath to calm the building rage. Her temper had always been a major drawback, and she couldn't allow it to explode here. This couldn't be personal. She had a mission to complete. A job. She had to do it to the best of her ability. Whether she lived or died didn't matter. Only the job. It couldn't be revenge. She couldn't operate out of anger. She was samurai and she had been trained for this very moment.

She needed to get close to Whitney without alerting his soldiers he was in danger. That meant she had to make it clear to everyone present that it wasn't her idea to get up and move around the restaurant. She planned out each move carefully, judging the amount of steps necessary to get in close enough to the table to use her speed to cut down Whitney's guards and kill him. She went over and over the moves in her mind until she was certain she could execute each one perfectly and complete the mission.

She palmed the drug she'd brought and, keeping it in her hand, slid her other one up along Frankie's thigh, fingers teasing and dancing their way higher and higher while she leaned toward him, her eyes smoldering with lust, her lips parted, tongue darting out to deliberately moisten her lower lip and give him ideas.

"Frankie. You're so . . . big. I like big." She batted her lashes, waiting for the inevitable. The moment his gaze dropped to the close proximity of her hand to his groin, she released the small vial of powder into his wine, using her body to jiggle the table. Fast acting, the powder dissolved with that small movement of the table.

"You have no idea, baby," he murmured, leaning closer to her.

Her hand brushed his lap while the other picked up his drink and held it to his lips. Watching her, he took a drink and licked the rim suggestively. She managed another giggle. "Too bad the table doesn't have long tablecloth. I could take care of this monster." She petted him and continued to hold the wineglass for him.

He drank another healthy swallow, and she lowered the glass to pick up a piece of nearly bloody steak with her fingers, holding that up to his mouth, breathing heavily, her lashes at half-mast as she gave him a sultry look.

He ate the piece of steak and drew her fingers into his mouth. She laughed and handed him his wineglass while she picked up hers, holding it up so they could touch glasses. "To later. I will make you feel so good, Frankie." She let her tongue tease her lip again. "Do you want to leave?" She knew he couldn't, but the drug was going to take effect very soon and he'd be on fire for her.

He grabbed her hand and placed it over his hard crotch, grinding it against him. "Damn it, baby, we have to stay for a few more minutes." He glanced toward Whitney and then over to Sheila and Melanie. All three were enjoying the great food. He leaned toward her, putting his lips against her ear. "Come with me to the men's room." He sounded a little desperate.

She let her eyes widen. She hastily shook her head. "Not there. The back parking lot has a little alley." She was taking a chance arguing with him, but she couldn't seem eager to go to the men's room with him. After all, she was a high priced escort, not a woman on a street corner.

His hand tightened over hers. She was definitely going to have a bruise. The drug was working. Right now, it was roaring through his body, settling in his groin until he couldn't think about anything but wanting her.

He jerked her closer. "You little bitch. You've been cock-teasing me all night. Get up and come with me to the men's room."

She drew back, pouting, shaking her head, a tiny figure next to his large, muscular body. She made certain she was on the inside so that when they passed Whitney's table she would be close to him. She struggled a little, interspersing her pitiful resistance with hysterical giggling. There had to be a delicate balance, where anyone watching would see she didn't want to go with Frankie. She kept breaking away and allowed herself to be recaptured as he dragged her toward the men's room.

She counted the steps. One step. Two. She was so close. Her blood thundered in her ears. This was it. Do or die.

"Frankie, no," she whined. "I'm not that kind of date." She managed to stop just a few steps from Whitney's table.

"Shut the hell up," Frankie snapped, "and do what I say."

Whitney looked up at her with no recognition whatsoever, but of course he wouldn't know who she was. For a moment she wanted him to know who was going to kill him, but then discipline took over. That wasn't important. Only getting the job done. Now she was close, close enough in another step to make her move. She took a deep breath and inhaled.

Confusion burst through her. Azami gripped Frankie tightly, fisting his belt, as shock poured through her. The man wore Whitney's face, but no way was that him. She'd recognize his scent and would recognize the energy surrounding him anywhere. The real Whitney felt "mad" to her. Insane. This man had to be a patsy, a double, someone placed here to draw her out, and she'd nearly fallen for it. She continued to stumble along with Frankie, bile in her throat as she realized she'd nearly blown everything in her eagerness to kill Whitney.

The men's room was looming close. Now she had to get back to her table and recover her purse and get the original job done. Furious with herself, she flicked a slight kick to the back of Frankie's knee as he took a step forward. He stumbled and both of them went down in a tangle of arms and legs. Azami cried out, a pitiful sob, and rolled away from Frankie. She was going to have to incapacitate him without appearing to do so, return to the table, collect her purse, and ensure Melanie's death without drawing any suspicion to her.

She glanced toward Whitney's table. He was talking to the bodyguard on his left. Her heart jumped again. Could she be wrong? She hadn't seen him in years, not since the trauma of her childhood. In profile this man looked *exactly* like Whitney, even to the curious reptilian way he moved his head. She couldn't make a mistake and kill an innocent man. He might be duped into posing as Whitney without knowing just what Whitney was like. Most people didn't know.

Several waiters rushed toward the couple on the floor. Frankie moaned and started to sit up, the effects of the drug making his mind slow and fuzzy. He looked very drunk. She sat, trying to look dignified and offended. The bodyguard Whitney had spoken with loomed over her, offering his hand.

"Frank, on your feet, now." His voice was filled with authority. "And start drinking coffee." He pulled Azami to her feet and dusted her off before the waiters got to her. "I'm sorry, ma'am. Are you all right?"

"She's a fuckin' escort," Frankie hissed, slurring his words.

"Most of the women in here right now are," the man snapped. "Go back to your table and we'll deal with this later."

Whitney would *never* have sent someone to rescue a woman, especially one he would consider a whore. She tugged her dress down and smoothed back her hair, trying to look as if she was affronted.

"I'm leaving. I just need to get my purse," she said, loud enough for the waiter to hear. "I've never been treated like this before." She pushed through the little knot of men and stormed past Whitney's table without glancing at him. She was certain the man was nothing more than a double.

"You'd better handle this, Frank," the bodyguard commanded.

Frank stumbled after her, apologizing as he caught up with her. "I don't know what got into me, Lila," he said, but his eyes burned with anger. "Stay and finish your dinner at least."

"I'm so embarrassed," she said, loud enough for Melanie and Sheila to overhear. "And I want to leave."

Frank caught her wrist and twisted hard. "You little bitch," he hissed. "I *paid* for you. You're going to sit in that chair and eat your food and smile at me and when we leave here, I'm going to teach you a lesson you're never going to forget."

She knew Melanie and Sheila overheard him. Both of them giggled like schoolgirls. Azami teetered back toward their table, stumbling when Frank yanked her, knocking into Melanie as she did so.

Melanie shoved her hard back toward Frank. "You're not much of a man if you can't handle that," she taunted, deliberately fanning Frank's anger.

Azami moved with blurring speed, sliding one hand over Melanie's arm as she stumbled back into Frank, her hands so fast, neither Melanie nor Sheila saw her.

Melanie scowled and rubbed her forearm. "Women like that give me the creeps."

"She's just making a living, Mel," Sheila pointed out. "Just like us. If you hadn't helped me, that could have been me."

Melanie nudged her with a little grin. "But you *like* sex. You would have gone into the men's room with him."

Both women burst out laughing. "Bitch," Sheila said.

Azami settled into her seat and brushed back her hair with a shaking hand, looking up at Frank imploringly through long lashes. "I just wish to go home."

"Well, you're not going home. You're going to do what I tell you to do." He pulled out his cell phone and, staring into her eyes, spoke into the phone. "Yeah, buddy. It's me. You feel like partying with a little china doll tonight?"

Azami thought it was a miracle she managed not to roll her eyes. She was Japanese, not Chinese.

"Yeah, I got one that needs a little lesson in manners. I

want her fucked up and begging to do anything I tell her by the time we're through. Are you in?"

Azami took a sip of her wine. She thought about making another scene, throwing the wine in his face, and stalking out. She knew she could get away with it, and it was what she should do. The poison absorbing into Melanie's skin right now would take time to work. She'd be long gone when Melanie died, and no one would connect her to the woman's death, but now Frankie boy had just managed to bring her nasty little temper out.

There were several women in the room from the escort service she'd used for her cover. Any one of them could have drawn Frank as their customer for the evening. She knew it was a hazard of their business, but still, the man was in serious need of a lesson in manners.

"We'll meet you out in the alley behind the restaurant. It will be fun." Frank snapped his phone closed and grinned at her. "Won't it, little china doll? We'll have a fun time partying. You'll like my buddy, Ross. He's has a thing for women like you."

Sheila nudged Melanie. "They're going to hurt that girl," she whispered.

"So what?" Melanie shrugged. "She's probably used to it. She wouldn't be in that business if she didn't like it a little rough. You just told me Sam Johnson is coming home in a coffin and yet you're all sad about a little ho. Are you going soft on me or what?"

Sheila shrugged. "I guess it reminds me of my childhood."

"Well, stop. You're so far above that little whore," Melanie stated. "Do you want coffee and dessert or shall we call it a night? They have that chocolate volcano thing I love."

"Dessert is fine," Sheila agreed. She signaled the waiter who was hovering just to make certain Frank and Azami didn't cause another scene. "It's important what you do, Melanie, you know that, don't you?"

Melanie smiled at her. "I know. Don't worry, I'm not

thinking about getting out. The money's too good. I get paid a good salary and Whitney has my retirement set for life. One thing about working for him, he pays better than anyone I know."

"You *really* have to be careful," Sheila reiterated, afraid Melanie wasn't listening to the warning. "We've lost a few people recently. I don't want anything to happen to you. Maybe you should lie low for a while, not contact us."

"I'm not in any danger," Melanie said. "I work in a secure building and live in one. I don't go out that often, and when I do, it's usually to meet you. We're friends. That has nothing to do with Whitney."

"I just think it would be a good idea for you to take a few precautions," Sheila warned. "It's not like I have a lot of friends and now that Violet's back in the fold, things aren't going to go well for me. She doesn't like women and she's absolutely fawning over Whitney these days, like she's mad crazy in love with him."

"There's always been something off about her," Melanie said. "And you're right to watch your back. She has a way of making people she doesn't like disappear. *Don't* get on her bad side. She's all kitten cute to men, but pure ice and nasty with women, even in Washington, but people love her."

"It's her voice," Sheila said. "I think that's part of her enhancement. She's one of them, you know, and for some reason, Whitney treats her differently than the others."

"He can use her ambition," Melanie pointed out. "But she's dangerous, Sheila. More dangerous than Whitney. He skates around the law for the sake of advancing science for humanity and his country. Violet simply wants power. She won't tolerate any woman around Whitney if she's set her sights on him. Seriously, Sheila, she's poison."

Sheila ducked her head. "She killed the senator. She had him living like a vegetable all those months in the hopes of saving him and then she just went into his room and yanked all the equipment off of him herself. I used to feel sorry for her. I thought she really loved that man."

"I thought so too," Melanie said with a small frown. "I used to watch her with him and she was totally into him. She never looked at other men unless he told her to flirt with them, which, just for the record, he did. I heard him once at a party. He said to 'go make nice' with another senator. He wanted her to make certain the other senator sided with him on some issue. She trotted off all smiling and had the other senator eating out of her hand."

Melanie clearly was the dominant in the relationship. Azami had studied Sheila Benet and had rarely seen her so animated with anyone. As a rule she was cool and aloof, rarely engaging even in small talk. She was Whitney's main go-between, and Azami had hacked her computer and phone, had been in her posh apartment numerous times— even stood over her while she slept in the middle of the night.

The woman had money, but she spent little of it on anything. She wanted to belong desperately, and she'd found that belonging and sense of purpose working for Whitney. But she clearly wasn't working for Whitney solely for the money. She wanted to keep and solidify her connection to Melanie.

Azami wondered idly how Sheila would react if she told her Melanie was already dead. There was no saving her now. Whitney and Sheila would have to recruit someone new to help murder an elite team of soldiers.

She enjoyed the salad, ignoring Frankie's threats. The man's head was definitely spinning now. Most of the time he just propped it up with his hands and moaned. His groin was on fire, a relentless ache that wasn't going away any time soon and would definitely slow him down when he tried to make his move on her. She considered kicking him hard under the table and walking off, but she needed to play the entire evening out. There were a dozen escorts in the room. She might be remembered, but no one would connect her with Melanie's death. Most likely, no one would connect the evening with Melanie's death.

"Are you seeing anyone?" Sheila asked, her tone a little wistful.

"Not regularly. I'm looking for the right man to hook up with, someone that will be of some use to Whitney, at least whatever information I can get from him, and he's got to be damned good in bed." Melanie laughed. "I'm selfish, Sheila. I don't want to have to share my apartment and time with a man. I don't want someone permanent, so if I invest more than a night or two, he'd better have something special to offer."

Sheila shook her head, spooning more chocolate. "Only you would say that out loud." There was admiration in her voice.

"Well, really, I don't need anyone. Do you want someone telling you what you can and can't do and always questioning you on where you're going? You call and I don't want to bring some man along to our dinners, but he'd want to horn in." Melanie took the spoon from Sheila and licked the chocolate off it. "That's just not going to happen."

"Aren't you afraid of growing old alone?" Sheila asked.

Melanie laughed again. "I've got you, silly. We'll be old ladies together, maybe get a ton of cats and rocking chairs. When we feel like it, we'll go on those cruises and eat ourselves silly and ogle all the young men."

Sheila nodded. "Sounds good to me."

Melanie held up her wineglass. "To our future as little old ladies." She smirked as she clinked her glass against Sheila's. "*Rich* old ladies. *Stinking* rich old ladies. Maybe we'll get a few Italian boy toys and they can feed our little pussycats for us." She laughed merrily at her innuendo.

Azami kept the disgust from her face, sitting there with Frankie squeezing her thigh and the two women who had sent a team of soldiers to their death, toasting their own futures. She didn't understand, especially Melanie, who saw the work the teams did all over the world, the lives they saved, how it was possible not to admire them and want to keep them safe.

And Whitney. She could barely look at his double without her stomach lurching. She found it hell sitting in that room with all of them. Whitney's supposed soldiers, men like Frankie, with no honor. Women like Melanie and Sheila, who took money and sent men to their death while they drank wine and ate chocolate. The realization came slowly to her: Thorn didn't belong here. She *was* useless to Whitney. She needed to rejoice in that. She needed to be proud of herself that she wasn't like those two women, or these men willing to do a monster's bidding for his money and approval.

What had she been thinking all these years? She had a father who had shown her the way to live with honor, two wonderful brothers who loved her, and Sam. *Her* Sam. She had a narrow escape when so many others suffered for years at Whitney's hands. Why had she made him so big? So omnipotent? She'd *allowed* Whitney to color her judgment of herself for years. These people were those he considered worthy and she despised them.

Melanie and Sheila rose to leave. Melanie looked right at Azami and pursed her lips to send her a kiss. Sheila laughed. "That's so mean, Mel." There was a slight nervous giggle in her voice, as if she really didn't like what her friend had done but was afraid to call her on it.

In all the time Azami had been following Sheila, no one had ever made her nervous. She'd seemed cold, without feelings and very little nerves, yet Melanie brought out her submissive nature.

Melanie deliberately winked at Frank. "You really enjoy yourself now," she told him.

Azami realized Melanie knew she was making Sheila uncomfortable and wanted to prove she could do it. They had an interesting relationship. Sheila seemed dependent on Melanie. Once she was gone, what would happen?

Frank tightened his hold on Azami's wrist and stumbled to his feet, jerking her close. "I do intend to have a good time, little China girl. And you'd better make me very happy.

You embarrassed me tonight and no one does that to me and gets away with it."

Azami let him yank her out of her seat. She caught up the small glittering bag, shoving it onto her wrist, allowing her hand free. Teetering on her heels, she took small, mincing steps as Frank dragged her toward him. The moment she was near the table where Melanie and Sheila had been seated, her fingers swept beneath the tabletop to acquire the tiny bug she'd planted earlier. Deftly she palmed it, allowing her purse to slide down her arm so she could shove it inside with a poke of her finger.

Frank was going to learn a little lesson in how to treat a lady when they reached the back parking lot. She hoped they'd get there before his friend, so she would be long gone and his friend could escort him to the hospital.

"Stop struggling or it will be worse for you," Frank hissed, giving her a little shake as they approached the table where the Whitney double was standing to leave.

"A little anticlimactic," the Whitney double said to his bodyguard. "I don't know what I expected, but the meal was good." He gave a little laugh.

She noted that the bodyguard ignored him. Whoever the man was, he was considered disposable. He'd been nothing but bait and no way were the bodyguards there to protect him. He would have been sacrificed in a heartbeat. Had she made her move on the Whitney double, the "bodyguards' " sole purpose would have been to kill her, not save him.

Out in the night air, Frank's head cleared enough that he realized if anything happened to her, the waiters had seen his face. He didn't care much if they identified him, the records would show he had died in South America two years prior, but still . . . He pulled Azami in close to him and walked her quickly toward the back parking lot.

She went willingly across the asphalt, weaving through the few cars there toward the narrowing alley. A broken wooden fence partially hid the alley behind the parking lot. The gate, hanging by one bracket, was long gone, splintered and broken like much of the fence. Frank thrust her through it and paused to lean against the rickety wood, sweat breaking out on his face. Every step had to be painful with his groin so full and heat rushing through his body, elevating his temperature.

Azami took the opportunity to step away from him, kicking off her heels as her heart sank. Not one but two men were already waiting, wearing evil grins. She was really growing tired of the entire mess. Frank would present no problem to her. He could barely stand, but these two men were a different story.

He grinned at the two men. "Ross, I see you brought a friend. The more the merrier."

Ross laughed. "Damn right."

Her phone buzzed in her purse. She pulled it out and looked down at the text.

Team Two called out of the country.

She sighed. There was no way that was a coincidence. If most of Team Two was away as Daiki indicated, that left both compounds vulnerable—and that left the babies at risk.

"Gentlemen, I'm going to give you a chance here and just say, let's call this a misunderstanding. Frank is in no shape to party and I'm not really up for it, so let's just all go home while you still can."

The grins faded. She wasn't running, screaming, or in the least bit scared. Frank made a grab for her and she slapped his hand away and slammed her foot into his groin. He shrieked and went down hard, the breath exploding out of him along with a sound much like an animal in pain. He lay writhing on the ground, holding his groin, the scream fading to moans.

The two men separated, Ross pulling a gun, the other a knife.

"You bitch. I'm going to fuck you up so bad no one will ever want to look at you again," the one with the knife said.

"Like I haven't heard that before," Azami said.

"Don't you move," Ross warned. "I'll gut shoot you and

we'll still fuck your brains out before you die. You'll just die hard."

Frank staggered to his feet behind her. She could hear his continual cursing directly behind her. She took three steps toward the gunmen and then put on a burst of speed, angling toward the man with the knife just as the gun went off.

Frank folded in half, screaming, a crimson stain spreading across his groin. She slapped the knife hand away as she went in, the tiny one-inch blade a ridiculous contrast to his ten-inch blade, but razor sharp, it went into the side of his neck easily. She turned the blade as she withdrew it, twisting behind the man as the gunman fired again at her. His second shot hit his buddy in the chest.

Azami kept moving, coming up behind Ross while he was still firing shots at the spot behind his falling buddy.

"Oh, no, oh, no," he chanted over and over, but continued firing as if his finger was stuck on the trigger.

She took him from behind, slicing his throat and stepping back quickly, moving out of his sight so that the shots wouldn't have a chance of hitting her.

She waited until the last shot had been fired and all three men lay still on the ground before she collected her heels and went over the fence to walk calmly away. She walked several blocks until she found a dark doorway. Quickly she shimmied out of the dress and pulled off the wig, sweeping her hair back in a ponytail. She wore a spaghetti tank under the dress. From her small bag she took out a pair of trousers rolled tight. The dress was rolled and put in her bag, the wig shoved in it as deeply as possibly. Scrubbing her face clean with the wipes, she pulled out her phone to text her brother.

On my way.

She came out of the doorway looking like any teenager out to meet friends.

CHAPTER 18

$\sim$

Kadan glanced at his watch. It was 02:30. "Suit up. Check your oxygen. We're thirty minutes out. Double-check each other's gear." He did the same and waited for Sam to nod that he'd made certain Kadan's gear was good to go.

At 02:50 Kadan signaled the men. "Make final in-oxygen check. We'll depressurize in five minutes."

Sam nudged Jonas with his foot. "Wake up there, circus man. Your snoring has been keeping me awake."

Jonas opened one sleepy eye and glared at Sam.

"In-oxygen check," Sam said. "Get on it."

"On it," Jonas conceded.

Kadan said, "02:55. Depressurizing mask up."

Sam kept his eye on Jonas. He appeared to be asleep again, but he obediently put his mask in place.

At 02:59 Kadan was on his feet. "One minute . . . thirty seconds. First jumper in the door."

Sam took a breath and looked out into the night. It was a damn dark, moonless night. The engines roared as the wind clawed at him, trying to jerk him out of the plane. Adrenaline poured into his body along with that familiar

tug of fear. The cold bit at him, the temperature at that eleva-
tion was about minus fifteen. He could smell the jet fuel and
felt the sting of the wind on his face. The aircraft was traveling around a hundred and fifty knots and he was about to
fling himself into that night sky.

"Go!"

At the command, he dove, and in a flash everything
changed. The wind hit him hard, buffeting him, pulling at
him, and he fought for control. He was carrying two hundred
pounds of gear. His rucksack hung between his legs, strain-
ing his movements. Then, just like that, there it was. He
realized the roar of the engines was gone and he was soaring
through the sky, freefalling, the feeling euphoric, his heart
racing with the love of the jump.

Sam pulled his chute and abruptly went from one hundred and twenty miles an hour to about twenty. The opening
shock hit his body and then he was flying, the wind rushing
by, his helmet muffling the sound so that he was flying in a
peaceful, surreal world. For a few moments there was freedom and absolute peace as he dropped through darkness in
silence. He was very aware he was suspended by a sheet of
silk in a commercial air traffic space, and the thought of
splattering on the window of a passing jet was there in the
back of his mind.

He went in and out of the clouds, a bad fog, and then he
could see the ground rushing at him. The jungle appeared
nothing more than a green sea spreading out in front of him.
Jumping without a strobe was always a tricky business. He
could tell the difference between trees and grass by the
shades of green. Thirty feet out he flared his chute, slowing
him down.

He landed with a light jolt, much like jumping off a single
step, reeling in his chute fast. He had the same reaction he
often did—thankful to be in one piece, and ready to go
again. He glanced at his watch. 03:02. Everyone should be
down.

Kadan was a few feet from him. Nico a meter away. Jonas

had his back to Sam and was pulling in his chute as fast as possible.

"Get coms up, Jonas; bury the chutes, Sam; and, Nico, you're on security," Kadan said.

"Chutes are good, Bishop," Sam replied to Kadan.

"Okay," Kadan said. "Let's get the hell out of this clearing. GPS has us thirteen klicks southeast of Kinshasa. This will be our RP if we get separated."

The rally point was a good one—plenty of cover but easily found should they need it.

Jonas spoke into the radio. "Valhalla . . . Valhalla, this is Reaper One. Do you copy? . . . Over."

Fort Bragg command answered immediately. "This is Valhalla, Reaper One. We have you five by five, over." A five by five was a signal report, telling the team how well they could be heard on a scale of one to five of strength and one to five of clarity.

Jonas responded. "Valhalla, Reaper One. We are up and on the hunt. Reaper One out."

"Let's recon," Kadan said. "We'll make a four-leaf clover pattern working counterclockwise. Be back here in fifteen minutes. If one of us doesn't make it back in fifteen, the others will wait five. If they're still not back and we can't make radio contact, we'll start looking for you. I have 03:30. Any questions?" When they all shook their heads, Kadan gave the go signal.

The jungle was hot and oppressive. The forest was made up of several layers, trees bursting toward the sky—the emergent level—anywhere from seventy to two hundred and fifty feet high. The canopy was sixty to ninety feet above him. If necessary, Sam could go up and run along those twisted branches that formed a highway far above the forest floor. Most of the birds and wildlife resided in the canopy. Flowers wound their way up the tree trunks toward the light, and moss and lichen crawled up the bark and over branches as well. Great ropes of tough vines dropped like snakes from above and hung in tangled twists and turns of grooves and crevices and elaborate loops.

A large snake wrapped around a branch above his head moved slightly to take a look at him. Monkeys clung to the branches and watched him in silence as he passed by. The air was heavy with moisture and rang with the steady drone of crickets and cicadas. Mosses and vines hung heavily over ribbons of water. Tangled ferns grew almost as tall as small trees, and on the floor thousands of insects moved rotting leaves and vegetation. The understory was an impenetrable, inky blackness. Tree frogs called to one another, hundreds of different sounds as various species vied for space on the airwaves.

Sam mapped out his assigned area in his mind, keeping an eye on the time. He made it back to the designated spot to find Kadan emerging from tall ferns. Nico was already waiting, but there was no sign of Jonas.

"There's a slight depression about twenty meters to the southeast, but other than that, it's all the same, trees, bugs, monkeys, and snakes," Sam reported.

"I've got the same shit," Nico said.

Kadan looked around him, clearly concerned that Jonas wasn't there. "It's the same to the north. There are a couple of small hills, that's it. We'll see what Jonas found and go from there, but from what I see on the map, I think that the depression would make a good hide site. We can use it for our patrol base. It's 03:50." He looked around again, and swore under his breath. "Where the hell is Jonas?"

Sam's heart dropped when only silence answered the question.

"Jonas, Jonas, this is Bishop, you copy? Jonas, do you copy?" Kadan spoke into the com.

This isn't good, Sam said, already starting to thread his way back through the jumble of downed trees and hanging vines. Anything could happen in that absolute darkness, surrounded by hostiles, and switching from speech to telepathy seemed a much better idea.

We'd better start looking, Nico agreed.

You two move clockwise. I'll go counterclockwise. Be back here in fifteen.

Sam nodded. *Fifteen minutes, check.*

Jonas pushed his way out of the jungle. "Hey, where are you heading?"

Kadan spun around, relief on his face. *What the fuck, Jonas. Where the hell have you been?*

We were about to go looking for you, Sam said. *Your fucking radio broken?*

Jonas flashed a small self-deprecating grin. *Yeah, actually it is. I tripped on a tree root and broke the battery case. The batteries won't stay in now. I can fix it once we get into a hide.*

Kadan let out his breath. *Well, glad you're good. I was afraid we'd have to hump your gear and your dead ass out of here.*

Jonas indicated back into the jungle. *The creek that's set as the meet point isn't far from here. I set my claymores up in case we need to "pop smoke."*

To pop smoke was to leave quickly, and given the circumstances, Sam was very much afraid that was exactly what they'd have to do.

The claymores are set on the edges of the creek. The first two are about three meters this side of where we expect the face-to-face to be. They can be popped as the team moves. I've got the detonator on remote. If needed, there's a second set ten meters farther, on a time delay. Stop, pull the ring, and haul ass.

Kadan flashed a small smile, the only indication that Jonas was forgiven for taking ten years off his life. *Okay. Good. Did you find an over watch position?*

Jonas nodded. *Yes, there's a small hill about twenty meters to the south. I think we should have adequate visibility from there.*

Kadan nodded his approval. *Good. We found a hide. Let's move. Fix your radio, genius. We'll call for the second*

team's insertion and then we'll settle in for some rack time.
One of us on guard at all times. Everybody good with an
hour rotation? He didn't wait for an answer. *Good.*

Once settled in their hide position, Sam made the call.
"Valhalla . . . Valhalla, this is Reaper One."

"Reaper One, this is Valhalla. Good signal. Ready to
copy, over."

The voice at the other end of the radio always gave Sam
a sense of being connected. "Valhalla, Reaper One . . . mission is a go, over."

"Copy. We have a green light for Team Two's insertion.
Valhalla out."

Sam never had a problem sleeping anywhere, anytime.
One got used to taking every opportunity because often,
you could go days without a safe place to catch a few minutes of sleep, but this time, when he closed his eyes, he saw
his foster father's face. The general was genuinely at a loss
as to who was selling him out and why. He couldn't conceive
of such treacherous behavior as burning a single soldier, let
alone an entire team.

Sam looked up at the branches swaying high up in the
canopy, the movement soft and subtle. As a rule he would
let the gentle wind lull him into at least drifting so his brain
would slow down and relax, but it was impossible. He knew
the president had been asked for aid—to send a covert unit
into the rebel held territory to wreak havoc and hopefully
break the back of the rebel army by destroying munitions
and vehicles as well as targeting the two men who vied for
leadership of the ragtag rebels.

Someone knew of those orders and had sent the plea to
Whitney. Whitney had his own agenda and had someone in
his pocket in the CIA with enough clout to make a deal with
one of the rebel leaders. The deal was to put Ekabela in
power in exchange for the diamond. Along with a clear path
to leading the rebels, Ekabela wanted a GhostWalker to pay
for his brother's death. Whitney had selected Sam and in

doing so, had tipped off the team that there was a double cross coming.

Had Whitney chosen Sam with the idea it would alert the team prior to the mission? It was entirely possible. He liked to play games. And if so, how far would he go? If the CIA was in charge of the operation and was deliberating operating out of Fort Bragg, what would they do when the team followed their orders to the letter and destroyed everyone, taking the package instead of turning it over to Whitney's man in the field?

Sam tasted anger in his mouth. They'd get burned. No doubt about it and they'd be left in hostile territory, a hell of a long way from home after stirring up a hornet's nest. He linked his fingers behind his head. It wouldn't be the first time it had happened.

He must have fallen asleep after all because he jerked awake when the radio came alive.

"Reaper One . . . Reaper One, this is Reaper Two."

Tucker's voice had never sounded so good. "Reaper Two, this is Reaper One, go," he answered.

"Reaper One, we're twenty mikes to TOT, over."

The team was twenty minutes to time over the target. "Roger that, Reaper Two, you are twenty mikes out from TOT. DZ will be marked with IR strobe, over." The drop zone would be marked with an infrared strobe.

"Reaper Two copies DZ marked with IR strobe."

"Happy landings," Sam said. "Reaper One out."

Ten minutes later Kadan addressed them in his hushed voice over the com. "All right, boys, team two will be here shortly. Is everyone in position?"

"In position," Jonas affirmed.

"See, Boss," Sam said, laughter in his voice. "I told you he'd get that piece of shit fixed. I'm in position. IR strobe is active."

"I'm looking at him, Bishop, right through my scope," Nico said, "and he looks like he's falling back asleep. I'm in position."

"All right, girls," Kadan said, "cut the chitchat and keep your ears and eyes peeled."

Tucker's voice broke into their coms. "Good evening, kiddies. How are we tonight? Warm, I hope. I still can't feel my damn toes. We're coming in from the south, southeast. I have the strobe in sight. We're at two thousand feet. See you in a second."

Kadan answered. "I'm at your seven o'clock. Knight is at your ten o'clock, Nico, your three o'clock, and Smoke at your five."

"Roger, we're on the ground. Rally at strobe," Ryland ordered.

"Glad everyone made it in one piece," Kadan said when all four men were down. "Let's get to the hide."

Chutes were buried and they moved quickly back to their hide, where Tucker called Fort Bragg.

"Valhalla . . . Valhalla, this is Reaper Two."

"Reaper Two, this is Valhalla, over." The disembodied voice came over the radio.

"Valhalla, we are in play and one hundred percent up." They let Joint Special Operations Command know they were ready to carry out their mission and everyone had made it into the field.

Kadan took over immediately in his no-nonsense way. "Okay, everyone, around the map. The creek is here." He jabbed the spot with his finger. "The expected meet site there. Here, about ten meters from the meet site, and here, another fifteen meters, we've set up claymores. The first two are on remote. The other two are on a time-delay fuse."

He indicated another spot with his finger. "There is a hill here that we'll be on for over watch." He hesitated a moment and then looked directly at Ryland. "I can go in with Sam, Rye."

Sam winced for him. Kadan was treading on thin ground asking, but Ryland had a bad habit of placing himself in the hottest spot.

Ryland's gray gaze settled on Kadan's face. "Are you implying I'm slowing down with old age setting in?" His voice was mild, but there was nothing mild about those steel gray eyes.

"No, sir," Kadan said.

"We'll stick to the original plan. Keep going."

Kadan knew better than to sigh. "Ryland and Sam will make the face-to-face about here. Move up the creek to this spot. You should be able to see where they make their stand. The rest of you will be concealed in the tree line here. If 'Murphy' "—of Murphy's Law fame—"shows up, you'll come up on line and engage the hostiles. At that point we will have fire on them from different points. That should be enough to help Sam and Rye, making the meet, break contact and get the hell out of there. At that point, we each pop white smoke and meet up here at the hide."

Ryland nodded his head. "Looks good to me. Before we leave for the meet, we'll have to set up to draw them back to the hide. Where you do you have the ambush planned?"

Kadan circled the site on the map. "Right here, sir. We will set claymores along this line here and here, using the terrain to bottleneck them into this funnel of claymores."

"If we don't need them, we pull them out when we move out," Ryland ordered. "Ground anything you don't need so we can move fast and quiet. Unless anyone has any questions, we leave in thirty minutes. Over watch, you leave now."

Sam and Ryland and the rest of the team made their way through the tangled vines and tall fronds to the creek.

"Over watch in position," Kadan reported.

"We're at staging point in the creek," Ryland answered. "We're splitting up here. Sam and I will slip up on them using the water for concealment."

Tucker, Kyle, and Gator melted into the jungle silently.

"In support position," Tucker announced first.

Kyle and Gator echoed him in seconds.

"Heads up," Nico said. "They are accompanied by twenty

armed men. All have rifles and sidearms. I see no packs, no other equipment."

"We copy," Ryland said.

"Copy twenty," Tucker said.

"All right, they set up right where we wanted them to. We are moving out. Sam, let's get this done."

They both slipped into the water, wading downstream, going into the deep, faster-moving stream, until they were fully immersed.

Ryland came up out of the water just at Ekabela's feet. He rose fast, a dark ghost, covered in black paint and dripping water as he caught the man in a tight grip, knife to his throat. He grinned savagely at the CIA operative who had orchestrated the double cross.

"I'm here for the package," he said, keeping his voice pitched low.

Ekabela had barely caught a glimpse of the dark shadow before his head was jerked backward, putting him off balance and exposing his throat to the very large, sharp blade sitting on his skin. Breathing, swallowing, any movement at all would result in the blade drawing blood.

The man in jeans and a light sports jacket raised his hand as if he could ward Ryland off. "Whoa, soldier. Stand down. I was supposed to meet you upriver and guide you here."

Ryland stayed perfectly still, letting his cold gray eyes say it all for him.

"I'm Duncan Forbes," the man from the CIA tried again. "Ekabela has the package for you. There's no problem whatsoever. Just put down the knife and we'll discuss this. We were told Sam Johnson would be picking it up. You're clearly not Sam."

"I am," Sam whispered from behind Forbes. "Don't move, sir. I wouldn't want to accidentally shove this knife through your kidney."

Forbes felt the tip of the blade stinging through his clothing. "There's no need for this."

"Just taking care, sir," Sam said. "We wouldn't want anything to go wrong like it did the last time one of us came into contact with an Ekabela. Give me the package and we'll complete the rest of the mission quietly. No one will know we were ever here."

"Your orders were to wait for me to guide Sam Johnson, and only Sam Johnson, to the rendezvous location," Duncan hissed. "You can't treat an important ally like this. I'll have you two brought up on charges. Put down your weapons. That's an order. Shit, you've messed up everything."

"Sorry, sir," Sam said. "I take orders from him." He brought his free hand sweeping past Forbes to indicate Ryland. "Give me the package. When it's secure, we'll go our way."

Forbes jumped a little, his eyes following the hand that pointed to the man holding Ekabela so still.

In the absolute silence of the jungle, the constant drone of cicadas and crickets returned full force. Sam felt exposed, his back to the creek, knowing Ekabela's men were ready to cut them down the moment Ekabela was released from Ryland's grip. He could feel them, more, smell their sweaty bodies as they crept into position, having been forced to shift to better protect their leader.

Ekabela was sweating and slippery, his eyes conveying both outrage and fear. He kept looking out to the jungle, trying to convey silently to his men to stay back. Forbes slowly nodded his head. Ekabela's hand crept toward his jacket.

"Be very careful," Ryland advised. "You bring your hand out of that jacket with anything but the package, you'll be the first to die."

Ekabela let out his breath in a kind of angry rush, but his hand was very steady as he reached into his coat and withdrew a small, brown paper–wrapped object. He slowly extended his palm. The package was small, no bigger than five inches in length.

"Please take that, Mr. Forbes, but be very careful," Sam

advised. "You don't want to reach for a weapon and blow it at this stage of the game. That will get you both killed."

Duncan Forbes's face twisted into a mask of anger. He stepped forward and took the package from Ekebela. "Now what?"

"Open it and make certain it's what it's supposed to be," Sam instructed. He had stepped forward with Forbes as the man moved, knife tip still pressed tight against his kidney.

Forbes didn't dare turn around, or look over his shoulder; instead he glared hard at Ryland. "This is absolutely preposterous. Both of you will be court-martialed for this."

"Do what you have to do, sir. We're just following orders." Sam's voice came from behind him, low, close to his ear, and the blade never so much as trembled or moved from Forbes's kidney. "But you open that package now."

Swearing, Duncan tore open the brown paper. Sam could see a large chunk of what looked like an uncut diamond. It was quite large and thick, maybe three inches in diameter. Keeping the knife pressed close to Duncan's kidney, he held out his palm. Duncan dropped the half-opened paper with the diamond into Sam's hand. He closed his fist around it and slid it inside his jacket.

Package secure, sir. He used telepathy.

Ryland gave the smallest of nods.

Sam stepped even closer to Duncan Forbes. "Do you have a vehicle close, sir?" he whispered.

Forbes nodded.

"I suggest you run to it and get the hell out of here fast. This is going to get ugly." That was all the warning Forbes was going to get. Sam released Duncan and slowly backed away.

Ryland drove his knife into the base of Ekabela's skull, severing the spine and killing him instantly. He held the body upright for an instant, his gaze drilling into Forbes.

"Geez. Oh, God." Duncan backed away from him, turning white under his skin, sweat beading on his forehead. "You have no idea what you've done."

Ryland's eyes met Sam's. Sam was very aware of the jungle around him, as if the world was still right, the sounds of the jungle, the constant shifting above their heads, the continual drone of the cicadas, the calls of the frogs, a cry of a monkey. His heart thundered in his ears.

Ryland let Ekabela's body fall to the ground, and just as if he'd triggered a bomb, the world erupted into hell around them. Duncan Forbes turned and ran for his life. Bullets tore bark off trees and vines, hissing through the air and spitting bark and splinters at them. Ryland and Sam both fired an entire magazine on full automatic, bullets spraying the jungle, driving the soldiers away from them.

Tucker, Kyle, and Gator had all gone to one knee and began to eliminate preselected targets. Simultaneously, Nico, Kadan, and Jonas on the hill in the over watch did the same. Smoke and red-hot streaks sizzled through the roar and shock of the guns, accompanied by high-pitched screams and explosions. Rock and wood chips rained down. Dirt flew around them as shrapnel hit everywhere.

Sam could tell how close the bullets were by the various sounds they made. The snapping sound was ominous, three feet or closer. The scent of cordite from the gunpowder grew strong. The distinctive smell of burned composition "B" from the grenades was heavy in the air.

Reloading. Bounding. Ryland called out telepathically to the others indicating he and Sam were moving and someone had to cover their targets.

Sam and Ryland retreated five meters, reloading as they ran. At five meters they both went down to one knee to place covering fire—rapidly aimed shots—at the swarming army of angry soldiers, giving the other two teams a chance to pull back. Once in line, they naturally became two teams and began to alternate covering fire.

The fighting was intense, an explosion of violence, and Sam just held on to one thing. He *would* go home to Azami. He was not buying it out here in the jungle.

Reloading. Bounding. The words were repeated often as one team would retreat toward their destination while the other provided cover.

The ragtag army didn't seem to have leadership, following in anger more than with any strategy. Clearly they felt they were a superior force, but they were scattered, not as well trained as the rebels Ekabela had had months earlier.

All clear of the danger range? Ryland asked as they continued moving into the trap, drawing the rebels into the funnel.

All members of both teams had to be a good twenty-five meters away from the first of the claymores.

Clear, the men responded one by one, using the telepathic link Ryland formed.

"Claymore," Kadan yelled as he detonated the first two antipersonnel mines.

Simultaneously Jonas pulled the igniter rings. The claymores had a range of fifty yards. Anyone inside that sixty degree horizontal fan was going to die or wish they were dead. As the claymores went off, the team hightailed it out of the war zone, back toward the hide.

Moving fast in their standard formation, cover and run, they made it past their second defense, the next line of claymores. Any combatants following would get caught in the next set of mines, and aside from taking out most of the rebels Ekabela had recruited, another devastating blow definitely would take the fight out of most that were left.

At the hide, Team One recovered gear while Team Two stayed on guard. They switched, working fast in silence while Team Two retrieved the rest of their gear.

We'll wait ten minutes and see if anyone was stupid enough to follow us, Ryland said, still using telepathy. He looked his men over. *Anyone hurt?*

Gator nudged Jonas with his foot. *Heard high wire here tripped over his big feet. He somersaulted down the hill this time.*

Fuck you, Gator, Jonas replied with a sheepish grin. *What the hell is that bloody streak on your face? You try to kiss one of those guys?*

The jungle bit me, Gator quipped back.

The relief of being alive crowded in while they did a quick inventory of body parts, hoping everything was still attached. Sam checked his gear, knowing they would be moving out fast, going somewhere a lot quieter before the next phase of their mission.

Ten minutes, Ryland announced. *Team One, gather all unused claymores. Team Two will cover. We go out in single file, four meters apart.*

They didn't want to give the enemy a large target, but it was more than that. If one person accidentally stepped on a pressure mine, no one else was going to take the blast.

Kadan, you're on point.

Kadan was a ghost, drifting in and out of shadows, up and down rocks, trees, any kind of terrain, never making a sound. He would be ten meters ahead, which would give the rest of them a chance if he came across the enemy. If he found anything, he would signal the rest of them to stop, move up on line quietly, or send Ryland up to investigate and make the decision which way to proceed.

The smell of rotting vegetation and mildew grew as they went deeper into the jungle. The jungle could be as deadly as—or even deadlier than—the enemy they were hunting. Everything seemed to want to kill them—bugs, snakes, crocs, and caiman, as well as larger animals and even the trees and vines. Monkeys had a nasty habit of giving away position with their screams.

The team kept their movements slow and deliberate, not wanting to stir up trouble while they slipped single file through miles of jungle. Kadan signaled Ryland when he found a good defensible position, and Ryland moved forward to consult.

We regroup here, Ryland decided. *We'll put phase two into operation from here.*

The men set up the base, took stock of supplies left, set their claymores, and posted guards while Sam made the call home.

"Valhalla . . . Valhalla, Reaper One, do you copy?"

"This is Valhalla . . ."

Sam gave his report as succinctly as possible. They were deeper into the rebel territory, and the chance of anyone listening was greater.

"Phase one complete, Reapers One and Two standing." He informed them of their remaining supplies and what took place during the first part of the operation.

"Copy that, Reaper Two. Phase two is a go."

"Phase two is a go, Reaper Two out."

Use hand signals or telepathy from here on out, Ryland commanded. *We're deep in their territory now.*

Sam let out his breath and turned to look at the men he'd spent so much time with doing this exact same thing. They were a long way from home and had a long way to go before they were finished.

Tucker winked at him. *Hell of a way to make a living and you with all those brains. Never know it, would you?*

Sam couldn't argue with Tucker's assessment. Hunting bloodthirsty rebels in the middle of their territory didn't seem like a genius idea right then.

Tucker snickered and took a swallow of water. *Getting shot at is thirsty work.*

They rested for a few minutes and then Ryland gathered them close again. *The rebel camp is here.* He tapped the map. *The compound is set in rows. Troop barracks are the first three on the north side of AO—area of operation. The command building with coms—communications— and the leaders' quarters is in the center. Vehicles and maintenance buildings are on the south side of the compound. Armine's house is thirteen klicks to the west.*

Ryland turned to Nico and Kadan. *I want you to set up shop up here on this hill a hundred and fifty meters to the east side of Armine's house and take him out.*

Nico just looked at Ryland. He was a man of very few words, but his reputation was renowned. Kadan gave a short nod.

Simultaneously, the rest of us will work in two man teams. Kyle, you and Jonas will make your way here to the munitions dump. Keep in mind that we need to use their mortar shells and explosives to our advantage.

Gator nudged Sam. *Kyle's all happy now. You know he likes to blow things up.*

Hell yeah, Kyle agreed. *Doesn't everybody?*

As usual Ryland ignored the byplay. *Sam, you're going to blow this shit up here. I want all enemy coms down. Take out the entire building. Use your ability to teleport, and get all the equipment in that building, I want the building gone completely along with everything in it. Get on the roof and wire their equipment if possible.*

Sam nodded, his stomach tightening. He was good at moving fast, but he would have to stay in one place to set explosives, and he'd be exposed on the roof.

Gator, you've got this small group of vehicles. Tucker and I will take this group here. He waited for all of them to nod understanding before continuing. *While pulling off the objective, we will place thermite grenades in the muzzle of each mortar tube. Any vehicles we don't have enough demo for we will place thermite on the engines.*

The term they used for demolitions was demo, and Ryland had fallen into the familiar pattern of speaking when working.

Kyle looked pleased. *Those things will burn straight through the whole engine.*

Ryland nodded. *That's what we want. We'll daisy-chain using det cord.*

Daisy-chaining was a way of connecting several explosive devices by explosive cord to detonate off the same fuse so that they all blow at the same time.

We want at least five minutes of time fuse so we can clear the objective and be gone before the thermite attracts too much attention. Once you have the demo set, you move back to ORP—objective, rally point. It's only a hundred meters from the objective, so noise and light discipline a must. If all goes according to plan, we are gone before they know we were ever here. At that point, we will make our way to the extraction point where the sniper team, Reaper Two at this point, will link up with us. From there we'll catch a ride with Task Force 160 to the USS Ronald Reagan *at sea in the Atlantic. We good?*

Ryland always tacked that last on, and everyone had better damn well be good with his orders. Everyone nodded and he waved them to gear up. They moved out in single file again, edging closer to the compound. Nico and Kadan slipped into the jungle, heading for their hill overlooking Armine's quarters. Everyone else, in designated two man teams, drifted through the thick vines to work their way in close to be ready for the signal to go.

Kadan's voice moved through their minds. *Reaper One, this is Two.*

Ryland answered. *Reaper Two, this is One.*

Kadan's voice was as calm as ever. Nothing ever seemed to shake him up. *Two is in position, we have a good visual on Armine's house. As soon as the fucker pokes his head out, we'll take it off.*

Ryland replied. *Happy hunting; once you've got him, get to the PZ.*

Roger that, Kadan acknowledged.

Ryland gave the command they were all waiting for. *Reaper One teams make ready. Go!*

Sam took off on his pre-chosen route. Sam had gone over and over it in his mind, studying the path he would take to the communications building. He knew every bit of cover possible to get to the building. He needed to get to a window and see inside the building to teleport into it. He had to have an actual destination. He had chosen his window ahead of time. The building sat smack in the middle of the rows of dilapidated huts, basically open. The north facing window appeared to have the most cover.

He moved quickly, getting the sickening jar of his physical body parts trying to catch up with his spirit. He emerged right outside the window in a crouch. He had only seconds before one of the guards spotted him. He lifted his head cautiously to peer through the dirty, yellowed pane. He just needed a spot where he could teleport inside unseen.

Two men sat at a small, rickety table, with a radio in between them. Maps were spread out along one wall. Papers were strewn around the room. In one corner, dirty dishes attracted flies. His heart dropped when he looked in the other corner. Two girls lay in a bloody heap—both were tied up and they stared at the two men with swollen, dazed, hate-filled eyes. Neither girl could have been more than fifteen, if that.

Bile rose in his throat. He shoved down the anger. It wasn't as if this was the first time he'd seen such things. If he left them there, they were going to die in the ensuing explosions. If he tried to rescue them, he was putting not only himself but his entire team in added danger. Swearing under his breath, he made his decision. If one of them made a sound, he'd kill them both and then do his job. But if he could, he'd get them out of there.

He took a breath, chose his spot, and moved with blurring, wrenching speed. He found himself in the corner, crouching behind a rusty water barrel, just a few feet from the girls. He made the smallest of movements, just enough to attract the nearest one's attention. He'd already planned his move if she screamed. He'd be across the room, slashing the two men's throats before he turned back to the girls. The compound had to be used to them screaming for a moment or two.

He had one finger to his lips, but he didn't hold out much hope. He knew he looked like another monster raiding their farm, killing their families, and subjecting them to a life of abuse and rape. The girl nearest him turned her head, her eyes widening until she looked as if only the whites of her eyes were showing. He shook his head, keeping his finger over his lips.

She swallowed hard and nodded, turning her head to press her lips against the other girl's ear. She whispered. The other girl jerked, her gaze jumping to him. Immediately she began to shake. For a moment time stood still while she battled for control. He willed her to be silent. She swallowed several times, and pressed her lips tightly together.

Now, he had no choice at all. He had to get the women out when they ignited the thermite, not before. He couldn't risk the other members of his team. He took a breath and moved, a knife in each hand. He was on the men before either girl could blink. He slammed the two knives simultaneously into the base of their skulls, severing spinal cords and killing them. Neither man ever saw him. He knelt to plant charges on the radios and added a few more to the structural beams holding the hut up for good measure.

Gator's voice came into his head. *Charges set, ready to drop thermite.*

Kyle was next. *Charges set, ready to drop thermite.*

Sam sighed. *Compromised. Cleaning up the mess. Go. I'll catch up.*

Not what I want to hear, Knight, Ryland snapped.

Go. Get it done. I'm right behind you, Sam assured.

Ryland answered. *Charges set. Drop thermite and fall back to the ORP.*

Kadan's voice slipped into their heads. *Reaper One, this is Reaper Two. Target neutralized with extreme prejudice. Reaper Two en route to PZ.*

Ryland answered him. *Solid, copy, Reaper Two, Reaper One oscar mike—on the move.*

The thermite triggered and all hell broke loose. From his window, Sam could see the explosion killed one of the guards and brought the entire compound to life. Rebels flooded into the vehicle holding area, trying to figure out what was happening. The charges on the vehicles and those in the munitions dump detonated together, sending a giant clap of thunder reverberating through the jungle and shaking the earth.

Sam slit the ropes binding the two girls fast, yanking the two of them to their feet, and indicating they had to leave fast, to stay behind him. He went out the door, triggering the thermite as he did, which only gave him two to four seconds. The two girls stayed close on his heels as the communications building lifted up off the ground. Wood, mud, and debris flew everywhere. Vehicles shattered. Munitions detonated, sending shrapnel in all directions. The flames, concussion, and flying chunks of white hot steel tore into flesh, searing many and leaving the few survivors too stunned to do anything. The two girls held hands, one moaning low and constantly, but they ran, barefoot, half naked, staying very close to Sam.

Reaper One, this is lost Knight, oscar mike—on the move. Sam reported to Ryland.

The GhostWalkers raced away from the war zone in two man teams. Sam used the cover of the chaos and mayhem of the explosions to make it into the trees. He stepped back to indicate the girls should run—and they did, in the direction opposite the one he wanted to go. He could only assume they had someone left to run to. He had to hightail it out of there before someone assumed leadership. He'd taken two steps when a bullet whistled past his ear and he heard it hit something solid. He dropped, spinning, just in time to see a rebel go down behind him.

Haul ass, Tucker advised.

Once everyone was back at the objective rally point, they moved out in single file, hurrying as fast as the jungle permitted, staying in cover, absolutely silent while the compound behind them roared with orange and red flames, lighting the night, heading for their pickup zone and their ride home. They were exhausted by the time they made it to the appointed clearing.

Ryland spoke into the radio while the others took up guard positions. "Valhalla, do you copy?" There was ominous silence. He waited a few heartbeats and tried again. "Valhalla, do you copy?"

Absolute silence. No static. No response. His eyes met Kadan's. "Kadan, try your radio. Mine doesn't seem to be working."

The men exchanged uneasy looks.

"Valhalla, this Reaper, over. Valhalla, do you copy, over."

Again there was that ominous silence. Adrenaline flooded their bodies as realization dawned.

Ryland shook his head. "The satellite link is down."

"That can't be," Gator said. "Those fuckers burned us."

"Forbes," Sam said. "Duncan Forbes. I should have killed him while I had the chance. He went running back to his master and Whitney pulled the plug on us."

Ryland scowled. "We were afraid this would happen and we've got a backup plan. It's just going to take us a little longer to get home. Sam, contact Azami." He sent the men a small smile. "She's got a freighter off the coast waiting for us and a company jet in Turkey. We'll make it home," he assured.

"The coast is a long way off," Kyle said, "and there's bound to be a few really pissed off rebels looking for us."

"We've been here before," Ryland reminded with a small, resigned shrug.

Sam used a small radio Azami had given him. "Firefly, Firefly, do you copy? This is Burning Man, over."

"This is Firefly. Burning Man, we have you five by five, over."

"Coming your way, over," Sam said. "It's a go."

"Copy that, Burning Man, it's a go. Waiting on you, over."

"Give me that," Ryland held out his hand for the tiny radio. He even snapped his fingers, impatience on his face.

Reluctantly Sam handed it to him. Ryland spoke into it. "Firefly, this is Burning Man leader. Are we secure, over."

"Totally, Burning Man, over."

"Duncan Forbes, CIA man holding hands with Whitney, made a call to someone at Bragg. I want them both. Do you copy?"

Sam sucked in his breath. Ryland had just included Azami in their trusted circle.

"Copy that, Burning Man, consider it done. Firefly out."

CHAPTER 19

Misery was tramping through hostile jungle for thirteen hours with the steady fall of rain. Long, silver sheets dropped from the sky, the drops making their way through the thick leaves of the canopy to fall in an endless, relentless stream. Everything and everyone was thoroughly drenched. The trees seemed closer at night, the tangled vines, thick and roped, hanging like nooses over their heads, ready to trap them.

The team walked in single file in absolute silence, continually alert for snakes, animals, insects, and hostiles. Sam had been in the rainforests hundreds of times, but he couldn't recall a more miserable journey. The feeling of being abandoned was strong, thrown away by an ungrateful government, left to die in a country they'd tried to help. He knew what Azami felt like, thrown away like so much trash. Anger mixed with trepidation with every step they took.

He was a man, trained for this shit. He'd signed on, knowing at any moment he could be burned. Azami had been an infant when Whitney had taken her from the orphanage. She'd been eight years old when Whitney had abandoned her on the streets of Japan. He'd experimented on her until he was certain her only use was a heart transplant the doctor was certain would kill her. Sick and dying, he'd had her flown in a box to Japan, taken by strangers to an alley known for sex trade, and dumped her—threw her away as he'd just been thrown away.

Anger smoldered in the pit of his belly—not for himself, but for Azami. Walking through a dark, hostile jungle couldn't be any worse than a child waking up in a country she didn't know, bruised and battered.

It was a four-day walk to Matadi and they wanted to find a car, but they needed a ride where a vehicle could actually travel, and most of the roads were blown to hell.

Kadan's voice hissed a soft warning in his ear. Sam went down on one knee, sliding his gun into firing position. They all remained absolutely silent. Their point man just indicated trouble.

A rebel patrol moved like wraiths, filtering through the trees just a few meters from them. The patrol continued on past them, and Sam let out his breath, his muscles relaxing a little. The rebels suddenly halted, one man moving out of the line into the trees, just off the animal trail they were using as a path. He opened his fly and suddenly looked straight at Kadan.

Kadan was no more than a foot from him, blending into the shadows as he often did. The man blinked and looked away. Kadan didn't move, remaining absolutely silent and still. Above his head the branch came alive, a snake lifting its head curiously to stare at the soldier. The reptile's movement drew the rebel's attention. He took a step closer, peering at the snake, machete raised. And then his eyes widened and he screamed, a high-pitched cry of absolute shock, to see a man so close to him.

"Contact, one o'clock!" Kadan yelled as he shot the soldier in the head.

The rebels opened fire simultaneously with the Ghost-Walker team, a mere five meters apart. The entire confrontation lasted forty-five seconds, but it seemed an eternity of hell with the shock of the bullets flying and men screaming. Monkeys screamed their fear and rage, adding to the chaos, and just that quickly, the jungle went silent.

Seven rebels lay dead, with the last one dying. Ryland signaled the men forward to quickly drag the dead deeper into the bushes and glean as much intel as possible, looking for maps and radio frequencies. The sound of gunfire could be heard for miles and they didn't want to stay there any longer than necessary, nor did they want to draw more attention to themselves than they already had.

They set out fast, putting distance between the dead rebels and them, making good time as the night began to approach. Ryland called a halt and signaled to Kadan to find a good hide for a few hours' sleep. They needed rest and food before they moved on.

Sam resisted the urge to use the radio just to hear Azami's voice. The rain refused to slow down, pouring down as if trying to flood the area. Small rivulets ran all around them. They had to watch each other for leeches, removing them in stoic silence. They took turns sleeping and guarding for four hours before starting out again. The quick catnap helped take the edge off.

Moving at night was slow, but moving during the day was far more dangerous. They had too long of a way to travel to engage with the rebels too many times. Kadan abruptly stopped as the sun came up, signaling to hold. The Ghost-Walkers dropped to their knee and waited.

We've got a fairly well traveled road here, Rye, Kadan reported. *We might pick up a vehicle if we keep close to it.*

Ryland considered the risks before he agreed. The distance to Matadi without picking up transportation would take too many days to walk and they were going to get lucky only if they were close to a road.

Let's stay close.

They didn't have long to wait until they heard the faint sound of an engine chugging toward them. Quickly they set up an ambush. As the rusty old pickup came into sight, Gator stumbled out onto the road, babbling, arguing with himself in his Cajun accent, seemingly oblivious to the truck. The truck lurched to a halt, four rebels spilling out, shouting at Gator and gesturing with guns. When he continued to babble, they looked at one another and one went up to him to deliver a blow into his midsection. The others spit on him. One punched and another kicked him as he went down. Engrossed in beating up the clearly insane idiot, none of them noticed the GhostWalkers slipping up behind them.

Gator's eyes cleared. From the ground he gave them a wicked grin and wiggled his fingers. "Bye-bye, boys," he said. "Been fun knowin' ya."

Four knives slit throats, and Sam reached down to help Gator as the bodies were removed from the road. "You all right?"

"Yeah. Next time you can be the insane guy."

Sam grinned at him. "Do I look crazy to you? You're so good at it."

"Get in the truck," Ryland called.

There were risks out in the open on the road, but it was far faster than "breaking brush"—walking in the jungle. As Kyle floored it, pushing the speed to cover miles, Sam breathed a sigh of relief. Every mile passing was a mile closer to going home to Azami. For the first time in his life he actually had a reason to go home.

They stayed as alert as possible with the pits in the road jarring them every few minutes. The rain fell in the same endless gray sheets, obscuring vision. At times the bald tires slid in the mud, sending them slamming into each other. They were packed like sardines in the back, but they weren't walking.

Three hours later, as they hit the top of a hill, the radiator began to steam and the engine abruptly seized.

"Okay, boys," Ryland said. "Time to put the LPCs back to use."

The men groaned and lifted their leather personal carriers out of the truck. Ryland laughed at them. "Too much good living. You're all turning into pansies. The truck saved us over a hundred miles of walking and a few days on top of that, so stop your bellyaching. We've got twenty-three miles until we get to Matadi. Let's get this sorry ass truck pushed over the edge so it looks like the abandoned wreck that it is. We need to get out of sight and make certain nobody saw us arrive."

After ascertaining they hadn't been spotted, they traveled twenty klicks from the truck, set up security, and settled in to wait for nightfall.

Duncan Forbes sank into his favorite seat at his favorite pub. "Whiskey." He needed it. And he had a damn good reason to celebrate. Everything had gone to hell in the Congo, but he'd gotten out alive and he'd had his revenge on the fuckers. Who did they think they were, anyway? They'd treated him like dog shit. "Elite, my ass," he said aloud. Yeah, they were so damned elite that they were going to die in that jungle, hopefully tortured by those equally idiotic rebels.

"Make that two," General Fielding said and slid his butt into the seat across from Forbes. He smiled at the woman seated at the bar. A pretty little thing. Delicate. Asian. The little cap of jet black hair was intriguing around her fragile face. She had the longest lashes he'd ever seen. Her lips were . . .

"You're staring," Forbes said with a tight laugh. "She's probably on the clock."

"I can find out after we have our drink. It was a long flight to Washington." He glanced again at the woman, catching her eye. This time she smiled. "I wish I was in uniform, but that always attracts undo attention. Women, however, fall all over me when I'm wearing it." He turned his head and suddenly he was all business, looking like the commander he was. "What the hell went wrong out there? I don't like leaving my soldiers behind."

"Sacrifices have to be made, General. If we're going to have a strong military, we need the right people leading," Forbes said. "These men not only blew a multimillion-dollar project, but more important, they blew months of negotiations. If the president gets those mines back, we won't have access to what we need for the weapon. He's not going to be so easy to deal with as a bunch of hotheaded rebels with no real agenda."

Fielding sighed. "Still. They were soldiers. Good soldiers."

Forbes shot him a look. "What do you know about them?"

"Not much." The general shrugged, his gaze straying back toward the woman at the bar. She was leaning over the bar, talking to the bartender, flirting a little as the man put the whiskeys on the bar for the waitress. She had picked up her clutch and seemed to be getting ready to leave. He didn't want her to leave. She was the only prospect he could see for salvaging the night.

The waitress scooped up the drinks and brought them over to the table. Forbes reached for his money, but she shook her head and indicated over her shoulder. "She bought it for both of you."

Forbes took his drink with a sigh of relief and downed half of it, before smiling an acknowledgment. "I don't think that uniform is going to matter one way or the other, General. That little tart is looking for some fun with you."

The general picked his drink up and waited until the little Asian girl had slipped off the barstool and was fully facing him. He raised his glass in a toast to her and took a large swallow. She smiled back at him and sauntered over, taking her time but holding his attention with her large, exotic eyes.

She stopped at the table as Forbes downed his drink and signaled for two more. The general managed another healthy swallow, looking her up and down over the rim of his glass.

"Good evening, gentlemen," she said softly, very softly, her voice just the merest thread of sound.

"Thank you for the drinks," Fielding said. He went to put his hand on her hip, but she glided a few steps and his hand fell through empty air.

She smiled. "You don't have me to thank. These drinks are courtesy of the GhostWalkers you thought you left behind in the jungle. Enjoy them, gentlemen, they'll be your last." She spoke so soft, so sweetly, it took a moment for her words to register.

Forbes opened his mouth to say something, but no sound came out. Alarm spread across his face. He clutched his chest.

The general scowled at her. "What the hell are you saying?"

She was already gone, walking out of the bar with unhurried steps, the bar door swinging closed behind her.

The waitress brought the second round of drinks to the table. Forbes half stood, still clutching at his heart. He suddenly fell, going to his knees, his chair tipping back. "Oh, my God," the waitress said. "Bill, I think he's having a heart attack. Call an ambulance."

As the words left her mouth, Fielding tried to stand and went down, smashing his head on the table, his hands gripping the edges so hard the table overturned. Several people ran to help. No one noticed the man removing the two glasses from the floor and pocketing them, leaving the newly spilled whiskey glasses beside the overturned table. He left the bar as the paramedics arrived.

Eiji walked out of the bar and down the sidewalk, using the same unhurried pace his sister had. He turned into the alley where she waited, once more in jeans, with her long hair pulled back in a ponytail. As he walked down the alley toward her, he reversed his light-colored coat to the darker blue side, slicked his hair back, and waited while Azami deftly changed the laces in his shoes to a bright pink. They both donned backpacks they had stashed. He dropped his arm around her shoulders, and they emerged onto the next street on the other side of the block, Eiji hailing a cab.

Daylight gave way to darkness, although there seemed to be little difference with the constant rain in the jungle. Sometimes the rain let up for a short while and then it would start again in earnest. They continued their journey toward the port where the GhostWalkers hoped to "acquire" a boat.

The rising sun found them four miles from town where they settled in for the day. It was far too risky in the more populated area to travel. With the sun, the rain faded into a mist and then gradually disappeared altogether.

"We'll rest here," Ryland decided. "Try to scavenge up some food, find a water source, and clean up a bit."

They all carried baby wipes and basic hygiene necessities and it felt good to take some of the grime of battle and travel off. Water came from a creek that ran into the nearby Congo River. Kyle, Jonas, and Gator went looking for food for everyone. Kyle managed to come up with a couple of dozen bananas and Jonas collected wild yams. Gator built a fish weir in the creek and captured a few tilapia.

Sam and Nico dug an oblong hole and built a fire in it. Using green limbs, they built a rack over the fire and cooked the fish and yams. They all sat back, finally satisfied, feeling as if they'd attended a virtual feast. The food was much needed, as it had been some time since they'd consumed any of their rations.

"We're going to revise our plan a little and go with a new strategy for the night," Ryland said. It was evident that while the others collected and cooked food, Ryland and Kadan had been working on a new plan. "We'll split into two teams. The teams will do independent recons of two different routes to port. We'd like to find a small boat to take us down the Congo River to the Atlantic. When we've completed our recons, we'll meet back up at a designated ORP and make a decision how to proceed. Any questions?"

Again there was no pause. "Good. Let's get it done, gentlemen."

Sam, Nico, Kadan, and Jonas headed out, traveling fast, as soon as they'd settled on an objective rally point. Sam slipped into the brush, close to the port. The place was heavily guarded, presumably to keep the rebels out. Armed men in uniforms paced restlessly. Several stood together, talking quietly, smoke and laughter drifting back toward him. He worked his way all along the river, trying to find some means of transportation, but the security had the place locked down tight. Cursing under his breath, he made his way back to his three team members. All of them shook their heads silently.

Kadan gave the signal to retreat back to the designated objective rally point. They could only hope that Ryland's team had fared better. They crouched down, waiting for Ryland's team when the radio gave a soft sigh.

"Burning Man . . . Burning Man . . . this is Firefly, over."

He closed his eyes for a moment. He was trapped in the jungle, no way to get out, the president's army all around them. The soldiers sure as hell didn't have a clue they were the good guys, and if caught, no one would claim them—not even the man who had asked for help.

He swallowed hard. She was right about the clarity of the radio. It sounded as if she was whispering in his ear. He hoped she was right about the audio capability—she'd devised some new audio device that if they stayed under fifteen seconds with each transmission, was supposed to be impossible to detect. Just the sound of her voice made him want to hold her close.

"Burning Man, over."

"Your ride is waiting."

"Copy that, Firefly, ride is waiting, over."

"Tell leader, problem taken care of. Home office clear as well. Firefly out."

His heart jerked. It seemed a hell of a lot easier to run around jungles with enemies surrounding him when he had nothing to lose. The freighter was anchored and waiting for them. They just had to make it out to the boat.

Ryland's team returned, looking as dejected as he felt. Kadan gave his report. Ryland's echoed it. The port was too heavily guarded to chance it. They'd have to move on.

Firefly has our ride in place. Sam was glad to give some good news. *Rye, the problem both in the general's office and the one you wanted addressed has been taken care of.*

Ryland's nod was barely perceptible, but he looked pleased.

It was a long, slow walk skirting the town. Several times they ran into dogs, but Gator quieted them before they could bark and give the team away. On the other side of town, they once again split into two teams for another recon. Almost immediately Sam spotted a van. The vehicle didn't look in much better shape than the truck had been, but it was transport. Old and rusty, the paint chipping, it would at least provide concealment as well as needed transportation. From what Sam had seen, most of the vehicles—and there weren't many—were in the same condition.

Gator and Sam crept slowly to the edge of town where the vehicle sat. A dog barked somewhere close and Gator turned his head toward it. The dog let out a soft whine and ceased barking. Sam went down on one knee and guarded Gator's back while the Cajun hot-wired the van. Gator sent Sam a triumphant grin when the van rumbled to life. Sam jumped in on the other side and they got out of there quickly. A quarter mile away, they paused at the edge of the road long enough for the others to jump in the open side door.

"Wonderful carriage," Kyle quipped.

"Nice work," Ryland commented.

The van creaked and moaned, but it was running and that was all that counted. They only needed to get another ninety-two miles according to the GPS. Having a vehicle, even though it was rusted in three spots on the floorboards, allowing them to see the road beneath flashing by, meant they would make their destination by daybreak.

It was a long trip as a few more cars occasionally shared the road with them. Once a truckload of soldiers rumbled past and all of them held their breath, grateful the van was closed and nearly impossible to see into in the dark. Gator simply slowed and moved to the side, allowing the truck to rumble past them.

"Stop strokin' that gun, Kyle," Gator said. "You're makin' me nervous. I'm thinkin' you're about to make love to the damn thing."

"She is purty," Kyle said, giving the gun one last caress, his eyes watching the truck ahead. "Slow down a little, and let them get ahead of us, Gator."

"What if they put up a roadblock?" Jonas asked.

Ryland opened one eye. "We'll cross that bridge when we come to it. Can the chatter and let me sleep. We've got swimming to do and I'm getting too old for this shit."

"Do they have sharks off this coast?" Jonas asked.

Sam snickered. "You and those sharks, Jonas."

"I have nightmares, man," Jonas protested.

"I'll feed you to a damn shark if you don't let me sleep," Ryland drawled.

Kadan and Nico exchanged amused glances.

Ryland opened both eyes. "I heard that. I'm not *that* old."

They all laughed and tension eased now that the truckload of soldiers was well up ahead of them. They drove through the night and made it to the coast just before dawn broke. Working fast, they filled the waterproof bag lining their rucksacks with air. The combination of inflated bags, empty canteens, and removing anything unnecessary would allow them to float their weapons and remaining gear out to the boat with them.

For what they couldn't carry, they dug a hole, piled in what was left of the gear, and used the remaining explosives saved for just such an occasion. They always destroyed anything that could later be used against them—or against another team—and anything that might identify them. They detonated the explosives as they waded out to sea.

Gator turned and waved with a big grin. "Nice meetin' y'all."

"Is Mari in the tunnel yet?" Lily asked.

Azami shook her head. "She's refusing to go and I can't say that I blame her. She wants guns and ammo. Briony took her twins down and she has Daniel. I've got Eiji with them and no one will get past him. He knows that they're the main target and he'll guard them with his life. We need all the available trained soldiers up here. I told Daiki to stay with Mari."

"Mari will lose those babies if they get to her and try to make her move."

"She'll lose them anyway if she moves into the tunnel. It's not like she can be carried in. She might let her husband, but she's not budging and we don't have time to argue. We have to get everything set for an assault on the compounds," Azami pointed out. "In any case, we're fairly certain Whitney doesn't know about her pregnancy. You've done a good job of concealing it to the outside world."

"I can't believe he's doing this," Lily said, her eyes shimmering with tears. "He's my father and yet he's willing to put Daniel and me in danger just to get what he wants."

Azami put her hand on Lily's shoulder. "You know he isn't the man you loved anymore, Lily. You've got to accept that. He's changed, gone a little mad . . ."

"Or maybe a lot."

Azami nodded. "The point is, once you can accept that he isn't that man you love, you can get past this. Then he becomes the enemy and you have to see him that way. What if he's standing between you and your child?"

Lily pressed her lips together and shook her head. "I just can't believe that he would hurt Daniel. What would be the point?"

"Dissecting him to see what makes Daniel tick." Azami

hardened her heart. Lily had to understand the true danger. The men surrounding her buffered her from the things her father did. "Right now your husband and Sam have been left in hostile territory on Whitney's order." She glanced around and unbuttoned her shirt. "He did this to me when I was three. These scars were acquired before the age of three."

She let Lily look her fill, her features twisted with horror, her eyes wide with shock. "He did that to you when you were a child?"

"My hair came in white," Azami said. She touched her hair a little self consciously. "There's a hell of a lot more, but the point is, pick up a gun and shoot the bastard if he gets near your son."

Lily swallowed hard and nodded. "I'll do what I have to do, Azami. They aren't coming into my home and trying to steal my son, or Briony's for that matter. I'll defend this place."

Azami buttoned her shirt. "Let's get to it then. Who's running the show?"

"Ian's in the war room now. I'm a strong telepath so I'll build a bridge to anyone who isn't," Lily said.

"You'll have to give Eiji and Daiki radios. I brought small ones for them. No one will pick up fifteen second transmissions. If anyone gets near the tunnels, which I doubt, or near Mari, they'll take care of it," Azami said with complete confidence.

She hurried in to find Ian directing his small army on the defense of both compounds.

"They'll come at us in small groups," Ian said. "Whitney doesn't want the babies harmed, so I'm guessing they'll try stealth to infiltrate. They have no idea we were warned that they're coming. They think a sweet bunch of ladies are here all alone."

"They've got another think coming," Flame, Gator's wife, said, with an indignant toss of her head. "Whitney always underestimates women." She had thick, wine red hair and vivid green eyes sparkling with something between mischief and determination.

"He thinks you're all flawed because most of you have problems with psychic overload," Lily pointed out. "He has no idea we've been working on that. I'll be with you, Dahlia. You have the most difficult time. Briony will be in the tunnels. She has a terrible problem when there's violence, but she'll defend the babies if she has no other choice." She looked at Azami. "Just as I will."

"I'll be of more use to you outside," Azami said.

"Me too," Saber Calhoun, Jesse Calhoun's wife, said. She was a small woman, extremely slight, looking more like a child than a grown woman. She had a cap of dark hair and large, violet blue eyes. She pressed her lips tight together and then looked Azami straight in the eye. "Do you remember me?" She swallowed hard, but refused to look away. "I practiced stopping hearts on you when you were just a toddler. Your hair was white when you were a child, but I'd know your eyes anywhere."

Azami nodded solemnly. "I remember. Every one of us had to do things we didn't want to do. I'm glad to see you made it out of there. You were always kind to me."

"I didn't feel kind," Saber admitted. "I hated those days he would force me to work on you. I tried so hard to make him stop, but the more I protested, the worse he got. We all thought he killed you."

"Apparently I don't die so easy. He thinks I'm dead, and I'd prefer it stays that way," Azami said.

"Ladies." Ian snapped his fingers. "Do you think we could conduct old home week a little later? We've got this little problem happening right now."

"Don't sweat it, Ian," Flame said. "These guys won't know what hit them."

He glared at her. "Do you plan on talking them to death? Damn, woman. You're giving me gray hair."

She looked him over judiciously. "You could use a little color there, Irishman. You're sort of bland."

Ian's face went as red as his hair. All the women burst out laughing. He groaned and wiped his hand down his face. "There is clearly a breakdown of discipline in this room."

The women burst out laughing again.

"Once you give women guns, Ian," Jesse Calhoun pointed out, "all bets are off. You be careful out there. Take a couple of weapons with you."

Saber leaned over and kissed him. "You take care as well. Don't be a hero."

"Stay to the north side," Ian cautioned. "If for any reason you come around to any other side, let us know, so no one accidentally shoots you." He glanced at Flame.

She gave another toss of her head. "I don't know why you're looking at me. I'm proficient with weapons. Wanna see?"

"Damn, woman, you've been living with that Cajun too long," Ian said.

She leaned in close. "It will never be long enough, Ian."

His blushed deepened. "Get out of here. And for God's sake, don't get shot or anything stupid like that. Gator would slice me into tiny pieces and feed me to the alligators."

"He might not do that, but he'd tell his grandmother on you and then no more free meals for you. She's pretty crazy about me," Flame teased.

"Yeah, well," Ian said gruffly, "all of you stick to the plan and we'll get through this."

Azami smiled at the man. He was surrounded by women and definitely out of his depth. Some men had a deep need to protect their women; Ian was clearly a man like that. He felt affection, if not love, for some of these women, Flame in particular, probably because he was so close to Gator, and he didn't like the situation much. He couldn't argue; the women were definitely capable and more than determined to protect their homes in spite of the fact that Whitney's experiments produced a few negative effects when around psychic energy overload.

"We'll be fine," Lily said.

Azami and Saber left the room together, falling into stealth mode, almost without conscious thought. They moved in silence, even in the halls, Azami pausing for a moment to retrieve the weapons she'd stashed when Lily had come to talk to her.

"I'm happy you're here, Thorn . . . Azami," Saber corrected. "I've thought about you nearly every day. I prayed you were alive and happy somewhere. I used to make up stories to comfort myself. I've had a lot of nightmares," she admitted.

Azami glanced at her as they slipped out the door and hurried into the woods. "I did have a great life. I was adopted by a wonderful man. He gave me two great brothers, a home, and a purpose. He trained, educated, and treated me with love and kindness. I'm guessing that's a lot better than most of the girls had."

"I wish I'd been a little older and could have stood up to him better," Saber said.

"My father once said to me, there is no use wishing away your past. Experiences shape us and build us into who we are. He always told me that it was my past that made me strong. He told me it is always best to live in the moment."

"Your father sounds like a very wise man," Saber said.

"He was. I wish Sam could have met him."

"Sam Johnson?" Saber stopped, crouching low in the brush. "You and Sam?"

Azami nodded.

They're making their way up the north side, a four man team, Lily reported.

Azami heard the whispers in her mind as Lily told each of the groups of defenders where the small four man teams were invading the two compounds. She pushed the sound to the back of her mind so she could be "in the moment" completely. She signaled Saber to her left, and Saber virtually disappeared into the brush.

Azami listened for the sound of the men moving toward them, fanned out, expecting to come up on a sleeping compound. These were Whitney's private army, growing smaller with each encounter with GhostWalkers, according to her informant. She was determined that these four men who had come to kidnap the infants would not be returning. Eventually Whitney was going to find himself without too many friends and then, for the first time, he'd truly be vulnerable.

A radio muttered and she heard the command. "Get the thermite in place."

Lily, tell everyone that they plan to blow up some of the houses as a distraction, Azami reported. The assault wasn't going to be on the two main gathering buildings, but on some of the outlying buildings probably to draw off anyone left at the two compounds.

The night was dark, swirling clouds blotting out any semblance of moon. The wind tugged at her face, cool, reminding her that fall was creeping toward winter and up in the mountains, it got cold. Out of the corner of her eye, she saw Saber go prone, wiggling beneath the brush into a small animal trail. One touch of Saber's hand and she could disturb a man's heart, disrupt it enough to actually kill him. Azami certainly knew what it felt like. Her heart actually jumped at the memory—and it wasn't the same heart.

She shook off her past. Her father was right. She had to be in the present, and thinking about something she had no control over did her no good at all. One enemy at a time. She heard a small rustle and then a murmur as the man approaching just to her right spoke into his radio in a soft voice, telling his leader he was in position and ready to invade the house. He was a good distance away, but clearly he expected to ease his way through the trees and rush to cover across the open space as soon as the explosions started. She expected fireworks, but it wouldn't be the same ones Whitney's men expected.

She waited, patient and still. To her left, in the direction Saber had taken, she heard a thud. Branches snapped. Her target turned his head toward the sound. Before he could say anything into his radio, she put an arrow through his heart. He went down gracefully, slumping over, still clutching his weapon.

In the distance, toward Team Two's compound, she heard gunfire. Bright, orange red flames danced, the night suddenly glowing from somewhere to the front of the main structure she was guarding. A fireball whooshed through the air, like a bright comet. Nico's wife, Dahlia, defending her home.

Azami moved to her right, falling back a little, to stay in front of the soldier making his way toward the helicopter hangar, determined to destroy the GhostWalkers' compound. *Her* home. She would be living here with these people who were like her, who could accept her differences. No one was touching her home.

She heard him coming almost before she could get set. She had no time to get out of his way. He was of medium build and moved easily through the forest, with hardly a whisper of a sound. He parted a bush and was face-to-face with her. She stepped into him, shoving his gun up as she drove the knife deep into his chest. His finger closed on the trigger and the gun roared in her ear, but his body was already slumping to the ground. He had one arm around her, and the deadweight nearly pulled her down.

Saber emerged from the bushes, twigs and leaves in her hair. She had a gun in her hand and fire in her eyes. Visibly relaxing, she helped Azami shove Whitney's man aside. In every direction, they could hear the firefight raging.

"You okay?" Saber asked.

Azami nodded. "You?"

Saber took a breath. "Yeah. I guess so. I really did promise myself I wouldn't do this again, but no one is going to take the babies from us. They aren't going to live the life we did. I got two of them."

"I'm with you," Azami agreed. "And I also managed to get two. That should be the four man team."

They did a quick reconnaissance of the area.

Clear, moving around to the west, Azami reported.

Negative, Lily said. *The boys are making a sweep, but we think we're good. They didn't get near either house. Poor Mari was really hoping someone would walk through her door. Come on in.*

They walked together, keeping a sharp eye on their surroundings, just in case someone had been missed.

"Did you have a difficult time trusting Lily?" Azami asked Saber.

Saber glanced at her. "At first," she answered honestly. "But she's shared all of her money to build these compounds and to make each GhostWalker independently wealthy. She's worked tirelessly to help those of us who aren't anchors be able to just walk down a street without freaking out. She's solidly on our side, Azami. I think all of us not only love her but have developed a very large protective streak where she's concerned."

Azami smiled at her. The hint of warning was subtle, but there. "I absolutely hear what you're saying, Saber, and I can understand it," she agreed mildly. "I'm planning on making this my home, so she'll have one more person looking out for her."

Saber's smile was relieved. "I'm glad you'll be here. I missed you. You were more like family to me than anyone I have. Jesse now, the GhostWalkers, and Jesse's family. I sometimes pinch myself to make certain I'm not in a fairy tale. He built a house for his sister, Patsy, right near ours."

"I am so looking forward to Sam coming home," Azami admitted. "I try not to worry about him, but I can't help it. I found myself wanting to contact him via satellite just to make certain he's alive and well."

Saber laughed. "Let's get inside and let the boys handle the rest of this. We can have tea and have a nice long visit. I want you to meet Jesse."

CHAPTER 20

Debriefing was a lot of bullshit. Sam wanted to leap out of his seat and go find his woman. He'd never actually had a woman to come home to, and now that he did, he had to sit like a kindergartener, wiggling around his chair, anxious to see her—inspect her—and make certain she didn't have so much as a scratch on her. Fucking Whitney, attacking the compound when there were just a few men and women to defend it. She wasn't hurt . . .

"Sam, you with us?" Ryland asked.

He wasn't the only one with a wife. Ryland had to be just as anxious. His son had been a target. He scowled at Ryland.

"He's got ants in his pants." Tucker snickered.

"He's got somethin' in his pants," Gator mocked, shoving at Sam's boot with his foot. "And I don' think it's ants."

"Go to hell," Sam said good-naturedly. "Like all of you aren't just as antsy."

Ryland sighed. "Our women fought off Whitney's men while we were in the field. It's getting a little old." He looked at Sam. "Get out of here." *And I want a full briefing from her later.*

Sam's nod was barely perceptible. He leapt out of the chair and rushed from the room, an arrow shot out of a bow. Laughter followed him, but he didn't give a damn. Nothing mattered but to get to her. Azami. His. He still didn't really believe she would be there. He kept expecting to wake up and find she was a dream—or that she'd come to her senses and run back to Japan where her life would make much more sense than his world did.

He sprinted out of the house, to the trail at the back leading into the woods. His five acres were to the west, and he rarely used a vehicle to travel the distance. He had worn a faint path in through the woods. When he wanted to go fast, he often teleported to keep in practice, and that's what he did now, setting his destination for just outside his home. He wanted to feel that amazing feeling she'd given him just days earlier of coming home. He needed to see the house lit up, telling him she was inside and waiting for him.

Dark clouds churned and spun overhead. Leaves on the trees swayed while some danced through the air with the wind, swirling their way to earth. The trees rose up like giant stick figures, branches reaching out, slowly shedding leaves as the season changed. A bite of cold touched his skin, but no matter how cold it was, nothing could stop the heat spreading through his body at the sight of those Japanese lanterns bobbing up and down the small stream running beside his house, the warm glow lighting the way home.

He stood on the worn path, his heart pounding, love flooding his mind. Azami. Sliding into his mind, holding him close. Her happiness spilled into him, filling him, driving out loneliness and doubts. She stood framed in the doorway, flickering candles dancing behind her, silhouetting her there in the dark. She wore only a short silken robe, her slender legs bare. Her hair fell in a silken waterfall around her face to spill to her waist. Her robe was open, exposing that wondrous, almost luminous spiderweb wrapping around all that bare skin. He really, really wanted to tattoo a couple more spiders to mark his favorite spots on her.

He walked slowly up to the house, his heart in his throat, his pulse pounding, savoring the feeling of coming home to her. Her dark eyes shone like a cat's in the night, a glitter of excitement—her heart in her eyes. Those extraordinary soft lips were parted as if she was a little breathless. She was so beautiful to him his chest hurt. A lump formed unexpectedly in his throat, threatening to choke him.

He wanted to feel love and he knew she was the one who would show him how. In his life, he had pushed aside his own needs, his own desires until Azami. He wanted to know love at its deepest, most profound, most elemental level. He needed Azami to give him everything, and from the look in her eyes, there was no doubt that she intended to do just that.

The moment he set his foot onto the porch, she launched herself at him. He caught her in midflight, drawing her into him. Her legs clamped around his waist and her arms circled his neck, her mouth settling on his. The world shifted and dropped away, as fire burst through his mouth, down his throat, and into his belly to race to his bloodstream, igniting an urgent need.

Now. Right here. Don't wait. I need you in me.

Her soft plea took his sanity. There was nothing left in his mind but her. She was everywhere. In his mind, in his heart, wrapped around his very bones. He kissed her over and over, drinking her in, devouring her, while the fire just burned brighter and hotter. He dropped his hands to his jeans, thankful he'd managed a couple of showers on the way home to rid himself of the jungle grime.

"Please, Sammy, hurry," her small, breathless voice whispered in his ear. Her small teeth bit at his earlobe and then her tongue stroked along his neck. "I've waited forever for you."

He managed to get his pants shoved down enough to free his aching cock. He gripped her hips. "Are you ready for me, honey? Are you certain?"

The urgency of her need was contagious, gripping him fiendishly, so that his lungs burned for air and his cock throbbed. He didn't wait for her answer, but pushed his hand between her legs. She was slick and hot, her hips already moving urgently. He laughed, the sound sheer joy as he steadied his cock.

"Lower yourself right over me, Azami," he whispered taking a gentle bite along her neck. She felt so perfect against his body. "Think of it like putting the sword into its scabbard."

She didn't hesitate but pushed herself down onto him. He was thick and hard, invading her feminine sheath, meeting that tight, exquisite resistance that squeezed him like a fiery hot velvet fist. He felt the rippling and bunching of her muscles as she lowered herself over him, her breath coming in ragged gasps, soft little moans like music in his ears.

He waited until she was fully seated and he was stretching her, pushing up against her cervix, giving her body a few moments to adjust.

She lifted her face to his again for those long, almost desperate kisses. He found himself eating at her mouth, drawing out all that welcoming sweetness. The wind rushed around them, blowing her hair in a whirlwind, cooling the heat of their bodies, but only fanning the flames into a firestorm.

He caught her hips as he pulled his own hips back. "Ride me, honey. And it's going to be a wild ride."

She answered him by holding his neck tighter and lifting herself to drop back down over him, sending red-hot fire streaking through his cock and spreading through his groin into his belly and down his thighs.

"I need you wild, Sammy. I feel a little wild."

That breathless confession was all it took. He forgot about holding on to control and took her hard and fast, his body slamming deep into hers, over and over, driving like a jackhammer, a steel spike, while the flames poured over and around him. Hunger clawed at him, making him a madman. Hot friction sent sensations careening to every part of his body while he pistoned into her tight, hot core.

Azami's breath rushed from her lungs in raw gasps as Sam's hands controlled her hips, driving her up higher than she imagined possible. There was no controlling the pleasure rising, pouring over her as he pumped hard and fast. She clung to him, her anchor in the storm of passion, her body tightening until she was strung out on a torturous rack. She heard her soft little pleas and couldn't stop herself, her moan rising to a crescendo as he thickened, stretching her, filling her until she thought he would find his way into her womb.

The explosion, when it came, was mind-numbing, her body clamping down hard on his, gripping with surprising strength, rippling around him, squeezing and grasping greedily, so that his seed jetted deep into her. She had known exactly what she was doing when she'd come to him begging for his body and she was fully committed to their life and their child—should there be one.

She laid her head on his shoulder and closed her eyes as the aftershocks took her again and again. She could breathe again now that he was home and safe. The world was right once more.

Sam held her, leaning his back against the wall, staring out at the last of the lanterns bobbing in the pond before they succumbed to the water pouring in from the small series of waterfalls. It took a few minutes to find his breath. He buried his face in her silky mass of hair.

"All I could think about, baby, was getting home to you," he admitted.

"That's good." She nuzzled his neck. "I don't want you to go away for a long, long time. Let's just stay here and make love forever."

He laughed softly. "Two great minds thinking alike. I like that." He carried her inside, kicking the door closed behind him.

Azami pulled back to look at his face. "I'm sorry, Sammy,

I should have greeted you properly," Azami said, her long lashes sweeping down to veil her cat's eyes. "I do have the bath ready for you. I just couldn't wait. Not even to let you relax."

He smiled at her, bending his head to find her mouth for another earth-shaking moment. "Silly woman, no welcome home could have been better." He carried her on through to the steamy bathroom. The air was scented and just the memory of their first ritual bath together made his cock jerk to attention all over again. "I know tradition is important to you, but we can bend a few things here and there as needed. And making love to you anytime, anywhere, is always a priority."

Her lashes swept up and her eyes gleamed at him. "Thank you, Sam. I needed to hear that."

He put her down, but kept her locked to him with one arm. "I hear you've been busy while I was gone."

"A little. With this and that."

He bent his head and kissed her. "That's no answer. I want details. And Ryland's going to want a report."

She looked up at him with that composed, serene look he found as sexy as hell. Sam drew her into the shower and took the handheld nozzle to begin their ritual, holding her still with one hand so that she knew he intended to have things his way this time.

"Don't give me that cute look of yours. It's not a great feeling coming home and finding my woman was out defending our home while I'm stuck in the jungle."

"Really?" Her eyebrow shot up and she leaned her head back against his chest while he took his time soaping her breasts. "I would have thought you'd be very happy you don't have to worry about me—or any of the others—when you're away."

He dropped another kiss on top of all that thick silky hair. "I suppose you have a point." His fingers traced the spiderweb down to her belly. "Tell me." He couldn't help that his voice had gone a little gruff.

"I found all the women extremely intriguing. Their individual gifts are amazing. Dahlia in particular. She actually built a wall of fire between the compound on the western facing slope and those trying to gain access. It was comical when I saw the video surveillance after. Whitney must have forgotten just how enhanced these women are." She squirmed a little as he brought his hand—and the nozzle with water—between her legs.

She gave a small gasp as he directed the spray against her clit. "Sammy, I can't think properly when you're doing that."

He kept up the pressure for a few more moments, until she was moaning, her hips moving subtly. He went back to washing her, enjoying the feel of her skin against his palms as he washed the inside of her thighs.

He bent his head to place his lips against her ear. "I plan to eat you up, Azami," he informed her. "Take my time and just enjoy myself."

Her eyes went darker than ever, turning to liquid. Her lips parted slightly as her breath turned a little ragged.

"Did you visit with any of the women in between holding off an assault and assassinating traitors?" His fingers stroked her thigh as he ran the water down her slender legs.

She nodded. "I liked them very much. I'm getting to know Lily, and Flame is very nice as well. Lily let me spend time with Daniel, and I've decided having a child is worth the worry."

He laughed softly. "I noticed."

She blushed. "I met Saber, from Team Two. We knew each other as children. She's a couple of years older than me and was good to me. It was nice to fight alongside her and catch up on her life. Her husband is very nice. I'm happy for her."

"Were they all welcoming?" he asked. His voice had gone husky. Washing her body, paying attention to shadows and hollows, using the water to thoroughly clean her, yet deliberately teasing her body with hands, mouth, and water had aroused him as much as it had her. He handed her the spray nozzle and sank down onto the little wooden stool.

"They were very welcoming, Sam," she said. "I'm going to love living here. Daiki and Eiji feel they can make this a second home."

She took her time, her movements unhurried and thorough. He didn't expect less from her. Caring for him was important to her, and she made certain that she attended him very thoroughly. This time, when she was washing his groin, her fingers and mouth were every bit as busy as the sea sponge, not so subtly paying him back for his arousing ministrations.

When she put down the spray nozzle and did that thing with her hair, knotting it up on her head before stepping into the steaming hot water, he realized that she had not only changed his world, but she'd changed him. He *loved* his home. He loved Azami and the way she cared for him. She didn't try to hide that she was overjoyed to see him or that she wanted his body every bit as much as he wanted hers.

This time, while they soaked in the tub, he allowed his mind to play out erotic fantasies, sharing them with her. The hot water had heated her skin to a rose color so he couldn't tell if she was blushing at his fantasies, but she shyly added a few details of her own that robbed him of his breath.

When he stepped from the tub, mostly because he *had* to have her again, his fist circled his pulsing cock, stroking with intent. Even though they'd made love hard and fast, it wasn't enough for him. He felt as if he might explode any moment. "Baby, you're going to have to help me out."

"You're very impatient," she observed, one eyebrow shooting up.

"Kneel up in the bathtub," Sam said, one hand anchoring in her hair, tilting her head back just a bit. "I need to feel your mouth around me. Just for a moment and then I swear, I'll be all about finishing cleansing the spirit."

That was a blatant lie. His mind wasn't going to be cleansed. Erotic pictures continued to dance in his head. He couldn't help it. Her body was there for the taking. His. Displayed only for him with her exotic tattoos and beautiful, delicate curves. There was no way to get rid of those pictures in his head, or the monster of a hard-on her ministrations had put there.

Azami slowly complied with his request, her movements flowing and graceful. He urged her head forward. Her hands were warm from the water, slowly surrounding the girth of his cock, and he sighed with relief. Her soft little hands felt a hell of a lot better than his had. She didn't have to do too much to put him in paradise. He watched her every movement. He'd never felt so much of a man as in that moment.

"I closed my eyes for five minutes out there in that jungle and all I could think about was this. How your mouth felt on me, the way you loved me. Show me right now." He nudged at her sinful lips with the head of his cock.

Azami smiled at his impatience, at his obvious hunger. He knew she deliberately waited a heartbeat, letting time stretch out before she slowly opened her mouth and licked at the pearly drops waiting just for her. His body jerked involuntarily. He anchored both fists in her hair, holding her to him.

Azami laughed softly, echoing the blissful sound he had made earlier. Simultaneously she drew hard flesh into the heat of her mouth so that the sound vibrated through his burning cock and traveled through his body, rocking him. He threw back his head and howled, making her laugh again.

He'd never learned to play like this. Never. He had never even considered it. Azami gave him such joy. She made life at home fun. He realized that element had been sadly lacking. He came home to an empty, dark house and sat in a chair reading his books or researching on the computer. There had never been the sound of laughter, or a woman who made him feel loved.

Azami loved him with that soft, sinful mouth of hers, taking him deep, her tongue teasing and dancing while her hands caressed and squeezed and cajoled. For a moment he closed his eyes savoring the feeling of the combination of love and lust rising. When she suckled him hard and then suddenly eased the pressure only to dance her tongue over the spot beneath the flared head, his hips picked up a rhythm he couldn't quite stop.

"Enough," he hissed, before it was too late. "I've got plans."

She pouted a little, looking up at him as she reluctantly released him. "I had plans as well."

"Later," he promised. "But right now . . ." He bent to lift her out of the tub. "You're all mine, woman." He wrapped a towel around her, giving her a quick, cursory dry before he picked her up again and brought her into their bedroom. He liked the sound of that—their bedroom. Already it smelled like heaven with whatever scent was in the lit candles.

He gave her a little toss so that she landed on the bed, legs sprawled out. Before she could move, he was on her, following her down, pinning her beneath him. His mouth closed over her breast, suckling strongly. His tongue flicked and caressed her nipple over and over while he tugged and rolled her other nipple until her voice came out in a gasping purr and she arched her back, pushing her breast deeper into his mouth.

He kissed his way along those filmy threads, following the web down to her belly, his hands caressing her thighs before pushing them apart. He locked down on her hips, holding her in place so he could indulge his whims. He bent his head for a long, leisurely taste. Her breath hissed out and she jumped, her hips trying to buck. He tightened his hold and took his time, licking, savoring the sweet honey spilling out of her for him.

"Coming home to you is heaven, woman. Look at you, so beautiful. And damn, you taste so good I could snack several times a day and never get enough."

Her fingers fisted in his hair, the muscles in her stomach bunching. Her breath came in a series of gasping pants. "I was going to feed you properly, Sammy," she confided.

"You are feeding me properly." He held her open as he bent his head to drink. His tongue drew out more honey, circled her clit while she wailed and tried to buck against the hands holding her tightly.

Azami thought she might not survive as his mouth ravaged her. There was no other word for it. She couldn't catch her breath or stay still, not even when he smacked her bottom, the wave of heat causing her to spill more hot cream. He murmured his appreciation, making hot, sexy noises as he lapped at her.

His mouth was pure flame, catching her clit on fire as he teased and stroked and suckled. She clawed at his shoulders, trying to stay still but unable to comply with his silent command. He was watching her, his eyes hot and dark and heavy-lidded with lust as he drove her toward her orgasm.

"That's it, baby, that's what I want. Fly for me." He pushed his finger deep, his thumb teasing her clit as the rush overtook her. He quickly replaced his finger with his mouth, tongue driving deep, increasing the strength of her orgasm until she writhed and keened his name over and over.

Grinning, he lifted his head and looked down at his woman. She was so beautiful with her hair coming out of that knot, spilling everywhere, her eyes glazed with pleasure, and the marks of his mouth, small strawberry brands, all over her body. He caught her easily in his hands when she started to move, flipping her over fast and hard, taking her breath. His handprint was on her buttocks, and he bent his head and nipped with his teeth right in the center of it before rubbing the sting away.

He dragged her hips up and back, forcing her toward the edge of the bed. Her buttocks were beautiful, round and firm and so enticing. He kneaded her pretty pink cheeks before wrapping one arm around her waist to hold her, while he pushed three fingers into her slick, damp heat. She cried out, panting, pushing back into his hand, wiggling her hips to entice and tempt him.

Sam licked his fingers greedily and then placed the head of his cock at that hot, slick opening. Azami tried to impale herself, pushing back with a small lunge, but he held her, laughing softly.

"Do you want me, baby? How much?"

He loved that she couldn't stop moving, desperate to get to him, uncaring that she was shamelessly showing him how much she wanted him. He wanted her every bit as much. Her need was an aphrodisiac, taking his lust and pleasure to a new high.

He took his time, slowly, oh, so slowly, pushing into her. He was long and thick and so damned hard, and she was exquisitely tight and fiery hot. He heard the growl rumbling in his chest when her silken sheath bit down on him, wrapping him in flaming silk.

He pulled back with equal slowness, a study in control, refusing to allow her hips to follow him as he nearly drew out of her before taking that slow, hot ride back while her body gripped him tightly, contracting and moving as if that silken sheath was alive.

She gave a little moan of protest, trying desperately to force him to speed up his pace. He craved her, hunger clawing deep, ripping at his belly, his body every bit as desperate, but he took his time, enjoying the way his hungry cock disappeared into paradise while flames ate his shaft.

He rubbed her bottom once, and then smacked her bottom lightly again just to feel that flair of honeyed heat flowing around him, hot and bright. She thrashed and pleasure burst through him. He plunged hard and deep. She cried out as her muscles clenched him tightly, hips rocking back to meet the brutal thrust. His cock burned, pushing through all those hot, tight folds, stretching her, going deeper than he'd ever managed.

"Is this wild enough for you?" he asked gruffly.

Azami lay facedown, chanting his name almost mindlessly while his cock slammed into her over and over, harder and harder. "More," she gasped.

The frantic pace set up a hot friction that sent sensation rushing to every part of her body, until there wasn't a place on her body that wasn't frantic for release. The heat from his hand only added to the erotic miracle he was giving her. Every thrust brought his shaft dragging over her enflamed muscles until every muscle tightened, pressure building like a tsunami. The explosion sent quake after quake ripping through her body. Her muscles convulsed around his thick cock, clamping down, taking him with her over the edge.

His hoarse cry was torn from his throat as his own body erupted like a volcano. He lay over the top of her, fighting for his breath while he tried to calm his pounding heart. He nuzzled her long hair out of the way to kiss the nape of her neck and then follow that beautiful bird across her shoulders with a trail of kisses. Beneath him, she shivered, aftershocks rocking both of them. He wanted to stay right where he was while her body contracted around his, sending pulses of pleasure through him. He was sated for the moment, drained, feeling relaxed and unbelievably happy. He was home.

"I love you, Azami, so much." He poured the emotion he felt, the intensity of it, into her mind, sharing with her the feeling he couldn't quite find a way to express.

She collapsed completely onto the bed, his body on top of hers so that he knew he had to force himself up before he crushed her. With great reluctance he slowly stood, allowing his cock to slide from that secret haven. Immediately Azami turned over, looking up at him with her dark eyes filled with love for him. In his mind, he felt that same intensity he'd given to her.

"You're sure, baby?" he asked. "You're really sure I'm what you want? I can be rough and we might be apart for long periods of time. You have to be sure, Azami. If you commit to me . . ."

"Didn't that feel like commitment to you, Sam?" she asked, her voice and demeanor once again serene. "I want your child growing in me. I want to live here, with you. I know we'll be apart; you're a soldier, and I have to continue on the path set before me, but I think that path is with you."

"Then you'll marry me immediately?"

She sat up slowly and pushed at the silky hair tumbling around her face. "I have promised you marriage and I don't go back on my promises." She suddenly looked alarmed. "Oh, Sam. I was cooking dinner for you and I've forgotten it entirely. It's probably ruined."

"You know how to cook too?" he asked.

She regarded him somberly for a long moment. "Yes. When I can keep my mind on what I'm doing, which clearly, when you're around, I can't."

He laughed, happiness bursting through him like a bright rocket. "Go take a shower. I'll see if I can salvage the dinner."

She rolled off the bed and started toward the bathroom. She half turned in the doorway, her tattoos gleaming in the candlelight. She sent him that small, mysterious smile that always set his heart racing. "I *love* you wild, Sam."

He watched her go, that fluid grace, her hair snaking down her back to below her waist, and his heart ached with pure contentment. He had found home and it wasn't the wooden structure surrounding him, it was a little slip of a woman who had forever taken his heart.

Keep reading for a special excerpt from
an exciting Carpathian novel
by Christine Feehan

DARK
STORM

Now available
from Jove

Evil permeated the very ground he slept in. Every breath he drew into his lungs brought the stench of malevolence deep into his body. Hunger crawled through him, clawing at his gut, pounding through every heartbeat, each pulse point. His fangs refused to retract. They had become permanent now, and with the edge of his tongue he could feel the slow lengthening of his canines. Sharp. Terrible. A heralding of the vile, foul abomination every male Carpathian feared, creeping relentlessly into his body and mind no matter how hard he tried to hold it back. Evil had an insidious way of creeping in at the very moment one was most vulnerable.

His world was one of absolute darkness, heat, and tremendous pressure. He'd been buried alive, trapped in the volcano for hundreds of years. Outside his prison, the world had changed and evolved, but he remained imprisoned in this eternal stasis, a mosquito trapped in an amber prison, if he was being poetic. But it was more like a hot lava bed of fire and stone and pure hell.

He searched his mind to remember his name—there had

been so many. Names meant nothing in his world; they never had. His species was immortal and they moved from century to century, shedding identities and acquiring new ones, taking on the customs, languages, and names of those around them so they blended into whatever world they lived in. Once, so long ago, he'd had a birth name—the name his family had given him—but then so had the vile creature he'd chased across continents.

Of all the names he'd called himself over the centuries, Dax was the only one left from his ancient heritage, a small part of the original very long name he'd been given at birth. After tracking the vampire to this continent, he'd taken the name of a fierce warrior of the Chachapoyas people and had become one of them. Later, when the Incas arrived, easily overrunning the Chachapoyas whose numbers had already been decimated by the vampire, he'd shed his Chachapoya identity and assumed an Incan persona, learning their language and customs by reading the minds of the people. Then, like always, he'd become what he must to hunt his prey.

All bloodlines save one—the Dragonseekers—knew the horror, the tragedy, of watching family members succumb to the curse of their species. The more powerful the lineage, the quicker, deeper, and more potently they grew once a warrior made the choice to turn vampire. This vampire, the one Dax had hunted all these long centuries, was the epitome of evil. He came from an extremely powerful line—second in command to the prince of the Carpathian people.

Dax had known the ancient Carpathian warrior, as had all warriors in their community. And they'd all known the moment Mitro Daratrazanoff made the choice to turn wholly vampire. All his life, Mitro had carried power like a mantle of authority, but his ego had been wounded beyond repair when the prince had passed over Mitro and chosen one of Mitro's younger brothers to serve as his second. Mitro's hatred grew, as well as his vanity, until he wanted his entire family and the prince dead.

Driven mad by his hatred, he rejected his lifemate, Arabejila, a beautiful Carpathian woman with astonishing gifts, and in doing so he'd rejected the salvation she could have given him. That alone was a crime unheard of in their world, but Mitro compounded his sins by trying to kill her, to drain of her blood and life. Mitro had the insane idea that should he murder his lifemate as he made the transformation, he would be the most powerful of all vampires and could easily destroy his famous family and that of the prince.

Thinking he could betray and kill Arabejila while still Carpathian proved impossible. He took her blood, but the lifemate bond refused to allow him to use his other half as his entry to transform to pure evil. But he'd killed her mother and father and left Arabejila dying, bleeding out on the ground beside their dead bodies. Worse, her mother had been pregnant with another long-sought-after female child. Arabejila had dragged herself to her mother and cut open her belly to save the unborn infant.

Dax had arrived to find blood and death everywhere, his oldest friend and partner's entire family savagely destroyed by Mitro Daratrazanoff. Arabejila and her mother were daughters of the earth, their female magick important to the entire Carpathian people. The unborn female child would carry that same gift, although she was several centuries younger than her only sister. Never before in the history of the Carpathian world had such a crime been committed. One Carpathian had deliberately killed *two* females and attempted to kill a third *before* he'd actually turned vampire. It had been murder—pure and simple. And once the bloodlust was on him, Mitro continued his killing spree across continents.

The infant was premature and Arabejila was near death. Dax had given both his blood to save them, tying them to him for all time, something few warriors ever did. The earth had reached for Arabejila, healing her so that she could make the journey with him quickly, her blood calling to that of her lifemate. They left her unnamed sister in the hands of another Carpathian couple and set out on the trail of Mitro. That trail led them from one killing field to another. Century after century, horrendous battles took place where both hunter and hunted nearly died time and again. Always Mitro managed to escape until they had at last trapped him here, in this volcano.

The plan had been Dax's, but it was Arabejila who had lured Mitro to the mountain. Mitro couldn't resist the call of his lifemate, no matter how hard he tried. Once Mitro was inside with Dax chasing him, Arabejila would call to the mountain to aid her in containing the vampire. She didn't like the plan, because it meant Dax would end his days there, but she obliged with the promise that as she knew she wouldn't be able to last long with her lifemate estranged, she would find a good human man among the remaining Tahuantinsuyu or Incas and have a child to carry on her work.

The stirring in his gut told him the vampire was on the move. The crust had grown thin, far too thin, and the pressure inside the volcano was appalling. The vampire's triumph could be felt through the mountain. Over the last few centuries, after Arabejila had allowed herself to die, each succeeding ancestor had been more human than Carpathian. The women had come to the mountain and, as Arabejila had insisted, had even given birth there to ensure their connection with the earth. The binding had grown weaker over the last few years, not lasting as it should.

Three times the woman had come just in time . . . but not this time. Mitro's vicious glee filled the volcano, his will pushing continually at the thinnest part of the crust. He sent out his evil, delaying the woman on her trip, finding weaker minds to entice to his bidding. Arabejila's blood relation was in danger and she wouldn't make it to the mountain in time to prevent Mitro's escape.

Dax searched for the vampire throughout the vast network of chambers and caves. The entire mountain stank of evil, completely obscuring Mitro's trail from the hunter.

Throughout the long years, they'd each done their best to kill the other, but they were evenly matched and they'd only sustained horrendous wounds, recovering in the heated soil time and again, only to engage once again.

Mitro was avoiding all confrontations now, seeing his chance to escape. While they were locked in the remote mountain, the world had passed them by. Dax could only hope that the Carpathian hunters had grown strong and much more skilled than Mitro. Dax was starved and would need recovery time to take up the hunt. He had kept his muscles in shape and practiced his hunting skills to keep himself sane, but he feared his mind was half animal now, and that the invasive evil had crept into his very bones. It would take tremendous discipline, if he found actual substance, not to drain the donor dry.

He prepared himself for the inevitable, but sent a prayer to whatever gods might be, to mother earth herself, that the woman arrived in time.

#1 *NEW YORK TIMES* BESTSELLING AUTHOR

CHRISTINE
FEEHAN

"The queen of paranormal romance...
I love everything she does."

—J. R. Ward

For a complete list of titles,
please visit prh.com/christinefeehan